Worth Her Weight

a novel

by

Janet Franks Little

TELEMACHUS PRESS

WORTH HER WEIGHT

The publisher does not have any control over and does not assume any responsibility for author or third-party websites or their content.

Cover designed by Telemachus Press, LLC

Cover art:
Copyright © iStockphoto/1657201/Palmer

Published by Telemachus Press, LLC
http://www.telemachuspress.com

Visit the author website:
http://www.janetfrankslittle.com

ISBN: 978-1-942899-30-3 (eBook)
ISBN: 978-1-942899-31-0 (Paperback)

Library of Congress Control Number: 2015946319

Version 2016.02.28

10 9 8 7 6 5 4 3 2 1

Table of Contents

Acknowledgments   i

Chapter 1   1
Chapter 2   11
Chapter 3   22
Chapter 4   32
Chapter 5   41
Chapter 6   51
Chapter 7   60
Chapter 8   68
Chapter 9   75
Chapter 10   82
Chapter 11   89
Chapter 12   98
Chapter 13   106
Chapter 14   114
Chapter 15   123
Chapter 16   134
Chapter 17   143
Chapter 18   154
Chapter 19   163
Chapter 20   172
Chapter 21   180
Chapter 22   189
Chapter 23   197
Chapter 24   207
Chapter 25   215
Chapter 26   223
Chapter 27   232
Chapter 28   242
Chapter 29   251
Chapter 30   258
Chapter 31   267
Chapter 32   276
Chapter 33   287

About the Author   295

Worth Her Weight

a novel

ACKNOWLEDGMENTS

IN LIEU OF baking everyone cookies, I'd like to express my gratitude here. After all, the cookies will only end up on your butts or thighs, whereas you will have my thanks in writing for as long as this book is in print, or until you sell your copy for a quarter at a garage sale, or until you delete the e-book from your electronic device; whichever comes first.

Thank you to MaryAnn Nocco from Telemachus Press for taking on this newbie author. With patience, professionalism, and promptness, you led me gently by the emails into this brave new world of publishing.

To Laurianne Macdonald, who invited me to the Coral Springs Writers Group, I owe many thanks. I am grateful for your red pen edits on my chapter critiques, for fighting an uphill battle to get me to eat and live healthier, for not snoring when we've shared a hotel room, and for laughing at my jokes.

To Roxanne Smolen, who edited my manuscript and educated me at the same time. Thank you for beating me up about changing the ending and making my female protagonist stronger, even when I was whimpering that she was just like me. Thank God, you're gracious when you're right. I love to hear you laugh after reading what I wrote because it validates the humor. You're a tough audience.

To Zelda Becht, Betty Housey, Cathy Kennedy, Greta Silver and Molly Tabatchnikov, the other infamous members of the Coral Springs Writers Group, I cannot express how much your support, critiques and friendship mean to me. I appreciate you uncapping your pens, opening your homes and hearts to an inexperienced writer who dared to become part of your long-standing circle. I'm sorry, Greta, that it cost you more tanked oxygen while reading the sex scenes, but heavy breathing is good for you.

To Dr. Dorina Varsamis, who was my first beta reader, thank you for your friendship, updates on sex and the single woman, and apologies before you said *I don't get this part.* You have no idea what you did for my ego when a brilliant, beautiful woman like you envied my forty-year marriage to the same man.

To the same man, Steve, the only one I've ever loved and who panicked when I told him I was writing a romance novel. Yes, some of the sex scenes are from my memories of when we were younger, thinner, energetic, hairy and carefree. Our bodies have changed and so have our emotions which are now mature, substantial, long term, smooth-running and permanent. Thank you for our personal HEA. (Happily Ever After in the romance genre)

Chapter 1

"WHY DID I let you talk me into this?"

"Come on, it'll be fun," Emma said when Brianne fastened her seat belt.

Fun was not a word Brianne ever associated with fitness centers. She hated the whole workout-at-a-facility environment. Mirrors everywhere you turned that pointed out the bulges you couldn't hide. Strangers' sweat that permeated the air until you went nose blind to it. The acoustical torture of unrelenting music and clanging of metal on metal. Brianne preferred her exercise to be a solitary endeavor. Watching, smelling, and listening to others work out was like being in an open restroom with people taking dumps.

"At least, you can see The Hunk." Brianne's sister leaned over the steering wheel to look out the passenger window then to the left again before crossing the intersection.

Emma tried out a new gym at least once a year, and this time it was Hardcort Fitness. Whereas Brianne forced herself to exercise four times a week, her sister taught Zumba or spin classes, sometimes in exchange for free membership.

Other than our brown hair, the only thing we have in common is our parents.

"Didn't you like watching The Hunk on TV?" Emma asked.

Brianne recorded the show *Weight Loss Wonders* during the two seasons when Cortland Hardison, aka The Hunk, yelled at or counseled obese adults. She exercised when the commercials played. This was her affirmation that a person didn't need public humiliation to lose weight. She never told anyone, including her sister, that The Hunk played a major role in fantasies with BOB, her battery-operated boyfriend.

"He was okay on the show," Brianne said with a shrug of her shoulders. "But, how tacky is it to have everything with your name on it? Hardcort Fitness? Cort's Kids, Cort's Store where you buy crap with Corters?"

The new facility looked impressive in the brochure Emma had handed her about the grand opening. It was a metal and reflective glass structure on the western edge of downtown Fort Lauderdale. The center's *innovative concept* was an area for children called Cort's Kids. It had Hardison-designed equipment and was staffed with trained instructors. In the photos, it looked like the human version of a hamster habitat. The equipment was all encased in clear, hard plastic that children climbed up, slid down, and crawled in.

The pamphlet read: *When a child completes the circuit, they receive a Corter, an electronic coin. They pass their personal rubber ID bracelet with a microchip through a reader, and the token is added to their account.*

Corters were redeemable in Cort's Store. It was stocked with child-sized hats, T-shirts, and sports paraphernalia imprinted with Hardcort Fitness.

What marketing gimmick would he have come up with if his name was even weirder than Cortland?

The parking lot was filled with cars. Emma found a space near the end of a row. "Let's hurry. I don't want to miss his speech."

Even with her longer legs, Brianne hustled to keep pace with her sister as she sped toward the front entrance. Emma held the door open and bounced from foot to foot in excitement. She grabbed Brianne's shirt sleeve and pulled her through the lobby. A Grand Opening banner was stretched across it with balloons everywhere. Emma speed-walked them around lines of shiny torture instruments and perspiring people. Unlike most fitness centers Brianne had visited in the past, there was a distinct lack of mirrors on the walls.

People like me know what we look like. It's the reason we sign up for gym memberships that we don't use.

There was no background music cranked up to mask the noises made by the equipment in use. People in sports-related jobs were often at risk for hearing losses from sustained exposure to noise. These same people also abused their voices. Without coaches, cheerleaders, and exercise instructors, her caseload as a speech language pathologist would be cut by ten percent.

Her sister talked like a tour guide stuck on fast forward. "This is the cardio area, treadmills, ellipticals, bikes, AMTs, rowers, X-trainers. Here's the strength training area, freeweights, plateloaded, racks, platforms …"

Brianne slowed to see what an AMT was, but Emma pulled her forward. Ahead was a neon sign in childish letters that spelled out Cort's Kids. Under it, a crowd was gathered. A speaker-enhanced voice was amplified above the sounds of feet that slapped treadmill belts and weights that clanked.

"I'd like to welcome everyone to the grand opening of the latest and greatest Hardcort Fitness center in Florida. We are pleased to …"

"Come on, Bree." Emma pulled her toward the crowd.

As they neared, constipated grunts sounded from an area where bulked-up weightlifters jerked and squatted. Based on the volume, intensity, and frequency of the voiced exhalations, she knew these Schwarzenegger wannabees were at risk for vocal nodules or worse.

Our private practice hasn't had a weightlifter as a client yet. I should tell Pam about this. Maybe the grunters are our next target market.

Up ahead, a beefy man with a bullet-shaped, bald head dropped his kettle bell close to her side of the walkway. He turned to his fellow grunters and pointed. "Look. That's my Tiffany up there."

Mounted from the ceiling was a large screen on which a video of children using the *innovative concept* equipment played. Brianne's eyes shifted downward from the film to where they were headed.

A harried woman rushed toward them on the serpentine path that wound between areas of grouped equipment. A crying preschooler in a tutu and tights was in her arms and sobbed, "I … wanna … stay."

Emma released her sister's shirt and feinted to the right. Brianne dodged to her left as the woman and child passed between them.

She forgot about the kettle bell.

The toe of her left sneaker hit the flat-bottomed cannonball. Her foot slid up the convex wall and lodged in the handle. Arms swinging like a pinwheel, Brianne hopped on her right foot as she tried to shake the grip of the thick wicket. The kettle bell rolled forward and released her. But her momentum caused her to stumble in a spastic linebacker run onto a life-sized cutout of The Hunk.

She flattened him.

An aluminum display stand with Hardcort Fitness DVD's teetered then toppled over. Plastic cases rained down on her. The crash and Brianne's cry of "Shit!" created a temporary hush.

The first person to reach her was Emma whose blue-gray eyes were wide with worry. "Are you all right?"

Brianne's view was suddenly blocked by a burly guy who straddled her. Plastic DVD cases snapped and crackled under his feet. He jabbed his meaty hands into her armpits and lifted her from the pile of debris like she was weightless. When she was on her feet, he picked up the offending piece of cast iron and disappeared without a word.

Red-faced, Brianne glared at her sister. "I can walk all over town without a problem. Look what happens the minute I set foot in a damn gym."

Emma pointed. "You're bleeding."

Brianne's right elbow throbbed. She grabbed her arm and twisted it to see what was wrong. A small flap of skin just below the joint was torn, and a trail of blood ran toward her wrist. The crowd who had gathered for the presentation parted as if cued. Cortland Hardison, in all his magnificent maleness, emerged. He frowned at the pile of damaged items that littered the floor.

How much is this going to cost me? Will they let me keep the bent cut-out? BOB and I would like the company.

"What happened here?" he croaked.

Emma stepped forward and held up Brianne's bloody arm. "My sister tripped and hurt her arm. I think she needs stitches."

Like a surgeon in a well-rehearsed operating room, Cort stuck out his hand. A white towel was slapped into it. He brushed Emma aside. As soon as he touched Brianne, an electric frisson raced up her arm. He wrapped the towel tight around her elbow, applied pressure and said, "Let's get you to the first aid area."

She knew something was very wrong, not with her arm but with his voice. As he led her away, Brianne took quick peeks at his six feet of awesomeness. His almost black, well-cut hair was brushed back from a patrician forehead. His dark, almond-shaped eyes carried the hint of an Asian ancestor. Despite a breathtaking face, he was shy of male-model beautiful.

Brianne's heartbeat quickened, and her stomach fluttered. She caught the whiff of something wonderful. It wasn't cologne, but a masculine scent that brought to mind finger-clawed sheets and toes curled in ecstasy.

He unlocked the door to a small office, ushered her into a chair, and opened a wall cabinet stocked with first aid supplies. When Cort turned around, he stopped dead. For several seconds, he stared into her dark blue eyes. Then his gaze dropped to her mouth and the beauty mark above the right corner.

From the doorway, Emma said, "Is there anything I can do?"

He blinked and in a hoarse voice said, "I'll take care of her."

Brianne tilted her head back as he came near. When his fingers closed around her wrist, her pulse leaped. Cort placed her arm on the table next to her and removed the towel.

"It's hardly bleeding now," he said. "I don't think it'll need stitches, but a doctor should check you."

Brianne listened to his harsh voice with an analytical ear. Then she was distracted by the coolness of the medicated wipe on her arm. It was in direct contrast to the damp heat between her thighs.

Cort ripped open two butterfly bandages and applied them. He wrapped a compression band around her elbow like the ones used after a blood donation. "That should do it."

Brianne cradled her injured limb against her. "Thank you."

His eyes bore into hers. "I'm sorry you got hurt."

"I'm sorry I ruined your grand opening. I'll pay for anything I damaged." She stared back, wide-eyed and breathless.

His right eyebrow arched. "Damaged?"

"You bent when I fell on top." She inhaled a sharp breath as her face heated.

He raised both eyebrows and smiled. "I what?"

"I mean, I bent the cardboard cutout of you." Brianne licked her dry lips and swallowed.

Cort's eyes followed her tongue tip along her bottom lip. "Don't worry. There's more that isn't bent."

Brianne forced her eyes away when her sister giggled.

An attractive, blonde woman in a tailored business suit elbowed Emma aside. "Cort, the photographer and reporter from the Sun Sentinel are here."

He leaned forward and in a soft voice said, "I wish we had met under different circumstances."

Brianne opened her mouth to say, "Me, too." Before she could shift her brain into action, he straightened and turned away from her. Emma moved aside, and The Hunk followed the blonde. Brianne rose as if she had an invisible connection to him. When he disappeared from sight, the spell was broken, and she dropped back into the chair.

Emma stepped into the room and held up her palm for a high five. "Way to go, Bree. We met The Hunk."

Brianne did not reciprocate the gesture. "I didn't do it deliberately. It was an accident." She stood up. "Are you ready to leave?"

Before Emma could answer, a handsome, well-muscled man who was slightly shorter than both women hurried into the office. "Hello, I'm Mark Diaz, the general manager here." He shook hands with them. "Let's all go to my office."

"Why?" Brianne asked as her eyes slid sideways to her sister.

"We need to complete an incident report. It's an insurance requirement."

"Will I have to pay for damages?"

"No, it's nothing like that." He held out his hand to usher them out the door then he locked it. "We're glad you're not seriously injured, but there is paperwork involved."

The forms took longer than expected. When they were done, Brianne and Emma walked over to the Cort's Kids area. Everyone was gone, the video screen dark. The DVD display that Brianne knocked over was nowhere in sight. A dozen children squealed and played on the equipment. Hardcort employees in khaki shorts and red polo shirts monitored them. Two mothers sat nearby engrossed with their cellphones.

"I'm sorry you missed the ceremony, Em," Brianne said.

"It's okay. All I really wanted was to see Cort Hardison in person. Thanks to you, I did."

They headed toward the exit. Emma stopped at a large, electronic screen that scrolled a list of classes and programs. She sighed and turned away.

Brianne asked, "Do you want to work out? I can go for walk."

"You don't mind? I feel like I should do something since I'm here. There's a Zumba class that starts in ten minutes. Why don't you join me?"

"No thanks. Give me the key to your car. I'll get my water and phone."

"You could use one of the treadmills in here if you want."

"I'd rather do it outside by myself."

As Brianne strode the streets of downtown Fort Lauderdale, she was unable to reach her usual speed because her left ankle was a bit sore. She returned to the Hardcort Fitness parking lot and waited by the car. Her sister emerged from the building a few minutes later. They stopped for frozen yogurt on their way home. Emma ordered a large chocolate with sprinkles and nuts. Brianne got the kiddie cup with plain, low fat vanilla. They sat on a metal bench outside to eat.

Emma said, "So what'd you think?"

"It's nice if you like that sort of place."

"No. I meant, what did you think of Cort Hardison?"

Brianne stared into her yogurt. "He's nice if you like that sort of guy."

"I wonder what he looks like naked."

"Emma!"

"Come on. You know he's hot."

"So what if he is?"

"I think he's hot for you."

Brianne scowled like Emma had said she was hot for chamber music. "There's no way."

"Way. I know that I-want-you-bad look."

"You're wrong. That was the I-don't-want-you-to-sue-me look."

They sat for a silent minute then Emma turned in her seat. "Let me ask you something. What's wrong with his voice? It sounded like more than just laryngitis."

"I suspect it is."

"Could it be serious?"

"He should definitely see a doctor about it." Brianne threw her empty kiddie cup into a trash bin next to the bench.

"Could you fix it with voice therapy?"

"It depends on what the doctor finds in the examination."

Emma's face sported a wide, white-toothed grin. "What would you do if you had Cort Hardison as a patient?"

"First, he would be called a client, not a patient. And what would I do?" Brianne screwed up her face in mock concentration. "How about stick my tongue down his throat and tell him to say, Aaahhh?"

#

Brianne's roommate, Pam, was doing paperwork at the dining room table when she entered the condo. She told Pam about her morning with Emma at Hardcort Fitness.

"*Chica,* something like that would happen only to you. Did you give Cortland Hardison one of our business cards?"

They were partners and therapists at The Voice Center, a private practice they started three years ago. Pam was in charge of marketing while Brianne oversaw the accounting.

"I didn't have my wallet on me."

"Did you, at least, tell him about The Voice Center?"

Brianne twisted in her chair. "It didn't seem like the right time."

Pam sighed. "He has a business where clients and employees may be abusing their voices and could use our training. On top of that, it sounds like he has a vocal pathology. You would have done him a service by letting him know."

"There wasn't enough time for me to tell him all that."

"You could have said something right after he told you to see a doctor."

"He probably thinks I'm some nut job who was trying to attract his attention."

"You had an accident because of someone else's negligence. That's not a reflection of your professional skills."

"Maybe not, but it still wasn't the right time."

Brianne headed down the hall to shower and change clothes. She couldn't get Cortland Hardison out of her head. He embodied her ideal man. Tall but not lanky. Muscular but not muscle bound. More than handsome but not pretty. The kind of guy with whom she wanted to do every nasty thing her mother said a lady never does.

Later that night she located an episode of *Weight Loss Wonders* she had saved. BOB got fresh batteries. She turned on the TV in her bedroom but muted the volume. Soft music from the CD player filled the room so Pam didn't know what she was doing.

#

Brianne woke at seven on Sunday morning to exercise. For her, it was like a God-directed decree. If she didn't attend church, then she had to do something else she didn't like. She dressed, pulled her sun-streaked brown hair through the back of a ball cap, grabbed a bottle of water, and headed down the stairs. She avoided the elevator whenever possible. It was the reason she liked living on the tenth floor. She had built-in stepper equipment.

Before heading out the lobby, she stretched in the privacy of the stair-well. It was a nice day for a walk because the humidity was low. It was still quite warm in south Florida, even in November. Brianne knew her route well and never listened to music or talked on her cell phone. Past experience made her vigilant for tourist drivers, sleeping vagrants, and loose concrete. She walked north for two miles then turned at a bakery and headed home. She was grateful that Sweeter Days Bake Shop was closed on Sundays.

If that isn't divine intervention, I don't know what is.

An hour later, Brianne opened her front door. The smell of freshly brewed coffee filled the condo.

Thank you, God.

For some reason, no matter how many times Brianne was instructed, she could not make a decent pot of coffee. Lucky for her, Pam had learned to brew *café cubano* from her *abuela* when she was eight years old. More than two years ago when she moved in, they defined the responsibilities which made their unique living and working arrangement successful.

Brianne grabbed a cup and headed to her bathroom. After her shower, she entered the kitchen dressed in loose jersey shorts and a tank top. Dark strands of damp hair lay on her shoulders. She poured herself another cup of coffee.

Pam sat at their two-seat bistro table with the Sunday paper. She wore a pink Victoria's Secret satin slip that glowed against her latte skin. Her dark hair was piled on top of her head in an artful tumble of curls. Pam was a *Latina* whose curves were similar to Brianne's, but she dressed to show them off. In the Holy Trinity of the female form, the two friends shared the same waist measurement. The difference was Pam had a Kim Kardashian bottom while Brianne sported Kate Upton boobs.

Why is it that Pam's butt sticking out is sexy, but my boobs spilling out are trashy?

Pam laid the folded newspaper on the table in front of her. "How's your arm? I see you put on a smaller bandage."

"It's fine."

"Did your foot bother you on your walk?"

"My ankle is still sore."

"Do you think Cort Hardison might be at his new fitness center today?"

Brianne's eyes narrowed. "Why?"

"Oh, I thought I could check him and the place out."

"And leave some business cards lying around?"

Pam shrugged. "Those weightlifters are a new market of clients. Do you want to go with me?"

Brianne shook her head. "One humiliation a week is enough for me."

But I wonder what they did with the bent Hunk. Would Pam check the dumpster for me?

Chapter 2

"WHAT ARE YOU watching?" Pam asked when she walked into the living room Tuesday evening. "Sorry. Did I scare you?"

Brianne placed a hand over her racing heart. "I didn't hear you come in."

Pam sat on the sofa and looked at the TV. "*Oh, Dios mio.* A Cort Hardison exercise video? Where did you get it?"

"I bought it." Brianne's eyes never wavered from the screen.

"Why?"

"I thought I might exercise to it."

"Sell it somewhere else, *chica.* You don't fool me."

Cort Hardison demonstrated a variety of positions for sit-ups to strengthen abs as he counted out the reps.

After several minutes with her eyes still glued to the TV, Pam asked, "Have you seen the whole thing?"

"Six times."

#

Wednesday was a busy workday. Brianne worked with clients all morning then rushed to her accent modification class at Sunshine Engineering. She greeted the three foreign-born employees as she entered the conference room. The men cleaned up their lunch remains, although the aromas of curry and other exotic spices lingered in the air. They set out their workbooks and homework on the long conference table. She loved motivated clients whose employer paid for their training.

When she returned to The Voice Center, Pam told her a new client was added to today's schedule. Dr. Rosenberg called in person and asked to have his patient seen as soon as possible. Since the otolaryngologist often recommended their services, the appointment was scheduled for five o'clock that day with Brianne.

"Why didn't you take it?" she asked Pam.

"Because Rosenberg requested you, and I have something important at four."

Brianne headed to her office. "Has he faxed over the prescription?"

"Not yet. But he promised you would have it and his report."

Brianne stowed her purse and briefcase. "What's the diagnosis?"

"Bilateral fold lesions. Kitty will open a file for you. She'll be here at four-thirty."

"You aren't coming back to the office?"

"I'm getting my eyebrows done at the salon on Las Olas."

Brianne rolled her eyes. "That's what's so important?"

"I had to book two weeks in advance so, yeah, it is."

#

Kitty, the part-time receptionist, interrupted Brianne as she finished her last client summary report. "Your five o'clock is in Room Two. File's on the door with Rosenberg's report. It was faxed a few minutes ago."

"Thanks, Kitty. I'm sorry you have to stay late so I'm not alone." She put her arms through the sleeves of her white lab coat to cover her black skirt and pink silk blouse.

"I'm glad to do it for *this* client." The gray-haired receptionist winked at her over the reading glasses perched on the end of her nose. She turned and left the office.

What was that all about?

At Therapy Room Two, Brianne lifted the file from the wooden rack on the door. She flipped it open and stepped into the room. Her eyes looked for the client's name.

"Hello, Mister … Hardison." When she glanced up, she was pinned by the smoldering gaze of The Hunk.

"We meet again." His voice sounded even hoarser than before.

Brianne's step faltered as if she bumped into an invisible wall. She recovered her professional demeanor and sat down across the table from her new client. "Let me introduce myself. I'm—"

"I know who you are."

How did he know? Did Rosenberg tell him? Did Kitty?

"Okay. Please give me a few minutes to review your paperwork and Dr. Rosenberg's report."

Cort Hardison wore a crisp, white dress shirt, collar open, cuffs folded back. A platinum Piaget watch glinted on his wrist. He looked even hotter than at Hardcort Fitness, very ubersexual. When she looked up from the file to Cort's face, he stared with such intensity she was speechless. Her skin prickled with an awareness of him. She cleared her throat, and his red-hot gaze lessened.

Brianne pushed a pad of paper and pen toward him. "I don't want you to speak again while you're in this room. When I ask you a question, nod or shake your head. Do you understand?"

Cort opened his mouth, shut it and nodded.

"Good. If you have a question or a response, Mr. Hardison, please write it on the paper."

Cort wrote on the pad and spun it around to face her. *Call me Cort*

"All right, Cort. According to Dr. Rosenberg's examination you have nodules on your vocal folds. Some people call them vocal cords. But they are actually folds of mucous membrane that stretch across your larynx. Do you understand what nodules are?"

He shook his head.

Damn. I wish he had seen the pictures already.

Dr. Rosenberg used a scope with a light to take photos of Cort's larynx. They were included with the report. Brianne knew the reaction a person, especially a man, had when he viewed the larynx and vocal folds for the first time. It looked similar to a vagina, and it was in his throat. Her responsibility was to ensure the client knew what was wrong for therapy to be successful.

Let's get this over with. Which photo is the worst?

Brianne laid down the one which showed the folds open. Cort's eyes widened when he saw the color picture. There was no way she could maintain eye contact while the gynecological-looking photograph sat between them. She was wet enough already.

With her eyes downcast, she said, "This is a picture that Dr. Rosenberg took of your larynx during his endoscopic examination." She didn't see it, but she knew Cort winced. Everyone did. "I know it was difficult for you."

Cort touched her hand. She looked up, and he nodded to confirm how bad the experience of being scoped was.

She pointed to the little bumps across from each other on the edge of each fold. "These are the nodules I was talking about. When you speak, the vocal folds open and close against each other. That's what produces sound. They meet in the middle first, like a jump rope hitting the ground. So this is the area most susceptible to problems."

She pulled the second photo from the file and placed it on top of the first one. It showed the folds closed except where the bumpy lesions kept them apart. It looked like a wet, red mouth with its lips together. In this picture, mucous pooled around the folds, like they dripped clear semen.

Oh God.

"Because the nodules don't allow the folds to close completely, your voice sounds rough or scratchy. In the photo, you can see your folds are irritated and swollen right now." Brianne put the photos back in the file and looked up at him again. "Do you know why you have this problem?"

He seemed to radiate heat with laser precision right at her. It came in waves. After a moment, he nodded with resignation.

"Do you want to avoid surgery to remove the nodules?"

Cort nodded again.

"Then let me explain our therapy program."

Brianne told him about the hour-long sessions every week. She said the number of sessions differed for each client from a few weeks to several months. There would be exercises to relax the muscles in his larynx and retrain his voice. His smile broadened.

Of course, he would like the idea of exercise.

"Once your voice improves, we have a vocal hygiene program for you to follow. It's to prevent this from happening again. This is important because your job causes you to overuse and misuse your voice. However, the first step in the therapy program is usually the hardest for most clients." She paused for effect.

Cort wrote: *What is it?*

"You've already started it. You can't talk, whisper, or make any verbal sounds for the next seven days."

He scribbled quickly on the paper. *Can't do that. I have commitments I can't cancel.*

She closed the file. "Then we're done here. Call Dr. Rosenberg tomorrow and schedule the surgery. That'll put you out of commission for more than three weeks after which you will still need therapy. Can you do that instead?"

Cort leaned back in his chair and lifted his face to the ceiling. He was a sex god who looked heavenward. Brianne waited. He lowered his hand to the notepad and wrote: *You're tough.*

She smiled.

And cute.

She frowned. "Are you willing to do our program or not?"

He smiled then jotted: *If you go to dinner with me tonight.*

"No, Mr. Hardison, it doesn't work that way."

He pointed on the pad where he had written *Call me Cort.*

"No, Cort."

He scrawled, *Just dinner.*

She wavered. *A dinner that might lead to bed … with his body against mine, in mine …* She snapped out of her fantasy as his pen scratched across the paper.

I owe you for the cut arm.

She bit her lip.

He wrote *pretty please* and then smiled at her as his dark eyes twinkled.

After a moment's hesitation, she pulled a paper out of his file. "This is our Patient Responsibility Form. By signing this, you agree to take responsibility for improving your voice. You promise to attend and participate in therapy sessions. It also says you are willing to try new techniques and behavioral changes."

Cort signed without reading and pushed the form across the table to her.

She said, "The vocal rest won't be too bad for the next week. You can text and use email. Many of our clients find it isn't the hardship they thought it would be." His eyes narrowed. "Believe me, it's true. Get your phone out. Text someone right now. Say you're under orders not to use your voice for one week."

He retrieved his phone from his pocket. She straightened the papers in the file. Her phone vibrated in her lab coat pocket. She had a text. It read: *I can't talk till Wed. Do you like pizza?*

Her eyes widened, and her mouth dropped open. "How did you get my phone number?" Before he could write his reply, she said, "The incident report."

Had he told Hardcort's general manager to get the information from her? Was an incident report actually needed for insurance purposes?

Oh my God, that's how he found out where I work and what I do. Her phone vibrated in her hand.

Cort: *You and me even.* He pointed to the open client file on the table with all his contact information in it. His thumbs flew across his iPhone's keypad. *How about New River Pizza?*

#

She followed him to the pizzeria in her car. Inside the restaurant, the young hostess stared at Cort with slightly parted lips.

She asked in a shy voice under lowered lashes, "Are you Cort Hardison?"

He nodded.

With a dreamy expression, her eyes roved over his face. Finally, Brianne cleared her throat.

The noise snapped the hostess out of her reverie. "How many are in your party?"

Brianne's head swiveled back and forth in an exaggerated movement. They were the only ones standing there. Cort raised two fingers. The hostess blindly picked up two menus.

Shit. I never thought about being out in public with him.

They were led to a table in the center of the restaurant. Cort shook his head. The perky hostess waited for him to say something. He pointed to his throat and shook his head again.

Brianne said, "He isn't able to speak right now."

Cort looked around the restaurant and pointed to a large, semi-circular booth in the rear corner. As they followed the hostess, a low heat warmed the small of Brianne's back where he placed his hand.

The young woman gestured with the menus she held. "Is this okay?"

He nodded.

Several people looked at them and pointed.

No matter where we are, we'll be the center of attention.

She stepped around the hostess and sat at the far end of the curved booth. Instead of taking the seat across from her, Cort motioned her to scoot over. She did, and he sat down. The menus were laid in front of them.

Cort's elbow touched hers, so she put her purse in her lap and moved farther to the left. So did he until his thigh pressed against hers. The hostess moved the menus. Brianne slid more to her left. Cort followed. The hostess pushed the menus to the middle of the table. Brianne moved again. He bumped against her.

"Stop it," she hissed.

He ignored her. The hostess gave up, left the menus where they lay, and walked away. Now Brianne's left butt cheek clung to the edge of the seat opposite where she first sat down.

What have I gotten myself into?

#

Brianne arrived home around nine.

Pam sat on the sofa, her iPad propped on her knees. "Who's your new client?" Her voice was smarmy with a sing-song cadence.

"Kitty called you."

"She sent me a text."

Brianne sat beside her. "Can you believe it?"

"I can't believe you went to dinner with him."

"It was just pizza."

"Well, I don't think that will violate any American Speech Hearing Association rules. But, just in case, I looked it up." Pam turned the screen to face Brianne.

On the iPad was the ASHA Code of Ethics. She pointed to where it said … *shall not engage in sexual activities with clients* …

"We didn't have sex, just veggie thin crust."

"So I guess that means you're okay." Pam flipped the cover closed.

"But not for long."

"What do you mean?"

Brianne rubbed her face. "You know he's on vocal rest for the next week."

"Of course, it's our standard protocol."

"Well, during dinner he wrote a text and asked if I was seeing anyone. I told him it was none of his business. Then he texted that he wanted to lick me from head to toe."

"Whoa. You've been sexted."

Brianne's arm and leg still tingled from where Cort's body rested against hers in the booth. It was a sexual pursuit long before he ever sent the lick message. "I know."

"What did you say?"

Brianne pointed to the iPad. "Pretty much what the ASHA Code of Ethics says. I told him our relationship was professional only. I'm really attracted to him, but don't worry. I won't do anything to jeopardize my license or our practice."

"I appreciate that. Does he understand the position he's putting you in?"

Brianne remembered how she quivered inside when Cort's hand lay against her back as he steered her toward the booth. A ripple radiated through her body when he squeezed her knee under the table. The heat of his thigh against hers burned through her skirt.

"Oh, he all but drew pictures of the positions he wanted to put me in."

Pam laughed. "He's got you tied up in one big come-fuck-me knot."

"You know, it was interesting having dinner with someone on vocal rest. I did all the talking, and he did all the texting."

Several times when she looked around the restaurant, the eyes of other patrons or the wait staff were on them. Did they wonder why he was with her? Why he was always on his phone? She was relieved when no one approached the table for an autograph or to ask questions.

Pam squirmed and adjusted her shorts.

Brianne leaned back to look at her friend. "What's wrong with you?"

"I didn't just have my eyebrows waxed today. I decided to get a Brazilian."

"How was it?"

"Not as bad as I thought. First, my pubes had to be measured to confirm they were long enough. Stop laughing. Once I passed that test, I got my landing strip."

"You decided not to do a full Brazilian?"

"Getting this done in addition to my eyebrows was enough. I didn't want that woman working on my hooha any longer than necessary."

"Speaking of hoohas, I showed Cort the photos of his larynx."

Pam giggled. "No wonder he sexted you."

#

The following morning, Brianne received a text from him. *Can't stop thinking about you. Want other SLP. Same appointment time?*

Brianne texted back, *Sorry. With me for duration.*

Cort: *I want to be with you. Just not in therapy.*

Brianne: *Got to go. Client here.*

She ate a chopped salad at her desk and reviewed client reports when her phone vibrated in her pocket.

It was Cort again. *Free to talk?*

Brianne: *Eating lunch.*

Cort: *Why can't I see other SLP?*

Brianne: *Rosenberg referred you to me.*

Cort: *Rosenberg referred the voice center. I picked you.*

Brianne: *Still can't change.*

During back-to-back sessions in the afternoon, Brianne's phone vibrated in her pocket. She knew it was Cort. When she returned to her office, she checked.

The text read: *What if I go to a different office?*

Brianne: *Take away your case? Think I want to see you then?*

Cort: *Bad idea. Getting desperate.*

Brianne typed chart notes for her last afternoon client. Her phone chimed in the pocket of her lab coat where it hung on a hook.

Cort: *How long till my therapy done?*

Brianne: *Not sure. 6-8 weeks.*

Cort: *Too long. Can I come 2-3 times a week? Be shorter?*

Brianne: *No.*

#

Her mother called later that evening. "Why were you having dinner with Cort Hardison last night?"

"Hello, Mom. How are you and Dad?"

"Brianne Gordon, how do you know him?"

"He's a client of The Voice Center. We had a late therapy session. Since Pam had another appointment, Mr. Hardison and I had pizza at the same restaurant. We were just two hungry people who shared a meal."

"That's not the way I heard it."

"What did you hear?"

"Mary Ann Williams' neighbor's sister saw you at New River Pizza. She said you two were very lovey-dovey."

"Oh, Mom, it was nothing like that. He wasn't able to talk. He had to lean close so I could read his phone texts."

"What's wrong with him? Why can't he talk?"

"You know I can't discuss his case with you."

"Well, that explains why the chairwoman of the Healthy Kids fundraiser called me all upset. She received an email from him today canceling as the keynote speaker. He said he'll still be there but won't be speaking. How are we to get someone else by Saturday night?"

"What about asking Dr. Adams to speak?"

Her mother snorted like a baby bull. "No one wants to pay a lot of money to listen to that old fart do his *Kids Say the Darnedest Things to Their Doctor* routine. Cort Hardison was going to be our celebrity speaker."

"He can still be your celebrity, just not your speaker. If I think of anyone who can, I'll let you know."

"There's something more that you're not telling me. What is it?"

"Don't, Mom." Brianne sounded a little sharper than she intended. "Have you seen him? What would a man like that want with a woman like me?"

Her mother sighed. "Oh, honey, when are you going to realize that you are a lovely, young woman? Any man would be proud to be with you."

"Well, nothing is going to happen because I have a responsibility to maintain a professional relationship. Let's talk about something else. How's Grandma?"

That ended any more questions from her mother about The Hunk.

Chapter 3

CORT'S PERSISTENCE PAID off Friday morning after a barrage of persuasive texts interspersed with sexts.

She knocked on the open door of Pam's office. "Do you want to take over Cort Hardison's therapy?"

"He finally got to you."

"I held out as long as I could."

"I'm surprised you lasted this long." Pam checked her schedule on the computer. "Tell him his current appointment time is okay for the next three weeks. I won't need another waxing for a month."

Brianne sent Cort a text when she returned to her office. *You win. Pam will take over your case. Same day and time.*

Great news! Dinner at my house tonight?

I'm a vegetarian.

Cort: *Don't worry. I cook mean salads.*

Brianne: *LOL. What time?*

Cort: *Six?*

Brianne: *See you then.*

#

After work, Brianne programmed Cort's address into her car's GPS. He lived in a neighborhood near downtown and the beach called Victoria Park. It was a combination of old Spanish style architecture and new construction. Cort's vintage house had white stucco walls. An arched, covered front entrance led to an oak door studded with ornamental ironwork.

Brianne was so nervous that the wine bottle in her hand quivered. As she looked for the bell to ring, the door opened without warning and startled her. Cort stepped forward and pulled her to him. Her nipples instantly hardened against his chest as his mouth sealed over hers.

His lips coaxed hers open with ease. His tongue moved inside and took gentle licks. The shoulder strap of her purse slid down her arm and dropped to the floor. After that, her awareness was concentrated on the wild beating of his heart and her grip on the wine bottle. Her body throbbed, and her breasts were heavy.

Don't drop the wine. Don't stop kissing me. Don't drop the wine. Don't stop holding me. Don't drop the wine. Don't stop … don't stop …

"Hi, Cort."

Someone was behind them on the sidewalk. Cort's arms released her, and he stepped away. Mortified, Brianne stumbled to the side of the front door. She gasped, and her chest heaved. Cort rested his forearms on the doorframe, bent forward like a runner trying to catch his breath.

Halfway between the street and the door was a young boy with his bike straddled between gangly legs. "I got your email 'bout how you can't talk. Are you still gonna come to my game tomorrow?"

Cort straightened. An impressive erection strained against his cargo shorts. His eyes followed hers downward. He pulled her partway in front of him then touched his index finger to his thumb and gave the okay sign. The boy's freckled face split into a big grin.

"You dropped your purse, lady." He turned his bike to the street and pedaled away with a backward wave.

One of Cort's hands moved to the front of her stomach, the fingers splayed, and pulled her back against him. Her breath caught in her throat. His arousal was thick and hard. It was like they were in that bubble again. The outside world ceased to exist, and she sensed only him.

Starved for air, she inhaled. It was the needed impetus that knocked her back to reality. Brianne took a step forward and crouched to pick up her purse. Her face flushed with embarrassment.

I better not bend over right now. Who knows what would happen. My God, that kid almost got the lesson of his young life.

Brianne tucked the wine bottle under her arm, hitched her purse strap onto her shoulder, and stood up. She took a deep breath, turned around, and smiled at Cort.

What is the rest of the evening going to be like? I haven't even gotten past the front door.

Cort gestured her inside. His home was lovely with high ceilings, ivory walls, terracotta tile floors, and deep archways. The furniture was traditional and fit the size of the rooms. A living room was on the right, a formal dining room on the left. Straight ahead, the hall was bisected by a stairway before it continued toward what looked like a kitchen at the rear.

He took the wine from under her arm and motioned for her to follow. The kitchen was small but well-laid out. Newer cabinets lined an outside wall with a large island in front. Cort picked up his phone from the counter. She pulled hers from her purse.

He hit a button, and a text message beeped onto the screen. *I'm happy to see you.*

She glanced at his still bulging fly. "I can tell."

His thumbs flew across the keypad, and then her phone lit up. *It's hard not to laugh out loud.*

"That's not the only thing that's hard."

He closed his eyes. It appeared he struggled to fight back his voice and maybe his woody also. When his eyes opened, they scolded her.

"Sorry," she said. "I know you're trying. I'll be nice."

He poured wine into two stemmed glasses from an uncorked bottle in an ice bucket. She followed him through French doors to an intimate patio space. The small backyard had a lap pool and lush tropical landscaping. His property was not waterfront, but there was brininess in the air so the ocean must be near. A cool breeze moved the palm fronds and made the area pleasant to be outdoors. The second stories and roofs of his neighbors' houses peeked through the dense foliage, but no windows or balconies looked directly onto his property. They sat in comfy wicker chairs.

"This is really nice, Cort."

Thank you.

"Have you lived here long?"

3 years.

"Did you have to do any remodeling?"

Put in lap pool.

This would be another interesting evening for a speech language pathologist. She had never socialized with someone on vocal rest. All her previous interactions were under therapeutic conditions.

Cort wrote *Hungry?*

"A little."

He returned with a cheese tray, crackers, and grapes. They drank the wine, nibbled on the appetizers, talked and texted about innocuous subjects. She helped him bring a wooden salad bowl filled with chopped vegetables and cheeses to the patio table where placemats and tableware were set. Eating or drinking with texting meant Cort had to set down his fork or glass to ask or answer questions. Often he used a nonverbal response.

He pointed. *Do you want more salad?*

He shook his head. *I can't believe it.*

He lifted the bottle. *More wine?*

It was like having dinner with someone who didn't speak your language. So that he could eat, she talked much of the time. "My family has been in the cattle business since the Civil War. My great-great grandfather bought a ranch outside of Fort Worth with money he earned fighting for the north. He was a city boy, and the family story is that he wanted to become a dairy farmer. He didn't know that the herd he bought was beef cattle until he tried to milk one."

Cort smiled and nodded. *Tell me more.*

"My Uncle Junior inherited the ranch after my grandfather died. His brother, Homer, runs a stockyard and slaughterhouse in the area. But my dad moved to Florida after he married my mother and owns PrimeTime Steakhouse on Federal Highway."

Her parents worked long hours when the restaurant started. After she was born, her grandmother, Inez, left the ranch and moved to Fort Lauderdale to take care of her, and three years later, her sister.

Cort wrote *And you're a vegetarian?*

"That was more traumatic for my family than when my cousin, Gary, announced he was gay. Most of them already knew because he wore a beret instead of a cowboy hat. But no one ever thought that a Gordon would stop eating meat."

Brianne recalled the family dinner at PrimeTime when her uncles and their wives were in town. She hadn't seen them since her high school graduation. Instead of gaining the typical freshman fifteen, she had lost thirty pounds. The sincere compliments from her family delighted Brianne. That ended when she gave her dinner order.

"I'll have the baked potato, plain. Salad, with oil and vinegar on the side. Asparagus, no Hollandaise. Broiled tomato halves, no sugar topping, just salt and pepper."

"And your steak, Miss?"

"No steak."

"Chicken or fish?"

"No chicken or fish."

Her father, who was seated beside her, leaned close. "Get the petite filet, honey. It's the smallest cut."

"I've stopped eating meat."

The members of her family were stunned, and the whispering circled the table like a game of telephone.

"What do you mean she doesn't eat meat? I've seen her do it," Uncle Junior said.

"Buddhists don't eat meat. Has she become one of them?" Grandma asked her mother.

"Is it because you took her to the slaughterhouse last summer?" Aunt Jean asked her husband, Homer.

"I say it can't hurt if she loses weight." Aunt Eileen said in a too-loud, booze-laced voice.

Brianne loved her rough-around-the-edges aunt, but often wondered if it was the booze or the setting sun which transformed her into a verbal predator. She was a different person during the day when she was sober. Dinners with her were brutal when Brianne was younger and more sensitive about her size 20 body. Her aunt seemed unaware how much her gin-fueled comments hurt.

"At least you have a pretty face, Brianne."

"Have you asked your mother to take you to Weight Watchers?"

"You're so smart, you don't have to worry about catching a husband."

"You're only twelve, and you look like you weigh more than me."

It took a while for her family to come to terms with her decision. Having her grandmother on her side helped. Grandma had no qualms telling her grown sons and their wives to back off. Brianne's trimmer, healthier body and obvious happiness were additional advantages.

Uncle Junior pulled her aside at the last family dinner. "I gotta admit, I thought this vegetarian thing was a fad. I figured when you got away from the liberals and Democrats at college, you'd eat meat again. But I was wrong."

She smiled with the knowledge that even a fifth generation Gordon who no longer ate meat was still loved and accepted by the family.

Cort sent her a new text. *How did you and Pam meet?*

"We were both in graduate school at UF. In one of our first classes, we were partnered for a presentation. We did a role play where I was the therapist and Pam was the client. She, of course, stole the show by making me look like I had no idea what I was doing. Actually, at the time, I didn't. By the end of the presentation, she was the client doing her own therapy."

She did not tell him about her battle with obesity and the bullying she endured. She did not tell him about the one night stands with drunken guys she met in college bars just so she could feel a male body close to her chubby one. She did not tell him about Paul, the chef, she lived with for two months until she found out he wanted the family business more than her. She did not tell him she was falling in love.

They carried the dishes into the kitchen. She rinsed while he filled the dishwasher.

Cort: *Ready for dessert?*

"Sure, what else have you *cooked* for me tonight?"

From the refrigerator, came a bowl of raspberries, blackberries, and blueberries, and a small dish of whipped cream. He opened a package of meringue shells and put everything on the island. Cort handed Brianne a plate and motioned for her to dish up the dessert. When she passed on the meringue shell, he reached around her and put one on the plate. The look in his eye told her not to fight him on this. She filled her shell with berries but hesitated at the whipped cream. Once again, his arm snaked out and plopped a decent dab onto the fruit.

He assembled his dessert and poured iced tea. Cort picked up both plates. He nodded for her to grab the glasses and follow. They went into a room with a step down from the living room. The walls had shuttered windows that overlooked the pool. It was set up as an office and TV room.

On one wall was a long table which functioned as a desk with two leather chairs on wheels. He put the dessert plates down and swiveled a chair around for Brianne. As she took her seat, he booted a computer monitor to life. He sat and pulled her chair close.

Cort put her dessert plate in her hand and pantomimed eat-eat. He typed *With this keyboard and screen we can communicate better. I want you to know I spent all day yesterday and today at this computer rearranging my engagements for the next week and notifying people about my voice. Many like my buddy, Sam, who you met out front were fine with it. Others not so much.*

"Like the chairwoman of the Healthy Kids fundraiser?"

His mouth dropped open. *How did you know about that?*

"My mother is on the committee. She called last night and told me you canceled as the celebrity speaker. They're trying to find a replacement." Brianne didn't mention that her mother knew about their dinner.

I feel bad about the short notice. I'm still going to attend.

"I wonder whose speech we'll have to listen to tomorrow night."

He stared at her then wrote: *You're going?*

"Mom insisted that our family buy four tickets. She didn't want any empty seats at her table. So I have to go, along with my dad and sister."

He sat back, his hands steepled under his chin. With a sudden movement forward, his fingers flew over the keyboard. His hands weren't chunky with thick fingers like Paul's. The skin wasn't calloused or stretched by knobby knuckles like her uncles'. They weren't girly and soft like her cousin, Gary's. Cort's fingers were blunt-tipped with clean cuticles. She pictured them dancing across her breasts, down her belly, parting her …

He nudged her to look at the screen. *Why don't we go together to the Healthy Kids fundraiser? I can still be their celebrity, as you called it, but you can give my speech. I have it written. I'll edit it tonight and email it to you so you can practice during the day.*

A jolt of panic radiated through her. She had no problem talking to clients, businessmen, doctors, and families in small group settings. A banquet hall with two hundred people scared her silly.

Before she could tell Cort no, he bent over the keyboard again. *I'll pick you up at your place. I have a car service that is driving me there. Can you be ready at seven?*

"Cort, I can't speak in front of that group." The money being raised was to fund exercise programs and summer camp tuition for overweight inner city kids. Would it matter if the fundraiser was for vaccinations or dental care instead? Maybe. She would be the adult spokesperson for childhood obesity prevention tomorrow night. Other than her family, someone might be there who would remember what she looked like back then. Would they say something to her? To Cort? She couldn't take that chance. "I'm sorry. I can't," she repeated.

Why not?

"I'm not a public speaker."

You wouldn't be a public speaker, just a public reader. You can read, right?

She was quiet.

He wrote, *Pretty please.*

When she didn't answer, he highlighted the words and made them **bold.**

Brianne laughed. "Do you ever say pretty please when you speak?"

Never.

"And yet you've written it to me twice."

Only you. Other women say yes right away.

After he wrote several more reasonable arguments on the computer, Brianne agreed to read his speech. What was it about this man that he could make her do anything he wanted? He seemed light-hearted after she said yes, like a weight had lifted off him. It affected his new communications to her.

Are you ticklish?

"No."

Panty or thong?

"Boxer or brief?"

You have the most kissable lips.

"So do you."

I can't wait to undress you.

No response from Brianne.

Have you ever made love in the shower?

She gave him a Mona Lisa smile.

I want to kiss every inch of you.

"Time to go." Brianne jumped to her feet. She peeked at the leather seat to see if she left a wet spot.

At the door, Cort took her into his arms. His kiss was tender. With his hands at the small of her back, he laid his forehead against hers and closed his eyes. It was as if he wanted to burn a memory of her into his brain.

Brianne wrapped her arms around his waist and relaxed against him. It was the first time all evening that she didn't teeter on the edge of a precipice. She needed more time to think about the unsettling way he affected her. After another consuming good-night kiss on the doorstep, she wobbled to her car on unsteady legs.

#

At home, she called her mother as Cort asked her to do. "Guess what, Mom? Cort Hardison has someone who will read his speech at the fundraiser tomorrow night."

"You talked with him?"

"He sent me a text."

Sort of.

"Why did he contact you?"

'He told me about his cancellations and mentioned the Healthy Kids fundraiser. I said our family would be going, and you were on the committee. When he got someone to read his speech, he asked me to let you know."

"That's wonderful news! I've got to call the chairwoman right away. Audrey will be *so* thrilled."

Her mother hung up without saying goodbye. She didn't ask Brianne who would be reading the speech tomorrow night.

Chapter 4

BRIANNE CRAWLED OUT of bed Saturday morning at five-thirty. She gave up trying to sleep. Worry about attending the fundraiser with Cort and giving his speech kept her restless most of the night.

I might as well exercise.

An older gentleman with a bushy white moustache was the lone person in the first floor workout room. He rode a stationary bike with the pedals making slow circles. "Good morning, young lady."

Brianne mumbled a greeting then faced the windows which looked outside. She kept her back to the mirrored wall. After she finished with ten pound reps, she turned to replace the weights. The old guy's eyes were still focused at the level of her butt.

Now his eyes are glued to my crotch. Yuck!

When he met her gaze, he smiled. "You look good for a big girl."

Brianne grabbed her towel and left.

After she climbed the ten flights upstairs to the condo, she showered and ate a bowl of granola. Then it was time to boot up her laptop to check for Cort's email. The Inbox had a message with the subject: *Healthy Kids Fundraiser.* She opened the attachment. Her horror grew with every line.

Brianne assumed the speech would be about his community fitness program. Or maybe he would plug his preschool exercise equipment and the Cort's Kids program at Hardcort. She never thought he'd write about childhood obesity. The damned speech read like her life story.

I can't read this. What the hell am I going to do?

Judging from the two AM time stamp on the email, he hadn't slept any better last night than she had. When Pam awoke midmorning, she asked Brianne about her dinner at Cort's house. They shared a laugh when she related the kiss interruption outside the front door.

"I was so embarrassed. I wonder what that kid told his parents. I'm surprised no one turned the hose on us, like dogs doing it in the yard."

"How did it go after that? Did texting to communicate get tedious?"

"It's why I ended up talking a lot. Later we sat in front of his desktop. He was able to write faster with that keyboard."

Brianne handed Pam the speech. Her roommate looked at the several pages of printed material. "What's this?"

"It's a speech I agreed to read at a fundraiser tonight. Cort was scheduled as the keynote speaker. Of course, now he can't do it."

"*You* agreed to do it? You've never willingly spoken in front of a big crowd before."

"Remember that CFM knot you said he has me tied up with? Last night it got a little tighter." Brianne pointed to the papers in Pam's lap. "It's for the Healthy Kids organization. My mom is on the planning committee. Any ideas how I can get out of reading it?"

"Forget to bring it?"

"Say the dog ate it?"

"Cramps?"

"Scared mute?"

Pam read what Cort had written while Brianne refilled their coffee cups and waited. When finished, she handed the pages back. "Did you tell Cort about your own childhood obesity?"

"Last night I told him a lot of things, but not that. I'm afraid if he knows, that'll be the end of us."

"Maybe or maybe not. Anyway, how much do you know about him?"

"Just what I've seen on TV and *People* magazine."

Pam got out her iPad and, with her usual Google proficiency, typed his name. "I can't believe you haven't done this already."

An Internet search revealed that he was born in Chicago thirty years ago. His parents were killed in a traffic accident when he was eight. After that, he was raised by his paternal grandmother in Boynton Beach. He started Hardcort Athletics and did two seasons on *Weight Loss Wonders*.

Photographs of him with other women filled the screen. There was a fashion model, a well-known TV actress, a local socialite, and several female fitness instructors. All the women were either tall and slender or short and petite. She bit her lower lip and a wave of insecurity washed over her.

I am definitely not his type. Why is he interested in me?

In the late afternoon, Pam wished her luck at the fundraiser dinner and headed to Miami. She planned to visit with her parents and then attend a party on South Beach. Before she shut the door, she said, "I'm spending the night at a friend's house. See you tomorrow afternoon."

Brianne didn't ask the friend's gender even though she was curious. Two hours later, she had finished her hair and makeup and was about to get dressed when her phone rang. She raced through the condo to the kitchen counter and answered the call before it went to voice mail.

The security guard at the front desk said, "Mr. Hardison is on his way up."

She had called earlier and put Cort's name on her approved guest list. When she hit the end button, she noted the time. It was six-thirty.

Why is he here so early?

The dinner at The Signature Grand, a large venue no more than twenty minutes from Brianne's condo, started at eight. There was a cocktail hour before, but they planned to arrive when it was almost finished so Cort wouldn't have to talk to people. That's why he said to be ready at seven.

As she put her cell phone into the clutch purse next to the folded pages of the dreaded speech, the doorbell rang. She wore only a short, silk kimono and lace panties. Cort raised his head when the door opened. He didn't move, but gazed at her from the brunette hair that flowed in loose curls past her shoulders to her red lacquered toenails. She, in turn, was stunned by his male beauty in formal wear.

When she could breathe again, she said, "You're early. It's not seven."

He shrugged and mouthed *sorry*. After kissing her cheek, he stepped inside. Cort walked around the living room, past the dining room, and peeked into the kitchen like a prospective buyer at an open house. Brianne stood in the foyer, her back to the closed door, unable to move. Her heart thudded in her chest. He was so elegant in a tailored black tuxedo with a snow-white tucked dress shirt. His long, slim legs in the knife-creased pants were topped by the well-fitted jacket over his wide shoulders. He prowled back to her like a sleek panther.

He tilted her chin up with one finger. His lips softened hers with gentle pressure. She responded with her mouth but kept her hands at her sides. As if she was as delicate as porcelain, he cupped her face with both hands. She wrapped her hands around his forearms.

Yes, kiss me like that again. Make me feel special.

As if he could hear her plea, he responded with long, slow strokes of his tongue. The taste of him filled her mouth. Brianne quivered with heat and need. She shifted her hands to his waist. Cort pulled the neckline of her robe aside and planted his mouth on her shoulder. He licked his way up her neck then flicked his tongue against her earlobe.

I want you to do that … down there.

He pulled her to him with one hand, the other cupped her breast. She trembled as a sparking desire grew inside her. Arched into his hand, she buried her face in his neck.

God, you smell so good, so male, so you.

Cort's dexterous fingers loosened her robe's belt. He spread it open and kneaded her bare breasts. He stared at his hands on her. His thumbs rubbed her aching nipples as bursts of sensation raced to her groin. His face melted with awe as her breasts spilled out around his fingers. She closed her eyes and whimpered from the passion that washed over her. He bent to suck one nipple into his mouth. She couldn't stop her low moans.

Over his head at her breast, she raised her eyelids. The clock on the opposite wall said it was a quarter to seven. "Cort, the time."

Her words seemed to shift him into a state of uncontrolled desire. His lips covered hers again as his hand pushed between her legs. The pleasure ricocheted between her mouth and where he moved the lace edge of her panties aside. His steel-hard shoulders flexed under her clenched fingers. He used her own lubricant as the pad of his finger rubbed her clitoris in gentle circles.

I need to stop him. I need more.

He slid one finger into her. His mouth closed hot and wet on her breast as his finger moved in and out. She moaned with delight. He removed his hand and angled her to the side where the hard edge of the foyer cabinet bumped the backs of her thighs. His hand pushed her panties down to her knees.

With one arm around her waist, he lifted her onto the marble top. It was cold against her heated body. He tugged her panties off. Her legs fell open, and Cort stepped between them. He pulled her hips forward as he stroked inside her with one finger then two. Her back bowed, and she raised her knees to give him greater access.

His fingers withdrew, and he stepped back. From his pocket, he removed a foil packet and ripped it open with his teeth. He tore at the opening of his pants and rolled the condom over his length. He spread her legs and probed, then pushed into her with one fluid thrust.

She wrapped her legs around his waist, her arms around his shoulders, and rocked her hips to meet his thrusts. His hands gripped her and lifted her to receive him. His body in the full tuxedo radiated heat like a fire out of control. Pleasure spiraled through her as primal instinct took over. She focused on nothing but the need to release the tension. As he surged into her again, she shattered. Her body jerked with pleasure.

"Cort … oh God, Cort."

He clenched a mouthful of her silk robe between his teeth seconds before his climax tore through him. She went limp in his arms, her head on his shoulder. He spit out her robe as his head dropped against her neck. They stayed in place, absorbing the aftershocks.

She waited for him to give her a gentle caress, a soft smile, or warm look. Nothing happened. After several minutes, she freed herself from him with fumbling effort. He stepped back, his face averted. She pulled her parted robe over her nakedness and hopped off the cabinet.

Cort removed the condom, tied it off, and zipped up. He looked around. She took it from his hand and walked on unsteady legs to the kitchen. When she returned, his back was to her as he straightened his clothing and finger-combed his hair. He continued to make adjustments in the foyer mirror and avoided eye contact with her.

Please turn around. Show me this meant something to you.

Instead, he emotionally withdrew by inches, then feet. She wanted to ask what was wrong, but suspected that even if he could speak, he would say nothing.

They never do.

She sighed in painful resignation. "I'll finish getting dressed. Have a seat. The bar's over there."

I guess he's sorry he fucked the fat girl. I'm still good at making 'em come and making 'em go.

She entered her bathroom and washed the smell of him off her at the sink. She cleaned all the makeup from her face and reapplied it. Brianne replaced her panties rather than retrieve the ones that lay somewhere out there. She put on a strapless bra. By the time she was dressed in a black one-shouldered, floor length gown, it was almost seven-thirty. She emerged from the bedroom to find Cort sprawled on the sofa. He held a glass from the bar with amber liquid in it.

She grabbed her purse from the kitchen, blanked her expression, and stepped into view. "I'm ready."

#

In the elevator, Cort pulled out his phone and sent a text. The limo driver, she guessed. A white Lincoln waited under the front canopy, the back door held open. An older man in a dark suit smiled as they walked toward him.

Does he suspect why it took us so long to come downstairs? Is that why he's smiling at me?

Brianne held the arm closest to Cort tight against her side. He tried to slip his hand between it and her body, but she stiffened her elbow in place. She dreaded the feel of his touch on her now. In the backseat, she scooted to the far side and leaned against the door. Unlike when they ate in the booth at the pizzeria, Cort did not try to move closer. He either didn't notice or didn't mind the chilly crevasse of leather between them.

He reached into the inside pocket of his jacket and held out a set of index cards. Last night she suggested that he prepare cards with responses he was likely to repeat multiple times during the evening. That way he could spend less time texting. She read all the cards by the passing street lights.

I am on vocal rest due to a medical condition.

I can answer any yes/no question.

I will be able to speak again by the end of the week.

I can be reached only by email or text until Thursday.

Healthy Kids is a program that means a lot to me.

I appreciate your support and attendance at this fundraiser.

A beautiful woman will be reading my speech tonight.

She nodded her approval and handed the cards back. During the remainder of the drive, she plotted how to get home without him. She wanted to leave before Cort knew she was gone, or he'd pretty-please her back into this car. She could hitch a ride with her parents. However, her mother likely had to stay late to wrap things up. Or her sister might be able to take her home unless she came with their parents. When she finished the speech, she could call a cab. Then she hit on a possible strategy.

The town car traveled along the lit entrance of The Signature Grand beside the tall queen palms that flanked the drive. As soon as the car stopped, Brianne unlatched the back door and stood. The chauffeur was startled that she blocked him.

In a soft voice, she said, "Do you have a card?" He handed her one from his inside pocket, and she dropped it into her open purse. "Thank you."

Cort's head rose across the rooftop. He raised his hands in the air as if to ask why she didn't wait. She shrugged like a woman who forgot the proper way to get out of a limousine. He guided her into the lobby with his hand on her back. A mini-crowd surged forward and surrounded him a few feet inside the entrance.

"We heard you might not be here tonight," one woman said as she clung to his arm.

"Is everything all right?" a man asked.

"I came just to see and hear you," a young girl gushed.

Cort pulled the cards from his pocket and distributed them. Some people read to themselves and passed them back to him. Others read the card then passed it to the next person. One group acted like they had just been given a script with each one assigned a line to recite aloud. Brianne moved off to the side and viewed with a clinical eye how people communicated in this manner. More guests filled the lobby, and she lost sight of Cort.

I might as well find my family.

When she entered the banquet hall, she spotted her mother at once. Candace Gordon still looked like the Miss Florida finalist she once was. Her tall, slender figure was striking in a deep emerald gown, set off by chestnut hair that was several shades lighter than in her pageant days. She and a woman in a mother-of-the-bride jacket and dress stood near a raised platform at the front. They studied a clipboard, obvious concern on their faces as they scanned the room. Brianne spotted her father and sister standing at a table on the right side. She headed their way.

"Hi, Dad. I see your tux still fits. You look great." His close-cropped dark hair and moustache were sprinkled with silver and coordinated with the gray cummerbund that strained slightly at his waist. Her father always wore a tux better than any man she knew. Tonight she moved Cort to the head of her best-dressed list.

Ted Gordon leaned over and kissed her cheek. "You look beautiful, baby."

Brianne turned to Emma and air-kissed near her sister's ear. "Is that dress new? It looks fabulous on you."

Emma's slim frame looked good in anything, including the pale pink, chiffon gown that floated into a full, floor-length skirt. With a stab of envy, Brianne compared her generous bust to her sister's. She had never tried to wear a strapless dress with a sweetheart neckline like Emma's.

My girls would be tumbling out of that.

"I got it on sale yesterday at Nordstrom's," Emma said. "It was …"

Her sister stared open-mouthed at something or someone behind her. Cort moved next to her and raised his hand to signal *excuse us.* He showed her his phone's screen.

Why did you come in here without me?

"You looked like you were doing pretty well out there with your cards."

He used the keypad then showed the phone to her again. *I want you with me.*

"Why do I have to be with you?"

A sick feeling filled her when she read what he wrote. *You are my reader.*

Not his date. Not his lover.

I'm his just fucked reader.

Chapter 5

BRIANNE WAS NO longer heartsick. *So that's all I am to him.*

The woman with the clipboard hurried to them as her mother trailed behind. "Ah, Mr. Hardison, I'm Audrey Nussbaum, the chairwoman of this event." She shifted her clipboard and put out her hand to Cort.

A waiter passed with a tray of filled champagne flutes. Brianne lifted one off, tilted her head back, and downed half.

Her mother frowned at her when her head came level again. She said, "Brianne, please introduce us."

It took a moment until she swallowed the champagne in her mouth. "Sorry … Cort, this is my mother, Candace Gordon. This is my father, Ted, and you might remember my sister, Emma, from Hardcort."

Audrey interrupted before Cort could shake her father's hand. "Mr. Hardison, I'm glad you're here this evening. I'm sorry about the problem with your voice, but was thrilled when Candace called to say someone would be giving your speech. Is that person here yet?" She looked around the room as if she expected to spot someone with a sign that said *Speaker*.

Cort held out his hands toward Brianne like she was the prize on *The Price is Right*. She took another gulp of champagne.

Her mother said, "*You're* giving the speech?"

Brianne answered with a dangerous edge to her voice. "Actually, I'm not the speech *giver*. I'm the speech *reader*." Cort frowned, and she narrowed her eyes at him. "Tonight, I'm the verbal equivalent of Cort's seeing eye dog."

No one said anything. Brianne finished her champagne, put the empty glass on a different waiter's tray, and picked up another. Cort plucked it from her hand, returned it to the tray, and shooed the waiter away.

"Ah, I see the dinner service is about to start," said Audrey in the awkward silence. "Mr. Hardison, we have you at the table over there."

She pointed with her clipboard to the front of the room. Cort keyed a message on his phone. Audrey cocked her head to read the screen. "Well, the Gordons are sitting right here."

Cort wrote more. Audrey looked upset. "Oh, but we planned to have you with the rest of the dignitaries."

Brianne resisted the urge to throw something. "They want you with the big boys, Cort."

"Brianne." Her mother elbowed her side.

Cort wrote. Audrey's frowned when she read his text. "Um, I suppose we can change your seat. Let me think."

Everyone waited as Audrey consulted her clipboard, flipped a page and then said, "Ahhh, I know what we can do. We asked Dr. Adams to speak tonight before you arranged for Brianne to give, I mean, read your speech. He's sitting at the Gordons' table. Do you want to switch places with him?"

Cort nodded his approval. He looked happy.

Audrey, on the other hand, did not look happy. She lifted the place card with Dr. Adams' name on it and stomped away.

"Let's sit," Brianne's mother said.

As it turned out, Dr. Adams' seat was between her parents. Before Cort could request additional seating changes, the other party of three arrived and sat down. Once again, Brianne was fascinated to watch the interactions with someone who was not allowed to speak.

Cort wrote something on his phone and showed it to her father. He read it, and without thinking, pulled out his phone and began to write a response back.

"No, Ted," her mother said. "You can talk to Cort. He just can't talk to you."

Emma leaned over and whispered in Brianne ear. "Mom said you're working with him on his voice. Is that why you're reading his speech? Are you mad at him about something?"

"I'll tell you later, Em."

Her sister eyed her. "Okay. And I also want to talk to you about coming up with a vegetarian menu."

"For what?"

"For PrimeTime."

"You're joking."

"We need to change with the times, Bree. You aren't the only vegetarian who eats there. Let's get together tomorrow."

Her sister had graduated in May with a business degree and was her father's assistant at the restaurant. The three family businesses under the Gordon Enterprises umbrella were PrimeTime Steakhouse, Double G Ranch, and HG Livestock. Every other month, the three Gordon brothers, and now Emma, met in either Fort Worth or Fort Lauderdale for a board meeting. Brianne was grateful her sister wanted to be a next generation Gordon to run the operation.

The server arrived at their table and asked each person if they ordered the beef, chicken, or fish. When she got to Cort, he had his phone ready with his meal selection choice.

Brianne said, "Bring me a plate with no meat on it."

The experienced waitress nodded. "No problem. How about I get you an extra salad?"

Brianne ate little. The strangers on her right ignored her after cursory greetings and introductions. When they began to ask Cort questions, he passed them his index cards to read. Emma leaned past her mother and asked Cort about his business. Brianne was impressed with her sister's ability to phrase her barrage of questions for a yes or no response.

As they finished dessert, Audrey tapped the microphone at the podium. "Ah, I want to welcome everyone to the annual fundraiser for the Healthy Kids program."

She listed the past year's events and upcoming activities. After introducing several major contributors, volunteers, and Broward County politicos, she said, "We are pleased to have with us tonight Mr. Cortland Hardison, who has supported our organization in many ways."

She gestured toward Cort and bounced her hands for him to stand. Necks craned around the room. Cort rose to a semi-erect position, twisted to look at both sides of the large room, and waved. When people spotted him, applause followed.

Audrey adjusted the microphone lower and said, "As you know, Mr. Hardison is the president of Hardcort Athletics and owns Hardcort Fitness centers here in Florida. He has started exercise programs in local parks and summer fitness camps for inner city youngsters. Just last week he opened his fifth Hardcort Fitness center with a special exercise area designed for very young children called Cort's Kids." More applause. "Well, Mr. Hardison was scheduled as our keynote speaker tonight. Unfortunately, a medical condition prevents him from giving that speech."

Murmurs hummed around the room. Perhaps people had seen old Doc Adams at the table with the event dignitaries. They regretted spending hundreds of dollars for a so-so dinner and thirty minutes of pediatric witticisms.

Audrey interrupted the grumbling guests. "Oh, but Mr. Hardison has made arrangements for his speech to be read by someone else. I would like to present Miss Brianne Gordon. Brianne, please come up."

Here we go.

She stood, picked up her speech, and looked at no one, especially Cort. As she walked to the steps of the raised platform, muted applause accompanied her. Audrey smiled and moved aside when she reached the podium.

After adjusting the microphone to her taller stature, she laid out the speech and took a deep breath. "Adults are responsible for turning fifteen percent of the children in the United States into junkies."

Good opening line, Cort.

"We have about two hundred people here for this fundraiser. Thirty of you have turned your children or grandchildren into junk food addicts."

Over not-so-quiet whispers around the room, she continued. "This is a growing trend with children from poor, middle class, well-to-do, and even famous families."

I hope my parents don't think I'm talking about them or Grandma.

Brianne did her best to read with vocal inflection and modulation while her face remained as expressionless as possible. "It is predicted that today's children will die younger than their parents. No one wants to experience the pain of burying their own child, especially from something preventable like obesity. However, for many today, that is a real possibility."

The room was quiet. She read some alarming statistics about the increased number of overweight children, particularly among young girls.

I was one of them.

Brianne then read the clinical definition of obesity in children. "Mr. Hardison witnesses and studies the obesity epidemic almost every day."

But I lived it and still worry about it.

The speech told about the children he worked with in schools and communities and their daily diets. He compared fast food with natural foods. "MSNBC reported that forty percent of parents say they turn to fast food because there is no time to cook natural, unprocessed meals."

She read about the fats and sugars in various fast foods marketed to children. "Portion control is out of control. In the 1950's, a soda was seven ounces. Some of you may remember the small glass bottles of Coke that are now prized antiques. Today, kids can get sixty-four ounce mega drinks in large plastic cups."

Now the speech got into Cort's area of expertise, exercise. "The lack of physical conditioning is widespread. How many kids do you see playing outside nowadays? Years ago children were sent out to play after breakfast and didn't go home until the next meal was served. Of course, today that would be grounds for an investigation by Children's Services."

Soft laughter and talking circled the room. She paused until it was quiet again. "Children prior to the 1970's were engaged in games that used their whole body, not just their eyes and fingers. These games required more than one player and were often scoreless. The average child today spends four hours a day watching TV, playing video games, or sitting at a computer. These activities also promote non-stop eating. Studies have

proven that television interferes with the signals to the brain that tell children they're full."

Okay, this is the last hurdle.

"Obese children also suffer from psychological problems, such as
eating disorders, depression, and anxiety. Twenty-six percent of overweight
teens teased at school or at home considered suicide. Nine percent of them
attempted it."

During the speech, Brianne either had her eyes on the written pages or
looked above the heads of the audience. Now she glanced down at the at-
tendees seated closest to the podium. They were focused on something behind her.

What's going on back there?

She looked over her shoulder. At some point while she read, the curtains on the back wall had retracted to reveal a large screen. A slide show
with photographs of overweight children played. The picture of a young girl
who was about twelve years old appeared next. Brianne swallowed hard.

She looks like I did at that age.

The girl had long, brown hair and smiled with a closed mouth. The
eyes reflected obvious pain. Her pudgy hands were held up as if to say *Please
don't take my picture.* The preteen showed potential beauty hidden under
puffy cheeks, which made her eyes smaller and her face boneless. A double
chin hid her neck.

Brianne found it difficult to tear her eyes away as the next photo
showed two young girls, one obese and the other slim. They were obviously
related, perhaps siblings. The slender child's face was lit with joyful abandon. The heavyset girl's smile appeared stiff and never reached her eyes.

I know how that felt, too.

To give herself more time for the film of tears to clear her eyes and
her voice to steady, she pretended she lost her place on the page. Despite
her best efforts, her voice broke when she read about the suicides of obese
children, some younger than twelve. In conclusion, the speech listed ways
that families, schools, and the community could help fight childhood
obesity.

And it was done. The audience clapped loudly.

They liked Cort's speech. I did it.

As she headed toward the steps of the platform, Audrey came up to her. With a perfunctory smile, she said, "Good job." At the podium, the fundraiser chairwoman angled the microphone downward accompanied by a loud squeal. "Well, thank you, Brianne. We're glad you shared with us Mr. Hardison's highly informative speech. The Healthy Kids program and its supporters have a little token of appreciation for him. We are grateful to you, Mr. Hardison, for your efforts to help improve the health and well-being of children in our community. Please come up here to receive this plaque."

Cort rose to his feet and walked toward her as the audience clapped.

I know he's going to hug me.

As he neared, she judged the exact moment to jog to the left. Cort wasn't able to make a directional change in time, so they passed each other with a table between them. He stared at her over the seated people. She glanced at him and walked on. Her father stood when she reached where her family was seated and enfolded her in his arms.

This is the hug I need.

"I'm so proud of you," he said.

"Thanks, Dad."

Her mother squeezed her hand. Brianne moved toward her chair as Audrey began the presentation to Cort. She picked up her purse and mouthed *bathroom*. Emma started to rise, but Brianne motioned her back down.

"Be right back."

She locked herself in the farthest stall and sat down. Brianne closed her eyes. As she calmed herself with deep breaths, several women came in, used the restroom, and left. When the old never-let-them-see-you-cry Brianne was once again in control, she opened the door.

A tall blonde who looked somewhat familiar leaned against the sink counter, her arms crossed on her chest. "Hello, Brianne."

"Do I know you?"

Brianne turned on the faucet to wash her hands and looked at the woman in the mirror. She wore a thigh-high, sequined dress that made her long legs appear giraffe-like. Her pale blonde hair hung straight to her shoulders. She looked like an ice queen, all silvery, glittery, and hard.

I think this is the woman at Hardcort Fitness who took Cort away to meet with a reporter.

"I'm Jacqueline Murphy, Cort's publicist. Do you have any idea how much you've screwed things up?"

"I assume you're going to tell me."

"First of all, I know you're the quack who told him he couldn't talk for a week. What kind of ridiculous therapy program is that?"

How dare a publicist tell me how to do my job! Who the hell did she think she was?

Brianne fought to contain her fury. She dried her hands then turned toward the Ice Queen with her hand outstretched. "Let me see your license, Jacqueline."

The publicist reared back. "What do want with my driver's license?"

"Not your driver's license, you idiot. I want to see your Florida license to practice speech language pathology."

Jacqueline stood straight. "You know I don't have one."

Brianne narrowed her eyes. "Want to see mine?"

Neither of them moved nor said anything for long seconds. Then Cort's publicist shrugged her shoulder. "You know, he'll just fuck you and dump you, right?"

Don't worry, Jacqueline-the-publicist. I'm used to that kind of thing.

Brianne picked up her purse and walked out. On the far side of the ballroom, a crowd gathered around the prizes for the silent auction and raffle drawing.

A man about her age with too-long black hair and an ill-fitting tuxedo stepped into her path. "Hi, Brianne."

Who's this now? His agent?

"You don't recognize me, do you? It's Alan, Alan Nussbaum. My mom, Audrey, is in charge of this shindig."

Then Brianne remembered him. He attended the same private high school as she and Emma. Alan hadn't been a scholar, artist, musician, or athlete. He just hung around the fringes of various groups.

"Hi, it's been a long time," she said. "I guess your mom insisted you come to this, too."

His eyes roamed from her neck to knees as he licked his lips. She steeled herself not to shudder from the lasciviousness of his scrutiny.

Finally, he said, "Yeah, she drags me to all these things. I wouldn't have recognized you without that introduction. Boy, you've really changed."

"What do mean, Alan?"

"Well, let's face it, when we were in school, you were a real porker."

Her mouth dropped open when he oinked twice.

Didn't you listen to the speech I read, you moron? Why would you think what you just said and did was in any way appropriate?

For the second time that night, Brianne froze her emotions. Her attention shifted from Alan's gleeful face to a tall figure headed their way.

Shit, I'm being saved by the other person I want to get away from.

Alan twisted his upper body around to see what Brianne was staring at behind him. Cort held up his phone. Brianne read *please excuse us* on the screen. He put it in Alan's face, then grabbed her hand and led her away.

When he found a quiet spot, he wrote: *Are you upset because we made love?*

"We didn't make love."

Cort looked perplexed and opened his hands, palms up.

"You want to know what we did? We fucked."

Cort's mouth dropped open.

Brianne raised her chin. "And, according to your publicist, I not only screwed you but your career, too."

Before he could respond, Audrey approached with her clipboard. "Ah, excuse me, Mr. Hardison. The photographer from *Society News* is here, and we need you for a picture."

She took Cort's elbow and led him away.

Brianne hurried to the nearest exit. In the lobby, she retrieved the driver's card and her cell phone from her purse. "Hello. This is Brianne Gordon. I accompanied Mr. Hardison tonight. Where are you parked?"

She strained to listen to the driver's reply above the conversations in the lobby. She exited through the front doors to the portico outside. "Okay. I'm headed your way … No, stay where you are … Stay right there … I see you." She walked as fast as she could in her long dress and four-inch Manolo Blahnik heels.

The driver was out of the car when she got there. "Is everything all right?" he asked.

"I need to leave, but Mr. Hardison has to stay for a while. You can come back for him after you drop me off."

Once seated in the back seat, Brianne texted Emma to say she was headed home then powered her phone off.

When the driver pulled up to her building's front entrance, he parked and turned in his seat. "Uh, listen, Mr. Hardison just texted me and asked if I knew where you were. What should I tell him?"

"Tell him you just dropped me off at my place and are headed back."

"Anything else you want me to tell him?"

She wiped a tear that rolled down her cheek then shook her head. Once again, she opened the door without waiting for the driver.

Chapter 6

ON SUNDAY MORNING, Brianne moaned aloud when the alarm buzzed for her church-skipping walk. Her head pounded. For two nights in a row, she had not slept well. While she exercised, thoughts about Cort swirled in her head.

When she returned to the condo, Pam waited for her in the foyer with two aromatic cups of coffee and a stern look. "We need to talk."

"Can I shower first? I stink."

Pam handed her one cup. "No."

Her friend wore a tropical print halter dress that Brianne bought for herself at an All Sales Final, Going Out of Business shop. She donned it only once for an art festival in downtown Delray Beach. The patterned fabric resembled a Florida landscape. Then she caught a reflection of herself in a store window as she walked by. With each lively step in her wedged sandals, her breasts bounced like two puppies trying to climb a high step.

That's why people smiled at me. I was Bobbing Boobies Brianne.

When the dress was offered to Pam, she asked Brianne why she didn't want it any more. "I don't like the way it looked on me," was her reply.

Now Pam sashayed in high-heeled, strappy sandals from the foyer to the living room. The silky dress swayed back and forth like it covered two Butterball turkeys on the move.

Brianne said, "I thought you'd be home later."

"I thought so, too. But after the calls I got, I came back to check on you."

Pam sat on the sofa, but Brianne lowered herself onto the coffee table in her sweaty state. "Who called you?"

"Your parents and Emma. All their calls went to your voice mail. Then I get here, and your phone is on the kitchen counter and you're not around. The security guard said you went out for a walk. Why did you leave your phone here?"

Brianne shrugged. "I figured it was turned off, so why take it?"

"Promise me you will always have it with you when you walk. You don't have to answer it. Just keep it on you."

Brianne put her hand over her heart. "I promise."

"Now tell me what happened and why everyone is worried. I knew reading Cort's speech would be trouble."

Brianne took a sip of her coffee. "First, I owe you an apology."

"For what?"

"Well, for my family bothering you, for making you come back early ... for having sex on your grandmother's cabinet."

Pam eyed her over the rim of her cup. "Please tell me it was with Cort and not BOB."

Brianne told her what happened when he came to pick her up.

"What is it with you two and front doors?" her roommate said. "Forget about the *gabinete*. From what I heard, my *papi* may have been conceived on it."

Brianne described how distant Cort became after they had sex. "He wouldn't even look at me."

"You know, most men don't want to talk after sex. Did you misinterpret the situation because he couldn't speak?"

"There was no smile, no hug, nothing. It was like he wanted to forget it happened as soon as he pulled out." Brianne leaned toward Pam. "Get this. At the fundraiser, he said he wanted me to stay by his side because I was his reader for the night. Not his date or his girlfriend. *His reader.* What do you think about that?"

"*Chica,* I don't know what to think about this *singao* you got yourself involved with. Maybe he was embarrassed that you guys had sex so soon?"

"Or he was embarrassed that he had it with me."

"No way. He wanted you more than world peace, and you know it. It has to be something other than the sex. We can guess all we want, but you won't know until you ask him."

Brianne emphatically shook her head. "I'm never speaking to him again."

"You need to find out what went wrong."

"No, I don't. It was just a one night stand. We both move on."

They sipped their coffee. Then Pam asked, "Did the reading of the speech go well?"

"It did." An image of the Ice Queen popped into Brianne's head. "Wait until you hear what happened *after* that."

"*Dios mio,* there's more?"

"After I walked off the podium, I needed to pull myself together, so I went into the ladies room. When I came out of the stall, Cort's publicist was waiting for me. This tall, skinny blonde called me a quack for prescribing seven days of vocal rest. Then she said Cort was going to fuck me and dump me."

Pam snarled. "I hope you told that bitch off."

"I did. When I went back into the banquet room, Cort asked if I was upset because we—" Brianne hooked her fingers into quote marks, "—made love. I told him we only fucked and even his publicist said I screwed his career."

"I better not ever meet this *puta publicista.*"

"That's why I turned off my phone. I didn't want to talk with anyone for a while. I'm sorry you had to deal with the fallout."

Pam set her empty cup on the coffee table. "Have you checked your phone or your email today?"

"No. A *loca* grabbed me as soon as I came in the door."

Brianne turned on her phone. There were three separate voice mails, one from her mother, father and sister. There were five text messages from Cort.

Where are you?

Answer me.

Are you all right?

Dammit answer me.

Why did you leave?

Brianne handed Pam the phone. She read the messages then handed it back. "Did he come here to see you?"

"Maybe. I told security to take his name off the guest list and turn him away if he showed up."

"Let's find out." Pam called the security desk and asked the guard on duty to check the log. She listened, thanked him, and hung up. "He did come. He was upset when they refused to let you know. There's a note in the log that the guard threatened to call the police unless he left."

"I'll check my emails after I shower."

"Well, I'm going to bed."

"Thanks for everything."

Pam waved over her shoulder as she walked to her bedroom.

After a shower and breakfast, Brianne opened her email account. There were ten messages from Cort which started after midnight and ended that morning.

From: Cortland Hardison
Date:11/12/2012 12:23:12 AM
To: Brianne Gordon
Subject: What is wrong with you?

From: Cortland Hardison
Date:11/12/2012 12:48:33 AM
To: Brianne Gordon
Subject: You're making me crazy!!!

From: Cortland Hardison
Date:11/12/2012 1:17:24 AM
To: Brianne Gordon
Subject: Will you tell me what the hell is going on?

From: Cortland Hardison
Date:11/12/2012 2:20:45 AM

To: Brianne Gordon
Subject: Please tell me what is wrong.

From: Cortland Hardison
Date:11/12/2012 2:55:08 AM
To: Brianne Gordon
Subject: Let me make things right.

From: Cortland Hardison
Date:11/12/2012 3:19:11 AM
To: Brianne Gordon
Subject: I'm sorry, so very sorry.

From: Cortland Hardison
Date:11/12/2012 4:10:15 AM
To: Brianne Gordon
Subject: Pretty please

From: Cortland Hardison
Date:11/12/2012 5:02:05 AM
To: Brianne Gordon
Subject: Pretty please

From: Cortland Hardison
Date:11/12/2012 5:44:36 AM
To: Brianne Gordon
Subject: Pretty please

From: Cortland Hardison
Date:11/12/2012 6:01:47 AM
To: Brianne Gordon
Subject: Pretty please

Brianne moved her cursor through the Inbox and deleted each one without opening them.

#

In the afternoon, she phoned her parents.

"How are you, honey?" her mother asked. "It's Brianne. Pick up the phone, Ted."

"Are you okay?" her father asked when he came on the line.

"I'm fine. I got emotional after giving the speech and didn't feel like sticking around for the auction."

After the two-way conversation with her parents, Brianne called her sister.

Emma asked, "Why did you leave without saying good-bye? Cort was looking for you."

"I was tired."

"Bullshit. It's because of what happened between you and him. You promised to tell me. I also need your help with the new menu."

"If you want, you can come over now."

"I'm on my way."

#

Upon arrival, Emma tossed her purse and some sample menus she collected onto Pam's foyer cabinet. "Now tell me what happened."

Brianne laid her hand on the marble top. "The problem started right here when Cort picked me up last night."

Emma looked confused. "In the cabinet?"

"Not in the cabinet. *On* the cabinet."

"On the cabinet? Ooohhh." Emma smiled. "Way to go, sis."

"Way to go until he regretted it."

"Why did he regret it?"

"No idea."

Maybe he thought whaling would be better than it was.

"Did you ask him?"

"No."

Emma shook her head. "Then how do you know he regretted it? Maybe it was something else entirely."

"Like what?"

"Birth control?"

"He used a condom."

"He wanted to wait until the wedding night?"

Brianne snorted. "Yeah, right."

"You always think the worst and that it's about you. It might be about him."

"Remember we're talking about The Hunk. What could possibly be wrong with him?"

"You never know, Bree. Everyone has issues. Some are just more obvious than others."

"Speaking of someone with obvious issues, do you remember Alan Nussbaum from high school?"

"I didn't until the creep tried to hit on me last night." Emma rolled her eyes.

"He said I looked really different. When I asked him to explain, he made pig noises."

"Forget him. He told me he still lives with his mother and is the proud owner of a comic book stand at the flea market."

Brianne picked up the menus and walked to the dining room table. She spread them across the tabletop and sat down. "Do you want to have vegetarian entrees on PrimeTime's menu that are similar to ones at these restaurants or different?"

They discussed various entrée options, the cost of new ingredients and preparation, how to make the dishes flavorful and whether to expand the meatless options to soup and appetizers. Brianne lent Emma her favorite vegetarian cookbook. The recipes she tried and liked were marked.

When they finished, Emma returned her iPad to her purse and asked, "Have you heard from Cort since last night?"

"He's texted and emailed me. I haven't read any of them. I don't plan to see or talk to him again."

"But you're his therapist."

"Pam is taking over his case."

She doesn't need to know the switch was done before last night.

#

Over the next three days, Cort sent more texts and emails. She deleted each one. On Wednesday, she planned to leave the office well before his five PM therapy appointment. In the morning, she met with The Voice Center accountant. From there, she went to Sunshine Engineering where she conducted her lunchtime accent modification class. Then she presented a proposal for a similar training program at a local software company.

It was almost four o'clock when she came in the building's unmarked rear door and went straight to her office. She was ravenous because she had skipped lunch. As she took the first bite of a vegetable sub, Pam walked in and sat down.

"Cort's here."

Brianne chewed and tried to calm her racing heart. "Did you move up his appointment?"

"No, he's been here since Kitty opened at ten this morning."

"Why?"

"He said he's not leaving until he hears from you."

Brianne laid down her sandwich. "This is crazy."

"No, crazy is that man out there. He brought his lunch and a damn pillow."

"A pillow?"

"He told Kitty it was in case he wanted to take a nap."

"What should I do?"

"What you should have done in the beginning. You need to talk to him. I know you hate confrontations. In the past, when you ran away, the guys just let you go. This one isn't. He left this letter for you. He said after you read it, if you tell him face-to-face to leave you alone, he will. By the way, I told him he could use his voice."

Pam stood and slid the envelope across the desk. She closed the door behind her. Brianne stared at the unopened envelope. Her heart pounded in her chest. The one bite she'd swallowed churned in her stomach. She tore the envelope open with shaky fingers. The letter was handwritten.

Dear Brianne,

I am so sorry. After <u>MAKING LOVE</u> to you, I was scared. No one has ever made me lose control like that. No one. When you wouldn't see me or talk to me I realized how much I hurt you.

Please forgive me and give me another chance. Let me show you how much you mean to me. I've never had to work this hard before, but you are so worth it. You're making me into a better person. I hope to be a man worthy of you.

Yours always, Cort

Chapter 7

BRIANNE SAT FOR several minutes before she jumped to her feet. She made a quick trip to the restroom then walked into the reception area. Cort sat in one of the cushioned chairs with his elbows on his knees. His head lifted when the door opened.

When she first met him at Hardcort Fitness, he was fit and in command. She was stunned by his civilized but sexy appearance at his first therapy appointment. When Cort entertained her in his home, he was casual chic and comfortable. Classy was the only word that came to mind when she pictured him in the black tuxedo for the Healthy Kids fundraiser. Now he looked haggard and worried, like someone awaiting news in a hospital.

He jumped to his feet when Brianne came through the door, a concerned look on his face. Without a word, she picked up his pillow and tucked it under her arm. With his hand in hers, she led him back to her office and pulled him inside. She threw the pillow on the floor, stepped around him to shut the door, and rushed into his arms.

Their mouths sought each other and kissed as if they were starved. Their bodies fit perfectly against one another, especially with her in high heels. He tore his mouth away and nuzzled her neck. His breathing rasped in her ear, his chest rose and fell under her palm.

"Brianne." His voice was rusty but hearing him say her name for the first time sounded wonderful. He pulled back, his face stark. "Thank you."

Although Brianne's heart still ached like an open wound, she couldn't deny how broken Cort seemed. No man had ever shown her such need before. It was thrilling and frightening, powerful and humbling.

His hands roamed over her back and down her hips. He trailed kisses down her cheek. Cort buried his mouth in the dip where her neck curved toward her shoulder. Brianne didn't realize how sensitive that part of her body was. He pulled back and gazed at her, his expression soft at first, then more intense. Brianne's desire for him pooled in her belly and between her thighs. He reached up and caressed her face.

"You're so beautiful." He kissed her again.

The muscles inside her clenched in anticipation of what Cort could and would do to her. He leaned to one side and slid a hand beneath the hem of her dress. When his fingers moved over her curves, he stopped and looked at her.

She smiled.

In the restroom, she had removed her panties. He backed her up and dropped to his knees.

She exhaled and said, "Not here."

"Here," he murmured, "Now."

He held her dress up with one hand and moved her legs apart. His tongue stroked up the inside of both thighs. Then it parted her folds and flicked over her. She gasped. He lifted her leg over his shoulder which bunched the dress at her waist. With both hands free, he tilted her hips toward him. Her hands pressed palm down against the door, and her hips thrust against his mouth. He squeezed her butt and positioned her for his plundering tongue.

Within a minute, Brianne's orgasm peaked. Her leg jerked in little spasms on Cort's back. She bit her lip to prevent a cry. A low moan escaped when the burst of pleasure flooded her body. Cort's arm circled her naked hips and held her upright until the tremors subsided.

When her knees wobbled, he stood and wrapped his arm around her waist. He sat down in a nearby chair and pulled her onto his lap. His length pressed against her thigh.

She whispered, "What about you?"

"Later. This was for you, sweetheart." His first endearment sounded wonderful. "Are you upset that we did it in your office?"

"Why do you ask?"

"You said *not here*."

"I went commando to get you, remember? I just didn't want to do it by the door *again*."

He chuckled. "I'm sure it's not a door fetish. It's just that I want you as soon as I see you."

They continued to cuddle. Cort used one hand to stroke the top of her thigh, over her knee, and down her leg as far as his reach extended.

After several minutes, Brianne leaned back against his arm and said, "I think we should talk, but I can't with my dress around my waist."

"And with you bare-assed in my lap, this hard-on will distract me."

"Are you sure you'll be all right?"

"Yeah, as soon as I admit what I jerk I was, this chubby will go right down." He helped her to her feet, and she smoothed her dress while he adjusted his pants. He pulled up a chair so they sat facing each other. "The past week has been the best and worst one in my life. Please understand how desperate I was to do what I did today."

Brianne said, "I'm sorry I refused to communicate with you. In the past I always just walked away. Everyone else let me go. You didn't."

"You're the first woman who showed me what a complete bastard I can be. It was a rude awakening. I got used to people telling me I was hot shit. I guess I believed it." He leaned forward and covered her hands with his. "I meant it when I said I never lost control like that before. The last ten years has been about controlling everything from my business to my relationships. I thought nothing could rock my world until I met you."

A firm knock sounded on the door. Pam said, "Sorry to interrupt whatever is going on in there, but it's almost time for Cort's therapy."

"He'll be right there," Brianne said. She spotted the pillow on the floor. "Would you really have taken a nap in our reception room?"

"Sweetheart, I would have done whatever it took."

Brianne retrieved her panties from the restroom while Cort had his therapy with Pam. She trashed her soggy sandwich. When his session was over, the three of them locked up the office.

"Would you like to join us for dinner?" Cort asked Pam.

"About as much as I'd like to watch my parents having sex." She turned toward her car. "I have grocery shopping to do."

After Pam waved goodbye and drove out of the parking lot, Brianne said, "I'm starving. I didn't get any lunch."

"What are you hungry for?"

She leered at him.

"Keep looking at me like that and we'll be doing it against your car."

"And you say we don't have a door fetish."

They drove to an Indian restaurant because of the variety of vegetarian dishes. Midway through the meal, both tried without success to hide their fatigue.

"I'm sorry." Cort yawned. "I haven't been getting much sleep."

"I've been sleeping but not well."

"I wanted to wake up with you next to me in the morning."

"I have an early client, and I need to be in the office by seven," she said.

"Seven? Who has therapy at seven in the morning?"

"Someone who has to be at work by eight-thirty."

"He can't come after work?"

"She's a single mom, and the afternoon and evening are for her kids."

He nodded, and they both finished their meals. After dinner, they stood in the parking lot between their two vehicles. Cort leaned back against his car and pulled Brianne between his legs.

"How does tomorrow night look for you?"

"Pretty good. I'm done with clients by two."

"I have a meeting tomorrow afternoon." He seemed to read her thoughts. "I promise I will follow Pam's instructions about my voice. I should be done by five at the latest. Will you spend the night?"

"Yes."

"One other question, are you on birth control?" His voice contained a tremor of hope.

"It's been a while since I've been in a relationship. So, no, I'm not on any form of birth control. But I could schedule an appointment with my doctor."

He pulled out his phone and thumbed the keys. Brianne stared at him, perplexed. He showed her the screen.

It said, *pretty please.*

Cort gave her a wry smile. "I can't say it, but it seems to work for me in writing."

#

Pam was surprised to see her when she walked in the door. "I wasn't expecting you home so soon."

"We're both tired and decided to call it a night. Besides, I have an early morning client."

Pam said, "You can tell me what happened between you two later. Before you go to bed, I just got off the phone with Marisol. She's having a party at her place Saturday night. Do you and Cort want to go?"

Marisol Santo Domingo was a wealthy socialite who had moved from Miami to Fort Lauderdale after her divorce. She and Pam had been friends since high school. When Marisol was in town for the season, she threw lavish parties at her home on the Intracoastal Waterway.

"I'll check with him and let you know."

#

Cort called Brianne at five PM on Thursday to say his business meeting was done. She was headed to his house when he texted: *Problem with AC at Hardcort. Meet me here.*

As she arrived, people streamed from the facility. Mark Diaz, the general manager, held the door open for them and appeared to offer apologies.

Should I go in or wait in the car?

She sent Cort a text. *I'm here.*

Long minutes passed before her phone chimed with a reply. *Where?*

Parking lot.

Come in.

Mark was about to close and lock the door when she walked up. She showed him Cort's text message to let her inside. The temperature was warm in the building. There was a large stain on the ceiling tiles. Equipment had been moved and wastebaskets placed to collect drips. Cort's voice was at a conversational loudness level, but the tension in his posture shouted his anger.

"Looks like we're gonna have to check out the unit on the roof," one of the repairmen said.

"Then let's do it. Every hour this place is closed costs me money and customers."

Cort greeted her with a kiss on the cheek before his attention was pulled away by a question from one of the repairmen. When the place got uncomfortably warm, Brianne moved outside. A cool breeze came off the nearby New River. It was almost seven when Cort found her sitting on a low concrete wall, her back against a pillar.

"I'm sorry. I had no idea it would take so long." He kissed the top of her head.

"Find the problem?"

"Finally, but it should never have happened in the first place. They installed something wrong. Anyway, Mark is staying here while it's fixed. I told him I would come back later. It'll take a couple hours to cool the place down. Do you mind if we go out to dinner and come back?"

"We can go in my car. It's right here."

She took two steps toward the parking lot then stopped because Cort hadn't moved. "What?"

"I'm thinking I may need my car," he said. "In case Mark calls."

"If he does, I'll drive you back." She waited. "Are you one of those men who can't stand to be driven by a woman? What about working on that control issue you have?"

Cort stood, hands on hips and his lips compressed. "You're right. Let's go." When they reached her Honda, he stood by the passenger door and tapped on the roof. "So this is your car."

Brianne's eyes narrowed. "Of course, it's my car."

"I've always wanted to drive a CR-V. Do you mind?" Cort held out his hand.

"Nice try, sport. You're riding shotgun tonight whether you like it or not." Brianne clicked open the door locks and got behind the wheel.

Cort got in, fastened his seat belt and gripped his knees. "Is this one of those relationship tests?"

"Relax, I'm a good driver." She started the engine and gunned it a little. She laughed when Cort's body jerked.

Brianne drove to a Greek restaurant with excellent hummus and vegetarian dolmades.

While they studied the menu, Cort asked, "If I order lamb, will it bother you to watch me eat it?"

"If it did, I couldn't have dinner with my family."

During the meal, he asked, "When you became a vegetarian, what was most difficult for you?"

Should I tell him the truth? How long before you reveal sensitive information to a man you're seeing? Hell, I haven't even told him about my obese childhood yet.

Cort waited, an expectant look arched his eyebrows. "Well?"

Why not tell him? The man has already been inside me.

"Farting."

Cort dropped his fork.

Brianne gave a self-conscious laugh. "It was tough in the beginning because I didn't realize that eating so many vegetables can affect your digestive system that way. I was in college, and sometimes I had to leave class and not come back."

"Did it go away when you got used to it?"

"Yes. There were other dietary changes that helped, too. I should have known to ease into it. One night it was so bad, I slept in the stairwell at the dorm. The next morning, no one would go in there. They thought something had died. I talked them into opening the outside door for a while before calling an exterminator."

Cort shook his head. "You have just destroyed one of my myths about women."

"Your other girlfriends never farted?"

"Or burped."

"How was that possible?"

"I couldn't say. They weren't around long enough. But they also weren't as open with me as you are."

Brianne changed the subject. "Have you talked with your publicist since Saturday night?"

"I still can't believe she thought it was okay to say what she did to you."

"I can't believe she questioned my professional judgment about your therapy."

"What? You didn't say anything about that."

Brianne said, "I guess your week of silence created problems for her. She called me a quack."

"I'm sorry. That was totally out of line. No wonder you were so upset." There was a new edge to his voice.

"Needless to say, you better keep her away from me and Pam."

"No problem. I made it clear that she overstepped her bounds. Now I'm debating whether to keep her as my publicist."

Brianne dropped her chin to hide her secret smile.

#

When they returned to Hardcort Fitness, it had cooled down. Cort turned on a few lights and walked to where the leak and offices were located. Brianne strolled around the area and stopped at a piece of equipment used for chin-ups. She laid her purse on the floor then grasped the padded handles of the high bar. With her calves raised behind her in a kneeling position, she did five chin-ups. Her arms quivered.

I need to work more on my upper body. Would it make my honkers smaller?

She switched to the other side where she jumped up, locked her elbows, and dipped down. Her arms trembled after only three reps.

Forget this. I don't need Cort to find me in a heap on the floor.

Brianne went to the free weights area and picked up two five-pound dumbbells. She completed a set of triceps kickbacks then shoulder presses. Halfway through bicep curls, a door closed at the back of the building. She stopped, replaced the dumbbells, and moved to where her purse sat in the shadow of an incline weight bench. She straddled the padded seat and waited for Cort.

Chapter 8

HE CAME INTO view from the back of the building and headed to the front.

Brianne said, "Over here, Cort."

He detoured off the walkway. A wide smile creased his face as he threw his leg over the bench seat and sat across from her. He wrapped his hands around her bare knees, and her breath caught in her throat. Cort scooted her toward him and lifted her legs over his thighs until their bodies were almost crotch to crotch. Brianne draped her arms around his neck and crossed her ankles behind him.

"The air conditioning must be fixed," she said. "It's cooler in here."

"Sweetheart, it's about to get hotter."

He grasped the nape of her neck. With his thumbs under her jaw, he lifted her mouth to his. Her breathing quickened. He skimmed feathery kisses from her ear down. The sensation was almost unbearable. She fought to not bend her neck or lift her shoulder to push him away. He reached beneath her top and deftly unfastened the front clasp of her bra. She closed her eyes as his hands stroked her bare breasts and plumped them together.

Brianne arched her back and rocked her hips with primal instinct. He rolled her nipples with his thumbs and forefingers. She gasped at the pleasure of this exquisite torture.

"I love your breasts," he murmured. "Lift your arms, sweetheart."

She did, and he flung her top and bra off. She undid the top three buttons of his shirt. Then he grabbed his collar and pulled it over his head.

Cort scooted her away from him, moved her legs off his, and swung them to one side. After he rose to his feet, he pulled her up with him.

Brianne wanted to feel his bare chest against hers. He had a T of dark hair that crossed his pecs and arrowed down toward his waistband as if it pointed the way. A small tattoo that looked like a sun sat above his left nipple.

Cort unbuttoned and unzipped her shorts. He pushed his hands into the back waistband. As he ran his palms down her derriere, the clothes slipped off and puddled around her ankles. She stepped out of them and kicked her sandals off.

He reached for his waistband, but she stopped his hands. "Let me."

She sank onto the bench and undid his pants. She laid her palm flat against the upright bulge of his erection. He closed his eyes and groaned. His pants dropped. She lowered his boxer shorts. The head of his penis appeared, and she enclosed it in her mouth. When she ran her tongue around the tip, she tasted his saltiness. Cort covered her ears with his palms as the muscles in his thighs trembled.

"Enough," he growled. "I want to be in you."

He lifted her head away from him, took a step back, and toed off his deck shoes. Before he pulled his feet out of his pants, he reached in the pocket, removed a condom and handed it to her. "Here's something for you to do."

She tore it open, pinched the end and unrolled it on him. When she finished, he lifted her off the seat. Cort sat with his legs straddling the bench. He moved her to stand positioned above him, one leg on each side.

He grinned up at her. "How are your squats?"

"We're about to find out."

He lowered his back against the incline. "Think you'll be able to count your reps?"

"No."

He held his cock upright as Brianne lowered her body onto it. Her emptiness was filled.

"Ah, Brianne, I'm crazy with wanting you. Show me how much you want me."

"I do want you, desperately."

She laid her hands on his chest and rocked her hips. The movement forced him against her G-spot and ignited vibrations of pleasure. She leaned her upper body forward, clenched her thighs, and lifted. He slipped out part way before she was pulled down and he slid into place. Eyes closed, she concentrated on the sensations that coursed through her.

He guided the up-down movement of her hips. "That's it."

Brianne lost all sense of time, place, and body image. She sat upright, placed one hand behind her on his thigh, and moved back and forth. She panted in time to her rhythm.

He slid his hand up her abdomen and laid it between her full breasts. Brianne clutched it like a lifeline. He arched his hips which caused him to go deeper. She whimpered as the tension in her built to unbearable tightness. Cort thrust hard as his head fell back.

"Ahhh."

He held her hips hard against his pelvis and pumped into her. The feel of his spasms drove the tremors she sought through her. She stiffened, cried out, and then sprawled in abandon on his chest. Cort held her to him while her arms dangled to the floor. They stayed connected. He stroked her back from neck to rump until their wild hearts calmed.

I love you. I love you. I love you.

At last, Brianne lifted her head and looked into Cort's face. "The reason most people do this in a bed is so they don't have to get up and get dressed."

He moaned. She laid her head back on his shoulder, and they remained still for several more minutes. Cort's breathing became slow and steady.

With her head still on his shoulder, Brianne said, "You're not falling asleep, are you?"

"Huh? No, no. I was just resting. I guess we better get going before the cleaning crew finds us."

"Cleaning crew?" She jerked into a seated position.

"Take it easy. They don't come in until after midnight."

Brianne extracted herself and rose with her legs on either side of him. She stretched her arms high above her head.

"Mmm, mmm, mmm," Cort murmured, a wide grin on his face as he scanned her up and down.

Brianne looked down her nude body straddled over Cort's like The Colossus at Rhodes. She ducked her head, scrambled to the side, and crouched to gather her clothes.

Where the hell did he toss my bra?

It was on a weight rack a few feet away. She slipped on her panties and shorts then went to where her bra was draped. When she turned around, Cort had just pulled on his boxer shorts. He bent to gather his clothes and shoes. She shrugged into her top.

He said, "Sweetheart, do you mind if I shower here before we head home?"

"I'd like to freshen up, too."

"You can use the bathroom in my office."

She ran her hands up his abdomen and across his chest. "Are you sure you don't want me to wash your back?"

"I can't think of anything I'd like better, but we really need to go soon. If you shower with me, we'll never get out of here in time."

Okay, but why does he have to shower here at all? Why can't he do it at home?

She picked up her purse and followed him to a door near the back of the building. He unlocked it and flipped on the light switch. The room contained a desk, several chairs, and file cabinets.

Cort grabbed a gym bag off the floor. "The bathroom's in there. I'll come back here for you."

Brianne touched up her makeup and combed her hair. When finished, she returned to his office. As she turned his desk chair to sit down, the arm hit an open drawer. A small pile of multi-colored foil packets were scattered inside.

So that's where he got the condom.

She was about to shut the drawer when she stopped.

Why does he have condoms in his desk here?

She pulled the drawer toward her. The foil packets lay on a folder marked *Fitness Sex*. After she stared at it for several seconds, Brianne sat down on the chair. She slipped the manila file out from under the foil packets and opened it. Inside were articles cut from magazines about sexual positions on various pieces of exercise equipment.

She gasped when she spotted a list in Cort's handwriting on the inside cover. He had ranked several pieces of equipment with the incline bench as number one and the names of several women under it.

Oh my God! Hardcort Fitness is his fuck pad!

An icy coldness washed over her. Brianne grabbed a thick marker from a mug filled with pens, added her name to the incline bench list in large, black capital letters. She laid the open file on the desk and grabbed her purse. Careful not to trip and fall like the last time, she hurried through the darkened facility. Brianne unlocked the deadbolt on the front door and raced to her car. She was about to exit the parking lot when she braked hard.

What the hell am I doing?

Cort pursued her for five days to apologize and ask for a second chance. He wrote a heartfelt letter that said he wanted to become a better man. Here she was, running out on him again without giving him a chance to explain.

If he wants to become a better man, shouldn't I try to be a better woman?

She parked her car out of sight, went inside, and locked the door. In the unlit reception area, she took a seat in the shadow of the check-in counter. Soon curses bounced off the walls of the empty gym from the direction of his office. Cort called her name several times in a voice used to locate a scared child or animal. He rushed into the reception area and pushed against the glass front entrance. He was knocked back when the door didn't budge. After twisting the lock open, he rushed outside and scanned the front parking area.

"Fuck!" After several beats, Cort stared at the door he held open and then peered out to the lot where her car had been.

He's wondering how I locked the door behind me.

Cort came inside and pulled the door closed. "Brianne?"

"Yes."

He tracked her voice to where she sat. "Thank you for not leaving."

"Actually, I got as far as the street before I turned around."

"Where's your car?"

"On the side of the building."

He snorted a laugh then said, "Can we talk about this?"

"It's why I came back."

He locked the door and then sat in the chair next to her. He opened his mouth, but before words came out, she laid her fingers against his lips.

"Let me go first," she said. "I have to tell you the drawer was open but the folder wasn't. I'm sorry I looked at it."

"You don't have to apologize. I'm sorry you saw it."

"How long have you had an office in this place?"

"Just a couple weeks. Why?"

Brianne crossed her arms over her chest. "Did you pack up the folder and condoms when you changed offices?"

"No. No." Cort laid his hand on her knee. "The desk and all its contents were moved just before this place opened. I didn't pack or unpack anything."

"Have you used the condoms here before tonight?"

In other words, have you used them since you met me?

"I can't remember the last time I used those in the desk. I think it was a couple of relationships ago."

"Can we take them home with us?"

He leaned over and kissed her cheek. "Yeah, let's get them out of here."

"I have two more questions for you, Cort."

"Shoot."

"What are you going to do with the folder?"

"How about we put in it through the shredder Mark has in his office? Do you want to do the honors?"

"No, I think you should. Second question: Why did you have to shower here rather than at home?"

"You'll see when we get there. The previous owners did a good job updating the place before I bought it. The one room they didn't do was the upstairs bath. It's the world's ugliest bathroom and my next project. Until then, I avoid it whenever possible."

Brianne rose to her feet. "Then let's go. I want to see the world's ugliest bathroom."

#

A short time later, they were crowded into one of the world's smallest bathrooms.

She looked around at the limited amount of open floor space and the outdated fixtures. "Now I see why you shower at Hardcort."

The full bath on the second floor of his house had a toilet, pedestal sink, and an old cast iron tub. Someone had squeezed a tiny acrylic shower into the corner between the tub and toilet. The bathroom walls were tiled in hideous peach and pale green.

Cort said, "Every time I use the shower, I have to stick my ass out past the curtain to wash my feet."

"When I was here for dinner last Friday night, why did you ask if I'd ever had sex in a shower?"

"I was hoping you'd tell me the one at your place is big enough."

Brianne laughed. "Mine is big enough, but I've never done it in a shower before."

Cort's mouth dropped open. "You've never had sex in the shower?"

"Or on a foyer cabinet or in my office or on a weight bench."

He looked pleased. "So when can we try out your shower?"

"It'll have to wait until a night when Pam is away. We have a rule that no one has a sleepover guest when the other roommate is home."

"I don't have to sleep over. We'll just shower together."

"The semantics are the same, sport."

Cort wrapped his arms around her in the tight confines between the sink and the wall. "Then I'm going to think of other interesting places for us." Twin chills of excitement and unease ran through her. He grabbed her hand and led her out of the tiled nightmare. "Come on, sweetheart. Let me show you my bedroom. We have lots of room in there."

Finally, a bed.

Chapter 9

THE MORNING LIGHT was different, the pillow too fluffy, the mattress too firm. Then Brianne smiled and turned over. The space beside her was empty. The digital clock on the nightstand read six-thirty.

Stretching, her hands grasped the squared headboard spindles as her toes pointed toward the foot of the bed. She flushed with the memory of holding onto those spindles last night with locked elbows so her head didn't bang into the bedrail.

Where is he?

Brianne rose and rummaged in her overnight bag. She dressed in Pam's satin slip. When she packed yesterday, her friend came into the bedroom.

"Here, take this," she said, putting the pale pink lingerie in the overnight bag. "You can't wear a ratty football jersey the first night you spend at Cort's house."

In the world's ugliest bathroom, she brushed her teeth. Her tousled hair looked good. With a light hand, she applied a bit of mascara and lip color. Brianne descended the staircase to the foyer. A continuous motoric rumble vibrated from the back of the house. The kitchen was empty, but a freshly brewed pot of coffee sat on the warmer. Brianne poured a cup and leaned against the edge of the counter.

Should I wait here or upstairs?

The noise outside stopped. Moments later, the door to the patio opened. Cort walked in with a towel wrapped around his waist. He dried his hair with another and smiled when he caught sight of her.

"You went for a swim?" she asked.

"In the lap pool."

That was the noise, the pump motor.

He came closer as he rubbed the towel over his upper body and kissed her. "How do you feel this morning?"

"Honestly?" She puckered her mouth into a moue of regret. "A little tender."

He frowned.

Brianne set her cup on the counter and put her hands on his cheeks. "Don't. I'm fine. Remember, I'm out of practice." He pulled her close, but she pushed away from him. "You're wet. You should take your swimsuit off."

He whipped the towel from around his waist then dropped it on the floor. "Sweetheart, I never wear one."

She stepped back into his embrace. "You must be real popular at the beach."

His hand ran over the slickness of the satin slip while his mouth devoured hers. Brianne's hand glided over his still damp back. She arched her body into his and clutched his buttocks.

He lifted his mouth from hers and ran it across her cheek to her ear. "We have to stop. You're too sore for more."

"But you're not, right?"

He lowered his forehead to hers. "What did you have in mind?"

She picked the towel off the floor and placed it on the granite counter of the island. "Hop up here, sport, and I'll show you." Brianne wrapped her hand around his burgeoning penis. "This is going to work out well. The tile floor is too hard to kneel on anyway."

She stepped between his knees. Her lips slid down over the purplish crest. She pulled him deeper into her mouth as he leaned back on one elbow. Brianne inhaled the mild bleach-like smell of chlorinated water on his skin. She sucked in her cheeks, and his cock bumped the back of her throat. Maintaining suction, she raised her head, until only the tip of him was still in her mouth. Again and again, this was repeated.

He moaned with pleasure as his hips pumped off the counter. His body coiled in blissful anticipation. He was at her mercy.

"Oh, God," he groaned.

As semen filled her mouth, she worked to swallow it. Spent, he fell back flat on the counter and covered his eyes with his forearm. She milked the last drop from him. While he brought his breathing under control, she lifted her cooled coffee and took a swig.

Now that might be something to try next time. Take a hot drink then swallow some of him.

He clasped her free hand and kissed the back of it. "That was great."

"I'm already thinking up variations on the present theme."

"What?"

"No, I think I'll keep it to myself and surprise you."

He squeezed her hand, flipped it over, and kissed the back. "I can't wait." He sat up and hopped off the counter. "I need to wash the chlorine off where you haven't licked it away already."

"Go," she said. "I'll make us breakfast."

When Cort returned to the kitchen, Brianne wore a chef's apron tied around Pam's satin slip. Steaming cheese omelets sat on the counter in front of the island's barstools. Slices of cantaloupe and kiwi lay on a plate between the two place settings.

"Good timing and good morning," she said.

He grinned. "It's been a great morning."

They sat side by side. Brianne put a forkful of omelet in her mouth. A long string of cheese stretched from between her lips down to the plate. With her eyes on Cort's, she sucked the strand upward. He stopped chewing and watched. Then she picked up a slice of melon, placed the tip of the crescent between her lips, and pulled several inches of the fruit into her mouth.

"You're killing me," he said. "You know that, right?"

She smiled and juice ran down her chin. Cort leaned toward her, lapped the liquid, and kissed her. His fork clattered to the counter. They were both a little breathless when they returned to their breakfast.

Brianne said, "We've been invited to a party tomorrow night if you want to go."

"Whose party?"

"It's a friend of Pam's, Marisol Santo Domingo. She's in town for the season."

Cort's fork was paused halfway to his mouth. His eyes darted around, like the answer to her question flitted in front of his face. "I … uh—"

Brianne said, "Marisol is one of your old girlfriends, isn't she?"

He nodded. "We dated, but it was before she got married."

"Do you want to go to her party?"

"I'll go if you want to."

"Let me think about it, and we can talk more tonight. Okay?"

#

At the office, Brianne called to schedule an appointment with her gynecologist. There was a cancellation on Tuesday afternoon, and she took it. She opened the newspaper to the *Society News* page. Pam put it on her desk with a Post-It note that said, *Check out Page 3*. There was a photo of Cort with Audrey Nussbaum and several other people active in the Healthy Kids organization. She scanned the article, but there was no mention of her. Pam was probably disappointed that The Voice Center didn't get some free publicity.

She and Pam ordered lunch delivered from a nearby deli and unpacked the food in the little break room.

Brianne poured dressing on her salad and said, "I still haven't told Cort about being a fat kid."

"Why not? Do you think he'll react differently than any other man you've dated?"

"Why wouldn't he? He works to help obese children, and his girlfriend was one."

"If you don't tell him, you risk him finding out some other way."

"Right now, I don't want him to find out at all."

Pam was silent, but a flicker of impatience narrowed her eyes and furrowed her brow.

Brianne said, "I know. It's not realistic. But I'm afraid I'll lose him because of it. Our relationship is still too new."

"How do you think he sees you as a woman?"

"As someone who isn't fat but isn't skinny either. I know I have bigger boobs than any of his other girlfriends." She looked down at herself. "They fascinate the hell out of him."

Pam laughed and shook her head. "Men."

"I still can't figure why he's interested in me."

"It's chemistry," Pam said. "Cort is a good-looking guy, but he doesn't rock my world like he does yours."

"I know I'll have to tell him about my past obesity soon. I just need to find the right time."

"Better sooner than later." Pam tossed her trash and left the break room.

While Brianne waited for her last client of the day, she received a text from Cort to call him ASAP. Was there was another problem at Hardcort Fitness? When he answered his phone, she asked, "Is something wrong?"

"One of my grandmother's caregivers called me. I'm on my way to Boynton Beach right now. I don't know how long it'll take."

"Call me when you can. I'll be at home."

#

Brianne made herself a salad for supper. While she ate it, Pam sent her a text. *At a friend's place till tomorrow. Be back @ 4pm for party. You and Cort going?*

Brianne: *Yes.*

At ten PM, she had her phone in hand to call Cort when it rang. "Where are you?" she asked.

"I'm in the lobby of your building. Security won't call or let me come up."

I forgot to put his name back on the guest list.

"Sorry. I'll get it straightened out."

A few minutes later, Brianne peeked through the door's peephole. Cort strode down the hall. She opened the door. He grabbed her around the waist, lifted her up, and kicked the door closed behind him. With her feet back on the ground, he held her and inhaled, his nose buried in her hair. He sighed and released her.

Her eyes scanned his strained face. "Is your grandmother okay?"

"Yeah, she's fine. I just hope I don't get another call tonight. Still have Scotch in your bar?"

She nodded. He poured himself a drink, took a swallow, and grimaced. Then he joined her on the sofa. She rubbed his leg. Tension coiled under his skin and made his muscles tight.

He laid his head against the back cushion and said, "I owe Lola so much."

"Lola?"

"That's my grandmother. I was eight when my parents were killed. She was getting ready to retire, but now she had this kid to raise. I'm all she's got, and she's all I've got. It's just that sometimes she drives me crazy." He ran his hands through his hair then reached for the Scotch again. "She's diabetic and doesn't follow the restricted diet or testing schedule. Two years ago, they had to amputate her foot. She keeps firing home health aides who won't bring her restricted food. I had to read her the riot act again."

"Does she live alone?"

"I had her house made wheelchair accessible. I wanted to move her down here, but she insisted all her friends are in that neighborhood. She's lived there for more than forty years, but I don't know how much longer she can. Her health is not getting any better and neither is her mobility." He stared into the swirling liquid of his drink. After several deep breaths, he turned to face her. "Let's talk about something else. What's new with you?"

"I was able to get an appointment with my gynecologist on Tuesday." She laughed at the excitement in his expression. "I've also decided we should go to Marisol's party tomorrow night."

He stretched his arm across the top of the sofa and caressed her neck. "You're sure?"

"You're a public person, Cort. I don't want to be your hidden girlfriend. I need to practice being out in public with you."

"I'll do my best to make sure nothing unpleasant happens. If you change your mind about going or want to leave at any time, just say the word."

"Thank you. Did you get something to eat? I can fix you a snack." Brianne rose part way off the sofa to head into the kitchen.

"I'm fine. I had supper with Lola after I did a junk bust."

She sat down. "A junk bust?"

"I went through the house looking for food she's not allowed to eat. It's in my car. I can't put it in her trash. She fishes it out. But I do have a favor to ask."

"I don't want that stuff around here either."

"It's not that. Would you mind if I used your shower before I go home?"

Brianne sat up straighter. "Is that why you came over?"

"It wasn't the only reason. But I told you I'm a shower groupie. You'll be lucky if I don't ask to use Marisol's at the party tomorrow night. I promise I'll be quick."

"I hope not." She stood, grabbed his hand, and pulled him to his feet. "Pam won't be home until tomorrow afternoon."

Chapter 10

WHEN BRIANNE WOKE up Saturday morning, she listened to the gentle huffs of Cort's breathing behind her head. The weight of his arm draped her waist. His hand still cupped her bare breast. As she wiggled her bottom, his penis woke up. Without warning, she was flat on her back. Cort stared down at her with dancing, dark eyes.

"Good morning, sweetheart."

"Good morning to you." She tried out endearments to herself but wasn't comfortable with one to say out loud.

Honey, maybe. Babe, no. Sweetie Pie, definitely no.

He looked at his watch, groaned, and rolled off her. "I have to leave in a few minutes." He scooted to the opposite side of the bed and stood up. "I'm taking my neighbor, Sam, and some teammates to their softball game this morning. His dad has to work, and his mom is home with the new baby."

Brianne propped herself on her elbow and admired his rear as he walked to the bathroom and closed the door.

Oh, good. He shuts the door when he uses the toilet.

He returned and began to dress. "What time do you want me to pick you and Pam up for the party?"

"How about eight o'clock? Earlier if you're planning to shower and get ready here."

He zipped his fly. "Now there's an idea. I wonder if we would even make it to the party."

"Remember, Pam will be here."

"Damn. And your shower is so nice." He put one knee on the bed and kissed her goodbye. "See you later, sweetheart."

Brianne stayed under the duvet and fell asleep for another hour. She swore when she looked at the clock. The building's air conditioned workout room would be busy now. So Brianne climbed steps in the hot stairwell. After ten top to bottom runs, she was drenched with sweat. She showered then searched through her closet for something to wear that night. Pam was the party girl and had way more outfits than she did.

"Time to go shopping."

#

By three PM, she hadn't found anything different or special at the mall. On her way home, she passed a vintage clothing store.

If I don't find a dress there, then I'll borrow from Pam's wardrobe.

As she entered the shop, the perfect outfit was displayed on a mannequin. It was a fifties sundress with a scoop neckline, double spaghetti straps and a deep V in the back. Tiny flowers were sprinkled across the white fabric background. The full skirt required a crinoline. She purchased an amethyst-colored one to go with the floral pattern. With the extra deep petticoat, the hemline fell just above her knees.

When her roommate returned home, Brianne modeled the dress. Pam gasped. "I love it! Where'd you get it?"

"I found it at *Still in Style*. It's the shop on Federal Highway."

"Please let me borrow it sometime."

"You can if you help me with my hair and shoes."

Pam urged her to wear a pair of pale pink heels with a high ankle strap and styled her hair in a tight, ballerina bun at the back of her head. She didn't put on panties even though the crinoline netting was a bit scratchy. Brianne sat down and then stood several times to practice with the crinoline. She had to put her hands on her thighs first so the front of the dress didn't jump up into her face and cause a wardrobe malfunction.

I see London, I see France, I'm not wearing underpants.

#

That evening, she had just inserted diamond stud earrings when the doorbell rang.

"Got it," Pam called to her.

Brianne entered foyer and stopped dead. Cort wore a pale linen shirt and cream-colored trousers that hugged his hips. He looked like a yummy vanilla dessert that needed to be licked before it dripped. His eyes lit up and a wide grin split his face as he scanned her from head to toe.

Pam had on a fitted strapless dress with a straight knee-length skirt also in a floral print. On the cabinet by the door sat their small purses. Pam patted the cabinet's marble top. "Cort, did you know this is my *gabinete?* It belonged to my grandmother."

No, Pam, please don't do this.

Cort said, "It's beautiful. I love fine furniture."

"I do, too." Pam's voice had a smarmy lilt to it. "My grandmother used it as a dresser, and my mother had it in her dining room. But I decided it would work well as a cabinet by the door. Isn't it great when furniture has multiple uses?"

"As far as I'm concerned, it's the best kind."

Brianne grabbed her purse, opened the door, and walked out without a word. Laughter rang out behind her as she headed to the elevator.

#

Cort hired a car service to transport them to and from the party. The driver was not the same one who took them to the Healthy Kids fundraiser. Marisol's mansion was the end cap property on a street that stopped at the Intracoastal Waterway. Cars and limos lined the road on both sides which created a lane for one-way traffic only. A police officer directed their car to enter the roundabout driveway, drop them off, and exit the other side.

Cort tapped the driver on the shoulder. "You can wait somewhere nearby. I'll call when we're ready to leave."

As they stepped inside, live music above them underscored their entrance. Waiters circled with trays of drinks and appetizers. There were groups of people in the large circular living room ahead and more on the patio beyond.

Marisol Santo Domingo stood in the marble pillared foyer and greeted her guests. She was a tall blonde with honey-colored skin. In her Jimmy Choo shoes, she stood at six feet but was rail thin. She leaned down to kiss Pam on both cheeks. "I am so happy you came to my party. Who did you bring with you?"

Her eyes skipped over Brianne and locked on Cort. Her gaze softened and went doe-like. "Cariño, Cort. It's been a long time."

"It's nice to see you again, Marisol. Have you met my girlfriend, Brianne?"

Marisol tore her eyes away from him. "Don't I know you?"

Pam said, "You've met Brianne before, Mari. She's my business partner, and we share the condo. Remember?"

"Of course, but you look so different tonight. I love your dress. Where did you get it?"

Pam shook her head. "Forget it, *mi amiga*. I'm wearing it next. And I don't want you showing up in a look-alike."

"So how long have you two been a couple?" Marisol said to Cort.

"Long enough," he replied.

She bent toward Brianne and in a low, conspiratorial voice, asked, "Has he fucked you at the gym yet?"

Pam was behind Marisol. "What was that?"

"I'll give you a word of advice, *mi bella*," the party hostess said. "If he asks you to hold onto the chin-up bar, only do it facing him." Marisol lifted her nose in the air and moved it side to side. "I got this beautiful nose after falling face first. Remember, Cort?"

Brianne grinned and glanced over her shoulder. Cort looked stunned. He took Brianne's arm and led her away as Marisol's laughter trailed them. On the way to the patio, Cort lifted two champagne flutes off a waiter's tray and handed one to Brianne.

He steered her to a secluded spot. "Whenever you want to leave, just say the word. I wouldn't mind if you said it now."

She wrapped one arm around his waist and laid her head on his shoulder. "Come on, sport. The worst is over." It was nice not to be the one embarrassed for once. "Let's mingle and see if I get any more good advice."

For the next two hours, they spoke to people who Cort knew and people who knew of him. They wandered through the open rooms and admired the interior design. The bathrooms were of particular interest. They discussed options that might work in the ugliest bathroom in the world.

"I know it's feminine, but this chandelier looks wonderful in here." Brianne pointed overhead. "But it doesn't matter what the fixture is. Having good light in a bathroom is what's important."

When they returned to the first floor, a deejay played music on the patio. They escaped to the dock behind the house. The wooden structure stretched the entire length of the double lot and up the side of the property. A small yacht was moored at the pylons.

Brianne let her fingertips skim the fiberglass hull. "Is this Marisol's boat?"

"I don't think Marisol's much of a sailor. She's either leasing the dock space to someone or allowing a friend to keep his boat here."

They strolled to the dock's farthest point. The nearest pier light was fifteen feet away where the yacht's bow was tied. They were hidden around a ninety degree turn and in the shadows from a stand of nearby palms.

Brianne leaned against the railing, threw her arms around Cort's neck, and kissed him. The fullness of her dress acted like a cock block. She couldn't get her lower half close to his. They mimicked the act of love with their mouths. Their tongues probed, withdrew, inserted, retreated. Brianne ached for him.

Passion roughened Cort's voice. "I hope you're not attached to your panties. I'm about to rip them off."

"I'm not wearing any."

Cort lifted his head from her neck. "When did you take them off?"

"I didn't put any on."

"I'm glad I didn't know until now. I would have been hard all night."

"Pam says if you don't wear panties to a party you're sure to have a good time."

He breathed into the shell of her ear. "Oh, you're going to have a good time." His lips glided down her neck along the column of her pulse. His breath became harsh and erratic. "Sweetheart, I need to be inside you."

He spun Brianne around so she faced the water. With her head bent over the railing, she breathed in the wet-wood smell of the dock, the salty ripeness of the water and sea life. He lifted her full skirt and crinoline to expose her bare bottom, caressed it, and stepped forward.

His laughter rumbled against her back. "This dress is the perfect shield."

With his hands on her hips, he directed her to step back a pace from the railing. She widened her stance as he unzipped his pants and put on a condom. Soon his erection sought entrance as he followed her wet trail.

I can't believe I'm going to do this, but I don't care.

He slid into her. "You're so beautiful."

Cort leaned forward and placed his hands on the railing next to hers. They danced an erotic bump and grind to the bass rhythm from the deejay's speakers. The voices on the patio, the squeaks as the yacht rubbed against its moorings, and the thump of the music amped up the tension in her body. Cort removed one hand from the railing and lifted the crinoline's layers at the front so he could reach her. As soon as he nudged her bud, she convulsed around him.

Cort grabbed her hips and pumped, one, two, three times into her. He almost contained his cry of satisfaction. After removing his hands from under her dress, he wrapped his arms around her waist and kissed her bare back.

Through the fog of their afterglow, someone at the far end of the dock said, "Let's check out the yacht."

Cort groaned then slipped out. He smoothed her skirts down and moved to stand beside her at the rail. She took the knotted condom and dropped it inside her purse. They rested against each other as the reflected lights from the houses across the waterway danced on the currents.

After several minutes, Cort held out his hand to her. "Let's find Pam and see if she's ready to go."

They were stopped by new people who hadn't seen or talked to Cort yet. By the time they located Pam, who nibbled on desserts at the dining room table, it was well after midnight.

"There you are," she said and wiped her fingers on a cocktail napkin. "Are you ready to leave?"

"Are you?" Brianne eyed the sugary display with yearning.

"Hell, yes. I need to get away from these calories and get a good night's sleep. Let's find Marisol to say good-bye."

Pam insisted on sitting in the front seat on the way home and chatted with the driver.

Cort said, "I'll call you tomorrow after my golf game."

"Not too early, sport. I plan to sleep in."

"I love that you call me sport. Is it because it rhymes with Cort?"

"Of course."

I've been using an endearment for him all along, and it's related to athletics. Go figure.

Chapter 11

BRIANNE MISSED CORT'S phone call at noon. She listened to the message then called him back. "Hi. How was golf?"

"I lost, but that's okay. The guy I was with is an investor. He likes me to lose at golf, but not in business. Were you still asleep?"

"I was vacuuming. What are you up to now?"

"I'm driving to Boynton Beach to check on Lola. When I get back, do you want to go out to dinner?"

"Okay. Where do you want to eat?" Brianne asked.

"I was thinking about PrimeTime."

"My *dad's* restaurant?"

"Sure. I want to see it. We also need to talk about this week."

"I know. Thanksgiving is this Thursday. I have to—"

"Shit!" Cort was silent for several beats. "Sorry, but traffic is stopped as far as I can see. Let's talk about it at dinner."

"What time should I be ready?"

"How about seven o'clock? Do we need a reservation?"

"Don't worry. I'll call. Drive safe," she cautioned.

"I will. Bye, sweetheart."

"Bye, sport."

#

The hostess at PrimeTime greeted Brianne and smiled at Cort who stood behind her. The flash of surprise in the woman's eyes seemed to be more for the boss' daughter having a date rather than who the man was. They were escorted to the table Brianne requested in a secluded corner of PrimeTime's dining room. With Cort's back to the room, they had a degree of privacy from the other restaurant patrons.

He opened the menu and asked, "What do you recommend?"

Before she could answer, a familiar voice said, "Hi, you two."

Her sister stood next to their table and grinned at them.

Brianne said, "When did you start working here on Sunday nights?"

Emma ignored her. "Hi, Cort, it's nice to see you again."

He rose from his seat and bussed her cheek. "Good to see you, too."

Brianne tugged on her sister's hand. "Why are you here?"

"Well, Dad, Mom, Grandma, and I decided to go out to dinner tonight. Just like the two of you."

When Brianne's family went out to dinner, they did not come to PrimeTime. Instead, the food and service at other restaurants was evaluated. They only ate here when her uncles were in town for a Gordon Enterprises board meeting.

"Actually, we have our usual table in the back room," Emma said. "Why don't you join us?" She looked to Cort for an answer.

He raised his eyebrows. "Should we—"

"No, we'll stay here," Brianne interrupted.

"Oh, but we thought—" Emma stopped herself.

When Brianne called in the reservation for this table, either her dad or Emma found out. They concluded that her guest was probably a man and not another woman. Her parents didn't know that she and Cort were dating, unless her sister told them.

"My family wants to check you out, Cort, especially now that you can talk to them."

He held out his hand. "Then let's go have dinner with the family."

"Remember, it was your idea to eat here."

They followed Emma to the back room. Her father, mother, and grandmother stood beyond the double doorway like a receiving line.

"Here they are," her sister announced as she led the way.

Brianne's step faltered. *How do I tell them not to bring up my obese childhood?*

When Cort bumped against her back, his warm breath tickled her ear. "Don't worry, sweetheart. It'll be fine."

While her parents greeted and introduced him to her grandmother, Brianne pulled Emma aside. "I haven't told him yet about being fat. Get the message to everyone."

Emma gave a silent *will do* with her thumb up. Cort held out Grandma's usual chair at the end of the long table. He took the chair around the corner from her and seated Brianne next to him. Her dad did the same for his wife and daughter across from them.

Emma whispered to their father, and he nodded. He turned to her mother and spoke in her ear. Meanwhile, Grandma held Cort's attention with a question about Hardcort Fitness. He didn't appear to be aware of the pass-the-message going on across the table.

Someone will have to tell Grandma.

Their drink orders were taken. Only Cort studied the menu as the Gordons knew it by heart. He leaned close to Brianne and whispered, "What can you eat here?"

"Side dishes."

Her sister must have overhead the exchange. "Brianne and I have been working on new items for the menu that don't have meat."

"What was that?" her father asked.

Emma said, "Cort asked why we don't have any vegetarian dishes for Brianne."

Don't put words in his mouth, Em.

Her father glared at her date. "This is a steakhouse. We have fish and chicken on the menu, but Brianne won't eat those either."

"I understand, sir," Cort said. "But you're losing part of your customer base. When people are dining with a vegetarian, they're not coming to PrimeTime if there are no meatless dishes."

Her father huffed. "So how long have you been in the restaurant business?"

"Ted, stop it," her mother said. "Cort is our guest and a fellow businessman. He's just making an observation."

Is this Dinner Disaster Number One?

Her dad glanced at Brianne. He must have seen the *please don't* look in her eyes. "Sorry. I have Emma talking my ear off about changing the menu. I guess I'm a little sensitive right now."

Cort said, "That's understandable. I think every business owner feels the same way. I know I do."

Brianne said, "Mom, when is your next Miss Florida meeting scheduled?"

"I have to be in St. Petersburg the first Saturday in December. I won't go to Texas that weekend with your father and Emma."

"You participate in the pageant, Mrs. Gordon?"

"I'm on a committee that plans Pageant Week."

"Candace was the first runner-up for Miss Florida the year before we got married," her father said.

"That explains why your daughters are so beautiful. You're a very lucky man, Mr. Gordon."

"Call me Ted."

"And me Candace," her mother added.

Dinner Disaster Number One averted.

Grandma said, "Tell us about your family, Cort."

"I lived in Chicago until my parents were killed in a traffic accident. Then I was raised by my grandmother in Boynton Beach."

The interrogation continued during the salad course and when their dinners arrived. Her father didn't come out and ask Cort his intentions toward his daughter, but he did pump him for details about their relationship. Brianne got her mother's attention and shifted her eyes between her father and Cort.

"Ted, you haven't given the poor man a chance to eat his dinner," Candace said. "Brianne is an adult. You don't need to grill her date."

Dinner Disaster Number Two eliminated.

Emma left the table in the middle of the entrée course. "Excuse me, I'll be right back."

Cort said to her father, "This is a good steak. Brianne told me about the Gordon history in Texas."

"My brothers own a slaughterhouse and the Double G ranch outside of Fort Worth."

Her mother said, "Did you know we'll be at the ranch for Thanksgiving?"

"No, I haven't told him," Brianne said. "We were hijacked before we could discuss it."

"Cort, you're welcome to join us," her grandmother said.

"Thank you for the invitation. But I'll be having Thanksgiving dinner with my grandmother."

Inez patted his arm. "Who's doing the cooking? You?"

Brianne giggled. Cort gave her a look that said: behave yourself. "No, a Thanksgiving dinner is way beyond my kitchen skills. My grandmother is in a wheelchair so she's unable to cook much anymore. I've ordered one from Publix that I can reheat for us."

Her father said, "So you don't know that Brianne will be away until next Sunday? We're staying the weekend because of my nephew's wedding on Saturday."

"Remember, Dad," said Brianne, "hostages aren't allowed to speak in a hijacking situation. So he doesn't know anything."

"Well, I know I'm going to miss you." Cort squeezed her hand on the table as he stared into her eyes.

When Brianne was able to break away from his smoldering gaze, her eyes shifted to her family. Her father wore a tight-lipped smile, her mother's head was tilted to the side with a sweet smile, and her grandmother had her chin propped in her hand with a knowing smile.

"I'm back." Emma took her seat once again. "What'd I miss?"

"We were talking about Thanksgiving," Brianne said.

Grandma turned to Cort. "The Gordons have been getting together for an outdoor dinner since Ted's father was a small boy. We cook a store-bought turkey on an outside spit and any other game his brothers manage to shoot the day before. You haven't had a real Thanksgiving dinner until you have to pick buckshot out of your teeth."

"Or taste Texas dust in your food," Dad added.

"Or step in horse shit on your way to the kitchen," Emma said.

Cort laughed and looked at Brianne.

She gave him a wry smile. "Can you see why I'm so excited about going?"

Grandma said, "Brianne doesn't like Thanksgiving because she still worries about her weight."

The laughter stopped. Brianne's heart stopped. She looked at Emma who mouthed *oops*.

Dinner Disaster Number Three strikes.

"Brianne doesn't have a weight problem," Cort said to her grandmother.

"When she was younger she struggled so much with it. As you can see, she has it under control now."

All Brianne could see was the back of Cort's head.

He asked, "How serious was it?"

"We were very worried, especially when she was bullied so much. We tried everything to help her, but ..." Grandma stopped. Everyone was silent, their eyes averted. "But, um, Brianne can tell you more about it."

"I'm sure she will."

The table grew quiet as everyone worked to finish the food on their plates. Brianne pushed her remaining vegetables around. When the server removed the dishes, it broke the knot of tension.

Cort wiped his mouth with his napkin and placed it on the table. "Well, thank you for the dinner invitation. It's getting late, and I have a seven AM flight, so we need to get going." He stopped the waitress before she left with the stack of dirty dishes. "You can bring my check."

"Dinner is on the house," her father said.

"Thank you, but I'll pay for my meal and Brianne's."

The server looked at Ted who nodded. She brought the bill for two dinners and left with a credit card.

Candace asked Cort, "Where are you flying tomorrow?"

"I'm headed to Los Angeles for meetings. I'll take the redeye back on Wednesday morning."

"We're flying to Fort Worth Wednesday morning. You'll miss seeing Brianne before we leave."

"I guess I will."

Cort thanked her family for the dinner invitation, kissed Grandma on the cheek, and waved good-bye to the others.

Emma came around the table, hugged Brianne and whispered, "Sorry."

"Not your fault."

They didn't talk on the way to the car. Cort started the engine.

Brianne said, "Can I—"

He held up his hand. "Let's wait until we get to your place."

"Pam will be home."

"Then we'll talk in the car."

They were silent on the drive to her condo. Cort pulled into a guest spot and turned off the engine.

Finally, he asked, "When were you going to tell me you had a pretty serious weight problem?"

She stiffened her spine, took a deep breath, and turned to face him. "I was going to tell you Friday evening, but then you had the issue with your grandmother. I didn't want to throw something else at you."

"Why didn't you say something before then?"

A knot of anger seized her chest. "When was I supposed to tell you that the obese child you attend fundraiser dinners for, have fitness programs for, and send to weight loss camps was me? When was I supposed to say that? Before sex? During sex? After sex?"

"I don't know. But you could have brought it up sometime during the last few days." He paused. "Just how bad was it?"

"At my heaviest, I weighed over a hundred pounds more than I do now."

Cort's eyes widened. "That much?"

"See." She pointed to his surprised expression. "That's the reaction that made me reluctant to tell you. Besides, it's not something I find easy to share with new people in my life. *Hi, my name is Brianne Gordon, and I used to weigh two hundred and fifty pounds.* The fact is, being who you are made it even more difficult." She waited for him to respond. When he didn't, she asked, "Is the obesity in my past a deal breaker for you?"

"I wouldn't say it's a deal breaker but—"

"But what? Is it not good for your image to be seen with someone who used to be fat?"

"It's just that—"

Her eyes narrowed. "You, of all people, should know that obesity is a disease. Food addicts are no different than people addicted to drugs, sex, or alcohol."

"Is that what you were? An addict? To keep the weight off, do you have to take it one day at a time, attend Weight Watcher meetings, recite the Serenity Prayer? Was food addiction your excuse?"

His sarcasm angered her and validated her unwillingness to confide in him. "My excuse was that I was a child. Do you remember your speech that I read at the fundraiser? It said if you over-feed children, they will eat twenty percent more. I was overweight as a three-year-old, and it worsened with hormonal changes in puberty. When I went away to college and was on my own, I lost the weight and kept it off."

"So just becoming a vegetarian did it?" Skepticism laced his voice.

"No, changing my diet alone didn't do it. I'm not an athletic person. I was bookish as a kid. So even if I wasn't overeating, I wasn't burning off calories. At college I walked everywhere and refused to take the campus bus. I didn't care how far away my classes were. That's how I lost the weight."

"Do you belong to a gym now?"

"I don't like exercising with other people around. But I've learned to eat healthy and do exercise that works for me."

Neither spoke for a long time.

"Is this it for us?" Brianne's voice was soft and hesitant. "If so, tell me now."

Cort ran his hand through his hair from front to crown. "I need time to think. This week apart will be good for that. I want to get our relationship in perspective without always having a hard-on."

I guess you can't think straight when the blood is flowing away from your brain.

"The reason I'm going to California is that a producer wants to talk to me about another reality show. But this is why I don't want to do another one with obese people. I know how bad they feel. I'm a fitness trainer, not a weight loss therapist."

"So I get to spend the next week in limbo while you decide if you can fuck a former fatso."

"Don't say it like that."

She opened her car door, stepped out and leaned down to look at him. "I gave you a second chance, Cort, because you wrote that you wanted to be a better man. While you're thinking about how important your image is, keep this in mind. I'm going to spend the next week thinking, too. I'm going to decide whether or not you have the potential to be worthy of me, regardless of my past, present, or future weight. Good night."

Chapter 12

PAM SWITCHED OFF the sound on the TV when Brianne entered the condo. "How was your dinner with Cort?"

Brianne dropped onto the living room sofa. "Awful."

"What did that *pendejo* do now? And I was beginning to like him again."

She told her about the whole dinner fiasco followed by their conversation in the parking lot.

Pam said, "Let me get this straight. He wants to rethink your relationship because you were a fat kid?"

"I guess he wants to evaluate the impact it might have on his image."

"What a hypocrite!" Pam added some expletives in Spanish.

Ditto, including the curses.

"So he's leaving tomorrow, and the day he gets back, I leave. We won't see each other for a week. I told him I'd be thinking about our relationship, too."

"Good for you, *chica*."

Brianne's cell phone rang in her purse. She pulled it out and checked the screen. "Shit, its Emma." She handed the phone to Pam. "Would you talk to her? I can't right now."

"Sure. Go take a nice shower. You'll feel better tomorrow."

#

Cort did not call on Monday. Brianne was determined not to be the one to contact him first, no matter how much she wanted a decision about their relationship. When she went to bed that night she powered off her phone.

In the morning, there was still no voice mail or text from him. After lunch, she left for her gynecologist appointment.

I'll be prepared whether Cort and I continue to see each other or not.

Following the examination, she was given the choice of oral contraceptives or the birth control shot administered every three months. In the end, she asked for a prescription for the daily pill. After she finished at the doctor's office, she went home to pack for her early morning flight to Texas.

#

"There you are."

Brianne jumped. "You scared me. I didn't hear you come in."

Pam waved her hand at the piles of clothes on the bed. "You're packing all this?"

"It's five days, including Thanksgiving and a wedding."

Pam sat on the one open spot on the mattress and examined a pair of cowboy boots. "How was your doctor's appointment?"

"I have a prescription for The Pill." Brianne stopped her folding. "How were things at the office this afternoon?"

"Fine. I had one appointment cancel for tomorrow."

Brianne held the T-shirt she started to fold against her chest. "Was it Cort?"

"No, and I checked before I left. As far as I know, he'll be there. Have you heard from him yet?"

Brianne shook her head, rolled up a pair of jeans, and put them in the bottom of her suitcase. "I've decided that maybe it's best for it to end now."

Before I fall more in love with him.

Pam stood and hugged her friend. "Don't worry, *chica.* Things will work out. Just give it time."

#

A van picked up the Gordon family early Wednesday morning and drove them to the airport.

Brianne placed her belongings in plastic bins at the security checkpoint then turned to help her sister. "Did Pam tell you what Cort said to me Sunday night?"

Emma took off her shoes and belt. "I can't believe that how much you weighed years ago would be an issue for him."

They cleared the walk-through scanner and waited for their possessions on the other side.

Emma lifted her purse and accessories out as the bin moved past on the conveyor rollers. "Has he contacted you since that night?"

"No."

"Asshole."

A TSA employee's head jerked in Emma's direction.

Brianne said, "She's not talking about you, sir."

As they waited for the rest of the family, Emma said, "I'm sorry I didn't warn Grandma. It's my fault this happened."

"No, it's not. I should have told him. I just kept hoping the perfect time would present itself."

Once they boarded the aircraft, Emma and Brianne were in a row of three seats with their grandmother in the middle. They waited for the rest of the passengers to stow their belongings and sit down.

Grandma patted Brianne's knee. "I'm sorry I mentioned your weight at dinner Sunday night. I thought Cort knew what you went through, especially since you spoke at that fundraiser."

"Don't apologize, Grandma. You didn't know I hadn't told him yet."

"He seemed upset."

"No, he was just surprised. We talked about it in the car, and he understands."

"Oh, I'm so glad." Grandma smiled at her. "After all, helping people with their weight is what he does."

"That's right. That's what he does."

Emma looked over the top of their grandmother's head to Brianne and mouthed *asshole*.

#

The flight to Dallas/Fort Worth arrived on time despite the hectic holiday travel. They found Uncle Junior and Aunt Eileen in the baggage claim area. Grandma was headed to the ranch with them where she had a one bedroom guest house on the property. Brianne, her parents, and sister had reservations at the Marriott in town. By the time they picked up two rental cars and checked into the hotel, it was two PM Texas time.

Emma stowed her empty suitcase in the closet of the room she and Brianne shared. "Mom and I are going shopping. Do you want to come?"

"No, I'm tired. I think I'll take a nap."

Emma left, but Brianne was unable to sleep. She checked her phone every fifteen minutes to see if Cort sent a message that he was back from California. After an hour, she gave up on a nap and booted her laptop to catch up on client summary reports. When her sister and mother returned, the family trooped downstairs for dinner in the hotel restaurant.

Brianne and Emma were dressed in jeans and boots. Instead of returning to their room after the meal, the sisters headed to Pearl's on the edge of the Stockyards. It was a great place for two-stepping with a friendly crowd of regulars, both young and old. When they entered the bar and dance club, the place was lively considering it was the day before Thanksgiving.

Emma moved her mouth close to Brianne's ear. "The band sounds good. The singer is pretty decent, too."

They had just placed their drink order with the bartender when an older bow-legged cowboy with a deeply tanned and creviced face approached them. "Which one of you darlins' wants to dance?"

Emma gave her sister a little push in his direction. "Go. I'll get the drinks and find a table."

Brianne tried to exit the floor several times as songs ended but was always pulled back by another dance partner until the band stopped for a break. Emma was at the bar in conversation with several men and women.

"There you are. Everyone, this is my sister, Brianne." Emma's new friends introduced themselves. "Are you feeling better?"

"This was just what I needed." She used a damp drink napkin to wipe her brow. "Where's my Texas Tea?"

"You mean the one I ordered for you an hour ago? Long gone."

Brianne got a replacement, and they chatted with an interesting mix of locals, ranchers, and farmers. Some of them knew at least one member of the Gordon family. They said their goodbyes at ten-thirty. For the first time in three nights, Brianne had a sound night's sleep.

#

They arrived at the ranch at nine AM on Thanksgiving Day. Everyone pitched in to help with either food preparation or set up. Brianne was thrilled to see her cousin, Gary, and his partner, Ray. Of all her relatives, she and Gary had a special bond. Maybe it was because of his sexuality and her obesity. They were the family misfits.

"Gary, Ray, I'm so glad to see you guys."

"Well, howdy do, Cuz." Gary kissed her cheek.

"Miss Brianne, you are prettier every time I lay eyes on you." Ray threw his arm around her shoulder and squeezed.

Grandma sat in a rocker on the porch with her grandson's pregnant wife, Diane. They were the only ones exempt from pre-dinner chores. The older woman leaned over the arm of her chair and talked to Diane's basketball of a stomach.

"What do you think Grandma's saying to the baby?" Emma huffed as she carried a chair under each arm out to the pavilion.

"She's probably telling him that she'll never let his father name him Cletus. That's what Andrew's been calling him since they found out it's a boy."

They had been ordered to add more chairs to the seating arrangement because their cousin Trey's future in-laws were coming. Kerry, who was the bride-to-be, her parents, and two older brothers were invited to this year's dinner.

Emma opened a folding chair and slid it under the table. "Wait till you meet Kerry's brothers."

"I've heard you talk about them."

"They are sex on legs." She fanned her face with her hand.

"Both of them?"

"Yep, one for you and one for me."

"I don't need one."

"You know what they say. Once you're bucked off a horse, you need to get right back on. Besides, Cort Hardison should know that your past weight problem doesn't bother other men. They're only interested in the current package."

"I appreciate you looking out for my love life. But right now, I don't know if I've been bucked off or not."

I may have been fucked off though.

Aunt Eileen's sharp voice called out from the porch. "Hey, y'all got more chairs to bring out. Stop gabbin' and get movin'."

When dinner commenced at one PM, there were twenty-two adults and Cletus the Fetus at the tables under the open air pavilion between the house and barns. To Brianne's surprise, one of Kerry's brothers, Kyle, was also a vegetarian. He stood behind his chair across the table from her.

Emma was right. He is sexy as hell.

He had the good, clean handsomeness of a California surfer with a mane of sun-streaked blonde hair. They were introduced as they waited behind their chairs until everyone was in place. He reached across the table to shake her hand, then unexpectedly turned it palm down. He pulled her to him a little, leaned forward, and kissed the back. His cool, aquamarine eyes sparkled at her as his warm lips pressed against her knuckles. She smiled at his courtly manner.

There was so much food no one commented that neither she nor Kyle had any turkey or duck on their plates. After dinner, the women carried dishes and food back to the kitchen. The men broke down the folding tables and stowed most of them back in the cellar.

The ten young people divided into two softball teams. The three Gordon brothers, their wives, Grandma, and pregnant Diane watched from the folding chairs still under the pavilion. Both teams wanted Angie, the twin sister of the father-to-be, on their side. She'd attended the University of Texas on a softball scholarship. Kyle managed to be on Brianne's team while his look-alike blonde brother, Keith, was on Emma's. Her fellow vegetarian was elected team captain to choose the batting order and field positions.

Brianne tapped his arm. "Listen, I'm lousy at softball. Put me where I'll do the least harm."

Grandma or ready-to-pop Diane would be better than me.

When she was at bat, Kyle stood with his arms wrapped around her to demonstrate a proper batting stance each time the ball was thrown. "Follow my directions and you can get to first base with me any time you want."

She missed the ball.

"Although I personally love it, you're choking up on the bat."

She missed the next pitch.

"If you just loosen up, I can get you into scoring position."

Strike three.

After a supper of leftovers, the lights were turned on in the pavilion. Speakers were hooked up to a CD player. Everyone danced, including Grandma and Diane. The aunts and uncles joined in line dancing and the Texas waltz. When the music's tempo increased, the cousins hit the floor with the Texas boogie. Brianne did a wild country swing dance with both Gary and Ray as partners. Everyone clapped and whistled when they finished.

It was midnight when people headed home. The church rehearsal was at four the next afternoon followed by the wedding party dinner. Kerry warned the bridal party that no one was to be hung over for the wedding on Saturday. Despite this, the secret plan was to meet after the rehearsal dinner at the Stagecoach Ballroom for drinks and dancing.

While Emma drove back to the hotel, Brianne pulled her feet out of her cowboy boots and rubbed her toes. "I hope my pinkies make it through the weekend."

"You've certainly made use of your dancing boots the last two days."

"It's been great. I really enjoyed myself."

"I wonder what Cort would think if he saw you dancing with all those cowboys last night and today with Kyle."

"At this point, I don't think he'd care. I haven't checked my phone to see if he left a message, but I doubt it." Brianne put her purse on her lap and rummaged through it. "Where *is* my phone?"

"Did you leave it in the hotel room?"

"I must have. I checked it before we went to Pearl's, but I haven't seen it since. I hope it's still in the room."

"I'm sure it is. I'm glad today was a good day for you, Bree. You deserved it."

The next thing she became aware of was Emma jostling her shoulder to wake her up. Brianne staggered out of the car and up to the room. She flopped spread-eagled onto the bed.

"Do you want to use the bathroom?" Emma asked.

"No, you go first."

When the shower started, Brianne sat up and pulled off her boots. She located the TV remote and turned it on. After channel surfing, she found an old episode of *The Big Bang Theory*. She scooted up the mattress, propped herself against the headboard with several pillows, and waited for her turn in the bathroom. Her eyes closed, and she fell into a deep sleep.

She never checked her phone.

Chapter 13

BRIANNE AWOKE ON Friday morning when the hotel room door clicked shut. She rolled over to look at the other bed. It was empty except for a note that rested on the pillow. She stretched. On the way to the bathroom, she shucked the clothes she had slept in. After showering, she read her sister's note.

Dear Dancing Fool,
    Gone to get my dress. Hope it's not too hideous. Will call you later.
Em

Starved and desperate for coffee, she dressed and went to the restaurant off the lobby. She ordered oatmeal, coffee, and juice then searched her purse.

Damn, I forgot to bring my phone.

After breakfast, she tore apart the room she shared with Emma. Her cell phone was not there. The concierge desk apologized, but no one from maid service had turned in an iPhone in a blue case. She called her parents' room on the hotel phone. Her father answered.

"Dad, I've lost my phone." Brianne's voice quivered with panic.

Has Cort been trying to reach me?

"Where did you last have it?" Ted asked.

"I know it was in my room Wednesday night. I checked it before I went to sleep."

"Did someone turn it in?"

"I called. They don't have it. Would you call Emma and ask if she knows where it is?"

A few minutes later, the phone on the bedside table rang.

Her father said, "Emma has your phone. She thought it was hers and put it in her purse."

"How did that happen? She has a pink case."

"Don't ask me. I don't know what you girls do with your phones and purses. Emma said she should be done at the bridal shop around one and will swing by to pick you up. She wants you to help her find shoes."

#

When Emma returned with her bridesmaid dress, she modeled it for Brianne. It was a strapless, floor-length, satin sheath with a matching wrap. Her sister viewed herself in the bathroom mirror. "Kerry says the color is gold. I think it looks like urine."

"It looks more like the color of beer to me. But it fits you nicely."

Emma returned to the bedroom. "Unzip me, and let's go find some piss-colored or Miller Lite shoes with a three-inch heel."

Shoe shopping took longer than expected. Gold heels that Emma was willing to buy were not a hot item in stores at Thanksgiving. They arrived at the church rehearsal with minutes to spare.

She opened the car door and told Brianne, "I'll call you when the rehearsal dinner is done, and we're headed to the Stagecoach Ballroom."

"You can't unless you give me my phone back."

Emma found the blue-cased device in her purse. "How could I have thought it was mine?"

"Didn't it ring while you had it?"

"If it did, I never heard it."

After Emma ran into the church, Brianne stayed in the parking lot to check her messages. She had one from Pam but no others. She called her back.

"Hi, how was your Texas Thanksgiving?" her roommate asked.

"Pretty good. My cousin's fiancée and her family were there. The bride's brother, Kyle, is a vegetarian, too. So nobody made any comments this year about the lack of turkey on my plate."

"Is Kyle cute?"

"Yeah, and he's a big flirt."

"So Cort is history?"

"I don't know what Cort is. I haven't heard from him at all. Did he come for therapy on Wednesday?"

"He was there and looked tired. He said he had couple hours of sleep before his appointment."

"Did he ask about me?" Brianne's voice sounded needy even to her.

"I think he knew he was on my shit list. I kept it professional during the session, and then he left."

A dull pain thudded in her chest. *My heart breaks again.*

"Are you okay?" Pam asked when the silence stretched too long.

"Not at the moment. But you know me. I'm like one of those clown bopping toys. I'll bounce back. I always do."

"It'll work out, *chi-chi.* Trust me."

#

Brianne walked to a steakhouse near the hotel with her parents. She ordered pimento cheese fritters, roasted corn bisque, and a kale and Brussel sprouts big salad. There was one vegetarian entrée, a falafel pita sandwich. Her father studied the menu at length.

He tasted her fritters and soup when they were brought to the table. She requested that her salad come with her parents' steak dinners.

Ted said, "I guess it would be nice if you could order something other than a salad or sandwich."

Brianne said, "This is fine for me. But many people like to have a meatless entrée when everyone else gets a dinner plate of food."

#

Emma's call came at nine PM. "We're done with the rehearsal dinner. Hurry up because the Stagecoach Ballroom closes at midnight."

Brianne found her sister, the brides' brothers, and her cousins, including tomorrow's groom, on the dance floor when she arrived. She danced several times as a couple with Kyle. He always claimed the slow, hold-me-tight numbers. The deejay announced that there would be one more song played before the place closed. Brianne was in the middle of a large line dance formation when she pivoted left and missed a step.

Cort stood at the edge of the large wooden floor, his eyes on her.

She worked her way through the dancers and launched herself at him. With her arms around his neck, he lifted her off her feet. She wrapped her legs around his waist, and he carried her away.

Someone yelled, "Get a room." It sounded like Emma.

When Cort reached a dark, empty corner, he set her down as their open mouths sought each other. She drank him in and moaned with need. He tightened one arm around her waist, and they held each other close.

"Do you have a car?" she said into his ear.

"It's outside."

Brianne stepped back from his embrace. "Be right back."

She dug the car key out of her pocket, found Emma, and put it in her hand. "I'm leaving with him."

"Remember the wedding is at one."

#

In the car, Cort slid the driver's seat back as far as it would go. He hauled her across the center console, and she straddled his lap. The steering wheel pressed her lower body tight against his. She could feel his erection between the V of her thighs.

He said, "I've been going crazy the last five days. I'm so sorry. Please forgive me again. I've been praying you'd give me another chance if I came here."

His hands roamed over her back and slid beneath her arms to cup her breasts. A rap at the window caused Brianne to jerk upright. Her elbow hit the horn, and a loud beep sounded.

A security guard scowled at them. "Take it home, folks."

They knocked foreheads as Brianne scrambled back to her seat. She lost her balance in her haste and tumbled bottom first. The back of her head bumped the passenger window, and her right foot knocked the rearview mirror askew. Cort jerked his head away in time to avoid her flying left foot.

"Are you okay?" he asked.

"I'm fine. Do you have a room somewhere?"

"I have a reservation at the Riverfront Marriott."

"That's where I'm staying. How did you know?"

He said, "Emma."

"Have you checked in yet?"

"No, I came here right from the airport."

"How did you—?"

Once again, he said, "Emma."

Brianne caressed his knee and thigh. "Please, get to the hotel as soon as possible. I hope you brought lots of condoms."

He laughed. "I have enough to get us through the night. We can buy more tomorrow."

Cort started the car and backed out of the parking space. The rent-a-cop glared, his arm cocked on the butt of his flashlight as they drove past. Brianne waved good-bye.

She turned in her seat to face him. "Why did you come, Cort? You didn't call or text me all week."

"I thought it best that I give us some time, especially while I was in California. Then I had my therapy session with Pam on Wednesday."

"I talked with her today. She said you never asked about me."

"I didn't have a chance. She refused to answer any questions about you before the session began. Afterward, she hustled me out of the office like I had B.O. She said something that later scared the crap out of me then locked the door."

"What?"

"She said Texas men love a smart, beautiful woman who can dance."

"Why would that scare you?"

"Take a look at the texts from Emma." He handed Brianne his phone. *Is this why she had my phone?*

She tapped on the Messages app then clicked on Emma's name. The last text included a photo of her clutched against Kyle tonight with the tag: *Everyone at the Stagecoach Ballroom tonight thinks Brianne and Kyle make a great couple.* The next picture showed Brianne asleep, still in her clothes, after Thanksgiving at the ranch. Emma's message was: *At the Riverfront Marriott Brianne is exhausted from dancing for hours with Kyle.*

As she scrolled backward, the photo montage continued. She was in a series of photos and a dance video with Gary and Ray with the caption: *Both men love her and call her Darling.*

"Do you know that the two men I'm dancing with in this video are my gay cousin, Gary, and his partner, Ray?"

"I do now."

She flicked through more photos from Thanksgiving Day. In them, she danced with Kyle, his brother, her cousins, and even one of her with Uncle Homer. Two photos showed Kyle with his arms wrapped around Brianne when she was at bat. Both of them had open-mouthed grins. The next one showed Kyle as he leaned across the table, his lips on the back of her hand. With her ruffled top and his white dress shirt, it looked like a cover picture from a western romance novel. The tag read: *The two vegetarian lovebirds meet.*

How in the world did Emma get this photo? Unless ... she directed the pose.

"I'm gonna kill her," Brianne said with conviction.

"Somebody needs to rein her in."

Brianne scrolled through more photos of her with a variety of dance partners, both young and old, at Pearl's. Brianne read Emma's tag aloud. "Texas men love a smart, beautiful woman who can dance. So Pam was in on this, too?"

"Apparently, and it worked. This morning I called a buddy of mine who owns a private jet. He gave me a ride, and I flew in this evening."

#

While Cort checked in at the front desk, Brianne went to her room, washed up in record time, and grabbed her toiletries bag. Her phone chimed with a text of his room number. She ran up the stairs rather than wait for the elevator. When she rushed around the corner from the stairwell, he stood by his open door, a garment bag slung over his shoulder and a carry-on at his feet. The excitement between them crackled in the air.

She ached with need for him. Her hormones were in overdrive since her period was due in a couple days. She had also gotten used to having sex again, and the weeklong dry spell transformed her into this wild creature. Regardless of the reason, the clothes that covered her skin were a torment. He appeared to suffer a similar agony.

He was on her as soon as the door closed. His tongue thrust between her lips as their hands stripped the clothes from each other's bodies. Both jockeyed for openings to kiss and lick bare skin as it was exposed. He walked her backward until the edge of the mattress bumped the backs of her knees. She tumbled with abandon. He followed and pinned her with six feet of aroused male.

She ran her fingers through his midnight hair. "I missed you."

Cort nibbled on her lower lip which curled her toes. "I thought about you, no matter where I was or what I was doing."

It was the same for her. Now her days were overlaid with the transparency of a relationship with him. He was part of her thoughts and actions every day, as if deep down in her brain, a little timer went off at regular intervals to remind her of him.

His hot mouth moved down her throat and latched onto a nipple. He supported his weight on his forearms while one thigh settled between hers. He shifted his weight to the side and ran his hand down her belly to cup her sex. His fingertip slipped into her cleft.

"Oh, Cort." Her fingers wadded the bedspread.

The grayness of the past five days faded and vibrancy came back into her world. He tasted sweet in her mouth. His labored breaths puffed into her ear. The body that anchored hers was a welcome and needed weight. She stroked the flexed hardness of muscle under his skin. His scent filled her nostrils. If only she could soak more of him into the essence of her.

I love you. I love you. I love you.

He licked a wet path between her breasts, down her stomach, and into the crease of her thigh. As he moved lower, he slipped off the bed and knelt on the floor. He grabbed her ankles and bent her legs so her heels rested on the mattress edge. His shoulders forced her legs to a wider V.

"Sweetheart, I've been dying for this." With his fingers, he separated her folds, and his mouth closed on her. He held her open as his tongue flicked her sensitive bud.

Her back arched. "Oh, God! Oh, God!" She writhed on the bed as he pleasured her with his mouth and fingers. Her hips thrust up, and her orgasm came in a sudden rush that took them both by surprise.

Cort rose to his feet with a condom in his hand and rolled it down over his erection. He leaned forward and placed his hands on the bed before he thrust for full, hot penetration. Brianne looped her legs around his waist. Her ankles locked behind his back. With straightened arms, he reared and pulled part way out. She used her crisscrossed feet to push him back in. He was deeper inside her than ever before. The bones of his pelvis bounced against the backs of her thighs.

She grabbed his forearms for leverage. Her hips twisted with each thrust until he hit the perfect spot. She had been empty for days. Now her body was filled to capacity with his heat. He reared, she pulled. He retreated, she advanced. The tempo increased. The rise of another orgasm spiraled in her. She screamed when she came, the ecstasy so violent that her legs fell away from Cort's body. He stilled. Her tremors stroked him. Then he groaned and shuddered. His back bowed as he pumped into her one last time.

The night passed in a kaleidoscopic blur. Demands became soothing comfort. Aches became pleasures. Frantic lust became relaxed loving. He touched or was in her body with a part of his until, in satiated exhaustion, they slept.

Chapter 14

BRIANNE AWOKE. THE waterfall sound of the shower leaked through the closed bathroom door. She opened her eyes to a room different than the one she slept in the past two nights. Her nipples were tender. A slight soreness burned between her thighs. Her fingertips skimmed along her jawline where it was chafed. She threw off the covers, climbed out of bed, and opened the bathroom door. Sliding back the shower curtain, she stepped into Cort's wet arms.

"How do you feel?" He touched a red mark on her shoulder.

In a Texas drawl, she said, "Like I've been rode hard and put away wet."

He laughed, then his gaze changed from humorous to tender. "You are so beautiful to me."

Still with a slow southern dialect, she said, "Shucks, I bet you say that to all the cowgirls."

He twisted around and shut off the water behind him. Then he pulled her in front of him and opened the shower curtain. When Brianne raised her eyes, she stared across the bathroom at their reflection in a wide mirror that stretched the length of the long vanity.

Her body glowed pale in comparison to the parts of his darker skin outlined around hers. His left hand was splayed across her abdomen, fingers spread from the bottom of one rosy-tipped breast to her navel. His gaze moved over her like warmed bath oil.

"Look how lovely you are, and how much I love you."

She looked at his face in the mirror. Tears filled her eyes.

"Sweetheart, don't cry," he said. "Don't you see what I see?"

"In your eyes, I do."

"How can you not know how beautiful you are?"

She looked at her reflection and then back to his. "I only see how beautiful *you* are."

He closed his eyes and shook his head.

She added, "But I'm happy *you* think I'm beautiful."

"Okay, we'll start there."

"Please say you love me again."

"I love you. I do. With all my heart." He leaned down and kissed her cheek. "It started in the first aid station at Hardcort."

She smiled back at him in the mirror. "I love you, too. But I have to admit, it's been a roller coaster of a ride."

He turned her around into his embrace. "I know I've been a bastard. All these feelings are new to me, and I've been fighting them. I'm sorry you got caught in the crossfire."

He helped her step out of the tub and wrapped her in a thick white towel then dried them both off. She wrapped a towel around her wet hair. Cort checked his watch on the vanity counter. "It's ten now. Are you hungry?"

"Starving."

"Let's call room service for something to eat. Then we'll get ready."

"What do you mean? Get ready?"

"I was thinking you and I could go to the wedding together. Emma says I can even take Ray's place at the reception tonight. He was called to take the afternoon shift. A co-worker's wife went into early labor."

"When did you talk to Emma?"

"She sent a text this morning before I got in the shower. She was checking on you since you didn't answer your phone."

Brianne pulled her cell from her jeans pocket and found the ringer volume was turned to vibrate.

Cort sat on the bed beside the nightstand. "Is it okay for me to go with you to the church?"

"Sure. I'm glad you want to."

He sighed. "Good. What do you want to order from room service?"

#

After breakfast, Brianne returned to her room to get ready. She shampooed her hair and took extra pains with her make-up. She had just spritzed on a delicate scent when there was a knock at the door. With her eye against the bullet-sized peephole, the big-headed image of Cort filled her view.

Dammit, he's fifteen minutes early.

She opened the door and stepped behind it. Cort strode in, magnificent in a gray pin-striped suit, white shirt, and bluish-silver tie. She shut the door and struck a provocative pose with one arm raised, her hand flat on the wall. The other hand rested on the hip which jutted out from her crossed ankles.

He turned. "Whoa."

She wore a pale pink bra with a matching thong and garter belt. Creamy stockings covered her legs except for the gap between their lacy tops and her thong. She wore nude-colored platform heels.

"Deal with it. You're the one who keeps showing up early." She walked past him and knew his eyes were on the cheeks of her behind.

He grabbed her arm and pulled her against him. "There's no way we can leave this room without me being in you first. I don't want to mess you up. Tell me what to do."

She was hot and wet as well after seeing him in his tailored suit. She spied the armless upholstered chair at a desk table. She wiggled loose from his embrace, strode several steps, and rotated the seat.

"Sit and don't touch my hair or makeup."

#

They were the last people to be seated in the church. A few minutes later, the music started as the groomsmen filed in from the sacristy and lined up at the altar.

Brianne pointed and whispered in Cort's ear. "The groom is my cousin, Trey. Next to him is his brother, Gary. The guy with the glasses is my cousin, Andrew."

"Which one of the blondes is Kyle?" Cort scowled when he said the name.

"He's the second from the end. His brother, Keith, is the last one."

The wedding march started. Heads turned to face the back of the church. As Emma strolled passed, she winked at them.

"Here comes my cousin, Angie. I don't know the last two bridesmaids. They're friends of the bride."

The ceremony was solemn and romantic. It ended without any hitches until the newly-married couple walked back down the aisle. The bride was on the side where Brianne and Cort sat. She stopped dead in her tracks and jerked her new husband to a halt. The bridesmaids and groomsmen behind them created a near pile-up.

Wide-eyed, Kerry stared then said to no one in particular, "What is Brianne doing with the exercise guy?"

In a dry tone, Trey answered, "According to Emma, just about everything."

"Remind me to kill my sister," Brianne muttered to Cort.

Trey tugged on Kerry's arm, and the processional continued down the aisle and out of the sanctuary. The bride looked over her shoulder at them, her mouth open, until she disappeared into the vestibule.

As people passed their pew, they smiled at Cort, gave awkward little waves, whispered, or pointed him out to others.

Brianne asked, "Do people often act like this when they see you in public?"

"Not so much in Fort Lauderdale because they're used to seeing me around."

They were the last ones in the receiving line. Brianne led the way and introduced Cort to Keith, the bride's brother. When she stepped in front of Kyle, he put his hands on her arms, pulled her forward, and kissed her full on the lips. Upon her release, he and Cort dueled with hard-eyed stares.

"Uh, Cort, this is Kyle, Kerry's other brother."

Their handshake took longer than necessary with whitening knuckles, like an evaluation of an opponent prior to an arm wrestling match. They were two rutting males in a show of one-upmanship at a church wedding.

That's all I need.

"Stop it," she hissed.

She grabbed Cort's wrist and dragged him along. He was introduced to her male cousins, Andrew, Gary, and the groom.

Cort asked Trey, "May I kiss your bride?"

Kerry's head bobbed in silent assent.

"Sure," Trey said. "Just don't ruin my honeymoon for me."

Cort leaned down and gave Kerry a quick smooch on the mouth. The maid of honor leaned toward him with a slight pucker to her lips, but he put out his hand to shake hers instead. Her eyebrows slanted toward her nose like a child's drawing of a bird in flight. He shook hands with the next two bridesmaids. When he got to Emma, he grabbed her in a hug and whispered in her ear.

As they headed outside, Brianne asked, "What did you say to Emma?"

"That's between her and me."

Cort and Brianne joined the line of people who waited along the church entrance for the wedding party. A pack of giggling, young girls in braces lead by a confident alpha redhead dashed toward them with cell phones in hand. They asked Cort to pose with them for selfies. He was pulled to the center of the walkway by his coat sleeve. The other wedding guests smiled at the girls' ambush.

When Cort bent low for the camera's view, a jowly, middle-aged blonde with a big Texas hairdo stared at his backside with a coquettish fluttering of her artificial eyelashes. Having strangers recognize her date and him posing with fans followed by delighted shrieks was still alien to Brianne. It was unsettling, like being lost in a foreign country. She stood alone, unsure what to do.

When the photo session ended, the girls bounced back across the sidewalk to high-pitched squeals and held their phones to bony chests. Cort returned to her side with a shrug and an indulgent smile. The wedding party emerged from the darkened doorway of the church. Birdseed was thrown in the air over their heads. The bride and groom ran to a decorated Ford truck with the Double G ranch sign on each door panel. The rest of the bridal party entered two white limousines parked at the curb.

Brianne's parents approached from across the sidewalk. Her father said to Cort, "I thought you were with your grandmother."

"I was on Thanksgiving day. Last night I flew in so I could be with Brianne for the weekend."

Her mother raised her eyebrows. "Was she expecting you? She didn't say anything."

"I wasn't sure I could come until the last minute."

Her parents looked at her.

She threw up her hands. "Surprise!"

"What do we do until the reception tonight?" Dad asked Mom.

"Let's get some lunch." She turned to Cort and Brianne. "Want to join us?"

They drove to a nearby Italian restaurant where they were the best-dressed patrons for Saturday afternoon pizza. Later at the hotel, Cort and Brianne crossed the coppery-colored marble floor to the elevators. They stepped inside.

"Hey, hold the door." Her father hustled across the lobby toward them.

His wife followed at a more sedate pace as warranted by her high heels. She called out, "Ted, what's your hurry? There's more than one elevator in this place."

Out of the side of his mouth, Cort said, "Meet me in my room later."

"Don't worry." She spoke through teeth held in a smile at her father's approach. "They get off before us." Her father stood against the door of the elevator to hold it open. "Dad, you're on the third floor. Why not use the stairs and get some exercise?"

He huffed. "I would, of course, but your mother won't because of her shoes."

When Candace entered, she turned to her husband. "We could have taken the stairs. Our room is only a couple flights up."

Brianne peeked at her father who looked straight ahead at the closing doors. Her parents got off on their floor and said they would see them at the reception tonight. Cort accompanied her to the room she shared with Emma two floors higher. She gathered what she needed to get ready that evening. When they entered the elevator again to go up to his room, Cort had her dress draped over his forearm.

Brianne pushed the button for the tenth floor. "If we get ready in the same room, I don't have to worry about you showing up early."

"Watching you get ready may mean we show up late or not at all." Cort nuzzled her neck and backed her against the elevator's side wall. "Sweetheart, have you ever done it in an elevator?"

"No, and I have no desire to either."

He spread his legs and pulled her between his thighs. His erection grew as he rubbed it back and forth across her. The elevator glided to a stop. Cort stepped away and faced the doors when they opened.

Two couples waited to enter. "Hey, it's the exercise guy."

Cort moved his arm so her draped dress provided coverage for the bulge in his pants. He took Brianne's hand as the party of four stepped aside for them to exit. One of the men moved forward to block their path.

"Who's your girlfriend, Hardison?" Before Cort could reply, a woman's arm jerked the jerk back and pulled him inside the elevator.

They took several steps down the hall, and then Brianne glanced over her shoulder at the closing elevator doors. "Do you see why doing it in an elevator is a bad idea?"

Cort hung up her dress while she put her toiletries in the bathroom. When she emerged, he was sitting on the end of the bed. He had removed his suit jacket and loosened his tie. Brianne stepped between his legs and pulled his head toward her breast. Cort fell back on the bed, taking her with him. He rolled to the side so they faced each other.

"I love you." She never meant the words more. With one hand, she opened the button at his waistband and lowered the zipper. Brianne reached inside his boxer shorts and wrapped her hand around him. "I'm not crazy about elevators, but I do love this big hotel bed."

He kissed her until she was breathless. "I want to watch you take off that pretty underwear you're wearing."

"You got it, sport."

Brianne scooted off the bed. With her eyes on him, she unzipped her dress and let it shimmy down her legs. She turned her back to Cort and bent over from the waist to pick it up and toss it on a chair. Cort groaned behind her. She unclasped her bra and pivoted so he had a side view. Brianne again bent forward and allowed the bra to slide down her arms and land at her feet. With her head at her knees, she reached between her legs and unhooked the back of one stocking and then the other. Her gaze locked on his as she sauntered back to the bed.

Cort propped himself on his elbows. His legs dangled off the mattress edge. She moved between his knees. One high-heeled foot was lifted to the small area of mattress between his thighs. She nudged the toe of her shoe down and forward until his balls rested on top. Brianne unfastened the front garter clasp. With deliberate slowness, she rolled the stocking down. She slipped her shoe and stocking off and dropped them to the floor.

She switched feet and repeated the stocking and shoe removal. Brianne tucked her bare foot back into the notch of his legs, slid her toes under him and wiggled them. His breath gave an audible hitch as she cupped her breasts and squeezed.

Will I be able to finish this strip tease for him?

His smoldering, heavy-lidded look told her how much he wanted to see this. She maintained eye contact as she moved one hand from her breast and skimmed it down her body. Her fingers slid into the front of her panties. She massaged herself in tight circles, first slow then faster. Her hips thrust upwards to an invisible lover.

Cort was pinned to the bed by her foot and leg. He dragged himself backward on the mattress and sat up. Reaching between her legs, his finger moved past the slight barrier of the thong and pushed into her. He stroked and panted, "Now, sweetheart, do it now."

Her orgasm jolted her. She collapsed on the bed and lay next to him. He stood, stepped out of his shoes, suit pants, and boxers. Then he tore open a condom and rolled it down his rigid length. He pulled off her thong and moved between her legs. She smiled at his attire.

Sport, there's nothing finer than you in a dress shirt and tie with a beautiful hard-on.

She pulled her knees up as he positioned himself and pushed into her. He shifted onto his elbows then eased back with exquisite slowness, groaned, and thrust again. Brianne flexed muscles that gripped and held firm. She watched his pleasure escalate with each movement.

His face grimaced with the effort to hold on a little longer. He sped up, called out her name, and drove into her one last time, his body shaking with erotic spasms.

"God, I love you," he said with a hoarse voice.

Cort pressed his forehead against hers, his eyes closed. His ragged breathing slowed and became rhythmic again. He placed a gentle kiss on her lips, pulled out, and laid next to her.

Brianne's phone chimed. She reached over to where her purse lay on the bed, found her cell, and read the text. "My dad is headed to the weight room downstairs. He wants to know if you're interested in joining him. I guess he knows you're with me."

"Ya think?"

Cort removed the condom. He spread the loosened knot of his tie apart then pulled it from around his neck. Brianne unbuttoned his dress shirt and put it on.

"Do you mind spending some time with my father?" she asked. "I think he wants to get to know you better without me around."

"It's fine. But you have to answer a question for me first. Did you keep your doctor's appointment on Tuesday?"

She laughed and rolled her eyes. "Yes, I did. I start on the pill when I get my period in a couple days. Then I'm protected a week later."

Cort tapped his index finger against his chin. "I have to wait another … ten days?"

"That's about right. Now, get ready for the exercise room. Go show my dad proper form, spot him, or whatever you do with weights. Just don't grunt."

"Ok, let him know I can come."

She poked him in the side with her elbow. "Oh, I know you can come, but I don't think my dad needs to."

Chapter 15

CORT LEFT TO meet her father just before five o'clock. While he was gone, Brianne showered, did her makeup, and put her hair in a loose topknot. Her last earring was inserted when the lock clicked, and he entered the room. She straightened from her bent position toward the mirror over the desk.

Cort pointed at her chest. "What the hell is that?"

She looked down in confusion. "This? It's a bra."

"That doesn't look like any bra I've ever seen. How are you holding it up?"

"Actually, it's holding me up." Her black lace bra was a backless push-up with flesh-colored side panels.

"How?"

"The sides are adhesive and stick to my skin."

"And it doesn't come off?" Cort walked around her and studied the bra like it was an engineering marvel.

"Not for a while. I can only wear it a few times. It's for specific dresses, not to be worn every week."

He studied her legs in black tights and lacy boyshorts. "I have a whole new appreciation for what a woman wears under her clothes."

As he reached for her, she held him off with a stiff arm. "We have to leave in thirty minutes. You need to shower and get dressed."

"We could be late."

"We almost missed the wedding. I don't want the same thing to happen for the reception. We're already the talk of the town."

While Cort showered, Brianne put on her dress. It was made of black sparkly fabric with an underlining from the bodice through the fluttering hemline that fell just above her knees. The slender, long sleeves were unlined and sheer. It was the back of the dress that required the specialty bra. A large diamond cutout exposed her from the clasp behind her neck to the small of her back. The front of the dress looked demure. The back was a different story. On her feet were high-heeled black ankle boots.

She sat in the room's armchair and checked her iPhone while Cort got ready. She had picked out his clothes. The reception was dressy but not formal. She suggested that he wear a white dress shirt, no tie, black jeans, and his gray suit coat. It was a shame he didn't have a good pair of cowboy boots.

Cort was ready at six-forty. He walked to the door and held it open for her. Brianne picked up her purse then walked out into the hall.

"Holy shit."

Brianne smiled. *I guess he likes the back of my dress.*

While they waited for the elevator's arrival, Cort leaned his head back to view his hand on the skin of her waistline. "Did you plan to wear this dress before I got here?"

"Yes."

"Another reason I'm glad I came."

#

The reception was at the Omni Hotel in downtown Fort Worth, not too far from the Marriott where they stayed. Guests milled around the ballroom that held circular tables draped in floor-length gold linens. Mirrors under votive candle centerpieces reflected light around the room which was decorated with amber wall panels and overhead hanging lights in wrought iron cages. The low hum of voices contrasted with the sharp clink of glassware. Soft music filtered from speakers.

Cort went to the bar which was three deep with people. Brianne headed to the appetizers station and filled a plate with brie in phyllo cups, fruit, and cheese. She prepared a plate for Cort with the same items plus the mini beef brisket. He returned with their drinks to the tall cocktail table where Brianne stood. They ate with gusto.

"I guess we worked up an appetite." He popped a pastry-wrapped appetizer into his mouth.

"How's my weightlifting buddy?" Her father clapped his hand on Cort's back like he expected him to giddy-up.

Cort's full mouth chewed at a furious pace.

Brianne answered instead. "He's fine, Dad. Just hungry from working out with you."

"There you are." Her mother joined them, a worried look on her face.

"What's wrong?" Brianne asked.

"It's Eileen. She's had a few drinks since the reception started."

Ted scowled. "Who are you kidding? She's had a few since lunch."

"But she promised Junior and Trey she would take it easy today."

Brianne paled. *Please, God, don't let her say something that will embarrass me in front of Cort.*

An announcer asked everyone to take their seats for the wedding party's entrance. Her mother led the way to the table where Brianne's aunt, uncle and grandmother were seated.

Cort leaned down and kissed Grandma's cheek. "Hello, Mrs. Gordon."

"I'm so glad to see you again. I apologize for blurting out about Brianne's weight problem when we had dinner. I didn't know she hadn't told you yet."

"Don't worry about it. I was just surprised. We're past that now."

Uncle Homer stood to shake hands. "I guess you're the boyfriend. I'm Brianne's favorite uncle, Homer Gordon, and this is my wife, Jean."

"I'm glad to meet you both."

Grandma said to them, "This is Cort Hardison."

Uncle Homer's expression did not change with the introduction of Cort's name, but his wife's eyes widened. Aunt Jean studied him in a more appraising manner.

"This beauty is my daughter-in-law, Diane." Uncle Homer pointed to the pregnant woman who sat down heavily next to his wife. "She's expecting our first grandchild soon."

Diane looked up at Cort as she rubbed her rounded belly. "I know you. You've been on TV. That weight loss show, right?"

"I did *Weight Loss Wonders* a couple years ago."

"Brianne looks wonderful. You must be giving her great workouts."

"I'm not her trainer. We're just dating."

She eyed him and then Brianne. "If you say so."

And I was worried about Aunt Eileen.

Cort pulled out a chair for Brianne and then sat next to her grand-mother. Her father pulled out her mother's chair. Candace took the seat next to her daughter, craned her neck and searched the room.

"Do you see Aunt Eileen yet?" Brianne asked her.

"No. Maybe Junior's trying to sober her up somewhere. I've never seen him so angry before. Trey was upset, too. I think she started nipping right after the ceremony this morning. Jean said she heard Eileen kept dis-appearing during the photo shoot."

The wedding party arrived to the accompaniment of Pharrell Williams' song *Happy*. The younger guests jumped to their feet, clapped, and cheered as the bridesmaids and their groomsmen entered the venue. They shook hands and hugged people on the way to the head table at the front of the room. The deejay announced the arrival of the bride and groom. Kerry raised her bouquet over her head, and Trey pumped his fist. After the wed-ding party was seated, the music became quieter. Conversation continued around the table until they were called to join the buffet line.

Cort scanned the array of food. "It looks like they're serving beef and turkey. Are you going to get enough to eat?"

"I should be okay. There's a meatless pasta dish. The bride's brother, Kyle, is a vegetarian, too."

Cort glowered but said nothing.

Before the wedding cake was served, speeches were given by the best man and maid of honor. Kerry's friend, Lisa, recited a weepy monologue about their long friendship.

Cousin Gary's speech to his brother was touching and funny. "Trey was my best friend growing up. It wasn't easy for him having a little brother like me. When I dressed up as Brooke Shields, he would put on a headband, grab a tennis racket, and pretend he was Andre Agassi. He told me there was nothing I could do that would ever stop him from loving me. That's why you are such a lucky lady, Kerry. When my brother loves someone, it's forever. So I wish you well on your honeymoon in Maine and for the rest of your life."

Trey and Kerry looked confused. The bride whispered in her hus-band's ear. Trey reached up and tugged on his brother's sleeve.

Gary leaned down and listened. Then, into the hand-held microphone, he said, "You're not honeymooning in Maine? But you told me you were going to Bangor for a week."

The room erupted in laughter, although Kerry's father didn't look very happy. As the dessert plates were collected, the deejay played music for the father-daughter dance. Kerry's father relinquished his daughter once again to Trey. The couple slowly glided around the wooden floor as they chatted to each other, smiled, and kissed for the photographer.

Gary startled Brianne when he clasped his hands around her and Cort's outer shoulders and squeezed them together like they were one wide person. He squatted between them, and they shifted in their seats to face him. "Here's my favorite cousin and her exercise man. Cort, I'm so glad you were able to come in Ray's place. When they start playin' some good music, you're going to see what a terrific dancer Brianne is."

Cort said, "Emma sent me a video of you and Ray dancing with her on Thanksgiving Day. I also saw how good she was last night at the Stagecoach Ballroom."

"Did you know she was my high school prom date?"

When Cort looked at her, she gave him a perfunctory smile with her mouth, but not her eyes. "No," he said, "she never mentioned that."

"She refused to go if we wore matching prom dresses. Even with me in a tux, we created quite a stir. When the music started, the queer and fat girl turned out to be the best dancers that school had ever seen." Gary, at last, looked at Brianne. She blew a gust of air upward to cool her hot face. "Darlin', you know it's true. There's nothing to be embarrassed about." He turned back to Cort. "They're still talkin' about us to this day. She's just as good a dancer now as she was then. She just doesn't sweat as much."

And I was worried about Aunt Eileen.

All the single ladies were called to the dance floor for the tossing of the bouquet. Brianne joined the group with reluctance. She sidled into an open spot near the back. As she moved into place and looked up, the bunch of flowers hit her on the forehead. It bounced off and landed in the hands of the woman next to her.

"I think this is yours." The stranger held up the bouquet.

"No, it's yours. It doesn't count if you catch it with your face."

She brushed the petal debris from her hair and spit off one that clung to her lips. When she returned to the table, Cort put his arm around her shoulder and gave it a squeeze. Her mother asked if she was all right.

Gary, however, was doubled over with laughter. "She is a klutz without music, Cort. It is plumb painful to watch her play ball or ride a horse."

Cort leaned over and whispered in her ear. "I got no complaints when you play with my balls or ride my horse."

She squeezed his knee hard under the table. He grimaced as he removed her hand. Next, the single men were called to catch the garter after Trey removed it from Kerry's leg. Unlike her, Cort joined the fray with eagerness and pushed his way into position. He leapt high in the air and caught the white, lacy elastic inches away from Kyle's fingertips.

Brianne stood at her seat to watch the action. Cort returned with the garter held high in triumph. "Do you want me to put this on you?"

She stood on tiptoe to put her lips close to his ear. "I thought you preferred the pink garter I wore earlier today. Remember?" She snuggled close to him and under the cover of his suit jacket, squeezed his ass.

"Let's sit down." He pulled out their chairs. "I need the cover of the tablecloth for a minute. Your parents are watching."

The deejay played several romantic pop ballads. Gary stood and frowned. "When's he gonna play some good dancin' music? I'll be right back."

Brianne recognized the start of the romantic song, *Don't Rush,* and tugged Cort to his feet. "Will you dance with me?" Then she stopped. "Do you know how to?"

"Don't worry, sweetheart, this isn't my first rodeo. I won't put you to shame."

"Well, let's dance to this song before Gary gets the playlist changed."

Cort removed his suit jacket. The edge of the floor was more open than the middle so they stayed there. Brianne and Cort locked eyes as they swayed to the beat. He anchored her waist as they did turns up and down the length of the wooden floor. He spun her away from him and snapped her back against his body. They moved as one, separated then came together again in a choreography that seemed to Brianne as natural as their lovemaking.

Our first dance. It feels so right, like we've been dancing together forever.

Brianne moved back from Cort but maintained contact with her hand flat on his chest. She walked him backward three paces, toes pointed as her hips swung side to side. Then she grasped a fistful of his shirt and pulled him forward several steps on each downbeat. The music paused, and Cort held her steady as he leaned toward her. She bent backward over his forearm, her topknot pointed at the floor. He snapped her back up and into several spins. They ended the dance as they started, eyes locked as they swayed in place to calm the pounding of their hearts.

The other dancers had vacated the area during their sensual pas de deux. They were alone. A smattering of applause accompanied their exit from the floor. The photo-seeking preteens from outside the church were huddled close together. Their faces were lit with bluish light as they watched the screen on one girl's cell phone.

Brianne's mother wiped tears from under her eyes when they reached the table.

"Mom, why are you crying?"

She motioned her to come closer. "Because Cort loves you."

"I know. He told me. And I love him."

Gary joined them again. "Kerry gave the deejay a preset list of romantic crap to play. He's got two more to go, then he'll put on some good country dance music."

Ten minutes later Gary asked Cort, "Do you mind if I steal her away from you?"

"She's all yours. Just be sure I get her back in one piece."

Brianne changed into her cowboy boots. On the way to the dance floor, she cautioned her cousin. "No aerials or lifts. Not with this dress and the underwear I'm wearing."

Gary gave her a leering grin. "Darlin', with that man of yours, I'm surprised you're wearin' underwear at all."

He led her at a sedate pace in the first dance. But with the next song, they stepped, spun, and whirled around the center of the floor. The other dancers were prudent and stayed at the sidelines. It was like when cowboys scattered and left the center of the arena to the bucking bull and the rodeo clown.

After the fifth dance, Brianne tapped her hands in a T shape to signal timeout. As she stood off to the side to catch her breath, she spotted Kyle and Cort together in conversation. When the bride's brother walked away, a thunderous expression marred her lover's face.

Brianne wove her way through the tables to him and put her arms around his waist. "Save me from my dance-crazy cousin."

"You look thirsty. Want me to get you something from the bar?"

"Water, lots of ice. But first, what did Kyle say to you?"

"He told me I was a lucky bastard because you obviously loved me. Then the son of a bitch said the minute I was out of the picture, he was stepping in and taking over."

And I was worried about Aunt Eileen.

"Cort, I never told him he has a chance with me."

"Well, I'll never be out of the picture, as he put it. That won't happen. You're mine." Cort kissed her. "I'll get your water. Be right back."

While she waited, Kyle appeared beside her. "Dance with me, pretty lady." He pulled her toward the dance floor.

Brianne dug in her heels and slipped her arm out of his grasp. "No."

"Why not?"

"I'm not dancing with someone who tells my boyfriend he's going to step in later."

"Brianne, he's not the guy for you."

"And you are?"

"Maybe."

"Maybe not. But that's my decision."

He walked backward away from her, his eyes locked on her face. "Just keep in mind that whenever you're ready, I'll be waiting."

Cort returned with her water. He didn't say anything about Kyle talking with her. Gary allowed her a short rest before he pulled her back on the floor for line dancing. Cort was with the preteens and Kerry's maid of honor at the back of the room. They demonstrated and practiced the repeated sequence of steps to a line dance with him. Soon he and his instructors joined the group on the floor.

At eleven o'clock, Brianne was ready to call it a night. She beckoned to Cort. As he broke away from the line, the adolescents whined in dissent.

One girl held onto his arm like a drowning swimmer. He extracted himself with a head shake and a smile.

When he reached Brianne, she said, "I'm ready to leave. How about you?"

The gaggle of pre-teens behind him crossed their arms over their flat chests and hid their orthodontia with exaggerated frowns. With dramatic shoulder shrugs, they exited the dance floor in the other direction.

"I'm ready any time you are," he said.

Uncle Junior and Aunt Eileen were seated together in chairs near the room's main exit. There was no way she and Cort could avoid them. Brianne introduced him and held her breath.

Aunt Eileen had a goofy smile on her face. "You're a very lucky man. She's a wonderful young woman."

And I was worried about Aunt Eileen.

They left the Omni hotel and headed back to the Marriott. Brianne stifled several yawns on the drive.

While they waited for an elevator in the lobby, Cort asked, "What time is your flight tomorrow?"

"Around noon, I think. Are you flying home on the private jet?"

"No. My friend dropped me off on his way to Phoenix. I have a commercial flight back at seven in the morning."

"I guess I better sleep in my own room tonight then."

Cort said nothing for several long seconds then asked, "Are you not sleeping with me tonight because of something Kyle said?"

So he did see him talk to me.

Brianne turned to look at him. "No. He asked me to dance, and I refused."

"Did he say he would step in when I was gone?"

"He said he'd be waiting."

Cort's eyes remained focused on the overhead panel of elevator lights. "Is he waiting in your room now?"

"What did you say?"

"You heard me."

A hot flash of molten anger hit her. Her face burned with the heat. The elevator dinged its arrival when Brianne whirled and headed toward the overhead stairwell sign. She banged through the fire door and was on the first step before Cort grabbed her arm.

"Let go." She tried to wrench away. "I'm late for my three-way with Emma and Kyle."

Cort wrapped her in his arms and held on tight. "I'm sorry, I'm sorry. I didn't mean it."

She pulled back slightly. "Then why did you say it?"

He tugged her to his chest again. "Because I've never been jealous before. Because I've never loved someone as much as I love you. Because I'm an idiot. Take your pick."

Brianne laid her head on his shoulder until her body relaxed. "Let me change my clothes. I'll pack for tomorrow and then come to your room. Okay?"

Cort heaved a sigh and kissed her. "I know we're both tired. I just want to fall asleep with you next to me."

Brianne opened the stairwell door back to the bank of elevators. "Good. I didn't want to climb five flights of steps anyway."

#

When she unlocked the door to her hotel room, she found Emma already there in her bra and panties. The beer-colored bridesmaid dress lay across her bed.

"When did you leave the reception?" Brianne asked.

"Keith brought me here a little while ago." Emma pulled a T-shirt over her head and slipped her legs into jeans.

"Where are you going?"

There was a tap from inside the closed bathroom door.

Emma said, "You can come out now."

The door opened, and Kyle's brother emerged dressed in jeans and a plaid shirt. His tuxedo was draped over his arm. "Hi, Brianne."

"Uh … hi, Keith." She shot questioning glances between her sister and the guy now pulling on cowboy boots.

Emma sat on the bed next to him to put on her boots also. "We're going to a club. You and Cort want to come?"

"It's eleven-thirty."

Keith said, "I have a buddy playing in a band. Their set is from midnight to two."

"Thanks for the offer, but I'm beat."

Emma jammed her phone, keycard, and some cash in her pockets. As she walked past Brianne, she patted her on the back. "Yeah, you've been busy since last night."

"Hey, I need to talk to you about sending pictures of me to Cort."

Emma never broke stride as she went through the door that Keith held open for her. "You can thank me tomorrow on the flight home. See ya."

Chapter 16

THE GORDON FAMILY rode the escalator down to the baggage claim area in the Fort Lauderdale airport. Brianne leaned against the handrail and talked to Emma who stood behind her.

As they neared the bottom, her sister pointed. "Look."

A man in a black suit stood off to the side with a sign that said *Gordon Family*. Cort stood next to him in shorts and a golf shirt. He held a sign that said *Sweetheart*. When she reached him, he kissed her and put his arm around her shoulders. They followed her family to the baggage carousel. Everyone but Grandma helped transfer all the luggage, except Brianne's, to a handcart and into the car service van. Cort and Brianne waved goodbye to her family. They entered the parking garage and rode the elevator to where he left his car.

After her bags were stowed in the trunk and they were seated inside, Cort said, "Where to?"

"Let's drop off my suitcase at home. I'll pack a bag and follow you back to your place."

"What time do you have to be at work in the morning?"

"I have a client at nine."

"I have a meeting at eight-thirty. I can drop you off around eight to get your car."

"That works for me."

#

When they entered the condo, Pam hustled around the arm of the living room sofa as she pulled her tank top down over her unzipped shorts. There was another person whose head bobbed as he also dressed in a hurry.

Who else is naked on my furniture?

"You're home." It was the first time Pam ever appeared flustered to Brianne. She looked like a teenager caught dirty dancing in front of a mirror.

"Cort picked me up at the airport. We came straight here. How was your holiday?"

"Good. Good." Pam glanced back into the living room. Her mystery guest made no effort to stand and greet them.

Cort and Brianne continued on their way to her bedroom. She spun around after the door closed. "Did you see who Pam had with her?"

"All I saw was a head of dark hair. Was it a man or a woman?"

"If it's a woman, then I don't know Pam as well as I thought I did. Let's give them a few minutes. I'll unpack and get my overnight things ready."

When they returned to the living room, Pam sat in a chair alone and held a magazine at an artificial angle. Over her shoulder, she said, "Cort, did you find that Texas men love a smart, beautiful woman who can dance?"

"I don't know about Texas men, but this Florida man does."

"Does what?"

Cort draped the outfit he carried on a hanger over the arm of the sofa. He walked over to Pam and pulled her to her feet. "I love Brianne, and thank you for helping me realize how much." He wrapped his arms around her and hugged.

When he stepped back, Brianne set down her overnight bag and embraced her friend. "Thank you."

"You're welcome," Pam said.

"Who was your guest?"

Pam waved a dismissive hand in the air. "Just a friend."

"We're leaving now so you can call your friend to come back."

"My friend is waiting in my bedroom. I knew you guys wouldn't be staying."

#

Cort stowed Brianne's bag in the trunk and laid her clothes out on top. She looked back at the condo building. "I wonder who's in there with Pam. She hasn't mentioned seeing anyone new."

Cort smiled with arched eyebrows and a wide-eyed look of pretended innocence. "I wonder *who* it could be."

"You know, don't you?" Brianne smacked his arm. "Who is it?"

"See that red car two spaces over?" Cort pointed to a sporty Toyota two cars away from his in the guest parking area. "It has a Hardcort Fitness sticker in the window."

"Whose car is it?"

"Mark's."

"Your general manager? But how does Pam know him?"

"He told me she came into the gym the day after your accident. She asked to leave some Voice Center brochures. I guess they hit it off."

They stopped at Whole Foods to pick up groceries for supper. Cort wheeled their cart through the store and followed Brianne. She walked down two aisles and didn't look at the shelves or put a single item in the cart. "Earth to Brianne. What do we need here in pet food?"

"Sorry. I can't stop thinking about Pam and Mark being together."

"Why?"

"Mark is good-looking and well-built, but he has to be almost a head shorter than her."

Cort raised his eyebrows. "Don't tell me you're a height bigot."

She gasped. "No. After what I went through with my weight, I don't judge anybody's body type. It's just that I've never seen Pam with someone … not as tall as her." Her face took on a look of thoughtful concentration. "It takes a special kind of relationship where one partner is physically different than the other."

"That's true. I remember the looks that my big, tall father and my tiny, little mother got."

"Well, if there's anyone with the self-confidence to handle the difference, it's Pam."

Cort leaned down close to her. "Would it help if I told you that Mark has the biggest dick I've ever seen?"

Brianne laughed aloud. "Pam can definitely handle that."

#

At Cort's house, he unloaded the groceries while Brianne took her clothes upstairs. When she came into the kitchen, they began to prepare supper. Cort cut up vegetables for a salad and Brianne boiled pasta while marinara sauce heated. The smell of garlic bread toasting in the oven filled the room. They ate on the patio as the daylight faded to dusk. Midway through the meal, Cort lit candles and turned on the underwater light of the lap pool.

Brianne eyed the bubbling water. "Is the pool only for laps?"

Cort's face crinkled with a smile, and he wiggled his eyebrows. "What did you have in mind?"

"I didn't have ..." Brianne wiggled her eyebrows "... *that* in mind. I just wondered if you could use it like a Jacuzzi or if it's only for exercise."

"You can relax in it if the jet pressure is lowered."

"I thought it would be nice to get in there since you have such a lousy shower. But we'd still need to use the world's ugliest bathroom to rinse the chlorine off."

"Not necessarily. On the side of the house, there's an outdoor shower."

"Really? Show me." Brianne followed him around the corner of the patio.

The shower had a roof overhang that jutted out from the wall of the house. Horizontal, vinyl slats formed the three walls that started about a foot off the ground and rose to eye level. Brianne opened the door and poked her head inside. A large diameter, rain shower head hung down toward the teak floor. The inside space was big enough to accommodate two people. A built-in bench lined one wall with a stack of towels on the end.

Brianne stepped back outside. "Please tell me it has hot water in there."

"No man likes a cold shower."

"Do you use it more than the shower upstairs?"

"It isn't always convenient. There's no sink, mirror, or light."

"Can we relax in the pool and then use this shower tonight?"

Cort nodded with a wide smile.

Brianne rubbed her hands together. "Let's finish supper."

After the food and dishes were cleared away, Brianne returned to the patio wrapped in a fluffy bath towel. Cort was in black boxer shorts. He adjusted dials on the pump while he held a penlight. There was just enough ambient light from candles in a dozen glass globes to navigate around the patio area. The light was off in the pool.

He sauntered over and wrapped his arms around her. "Ready to relax, sweetheart?"

"I get the feeling that relaxing isn't in your plans."

He loosened her towel, and it fell around their feet. She skimmed his shorts down to his ankles. Cort took her hand and led her down the steps into the pool. The lukewarm water reached her shoulders.

"I thought it would be shallower." She spun in the water, her arms opened wide.

"I wanted to be sure I could do flip turns without hitting the bottom so I had it made deeper than usual."

Cort moved to the center and pulled her into his arms. She wrapped her legs around his waist. They bounced in the bubbly water. She once calculated her weight with the moon's gravity. It was about twenty-two pounds. That's what her body seemed to weigh as Cort held her buoyant in the water.

She glanced down their bodies. The dark sun tattoo on his chest caught her eye. "I've been meaning to ask you about this." She outlined the eight rays with her fingertip. "Is there any significance to it or do you just like the symbol?"

"It's a common Filipino tattoo when done in black. I wanted something small to represent my mother. When I look at it, I remember the last time she kissed me goodbye."

"That's a lovely sentiment."

"I see you haven't been inked. Trust me, I've looked."

Brianne flicked water at his face.

He dropped his arms from around her waist. "Stand up, sweetheart."

When she was upright, Cort put one arm under her knees. He cradled her against his chest then sank in the water. Her breasts rose closer to his face. He lowered his head and licked water droplets from her nipples. Brianne shut her eyes to savor the sensations. Cort kept her afloat on the water's surface while his mouth nursed, nibbled, and nipped. The top step of the pool nudged her shoulders.

She opened her eyes. "Are we getting out?"

"No, just lie back and relax. If you need to, grab the handrail."

Cort sank down in the water, spread her knees open, and moved between them. Only his head was above the water. He placed his hands under her hips and lifted her to his mouth. The initial touch of his warm lips on her cool skin bowed her back. His tongue traveled up the inside of her thigh. His hands squeezed her cheeks.

"Ahhh." Her head fell back and lay in the water, half submerged.

His tongue swirled around and around. The water lapped against her body in rhythm to his touch. Her limp legs went rigid when his finger slipped inside. A litany of low moans escaped her.

"That's it, sweetheart." Cort lifted her pelvis farther out of the water. His finger kept time with his tongue, one circled, one stroked. The feel, the friction was different as her natural lubricant washed away with each touch.

This is too much. I can't take it.

Brianne was seized by her orgasm. Cort skimmed up her body, covered her mouth with his, and muted her cry. He held her against his body as the water rocked them. At last, she looked at him. "I love you, and I love your pool."

"Wait 'til you try my shower."

Hand in hand, they walked across the patio. Cort stepped inside and turned on the faucet. They stood beyond the spray until the water warmed. When the room became a dark, steamy cocoon, they moved under the water cascade. Cort had placed several lit candle globes outside the walls which let a pale horizontal light inside through the gaps between the slats. He flipped her wet hair behind her ears and exposed the column of her neck. His tongue ran down it and back up to her jaw.

Damn. He knows all my weak spots.

The muscles in Brianne's belly clenched in anticipation. Cort reached for a bottle on a shelf. He squirted gel into his hand and washed her hair. She closed her eyes and succumbed to the massage of his strong fingers. His soapy hands ran suds across her shoulders. He turned her back to his chest and continued his cleansing rub down her front.

He handed her the shower gel. "Do me, now."

She turned to this glorious, wet man of hers. She lathered her hands and ran her fingers through his hair. He leaned his head back under the shower head to rinse. Brianne soaped his shoulders, down his chest and back. He stood statue still with closed eyes. When she finished, he pulled her into his embrace and stepped under the water as it rained down on them. Cort gazed at her in the warm, moist darkness. She sensed rather than saw his carnal expression. The pool had washed away her dampness, but now it gathered between her thighs.

He turned her around. "Put your hands on the bench."

As she bent forward, she widened her stance. He reached toward a pile of towels. The distinctive tearing of a condom wrapper whispered in the dark enclosure.

Seconds later Cort kissed along her spine's length. "My beautiful girl."

His hands moved to her front. He palmed circles on her breasts, and her body came alive for him. He held her hips steady and eased himself inside. For several seconds neither of them moved, then he pulled out slightly. The rhythm was slow at first but soon picked up speed and intensity. Brianne gripped the bench slats and pushed back against him. A coiling deep inside her grew tighter.

"Come on, sweetheart." The command was uttered as a groan.

The urgent endearment sent her over the edge into a world of mindlessness. When her senses returned, Cort lay on the bench, his head on the towels, and she was on top, her back to his front. She could see the stars in the night sky over the top of the shower wall. Minutes passed.

She sighed. "Another new shower adventure for me."

"Anything for the woman I love."

He pushed on Brianne's shoulders to help her sit. She rolled to her feet with one hand on his chest until she was steady. Cort rose, turned off the shower, and grabbed two long bath towels. He wrapped one around her shoulders like a long shawl. The other he used to dry her hair before he fastened it around his hips. He led her to a cushioned recliner, where he laid down and pulled her next to him. They cuddled with faces upturned to the night sky.

"Brianne, you are everything I ever wanted. I need and love you so much."

His statement stunned her. She closed her eyes, unable to process his words and all he had done to win her back. Even her mother said he loved her.

I don't get it.

Cort was successful, sexy, and attractive, even to preteens. He could have any woman he wanted. From the photos posted on the Internet, it appeared he'd been involved with a number of different beauties. Brianne doubted that any of them suffered from obesity at one time. They all projected self-confidence, poise, and assurance in their ability to attract a man like Cort. Former fat girls like her were never given the How to Date a Hunk instruction manual.

It's why we settle for dates with chubby chasers or no one at all.

Cheerleaders, prom queens, and tramps knew how to get and keep the hot guys. Not nerdy, overweight girls who always experienced life and love through the View Master of their body image.

He thinks I'm everything he wants and needs right now, but what about weeks or months from now?

Her panic became audible. She choked on unshed tears. A chilled numbness spread as an avalanche of fear slammed into her. Her chest heaved in shallow breaths.

I can't bear to lose him. But I will. I know it. It's just a matter of time.

He sat up on one elbow and looked at her wide eyes. "What's wrong?"

The concern in his voice should have made her feel better. Instead, she closed her eyes and fisted the towel tighter around her.

He stroked her cheek. "Brianne, what's happening?"

Tears trailed down and wet his fingers as her sobs broke through.

Oh, God, he's going to see my ugly cry.

"Sweetheart, talk to me." Cort pulled her into a seated position.

"I'm so tired, and I'm PMS-ing like crazy."

Shit, why did I say that? Men don't want to hear about hormones.

He held her tight against him. "Let's get you into bed."

The past week had been an emotional roller coaster. Despite the reasonable explanation she gave for her moody tears, Brianne was convinced her psyche was in rehearsal for losing Cort. If she was not blindsided by the pain to come, she might be able to endure it.

Chapter 17

BRIANNE WAS STILL tired and somewhat blue on Monday morning. She did her best to appear cheerful and less hormonal than she was. After Cort dropped her at the condo, she drove to The Voice Center. Kitty poured water into the coffee maker as Brianne passed the break room.

"Bless you." She hugged the receptionist from behind. "I want caffeine so bad right now."

"Do you also need a vacation from your vacation?"

"You have no idea."

Brianne was with her morning client when her period began. While he practiced the yawn-sigh technique with vowels, she excused herself. As the work day continued, her cramps worsened.

After lunch, she went home to a heating pad and ibuprofen. She sent Cort a text: *Left office early. At home.*

He called later that afternoon. "Are you okay?"

"My period started. I'll be fine tomorrow."

"Can I come over after work?"

Brianne paused. *I don't want him to see his bloated girlfriend with cramps. Besides, I look like shit.*

Her cell phone chimed with a text message from Cort. *pretty please*

"How can you talk to me and send a text at the same time?"

"I'll show you when I get to your place. I won't stay late. You need your rest."

"Did you sit with any of your former girlfriends when they got their period?"

"No, but it'll be a good experience for me. Have you taken your pill yet?"

A pain pill? No, he means my birth control.

"Not yet."

"Take it and wait for me. I'll get us some supper. See you in about an hour."

That gave her time to take another ibuprofen as well as her new prescription and change clothes. She dressed in a camisole top and lounging pajama bottoms. After she washed her face, applied lip gloss, mascara, and combed her hair, she looked at herself in the mirror. The reflection didn't scream *here's a bloated, crampy woman.*

Cort arrived with a large container of butternut squash soup, chopped salad, and mushroom risotto cakes from Sublime, her favorite vegetarian restaurant. He edged in sideways when she opened the door for him.

"What do I smell?" She sniffed the air.

He gave her a sheepish look and showed her another bag he held behind his back. "I stopped at McDonalds for me. I ordered extra fries if you want some."

She kissed him. "I'd love some. Thank you."

While they ate, Cort told her, "I changed my appointment with Pam to Tuesday afternoon because I have to be in Los Angeles on Wednesday. I have a meeting with another producer about a reality show."

"Do you want to do another one?"

Will it mean you have to leave Florida and me?

"I haven't decided yet. It's good for business to keep my name and face on TV. But it would have to be the right project."

Pam arrived home and was invited to share their meal.

Brianne asked, "When are we going to meet your *friend?*"

"You know who my friend is. Cort told Mark he saw his car here yesterday."

Brianne glanced at Cort whose eyes were focused on his food. She turned back to Pam. "Why didn't you tell us it was Mark who was here?"

"Maybe because I hadn't told you I was seeing him in the first place. Or maybe because it took him a while to get his dick back in his pants." Brianne nibbled on her rice cake while Cort hid behind his Big Mac. Pam grabbed several of his fries. "I'm sure Cort also told you that Mark is hung like a horse."

Cort's eyes bounced back and forth between her and Pam. There was a spark of amusement in them.

Since the subject was on the table, Brianne asked, "Is his big dick the reason you're seeing him?"

"It's one of them."

"Are the other two reasons in his scrotum?"

Cort choked. Both women eyed him as he drank some soda to clear his throat.

Pam said, "He's a great guy. Good looking, smart, fit."

Brianne stared at her chopped salad, speared a forkful and put it in her mouth. When she raised her eyes from her plate, Pam stared at her with a steely gaze. Brianne hadn't seen that look since she suggested they call their practice *The Larynx Ladies*.

"What?" she asked.

"Go on. Say it."

"Say what?" Brianne asked.

"Say that Mark is shorter than me."

"He's shorter than a lot of people, including you." Brianne put down her fork. "I guess I'm surprised because he's not like the guys you've dated in the past."

"You mean the tall assholes I've dated in the past?"

Brianne gave a sideways glance at Cort who shrugged. She said, "Have your parents met him?"

"Not yet. We've just been together here or at his place."

"You haven't gone out in public with him?" Brianne blurted. Cort's foot nudged hers.

"We're getting used to each other in private first. If things work out, then I'll decide if I want to go public with him."

"You called Cort a *pendejo* when he was rethinking our relationship because I was a fat kid. How is this different?"

Cort held up an index finger to interrupt. "What's a *pendejo*?"

Pam ignored him. "Mark hasn't asked me to go out with him yet."

Brianne winced.

"What's with the look?" Pam said. "So he hasn't suggested we go out on a date. There's nothing wrong with that."

"You're right. There's nothing wrong that."

Cort bumped his foot against hers again, a little harder this time. She tucked it under her chair and out of reach.

"Are you saying that maybe he doesn't want to be seen with a giant *Latina*?"

"No. I'm just surprised that you're okay with a relationship that's just sex."

Pam reached across the table for the butternut squash soup container and eyed the remaining contents. "Are you done with this?"

Brianne nodded and handed her an unused plastic spoon.

Pam tipped the container and scooped several mouthfuls. "Actually, it's kind of nice not worrying about introducing him to my parents or meeting his family. We're not running into old boyfriends of mine or girl-friends of his. It's like we're having an affair. The only thing secretive about it was not telling you." She turned toward Cort who jumped like an eaves-dropper caught with his ear against the door. "You know, men rarely get to listen to girl-talk like this. Are you taking notes?"

He looked baffled, like he wasn't sure if her question was rhetorical or not.

When all the food he had brought from McDonald's and Sublime had been consumed, Pam said, "Thanks for feeding me. I'll leave you two alone."

After the takeout dinner was cleaned up, Cort and Brianne cuddled on the sofa.

She asked, "What time is your flight to L.A?"

"Around four-thirty. I'll go from The Voice Center to the airport. I'll be in meetings all day Wednesday and part of Thursday."

"I'll miss you." Brianne laid her head on his shoulder and hugged his arm against her breast.

That's the trouble with being this much in love. I'm already sad thinking about being separated from him, even for a few days.

Cort kissed her forehead. "Do you want to have dinner Friday night? I should be coherent by six o'clock if I'm able to sleep during the day."

"Sounds great."

#

At eleven thirty Wednesday night, Brianne's cell phone woke her. "Hello." Her voice was groggy with sleep.

"Sweetheart, I'm so sorry for calling this late. I have a huge favor to ask."

"Cort?" She came awake in an instant. "What's wrong?"

"My grandmother's aide called an ambulance and had Lola taken to the emergency room. I can get a flight home later this morning, but the hospital wants someone there now. The aide couldn't stay past eleven o'clock."

"I'm not a family member. The hospital won't tell me anything."

"I know. They faxed a HIPAA form to the hotel. I signed it and sent it back. They have my permission to release information to you. The emergency room nurse said Lola's disoriented and speaking gibberish. They're checking to see if she had a stroke. Can you go?"

"Of course. Which hospital?"

"Bethesda West. Do you know where it is?" Cort's voice sounded strained.

"I know exactly where it is. I'll get dressed now and call you as soon as I find out anything. Relax your voice. It sounds hoarse."

"It's been a long day of meetings. I'll do my exercises as soon as I hang up. I can't tell you how much I appreciate you doing this for me. I love you."

#

Despite the time and light traffic, it still took Brianne an hour to reach the hospital in the next county. She drove past rows of royal palms that lined the entrance to the hospital. With its landscaping lighting and even a sculpture, the cream and peach-colored building looked like a hotel. She parked in the visitor lot closest to the emergency room.

Despite the late hour, a clerk behind a contemporary wood desk greeted her with a smile. "What can I do for you?"

"I'm Brianne Gordon. I'm here to check on Lola Hardison. She was brought to the ER earlier this evening."

The clerk tapped her keyboard and checked the monitor. "Have a seat. I'll let them know someone is here."

Brianne sat on an upholstered chair welded in a row to three others. A sleepy security guard sat in a counter-height chair. He swiveled back and forth in a hypnotic rhythm. Several other people scattered around the room dozed or held cellphones close to their faces while their jittery knees bounced.

Twenty minutes later, she was called to the desk. The clerk ran her driver's license through a scanner, photographed her, and issued an adhesive label ID.

The pleasant woman pointed to her left. "You can go through those double doors."

A wall sign directed her to push a plate-sized metal button to operate the automatic opener. The double door closest to her moved inward while the other swung out with a whisper. Two nurses and a doctor were behind a glass-walled office. No one else was in the corridor that was lined with closed doors.

Even with separate treatment rooms, Brianne expected to see people on gurneys, family members sitting or standing in the hall, or staff running around like on TV hospital shows. But this ER was eerily calm and quiet.

A pretty African-American nurse in scrubs with a wild floral-design top was seated behind a counter and looked up at Brianne's approach. Her name tag read: Aurora Davis R.N.

"Can I help you?" she asked.

"Hi, I'm Brianne Gordon. Is it usually this quiet?"

"Are you kidding? This is the calm before the storm. It'll probably be hell in here right as I'm due to go off duty."

"I'm here to check on Lola Hardison. Her grandson called from California and asked me to come."

"Are you family?"

"No. There is no other family. I'm his girlfriend. He faxed a HIPAA authorization with my name."

Nurse Davis tapped keys on a computer. "It's here. They're running tests on Mrs. Hardison right now. I expect her back any minute."

"I was told she was confused and her speech was affected. Is she showing any signs of hemiparesis, numbness or a headache?"

The nurse looked at Brianne with raised eyebrows. "When she was taken to radiology, her speech and confusion were improving slightly. She didn't appear to have paralysis or weakness in her face or limbs."

"Was she able to understand what others were saying to her? Could she follow verbal directions?"

"Pretty much. We had difficulty understanding her speech. It was garbled. Are you in the medical field?"

"I'm a speech language pathologist."

The nurse nodded. "As soon as we find out more, I'll let you know. You can wait in the lobby until she gets back. It shouldn't be too much longer."

"I'll call her grandson and update him."

Brianne went outside. She stood off to the side so she didn't block the entrance doors. Although the night air was cool, she was warmer than when she sat in the frigid waiting room.

She tapped Cort's name on her favorites list and the phone dialed his number. He answered after one ring.

Brianne said, "Cort, I'm here at the hospital."

"Have you found out any more?"

"Your grandmother is having tests done in radiology right now. The ER nurse said her confusion and speech were somewhat better than when she was brought in. She didn't have any weakness or paralysis so it doesn't sound like a stroke to me."

"I feel so helpless being this far away. The flight got in late last night. I was in meetings all day. I'm exhausted and now I have to deal with this. Thank God, you're there."

"I'll stay as long as needed. We should know more when all the tests are done."

"Thank you, sweetheart. I have another call coming in."

"Don't worry. I'll handle things here."

When Brianne went inside, the clerk said, "You can go into the ER."

Nurse Davis smiled when she saw Brianne. "Mrs. Hardison is back. I have good news. No sign of a cerebral hemorrhage. The urine test confirmed she has a bladder infection."

Brianne stared at her dumbfounded. "A bladder infection?"

"We see it all the time. Urinary tract infections in the elderly mimic the symptoms of dementia. We have her on an antibiotic IV and she's showing improvement. Older folks usually don't have the pain that younger people experience. But as the UTI progresses, it affects their cognition and speech."

"So this had nothing to do with her diabetes?"

"Well, the fact that she's wheelchair-bound and diabetic doesn't help. Would you like to see her?"

Brianne hesitated. "To be honest, I've never met the woman. Her grandson and I have been dating less than a month."

"I see from her records that her grandson is Cortland Hardison. Isn't he the hunk from *Weight Loss Wonders?*"

Brianne nodded.

Nurse Davis grinned at her. "Damn, you are one lucky girl." She came around the counter and gestured forward with her arm. "Follow me."

Brianne's heels were noisy on the tiled floor. The nurse's white plastic clogs made almost no sound. They stopped at a treatment room with a closed door. Nurse Davis opened it and Brianne went inside after her.

"Lola, I brought someone to see you," the nurse said with a cheery voice.

Brianne's smile froze on her face. *Oh, my God! Cort's grandmother is huge!*

The woman on the gurney weighed at least three hundred pounds. With both side rails up, her body overflowed between the metal stanchions. Her stomach ballooned beneath the sheet and a puffy face melted into her chest with no visible signs of a neck.

Nurse Davis said, "How's she doing, Rita?"

A woman in pink scrubs rose from a chair beside the bed. Her tag identified her as Rita Menendez, LPN. She said, "Her espeesh es better."

Nurse Davis touched her patient's shoulder and pointed to Brianne who stood at the foot of the bed. "Lola, this is your grandson's friend."

Brianne found her professional voice. She wanted to first assess how much verbal information Lola could process. "Hello, Mrs. Hardison."

Lola's head moved from Nurse Davis to Brianne. She blinked and furrowed her brow. Her mouth frowned. "Who you?"

"I'm Cort's friend, Brianne."

"Where he?"

"He's still in California."

"How … know Cor?"

"We're friends."

"Where my gran … on?"

Nurse Davis interrupted before Brianne could repeat her answer. "You rest here a little more. We'll be right back."

Lola reached out with startling quickness and grabbed the nurse's sleeve. "Call Cor."

"We did." She loosened Lola's grip. "He's on his way. Rita will stay with you until he gets here."

The white lie seemed to relax Cort's grandmother who deflated like a cooling soufflé of flesh. As they exited the treatment room, Brianne took one last look at the woman who raised Cort.

Out in the hall, the nurse said, "You can see she's still exhibiting symptoms. Let me check with the attending physician."

Brianne leaned back against the wall by the treatment room door after Nurse Davis left. It was about fifteen minutes later when a thirty-something, white-coated doctor with a neat goatee approached her.

"Hello. I'm Dr. Sotomayor. We're going to admit Mrs. Hardison tonight. She definitely has an infection which the intravenous antibiotics will clear up pretty quick. But I'm concerned about her sugar levels and EKG results. I understand she lives alone."

Brianne nodded.

He said, "We're going to monitor her for a day or two. When is her son—"

"Grandson," she corrected.

"Yes, when will he back?"

Brianne's head was so foggy with fatigue it took her a moment to figure out what day it was. Her watch said it was four-ten AM Thursday. "He's scheduled to return Friday morning unless he can catch an earlier flight."

"They'll be taking Mrs. Hardison up to a room shortly. She'll be here for at least the next twenty-four to forty-eight hours."

Brianne asked, "Should I stay until he gets here?"

In the usual noncommittal manner of a physician, Dr. Sotomayor said, "If you want, but she's going to resting most of the day. Her regular doctor will check on her during morning rounds and call afterward."

The ER doctor spun on his heel and headed down the hall. Brianne followed and stopped at the desk where Nurse Davis sat.

She leaned her arms on top of the high counter. "Can I ask you a question?"

The nurse smiled. "All right. I'll take your boyfriend off your hands. My husband won't like it, but who cares?"

Brianne laughed then turned serious. "Should I stay here with Lola?"

Nurse Davis reached up and patted her arm. "That's not necessary now that we know her medical condition is not that serious. Go home and get some sleep. She's in good hands."

Brianne hesitated, bit her lip and looked down the hall to where Lola was.

"Listen," the nurse said, "She needs rest right now. Her doctor is not going to release her before her gorgeous grandson gets home. They'll discuss that later today."

"Thank you."

Brianne left and called Cort from her car. She told him about Lola's urinary tract infection and admission to the hospital.

"I'm not going to change my flight until I talk with the doctor." He paused. "Did you see Lola?"

"The nurse took me back and introduced me. Your grandmother was still somewhat disoriented, although her speech was clearer. She kept asking where you were. I'm sure that given more time for the antibiotic to work, she'll be much better. Do you want me to come back and visit her later today?"

"You don't need to. I'll call Camille, one of her daytime aides, in the morning. She can go to the house and get her things. We've been through this before."

"I can keep her company during visitor hours this evening."

Cort answered with uncharacteristic abruptness. "That's not necessary."

"I'm glad to do it. I can drive here after work and let you know how she is."

"You've done enough. I've got to go. Bye."

The line went dead.

Chapter 18

BRIANNE GOT HOME at six in the morning. She set her alarm for ten AM but was unable to fall asleep until after seven. She kept herself caffeinated to finish her schedule of clients. Cort hadn't contacted her all day. Brianne yawned and rubbed her eyes as she worked on client summaries. When she opened them again, Pam stood in the doorway.

"You look tired," she said.

"I didn't get much sleep. I drove to Bethesda Hospital in the middle of the night."

"And you did this because …"

Brianne yawned again. "Cort called from California and asked me to check on his grandmother. She had been taken to the ER. Did you know that urinary tract infections in the elderly cause symptoms of dementia?"

"I do know about that. It was kind of a funny story. My *abuela's* brother was in Walmart when someone noticed him acting disoriented. They couldn't understand him and thought because he looked Latin that he was speaking Spanish. Then one employee said, *he no espeak Espanol.* That's when they called the EMTs."

"I left after Lola was admitted to the hospital. I called Cort to let him know before I drove home." Brianne frowned and shook her head.

"What's wrong?"

"The first two times I talked with him he was sweet and grateful. When I called to tell him about the diagnosis, he was cool and abrupt." Brianne rubbed her forehead where a fatigue headache throbbed.

"Why?"

"Maybe because I now know his grandmother is morbidly obese?"

"So he's got a fat grandmother. Who doesn't?"

"The guy who owns fitness centers," Brianne said.

"Come on. Do you really think he'd be mad because you found out his grandmother is fat?"

"I don't know, but he was adamant that I not visit Lola tonight at the hospital."

"*Chica,* I'm sure there's good reason and that it has nothing to do with his grandmother's weight. Let it go until you can talk with him about it."

Brianne sighed. "You're right."

"I'm heading out now. Can you lock up?"

After Pam left, Brianne finished her file updates then sent Cort a text. *When are you flying back? Is there anything I can do?*

He didn't reply before she locked up the building. There was still no message by the time she arrived home. She respected his request and didn't drive to Boynton Beach to visit Lola. As she got into bed Thursday night, her phone chimed.

Just landed. Going home to sleep. Will talk tomorrow.

#

Brianne left the office on Friday determined to call Cort as soon as she got home. Instead, she was surprised to find his car parked next to hers. She halted just outside The Voice Center's rear entrance.

He opened his car door and stood up. In a low, flat tone, he said, "Get in. We need to talk."

Uh-oh. This is bad.

She walked to the passenger side and steeled herself.

Don't let him see you cry.

Her heart thundered in her chest as she slid into the passenger seat. She gnawed on her bottom lip and twisted her fingers in her lap. Cort draped his wrists on top of the steering wheel and stared out the windshield.

He can't even look at me.

After several more seconds of viewing his profile, she turned and looked straight ahead also. Each heartbeat was a painful hammer blow as she waited for the words which would end her romantic dream.

"Have you recently Googled my name?" he asked.

She blinked her eyes several times in bewilderment. "Uh, no."

"If you had, you would have found photos of us on the PrimeTime website. It said I'm a regular customer and recommend their food."

Brianne closed her eyes as acid roiled in her stomach.

Oh, no. Emma's new marketing campaign.

Cort said, "My publicist told me about this unauthorized use of my name and image while I was in California."

"Your publicist, Jacqueline?"

The bitch who called me a quack.

"Yes. I never agreed to endorse PrimeTime and no paperwork was signed authorizing what is called the Right of Publicity. No one, not even your family, can use my name or image without my knowledge or permission."

Even though she had nothing to do with this, Brianne was awash with humiliation. She'd say she was sorry, but it would be meaningless. "What did you do?"

"I told Jacqueline that I didn't want to pursue legal action against the restaurant. Your father was contacted today. He was advised to remove everything about me from the website. It's already been taken down."

The silence stretched between them as Brianne looked out the passenger window and mentally cringed with the implications of what Emma had done.

Cort said, "Say something."

Brianne turned her head and focused on the back wall of The Voice Center. "What do you want me to say? My sister had this idea for a new marketing campaign using endorsements from public figures. I'm sure she never ran it by my father before she posted you on the website. I hope she's learned her lesson."

There.

"Why did *you* agree to it without asking me first?"

She looked at him in disbelief as he stared out past the hood of his car. "I did *not* agree to it. I knew nothing about it."

He glanced at her with raised eyebrows before he looked out the windshield again. "There were pictures of the two of us at the restaurant."

"I don't care what there was." Brianne's voice rose in volume. "I did not agree to be photographed nor did I give consent on your behalf. Since I can eat almost nothing on the menu, why would I want to be part of the advertising?"

"The posting also announced the new vegetarian menu. I thought you helped with that."

"Emma asked for my input on possible non-meat dishes. That's it. I'm just as blindsided by this as you are."

There was a long pause before Cort spoke. "Okay. I believe you."

She wanted to say *thank you* with sarcastic insincerity. Instead she asked, "Is there anything else?"

"Actually, there's one more thing."

Brianne took a deep breath and turned to look straight ahead. *Here it comes.*

"There's a video of us on YouTube."

Brianne's body jerked in surprise. "Emma did a video, too?"

"It wasn't of us at PrimeTime."

Oh shit. Were we having sex?

"Where were we?"

"Remember that first dance we had at the wedding reception?"

"Of course."

It was the most romantic and best dance of my life. Is that memory now in the crap pile, too?

"I think one of the teens videotaped it with her cell phone and put it on YouTube."

Brianne's shoulders slumped in defeat. "Are you having it removed?"

"No. I wasn't identified by name in the title."

"Then how did you find out about it?"

"Someone from *Celebrity Dancers* saw it and contacted my agent," he said.

"Is that a good thing?"

"It's always better to have producers approach you with proposals than the other way around."

Brianne continued to stare straight ahead. "So not everything about me and my family is bad for you or your career?"

His leather seat squeaked. "What do you mean?"

She stiffened her spine and turned to face him. There was a deep crease between his eyebrows.

Brianne said, "When you were put on seven days of vocal rest, it created havoc with your business schedule. Finding out about my weight problem made you consider the possible impact on your image." He opened his mouth to speak, but she held up her hand. "Let me finish. My sister oversteps her bounds by posting you on PrimeTime's website without your permission. As far as the video is concerned, it's not a problem at this point. But TMZ may get it and make fun of you yet. After I go to the hospital and see your grandmother, you make me feel like a hookup you'd rather she didn't know about. I get the feeling that you think my family and I are not worth the trouble we're causing you." She turned away from him and crossed her arms on her chest.

Finally, he said, "I don't know what to say."

Say I'm worth the aggravation. Say nothing else matters but that we're together. Say that you love me.

She counted one Mississippi, two Mississippi, three Mississippi, four Mississippi, five Mississippi. She blinked to push back the tears that threatened to surface. In a weary voice, thick with resignation, Brianne said, "Why don't you *just* say it's over between us?"

A long moment passed where no one moved or said anything. Then his car door opened and slammed shut. She looked around.

Shit! Where'd he go?

The passenger door was wrenched open, and he pulled her out of her seat. A feeling of panic raced outward from her chest.

All he had to do was tell me to get out of the car. He doesn't have to throw me out.

Instead of being flung away as she expected, Cort wrapped one arm around her waist and pulled her close. Brianne's eyes darted around as he held her head pushed forward toward his shoulder. Pinned against him, she waited. At last, Cort released her.

He put his hands on the sides of her face to tunnel his eyes into hers. "There will be no goodbye for us. I told you that before. I won't allow anyone or anything to ruin what we have." He must have seen the confusion on her face. "Why would you think I wanted to break up with you?"

"Isn't that what *we need to talk* means?"

He gave her a quick kiss on the lips. "No, sweetheart, sometimes it just means we need to talk."

He shut the car door, leaned against it, and locked his hands behind her back to pull her close.

Brianne stiff-armed her upper body away so she could look in his face. "After I offered to visit your grandmother, you were so insistent that I not go back. Were you upset that I met her?"

And found out she's obese.

His dark eyes crinkled. "I knew you'd drive back to the hospital if I didn't say no. You had been up most of the night, and then you were going to work all day. Lola is hard to handle when you're rested. Trust me, I just spent the day with her."

"Was she sent home from the hospital?"

"No. They're doing more tests. The doctor is concerned about her heart and mobility. I'm afraid they aren't going to release her until she goes to rehab first. She's not going to like that."

"Okay. I understand why you didn't want me to visit her last night, but you should have told me."

"You're right. I should have."

"Then there's the other reason for breaking up. Emma's posting on PrimeTime's website."

"What your sister did would not make me call it quits. She was the one who got me to go to Texas for you. I owe her."

"Cort, telling me that using your image was actionable in a lawsuit and thinking I was part of it *is* a reason to break up."

"Not for me. It wasn't defamation or libel. It was unauthorized use of my name to promote a good restaurant. I admit it bothered me when Jacqueline said it must have been your idea."

Brianne's spidey sense went on high alert. "She said that?"

"Well, the website's promotion was about the new vegetarian menu, and you were in the picture so she assumed you approved it. But now I know that you didn't have anything to do with it. So is everything okay now?" Cort raised his eyebrows.

"Not yet. When did you find out about the website and the video?"

He looked skyward. "Jacqueline called me late Thursday evening."

"Was it before or after you asked me to go to the hospital?"

"It was after you arrived there but before you called me to tell me what was wrong with Lola."

"So after you found out about the website and video, we had our last conversation. That's when I offered to visit Lola and you said to me, *you've done enough.*" Brianne mimicked the same clipped, cold tones he used.

"Did I sound like that?"

"Yes, and that's why I thought you were breaking up with me."

He hugged her close. "I'm sorry you felt that way. It was not how I intended it."

He's not sorry he said it. He's sorry that I took it that way. Do I want this argument to continue over semantics?

"Are we okay *now*?" he asked.

"I guess."

Will he pick up on my vague response?

"Then let's eat."

Men.

She sighed. "Where can we go on a Friday night with no reservation? Remember it's *the season*?"

It was the time of year that locals dread. Snowbirds and tourists descended on South Florida and clogged the roads and restaurants. Cort and Brianne ended up at a salad buffet and were able to eat without waiting. The place was noisy and distracting as every patron paraded to and from the food stations. Brianne had just returned with frozen yogurt when her cell phone rang.

"It's my sister." She answered the phone. "Hi, Em. Hang on, I need to step outside." She went out the exit door. "Are you still there?" No words, just soft sobs came through the phone. "Emma? Are you okay?"

"I'm soooo sorry."

"I know you are."

"Is Cort mad at me?"

"Well, he didn't appreciate what you did, and neither did I," Brianne scolded.

"I'm glad he isn't going to sue PrimeTime. Is he going to break up with you?"

"No."

At least, not today.

"I've never seen Daddy so mad. He told me I was fired if Cort sued or you guys broke up."

"I guess you still have a job then. But, Emma, what were you thinking?"

Her sister heaved a dramatic sigh. "I got carried away after Daddy agreed to the new menu. I snapped some pictures the night we ate with you and Cort at the restaurant."

"Is that what you were doing when you disappeared from the table?"

In a little girl voice, Emma said, "Yes."

"Are you in Fort Worth with Dad right now?"

"He said I couldn't go. He was too upset to spend the whole weekend with me. I'm supposed to call and tell him if you and Cort are still together."

"We're having supper. Cort is the one you really owe an apology."

"Do I have to?" Emma whined. "Can't you just tell him I'm really, really sorry, and it won't happen again?"

Brianne headed back inside. "I'm going to put him on, and you own up to what you did." She handed her phone to Cort.

He walked outside. A few minutes later, he sat down and slid her phone across the table. "I feel bad for her."

"Don't. Emma needs to learn chain of command. This experience will teach her a valuable lesson."

"She was crying."

"Yeah, she did that with me, too. My dad threatened to fire her."

"Emma is just inexperienced, not malicious."

That's right.

Her sister didn't impugn his professionalism. Emma didn't tell him he was going to be fucked then dumped. She didn't accuse him of legal improprieties without verification.

When are you going to see who really should be fired?

Chapter 19

BRIANNE AWOKE EARLY Saturday morning and headed to the exercise room on the first floor. The only person present was the geriatric bike rider who watched her rear end the last time she worked out there. She hid behind equipment as she exercised, so he never had a clear view.

When she entered the condo, Pam called out to her from the kitchen. "Go take your shower. By the time you're finished, the *huevos habaneros* will be ready."

They ate the tomato and egg dish with crispy slices of *pan cubano* slathered with butter.

Pam cupped her hand at the table's edge and brushed stray crumbs into it. "Do you and Cort have any plans for this weekend?"

Cort was an umpire for his neighbor's Little League game that morning. The rest of the afternoon involved Lola's discharge from the hospital and transfer to a nursing home for rehab.

"Nothing definite. Why? Is Marisol throwing another party?"

"No, Mark and I wanted to ask you guys to go out to dinner with us either tonight or tomorrow night."

"Will this be your first time out in public with him?"

Pam had her back turned to Brianne as she loaded the breakfast plates into the dishwasher. "We had lunch once."

"Are you sure you want to double date?"

"We thought it might help. You know, if conversation lagged, we can talk with you and Cort."

"Do you and Mark run out of things to say when you're together?"

Pam shut the door of the dishwasher and straightened. "We don't talk a lot when we're together. Unless you count the number of times I say *Oh God* and he says *I'm coming*."

"I'll ask Cort." Her text read, *Are you free for dinner tonight or tomorrow with Pam and Mark?*

His reply was, *Don't know how long it will take with Lola today. Sunday night better.*

Brianne said, "He can't tonight, but tomorrow is okay. Where do you want to go? Remember it is *the season*. We'll need a reservation."

"Let's go to PrimeTime, and you can try one of those new vegetarian dishes. We can always get in there," Pam suggested.

"That's not a good idea so soon after what Emma did."

"What about that restaurant by the Galleria Mall where you got that roasted tofu? That was a nice place. What was it called?"

They looked up the name of the restaurant online, and Pam called in the reservation. Both men confirmed via text messages that they would come to the condo at six PM for drinks before dinner.

#

Brianne was in her bedroom reading her Kindle that afternoon.

Pam knocked on the doorjamb. "Can I come in?"

"Sure."

Pam had her laptop cradled across her forearm. "Talking about PrimeTime reminded me of the video you said was on YouTube. Have you seen it yet?"

"No. Did you find it?"

"I typed in wedding, reception, dance, Texas. It's listed as Sexy Hunk Wedding Dance." She looked at Brianne with raised eyebrows. "Sexy hunk, huh?"

"Hey, I didn't title it, but he is."

Pam sat on the edge of the mattress with the laptop perched on her knees. Brianne scooted next to her and hugged a pillow to her chest. The video started with the unexpected jarring of sudden music.

A preteen voice was captured on the audio, masking the song. "Are you getting it? OMG, he is so sexy!"

The videographer shushed her. As Brianne and Cort moved around the dance floor, camera girl slid along the sideline like she was on a track dolly for a low budget film. If Brianne didn't know better, she'd think the girl used a steady-cam. The picture was not affected by the usual nauseating camera shake.

When the film ended, Pam closed her laptop. "You guys looked great. I can't believe you didn't practice beforehand."

"That was our first dance together."

"You always say you're a klutz. How come you're such a good dancer?"

"According to my cousin, Gary, I'm only graceful when there's music playing."

"Do you make love to music?"

"We haven't tried it yet. I'll have to see if there's a difference."

Pam laughed. "I talked with Mark this morning and told him there was a secretly recorded video of you and Cort on the Internet. He got upset because he thought it was porn."

"I was afraid of that when Cort told me about it. You hear about all these unauthorized sex tapes of celebrities being released. That's all I need, a film of me having sex out in cyberspace."

#

Cort called at nine PM. "I'm back home at last. I got Lola settled at the rehab center."

"How's she doing?"

"She's telling everyone I put her there to die."

Brianne laughed. "Give her some time to adjust. She may like it better than with the home health aides coming and going."

"I don't know. She said she'd rather die alone at home than during a Bingo game with some old guy trying to feel her up. I just hope I don't get a call to come get her because they've kicked her out."

"I don't think you have anything to worry about."

"Let's hope not. Can we talk about tomorrow night?" With a note of hope in his voice, Cort asked, "Will it be ten days since you started the pill?"

"Sir, you are correct."

"Ahhh." He sighed. "I can't wait to get you in bed. But I do have a question about our dinner date."

"Shoot."

"Have you and Pam ever double dated before?"

"Once."

"How did it go?"

"Badly."

Cort cleared his throat. "Do you want to tell me about it?"

"It was a wake-up call for me. That night I realized my live-in boyfriend, Paul, wanted to get his hands on PrimeTime more than on me."

"How'd you find out?"

"Pam's date talked about having to sell the insurance company he inherited. He was a fireman and had no interest in running the family business. Paul turned to me and asked who would get PrimeTime when my father died. That question and others he had asked added up. A week later, I kicked him out of the condo. Pam moved in, and my dad fired him from the restaurant."

"He worked for Ted?"

Brianne said, "He was a chef. That's how I met him. I guess he figured if he was tight with the owner's daughter, PrimeTime would be his one day."

"He was a fool. You're the prize, not the restaurant."

#

On Sunday morning, Brianne went for her usual church-skipping walk. Since Pam spent the night at Mark's place, there would be no fresh pot of coffee when she got home. She planned to detour to Starbucks for a grande brew to go. Before she got there, she ducked into the doorway of a closed restaurant. With her back to the sidewalk, Brianne fished crumpled dollar bills from her sports bra. She ironed the wrinkles out on her thigh and waved them to air-dry any dampness away.

She proceeded to the coffee shop and ordered her caffeine fix. When she exited, she stopped just outside the door to take tiny, cautious sips of the boiling brew. There were no seats inside so she looked for a free table in the open air.

"Brianne. Brianne, over here."

The Ice Queen stood by the corner of the building where café tables sat inside a metal fenced-in area. Jacqueline was dressed in pale linen pants and a tank top covered by a sheer blouse. Her hair was drawn tight into a chignon.

Brianne wore calf-length leggings and an oversized UF T-shirt. Her hair was skinned into a ponytail. She was makeup free and sweaty. She remained rooted in place and lifted her coffee cup in greeting. "Hi."

Jacqueline motioned her to come closer. She hesitated. The Ice Queen put her hands together in a pleading gesture. "Please. It's important."

With reluctance and a scowl, Brianne went closer. Cort's publicist waved a come-on gesture and disappeared around the corner of the building. With her hot cup of coffee held at shoulder level, she negotiated her way around the chairs, people, and canines with care. The Ice Queen sat alone at a table for two on the side of the building.

When Brianne stood next to the table, Jacqueline used her foot to push out the chair opposite her. "Sit."

Sit? Brianne turned to walk away. *Try to chase me in your Choo's, Jacqueline.*

"I owe you an apology."

Brianne stopped, put her cup on the tabletop, and sat down.

Jacqueline said, "I saw you walk by. We need to talk."

I'm here to listen to an apology, not talk.

Silence was her best advantage right now. She sipped her coffee while her gaze fixed on the woman across from her.

Despite her statement of contrition, Jacqueline projected an aura of intimidating, self-contained arrogance. "I'm sorry for what I said at the fundraiser. I was totally out of line and had no right to question your professionalism."

You didn't question it. You called me a quack.

"Obviously, you know what you're doing. Cort's voice sounds like it used to, and he's only had a month of therapy."

I don't want her to think that I'm sleeping with a client. I wouldn't put it past her to report me to the licensure board.

"I'm no longer Cort's speech pathologist."

"You aren't?"

"No. Ethically I can't be personally involved with a client. A colleague took over his case."

"Well, both of you have done a great job. He says he won't need surgery now. Is that right?"

Brianne wasn't going to share anything about Cort's prognosis with this woman. After all, HIPAA rules applied to her also. She drank some coffee then turned sideways in her chair to stand. "I need to get going."

Jacqueline stretched her arm across the table to halt her. "A minute more. I'm meeting a friend who should be here shortly. I wanted you to know that the other thing I said was because I was jealous."

Now this might be worth waiting to hear.

"Cort and I broke up a few months before the Healthy Kids fundraiser. It was hard seeing him with another woman for the first time. Please forgive me for lashing out at you like that and forget that I said such a … a coarse thing."

Fat chance. I'm not God, and I don't have Alzheimer's.

Then Brianne recalled that Cort found out about the pictures posted on PrimeTime's website from this woman. "Why did you tell Cort I authorized the use of his name and image on the restaurant website?"

Jacqueline seemed taken off guard by the question. "What?"

"You said I knew about the posting and agreed to it without his knowledge or asking for permission."

"I thought that you *did* know about it. After all, you were in the pictures, and it is your father's restaurant," she said in the tolerant but slightly exasperated manner of a government official to a concerned citizen.

"I didn't even know we had been photographed until Cort told me."

"Oh. Then I guess I have something else to apologize for." Jacqueline sat back in her chair and folded her arms across her chest. The woman's animosity was undisguised now.

Brianne waited, but it didn't appear that another apology was forthcoming.

Then the publicist's expression eclipsed from a sour look into one of delight. Her long, slender arm shot up into the air. "Over here."

Their little talk was over. Brianne stood, picked up her almost empty cup and turned to leave. A model-thin woman with a waterfall of inky-black hair and also dressed in resort chic headed their way.

"Bye," Cort's publicist said in a dismissive manner.

Jacqueline's exotic friend gave an imperial nod when they passed each other. Brianne stopped at a trash can and took a final swallow of coffee. Her ears seemed to be like giant microphones tuned to the voice of the Ice Queen.

"Dorma, you made it."

For all her regal bearing, the woman's voice vibrated with a high-pitched, nasal whine. "Who was that?"

"Believe it or not, she's Cort's new girlfriend."

"Her? You've got to be kidding."

"He says he's in love."

"What does he see in her, other than big tits?"

"Beats me. Maybe she gives great head."

That's the problem with eavesdropping. You better be prepared to hear what you'd rather not.

All the feelings of superiority that buoyed Brianne when she listened to Jacqueline apologize evaporated. She plodded home with the heavy steps of the big girl put down by the pretty ones again.

#

Sunday evening, Brianne opened the condo's door at six when the bell rang. Mark held a fragrant floral bouquet. Cort waved at her empty-handed.

"Hi, Mark. Pam's in the living room." She pointed and he headed there.

Brianne put her arms around Cort's neck, and he pulled her tight against him. He backed her up against the foyer cabinet and kissed her.

They were lost in their passion until Pam said, "Stay off *mi gabinete de abuela*." She stood behind them, a vase filled with her flowers. She placed it in the center of the dining room table. "I'll get the wine while you guys join Mark."

In the living room, Brianne headed toward the sofa. Cort followed with Mark behind him.

Should I sit on the sofa or leave it for Pam and Mark?

Since she was between the sofa and coffee table, she walked to the end, rounded the corner and moved toward the chairs on the other side. Cort followed, and so did Mark. She sat in the far chair. Cort stopped, took a step backwards and sat on the remaining chair. Like the next to the last person in musical chairs, Mark stood at the end of the coffee table. He quick-stepped backwards and sat on the sofa, just missing the arm.

Pam watched with an open bottle of Merlot and shook her head. "Awkward."

Brianne giggled with nervousness. "At least, I didn't trip or make anyone else fall."

"And there wasn't even any music playing," Cort added.

Everyone laughed, and the shared mirth seemed to relieve the tension. Pam poured wine into the stemmed glassware on the coffee table and passed them around. The conversation drifted into talk about their families after Brianne and Cort shared stories from their weekend in Fort Worth.

Mark said, "My sister, Yvette, is really into country western. My Puerto Rican family doesn't get it. She came to our cousin's fifteenth birthday party, her *quinceañera,* dressed in boots, a denim mini skirt, and a cowboy hat. You have to understand that the dress code is black tie and formal gowns. My mother almost had a heart attack."

Cort tipped his wineglass toward Pam. "Did you have one of those parties?"

"No way," Pam said with a grimace. "My sister began planning her *quinceañera* when she was thirteen. My mother said it was important to celebrate becoming a woman. I told her I didn't need an expensive party when a push-up bra and thong would do the trick."

They left thirty minutes later. Cort carried Brianne's work clothes for tomorrow and an overnight bag to his car. Pam and Mark climbed into his little red roadster.

At the restaurant, the hostess said, "Your table isn't quite ready. It will be a few more minutes."

Brianne said, "That's restaurant-speak for we used your table and hoped they would be finished by your reservation time."

Fifteen minutes later, the hostess led them into the Art Deco dining room. The floor had a chevron design of hard woods. Upholstered chairs circled round tables laid with crisp white linens, and chrome lamps hung from the coffered ceiling. White-jacketed and bow-tied waiters and waitresses took orders and served food. They were seated at a table in the middle of the room.

As they read their menus, someone close by said, "Look who we have here."

Brianne cringed.

Chapter 20

BRIANNE LOOKED UP into the smiling face of her old boyfriend. "Hi, Paul."

Cort's head swiveled from the man who stood next to their table, to her, and back to Paul. Pam stared at him with a tight-lipped, narrow-eyed expression. Mark must have sensed the tension that swirled around the table because his eyes jumped up from his open menu. Paul wasn't wearing a chef's coat and the ubiquitous black-and-white pants. He was dressed in a black suit with an open-collared white shirt.

"How ya doin', Brianne?"

"Good. Are you eating here, too?"

"Naw, I've been workin' here for almost a year. I'm in the kitchen during the week. On Sundays, I'm the dining room manager. How are you, Pam?"

"Fine." Pam looked at him with hard eyes. "So tell me, Paul, does the owner of this restaurant have an unmarried daughter?"

He gave her a feral grin and cocked his finger at her like it was a holdup. "Ya still gotta mouth on you."

"That's right." Pam slipped her hand under Mark's arm and cuddled close. "And the man I like enjoys it."

While Pam sparred with Paul, Brianne studied him. He'd put on a few inches around his midsection and his dark, curly hair was thinning, but he was still an attractive man.

"Let me introduce you," said Brianne. "Paul, this is Cort Hardison. Cort, Paul Mancuso."

The two men shook hands, but there was no whitening knuckles. It was a simple handshake between two newly introduced men.

"I recognized you first." Paul released Cort's hand. "Then I saw Bree and Pam."

"And this is Mark Diaz." Brianne pointed with her palm open across the table.

Paul shook Mark's hand. "So what brings you guys to my restaurant?"

My restaurant? My God, he's still an arrogant prick.

Brianne responded first. "I love the roasted tofu here."

Paul barked a laugh. "You must still be a vegetarian."

"Yes, I am."

Paul's head snapped up, and he nodded to the back of the restaurant. "Well, folks, have a great dinner. Nice seein' you girls again. If you need anything, ask your server or have her get me."

After several long beats when Paul was out of sight, Pam said, "That went better than I thought it would."

Brianne and Cort remained silent.

Mark looked at each of them. "What am I missing here?"

Pam put her hand on Mark's arm. "The last time we double dated, Brianne was living with Paul. During that date, she found out what an asshole he was. A week later, she broke up with him and kicked him out of the condo."

Cort leaned forward toward Mark as if to share a confidence. "That's why I'm on my best behavior tonight."

Brianne burst out laughing, followed by the others. They were still giggling when their waitress came to take their drink orders. During dinner, the talk turned to exes and crazy dates.

Pam said, "In high school, I went with a guy to a movie theater for our first date. I excused myself to go to the restroom and when I came back, he was making out with the girl next to him. I left without saying a word."

"C'mon, Pam," Brianne said. "That doesn't sound like you."

"Well, that wouldn't happen now. I just walked out the door and called my dad. The jerk acted like nothing was wrong the next time I saw him. He didn't even ask me where I went."

Mark said, "I dated a girl I knew from high school for about six months. She made me laugh and was a little crazy, too. My mother hated her. One Sunday morning, my parents burst into my bedroom, yelling at me. I didn't know what was wrong until my father shoved the newspaper in my face. There was an engagement announcement saying Corky and I were getting married."

Pam had her elbow on the table, her chin in hand. "Had you asked her to marry you?"

"No way. She had been dropping hints that I ignored. We were working part-time, going to school, and living at home. She decided the announcement would give me a jump start."

"And did it?" Pam seemed very amused by this story.

"Yeah, I called her up and said I never wanted to see her again."

Pam looked at Cort. "Your turn next. What's your worst dating story?"

"One of the production assistants who worked on *Weight Loss Wonders* invited me to her house for dinner. She was a gourmet cook, and we had a great meal. Afterwards, I asked where her bathroom was, and she led the way rather than point down the hall. As I was about to go inside, she asked if she could watch."

Brianne smiled because she knew how private Cort was when it came to the bathroom. "What did you do?"

"I left. I wouldn't put it past her to have a peephole somewhere."

#

In the parking lot, they hugged and shook hands with each other.

On the drive to Cort's house, Brianne said, "I can't believe of all the restaurants in this city, Pam and I picked the one where Paul works."

"I have to admit I felt a little jealous when you introduced him."

Brianne's head jerked toward him. "Why?"

"Because he's seen the woman I love naked. He's been with you in bed. I never cared about that before. Being in love has made me possessive."

"Cort, you—"

He reached over and squeezed her knee. "Don't worry. I trust you completely. I just want to be honest about my feelings since they're so new to me."

When they arrived at his house, Cort opened Brianne's car door. He draped her work clothes over his arm, grabbed her overnight bag, and led her upstairs to his bedroom. He hung her dress over the back of a chair and dropped her bag on the seat. Then Cort grabbed her around the waist and pulled her to him. She plowed her fingers through the silky strands of his hair as he claimed her lips.

She tore her mouth away. "Wait."

He heaved a deep breath. "Why?"

She tried to look serious. "We can't have unprotected sex until Monday, and it won't be Monday for another two hours."

His mouth curved into a crooked smile. "Let's risk it. I'll make an honest woman of you if we get pregnant tonight."

"You got a deal, sport."

She pushed his jacket off his shoulders. He pulled the V-necked shirt he wore over his head. His eyes stared deeply into hers when she slipped her finger behind the waistband of his jeans. She rubbed her knuckle against his skin.

"I want to kiss you down here."

Let me do what I'm great at, according to the Ice Queen.

Brianne backed him up to the bed by pushing her finger against his abdomen. After he flung the duvet off the bed and pulled back the top sheet, he sat on the edge of the mattress. She stepped back, reached behind and unzipped her dress. Hunching her shoulders, she let it slide to her waist, exposing her lacy, red demi-bra.

Cort smiled. "Seeing what you wear under your clothes is like opening presents on Christmas morning."

She wiggled out of the dress and laid it on a nearby chair with her clothes for work tomorrow. When she moved back to him, Brianne tipped up his face and kissed him. He slid her panties down her legs. She raised each foot to slip her shoes and underwear off but never broke contact with his mouth. He eased a finger inside until she was moist, swollen, and ready.

Cort stood, lifted her off her feet, and placed her on the bed. Then he pinned her beneath him. While his tongue circled hers, his fingertips crawled from her thigh to her belly and zeroed in on the front hook of her bra. He suckled on each nipple as it was exposed.

Brianne pushed her pelvis against his. "I was going to kiss you here."

"I'd never make it. First, I want to feel myself inside you."

He flexed against her several times with his jeans and erection. It created a friction that made her moan. He rolled from the bed to his feet, bent his knees and flipped each shoe off by the heel. He flung them backwards. One hit the wall with a loud thud. Then he shucked off his jeans and boxers.

"Oh God, I want you so bad, sweetheart." He climbed on top and spread her legs open with his knees. With his eyes closed, he entered her.

Her chin lifted, and she reveled in the full feeling of him. He eased back carefully and pushed in again, his forearms pressed into the pillow on either side of her head. He continued to move in an unhurried pace, as if he cherished every inch of his possession.

"Faster," she panted.

"Want to … last forever."

He kissed her with such love that her eyes moistened. Her hands gripped the bunching muscles of his behind as they contracted and relaxed with the carnal rhythm. Her pleasure increased with each stroke of his powerful body. Her hips rose to his downward penetration, which gradually increased in speed and intensity until she came apart around him.

He breathed, "Bree," and found his release.

After a time, he rolled off. She curled into his side with her leg over his thigh. Cort lifted the sheet with his foot and pulled it over them. They stayed that way for a long time.

I don't want this feeling to end.

Memories of the times they had sex and made love in the past weeks flooded her. None of those experiences had the same impact as this one. This was so tender and sweet.

He kissed her temple. "I know I'll never get enough of you."

"I know I'll always love you."

"Thank God, you fell for me at the grand opening."

"I didn't fall for you. I fell on you." She sat up. "Let me show you how much I love you."

He used the sheet to dry himself before he pushed it to his knees and opened his arms wide. "I'm all yours, sweetheart."

She brushed her fingers over the patch of pubic hair to his rising erection. As she grasped him tightly, he made a throaty sound. She pulled her legs under her and knelt at his side. When she bent her head, the long, silky veil of her hair spread over him. She ran a trail of kisses from one hip bone to the other. Their co-mingled scents wafted from his flesh. She took him in her mouth. Her tongue spun around him, over and over.

Without warning, he jackknifed into a seated position and lifted her astride his lap. He thrust and was sheathed in one smooth stroke. "Ahhh. That's better."

Brianne curled her arms around his neck. He placed his hands on the bed behind him and braced himself on his locked arms. She tightened her core and thrust her pelvis forward. He timed his movements to synchronize with hers. They were like counter-balanced pendulums meeting at the mid-point. She froze in place when her orgasm rippled through her. He kissed her shoulder then bucked upward into her for his own release.

As she sat with her head on his shoulder, his lap grew wetter. "The nice thing about a condom is that it's not as messy. I'm getting you all wet."

He unlocked his elbows, sank back to the mattress and took her with him. "I don't care. It felt so good loving you without one." He wadded the pillow under his head. "I'll need to get some more sheets for the bed. I only have this one set."

"That's very bachelor of you."

"I only needed one. I washed and put them back on as soon as they were dry."

"Speaking of dry, we have to decide who's going to sleep in the wet spot."

Cort wiggled under her. "I guess it'll be me. I think I'm lying in it."

"Stay right there." She climbed off him and the bed. When she returned from the world's ugliest bathroom, she had a wet washcloth and towel. He lay back on the pillow and smiled as she cleaned him up.

"My turn," he said.

"I took care of myself in the bathroom. Hang on. I want to brush my teeth and take my pill."

"I'll be waiting."

Cort was propped against the headboard with his lap covered by the sheet when she returned to the bedroom. He was fast asleep with his head canted to one side, his black hair mussed, and his face dark with whiskers.

He is so beautiful. And for now, he's mine.

Brianne turned off the bedside lamp. By the moonlight which filtered through the curtains, she went to her side of the bed and climbed in. As soon as she lay down, Cort must have sensed her presence. He slid to a prone position on his side, palmed her breast, and exhaled deeply in his sleep. She covered his hand with hers and closed her eyes.

#

Brianne didn't get to The Voice Center until Monday afternoon. She started the workday with her new lunchtime accent modification class. Both she and Pam had clients scheduled until eight PM that evening. They had an hour for supper and called for deli takeout.

After a bite of her grilled cheese sandwich, Brianne asked, "Did Mark spend the night with you after dinner?"

"You didn't notice me walking bow-legged today?"

"Really? Or are you just joking?"

"We've decided, or I should say, I've decided we can't have sex more than two days in a row. I think I'm getting callouses."

"Pam!"

"Hey, you're the only person I can talk to about this. So deal with it."

"Okay. Then despite all the monkey sex, how do you feel about each other?"

"He's really growing on me. Shit, that's a poor choice of words. I mean, I'm beginning to like more of him than his stamina and big dick."

"You are sooo romantic."

"What?" Pam wiped a napkin across her mouth. "Sex was the only reason we hooked up in the first place. Now, we're enjoying each other's company, too. That's why we asked you and Cort to go to dinner last night. It was fun, wasn't it?"

"We had a good time. I wasn't sure how Cort would feel about socializing with an employee, but he didn't say anything."

Pam slapped her palm against her forehead. "Duh. That never even crossed my mind. Mark never said a word either."

"I don't think they'll be doing a boys' night out any time soon, but the four of us getting together is probably not an issue." Brianne gathered the paper remains of their dinner and put it in the trash. "How's Cort doing in therapy? His voice sounds pretty good."

"He's been a very conscientious client. I think his session on Wednesday will be the last one. You can let me know if you think he'll need a checkup in a couple of months. I figure having an SLP for a girlfriend made him follow the vocal exercises I prescribed."

"My only concern is if he gets involved with another reality show or project where he's expected to yell a lot. Right now, he only has to talk at conversational levels, but that could change."

"Is this something I should know about before dismissing him?"

"He's been out to California twice, talking to TV people. He said he won't do another show unless it's the right one. That's all I know. So during his appointment, you might really stress to him about maintaining his vocal hygiene."

"If he does another show out in California, what's that going to mean for your relationship?"

"Good question. I don't know."

Chapter 21

BRIANNE CALLED CORT when she arrived home at 9 PM.

He said, "Long day for you. Are you tired?"

"A little. I don't like late appointments, especially on a Monday. But, just like with early morning appointments, I sometimes have to accommodate the clients' schedules."

"What's your workday like tomorrow?"

"I'm finished by four o'clock."

"I have to go see Lola. Would like to join us for dinner?"

"At the rehab center?" Brianne asked.

"No, I'm going to pick her up and take her out to eat. Do you want to come?"

"I'd love to."

Cort paused. "I have to warn you. She doesn't remember you at the hospital. She swears no girlfriend of mine talked to her in the ER, just the nurses."

"I understand. Where's the restaurant?"

"Lola loves this Chinese buffet near I-95 and Woolbright Road. It's not too far from the rehab center. I know you would be able get something to eat there. They have a hibachi grill and the typical Chinese dishes and sushi."

"That sounds fine. What time?"

#

Cort and his grandmother were already seated at a table when she arrived the next day after work. A chair had been removed, and Lola's wheelchair was rolled in its place.

Cort stood when she reached them and kissed her cheek. "Lola, this is Brianne Gordon, my girlfriend."

She sat on Lola's left and across the table from where Cort was seated. It was polite to greet a wheelchair-bound person at eye level, if possible, to allow them a face-to-face introduction. "Hello, Mrs. Hardison. It's nice to meet you."

"Cortland tells me that we met before."

"I did see you briefly at the hospital, but you were sick so I don't expect you to remember. Cort wanted me to make sure you were getting the best care possible since he couldn't be there."

Lola smiled at him. When she turned to Brianne, her sunny expression disappeared. After the waitress took their beverage order, Cort pushed his grandmother's wheelchair to the buffet tables. Brianne looked over all the items before she picked up a plate. The salad bar didn't interest her. The steam tables contained the usual dishes she avoided. They had meat in them and a high fat content.

Lola said, "I want a little bit of macaroni salad."

"It's not on your diet," Cort answered.

"That diet is for the death camp you put me in, not when we go out to eat."

"Pick a meat instead of something high in carbs and fat."

Lola's querulous questions continued as he wheeled her chair around the various stations.

"What about Sweet and Sour Chicken?"

"Breaded, fried, and sugary. Pick something else."

Brianne selected a sample of every available raw vegetable and cubes of tofu. When she gave the plate to the hibachi cook, she asked that the tofu be grilled before stir-frying it with the vegetables. She returned to the table with a bowl of miso soup. Cort pushed Lola's wheelchair into place. He rolled his eyes at Brianne over her head.

"I'm going to get my food now." He nodded to his grandmother and mouthed *sorry* to Brianne.

"Go." She waved him away. "Mine is still cooking."

Lola's eyes followed a spoonful of miso soup from the bowl to Brianne's mouth. "You like that stuff? It tastes like sour dishwater to me."

"It's good for your digestion if you have some before a meal."

Lola scowled. "There's nothing wrong with my digestion."

"I didn't say there was. But soy is known to help people who do have a problem."

Don't mess with me, Lola. I've worked with people more hostile than you.

"You have stomach problems? One of Cortland's other girlfriends was skin and bones. She just picked at a salad during the whole dinner. You don't look like one of those women who don't eat hardly anything or throw it up afterwards."

"Not me. I have a healthy appetite and enjoy my food."

With Cort gone from the table, Lola subjected her to a brazenly critical stare that old people feel entitled to give. Brianne chose her dress today with careful consideration. It was a royal blue sheath with cap sleeves and a modest neckline. Her bosom filled the bodice, and Lola zeroed in on it.

"Are those real or paid for?"

"All me."

Lola harrumphed. Did Cort's grandmother think she was lying? Or was she surprised her grandson dated a woman with bigger-than-average tatas?

Cort returned with a bowl of soup and a plate of boiled shrimp. He rushed to take his seat as if he expected chaos in his absence. "Is everything okay?"

"I didn't get any ribs," Lola reminded him. "You said I could have one."

A bell dinged at the grill. Brianne pushed her soup bowl to the side and scooted back her chair. "I think my food is ready. I'll get you a sparerib while I'm up."

His grandmother is no match for me.

As a graduate student during her two externships, she learned how to deal with elderly clients, even the ones who told her therapy was a waste of time. She had one senior citizen reach over and slap her face while she worked with him. His wife was appalled and apologized several times. Brianne continued the session but remained out of his reach after that.

When she returned to the table, she gave Lola the demanded piece of meat.

Cort pointed to Brianne's plate of grilled vegetables. "Doesn't that look good? It's healthy and filling. I could have the chef put shrimp, chicken or steak in it for you."

Lola picked up the sparerib and bit into it with the intensity of a big cat with its prey. She eyed Brianne's food when she came up for air. "What kind of meat is in there?"

"None. I don't eat meat."

"Is there shrimp in there?"

"I don't eat fish either."

"How can you live on just vegetables?"

"I have tofu in it for protein."

Lola's nose wrinkled when Brianne mentioned the soy product. She turned to Cort. "I thought you said her family owns a steakhouse."

"Her—" started Cort.

"My father owns PrimeTime in Fort Lauderdale," Brianne interrupted. "One of his brothers owns a cattle ranch, and the other a stockyard in Fort Worth, Texas."

"Then it's crazy that you don't eat meat."

"Why is it crazy?"

Cort looked like he wanted to jump in to mediate but kept quiet.

"It just doesn't seem right," Lola said. "It's like you don't support your family."

"Mrs. Hardison, I ate meat until I was eighteen years old. When I stopped, I lost weight, my skin cleared up, I had more energy, and I just felt better. I didn't stop eating it for any ideological reason. It doesn't bother me that other people eat meat. Those people keep my family in business. It just doesn't work for me."

Cort eyed his grandmother like she might lunge out of her chair and attack Brianne. They ate a minute more in silence.

When it appeared Lola was calmed by the calories she consumed, Brianne continued in her pleasant, you-can't-intimidate-me voice. "My family gave up a long time ago trying to get me to eat meat again. In fact, my uncle recently told me he expected me to change my mind by now. So far I haven't. I never preach to them about their diet and I won't do it to anyone else either. Everyone has the right to eat whatever keeps them healthy. So how about we talk about something we both agree on?"

"What's that?"

"We both agree that Cort is wonderful. Tell me something about him that I probably don't know yet."

"Hey, wait a minute—" Cort said.

"Shush!" Lola sat up straight in her wheelchair and lifted her neck like a rooster about to crow. "Did you know his mother was Oriental?"

"Lola, remember—"

She held up her hand like a crossing guard to stop him. "I forgot. An Oriental is a thing like a rug. His mother, Nita, was Asian."

Brianne didn't mention that she had seen the Filipino tattoo on his naked chest. "What nationality was she?"

"She was from the Philippines. My son, Frank, swore she wasn't a mail order bride. He said he met her here in the States. Where would he meet a Filipino in Chicago? He was an accountant, for God's sake. I suppose those people need their taxes done like everybody else." Lola took a deep breath. "Did Cortland ever tell you how he got his name?"

Brianne glanced at him. "No, he didn't."

Cort looked like he faced a runaway train.

Lola was on a roll now. "The Hardison family has a tradition of naming the first-born son with the mother's maiden name. That's why my son was named Franklin. I was Lola Franklin before I got married. But poor Cortland was almost named Corotan until I put my foot down and insisted that his parents Americanize it. Can you imagine having to go through life named Corotan Hardison?"

Cort shook his head and peeled a steamed shrimp.

Before Brianne could respond to the question, Lola asked, "Your last name is Gordon, right?"

"Yes, it is." She knew where Lola was headed.

"Your first son would have a nice name if you married my grandson. Gordon Hardison. I like the sound of that."

Cort's eyebrows shot up like window shades. "Lola, it's way too early for you to be talking with Brianne about this."

"Hey, I may be old, but I'm not stupid. I know you're sleeping with her."

The heads of a couple at the table across the aisle snapped their way.

Lola said, "All young people jump into bed together right away. In my day, we waited until after the wedding. That's not to say some brides didn't have a bun in the oven when they walked down the aisle. When you're having sex, anything can happen."

The woman at the next table held up her crucifix necklace as if to ward off a demon. "You tell them! Premarital sex is godlessness and will send them straight to hell."

Lola gave a rumble of disgust. "Mind your own bee's wax. This is a private conversation." She lowered her voice. "You can't go anywhere without running into wackos. Just know, if you two have a boy, he should be called Gordon to carry on the tradition. What do you think, Brianne?"

"I promise you, that should I have Cort's son, he'll be called Gordon. Actually, with having two daughters, my dad would like that, Mrs. Hardison."

For the first time, Lola smiled with genuine warmth. "Call me Lola. Everyone does, including my grandson."

She and Cort chuckled at some private joke.

"What's so funny?" Brianne asked.

Cort said, "*Lola* is a Filipino word for grandmother."

"The first time I met Nita, my daughter-in-law," his grandmother said, "she asked why I was called grandmother before I was one."

Cort laughed. "When I went to live with her, my friends were surprised that I was allowed to use her first name."

"One of the neighbor ladies gave me an earful about him doing that. I told her I was too young to be called Granny like her, even though I was two years older."

"Remember Dan who lived across the street?" Cort asked Lola.

"The kid with the big ears?"

"That's the one. He once tried to call his grandmother, Harriet. She took off her shoe and beat him with it. After that, he thought I was cool."

"Do you have any unusual names in your family?" Lola asked Brianne.

"My mother is named Candace, and her maiden name was Applegate. Needless to say, she never let anyone call her Candy before she got married."

"Candy Apple … gate." Lola chortled. "I've never heard the name Brianne before. It's pretty, though."

"I was named after my mother's brother, Brian. He died of cancer as a child. Since I wasn't a boy, I got the feminine version of the name."

I'm not telling them my middle name is Inez, like Grandma's. When I was a fat kid I hated that my initials spelled B-I-G.

Lola talked about her job as a school secretary. "I saw three generations attend that school before my retirement. The kids stayed the same, just the parents got worse."

She told about her deceased son. "There is nothing in life as hard as burying your child. As awful as that was, I thank God every day that Cortland wasn't in the car with Frank and Nita."

She spoke about watching her beloved grandson on TV. "I used to invite some neighbor ladies over to watch that show with me. They would ooh and aah over Cortland. For heaven's sake, they were my age. Gertie said she liked to look at his *package* in those shiny, black shorts. That's when I told them I wanted to watch the show by myself because they talked too much."

Cort's head jerked up when his grandmother mentioned his *package*. He tried to look unfazed, but his face reddened as if he had just eaten a Chinese hot pepper.

"I never heard how you two met," Lola said.

Brianne recounted her fall at Hardcort's grand opening and Cort's subsequent referral to The Voice Center for therapy.

"Do you still go to Cort's gym?" his grandmother asked.

"I … I …"

"Brianne does work out but doesn't like fitness centers," Cort said.

"I walk, climb stairs, and use weights in the exercise room at my condo."

Cort stretched out his fingers and studied them. "She loves to do squats on an incline bench."

With her voice pitched slightly too high, Brianne said, "Lola, would you like some fruit or yogurt for dessert?"

After dinner, Brianne accompanied them to the parking lot. She held the wheelchair steady as Lola transferred herself with difficulty into Cort's car.

While he stowed the chair in the trunk, his grandmother held out her hand and pulled Brianne close. "I like you. You're a level-headed, smart, good-looking woman and just what Cortland needs. I'm going to tell him you're a keeper."

"Thank you, Lola. I care about him a great deal."

"Who're you kidding? You love him, and he loves you. We'll do this again sometime. Cort, turn on the air then go kiss her goodbye."

He slung his arm around Brianne's shoulder as they strolled to her car. "I can't believe how well you handled Lola. It was amazing."

"She just wants what's best for you."

"She also didn't ask to be taken back to the buffet for thirds, fourths, or fifths. Getting her to talk so much gave her a chance to feel full."

"It's easier to carry on a conversation with someone new than a family member. There's so much more information to share."

"I don't know, Brianne. I brought one other woman I was dating to meet Lola. It was a disaster. The dinner couldn't end fast enough. That's why I was reluctant to do it again. I should have known it would be better with you."

They were beside her car now. Although the parking lot was busy, the darkness of the evening cocooned their embrace and kiss.

"What's your day like tomorrow?" Cort asked.

"Seven AM to four PM, back-to-back clients. When is your appointment with Pam?"

"Three o'clock. She says she has to be somewhere at five so she moved me up." Brianne smirked. Cort took a step back. "What's so important that I have to come in earlier?"

"Her Brazilian."

"She has another Latin lover?"

"No. Her Brazilian wax. It's been a month, and she's going in for a touch-up."

Cort looked at her like she might reveal a long-kept female secret. "Is that where they take off ... everything?"

"You can go as hairless as the day you were born if you want."

His face displayed a look of pained squeamishness. "Doesn't that hurt?"

"I guess it depends on the expertise of the person doing it. That's why Pam doesn't want to miss this appointment. The woman is good and booked solid."

I can't believe we're standing in the parking lot of a shopping center, while his grandmother waits in the car, discussing Pam's pubic hair.

"I gotta ask—"

"No, I've never done it. Yes, I would consider it."

"Really? And without me having to write pretty please?"

"After it's done, sex is out of the question for several days or more."

"Forget it."

"I could do it when you're out of town and surprise you when you came home."

"I don't know. I like the way it looks down there. Just enough for you to look like a woman but not so much that I have to floss afterwards."

I can't believe we're standing in the parking lot of a shopping center, while his grandmother waits in the car, discussing my pubic hair.

"Do you want to come to my house when you finish work tomorrow? I'll cook supper."

"That would be wonderful. The following day I have a light schedule."

They kissed goodbye again. She glanced into her rearview mirror as she drove out of the parking lot. Cort waited by the passenger side door of his car. He waved goodbye next to a meaty arm that hung out the open window and waved also.

Chapter 22

ON WEDNESDAY BRIANNE brought her lunch to work because she knew she wouldn't have time even for takeout. She finished with her last morning client, grabbed her salad, and was about to enter the break room when her phone vibrated. It was a text from Emma.

Call me as soon as you can. 911

A message with the emergency numbers was their code for immediate contact. She quickly dialed her sister. "Em, is everyone okay? Grandma?"

"They're all fine, as far as I know. Are you sitting down?" Emma's voice had a serious note to it.

A tremor of dread raced through Brianne. "What now?"

"I didn't want to tell you this, but Alan Nussbaum put pictures of you from high school on Facebook. I think they were probably scanned from the yearbooks. There are also pictures he took of you at the Healthy Kids fundraiser. Brianne, he paired a photo of you walking off the dais after the speech with one where you were walking down the hall at school. He tagged them as before and after shots."

"How did you find out about this?"

"I had put Cort's name in a Google search, and the notification popped up my computer. I wouldn't have known except Alan tagged Cort's name in that one picture. He wrote that you were reading his speech," Emma said.

"Oh, God. This is why I hate social media." Brianne rubbed her eyes. "What I should do?"

"The photos he took were in a public place so he has the right to post them. The yearbook shots probably fall under the same category. He's not using them for commercial purposes so you can't go after him with a Cease and Desist motion, and I ought to know. At best, you can ask him to remove them."

Brianne shuddered. "I don't want to contact creepy Alan."

"One good thing is that you don't have a Facebook account. However, I don't know if the same is true for Cort's Facebook page. He might have his profile settings edited so that a notification pops up when somebody tags him. If he doesn't allow it, then the picture won't appear on his timeline, and he doesn't have to de-tag."

"I have no idea what you just said."

"Never mind. I think you should let Cort know about this. It doesn't look like Alan has made any connection between the two of you. You were just his speech reader at the fundraiser," said Emma.

"If I were to get in touch with Alan, he might realize there *is* something going on with Cort and me."

"And he's sleazy enough to exploit it, too."

Shit, is this going to involve the Ice Queen again?

Brianne sighed. "I'll talk to Cort about it tonight."

"I'm sorry." Emma sounded like she was on the verge of tears.

"It's not your fault."

"I know. It just seems that you guys can't catch a break. It's like you're star-crossed lovers."

"Shit happens in every relationship, Em. What matters is how you deal with it." Brianne ended the call.

Are we unlucky lovers? Is this the price I pay to be with The Hunk?

#

She arrived at Cort's house just as he hauled his trash can out to the curb. He kissed her and carried her overnight bag inside.

Brianne sniffed when she entered the foyer. "I smell something cooking. What is it?"

"The one dish Lola taught me how to make, her famous mac and cheese. Of course, I left out the pound of bacon she puts in it."

"Sounds great. Do I have time to change and freshen up?"

"Plenty of time. I still have to put the salad together. But first …" He put her bag on a small wooden foyer bench and lifted her purse off her shoulder to place it on the seat also. With soft lips, he kissed her. She caressed the nape of his neck, moved to his broad shoulders, under his arms to the expanse of his back and down to his buttocks. As she explored his body, his kisses became more urgent, and his arms tightened around her. Their breathing quickened.

Cort pulled her blouse out of her pants. Then his warm palms were on her back as his fingers moved up to her bra clasp.

She murmured against his mouth. "Why are you undressing me in the front hall?"

"Just helping."

Her bra loosened around her. "I wasn't going to change my bra."

The muscles deep inside her belly fisted in that familiar way. He moved his hands from under her blouse and unbuttoned it while he kissed her jaw from ear to chin. She remained motionless as he peeled her blouse and bra off and let them fall to the floor. He stood back, licked his lip, and gazed at her.

"Oh, Brianne, I love every inch of you."

I had a lot more inches to love in the Facebook pictures I have to tell you about.

He slanted his head, and his tongue probed as his kisses demanded more. One of his hands ran down her back and pulled her against his erection. Brianne moaned into his mouth. Desire raged through her body.

She flexed her fingers into the rock hardness of his biceps, moved them up to his face, into his hair, and tugged. His mouth dropped to her neck as his hands moved to her front. He flipped open the belt on her pants, undid the button, and pulled down the zipper. When her slacks dropped, the belt buckle clanked on the tile floor. Now she wore only panties and shoes while he was fully clothed.

She leaned away from him, pulled his shirt out of his jeans, and undid the button on his waistband. While she unzipped him, he pulled his shirt over his head. She heaved a sigh of relief when they both stood there top-less with their pants pooled on top of their shoes.

He gave her a seductive, lopsided smile that implied he found her sexy and funny at the same time. "Happy now?"

"Almost." She crouched, untied his sneakers and helped him slip them off while he stepped out of his jeans. She stood, toed off her heels, and lifted her feet out of her pants legs.

"I've got an idea." Cort backed her up to the staircase. The dark wood steps had a thick wool runner on each tread. An ornate iron railing ran down the outside edge. "Turn around." He pulled her panties down and off. "Put your knees on this step. A little further apart."

Brianne put her hands two steps above her to steady her position. She glanced over her shoulder to see Cort remove his boxers and kneel on the step below her. His hand traveled up the back of her thigh then his fingers slid between her legs. His other hand reached around to gently massage her in slow circles.

In reflex, her hips moved in time to the pleasure he created. He inserted his thumb and stroked the front of her vagina. She moaned. Her world condensed into the small space he controlled. She closed her eyes. His fingers unleashed wild sensations that made her pant and gasp.

He nibbled her ear. "I love you like this."

His thumb withdrew and he eased into her until his full length was inserted. The position of being above him caused him to enter her at a unique angle. He touched the sensitive bundle of nerves within. She bore down on him, which increased the pleasure that spiked through her. He circled his hips, pulled back, then eased in. He repeated the motion, again and again, always with the circle first. It drove her insane with delicious torment.

"Oh, please." She was not sure how much more she could take.

He increased his rhythm as her insides quivered. Her upper body arched as she convulsed around him and called out his name. Cort stilled when her orgasm gripped him, then he poured himself into her. He collapsed on her back with ragged breaths. When he pulled out, she rested her hip on the step and turned to face him.

Cort leaned forward and kissed her. "Ready for mac and cheese?"

She laughed. "Now I really do need to freshen up."

When she stood, a yellowish-white circle was on the dark carpeted stair. "Uh, oh."

"Don't worry," Cort said. "It'll come out with baking soda."

She cocked her head at him. "And you know this because …?"

Cort ducked his head and stared at the stain. "I … uh … I looked it up on the Internet before."

"I'll have to remember that, Heloise Hardison." She kissed his cheek, grabbed her bag from the foyer bench, and headed upstairs.

#

They ate salad, steamed broccoli, and Lola's famous macaroni as the night darkened. The only light came from candles in glass globes around the patio.

This is as good a time as any to tell him about the photos.

"I have something to tell you. Emma called today because she found pictures of me on someone's Facebook page."

He paused after emptying the last of the wine into their glasses. "What … kind of pictures?"

"Not that kind. Pictures from the Healthy Kids fundraiser and photos from my high school yearbook."

He breathed an audible sigh of relief. "Who posted them?"

"Do you remember the guy I was talking with after the fundraiser dinner?"

"If you mean the one right before you left, I don't remember much about him."

"His name is Alan Nussbaum." When Cort's head jerked toward her, she said, "Yes, his mother is Audrey, the chairwoman of the fundraiser. I went to high school with Alan, but I didn't recognize him until he reminded me who he was."

"Why would he post pictures of you on Facebook?"

"Good question. Alan was a little weird back then and maybe still is. Anyway, he didn't know who I was until his mother introduced me before the speech. Then he said … he said … I looked really different." She rubbed the teak surface of the table as if she wanted to polish the wood with her fingertips. "He said in high school I was a porker, and then he oinked at me." When she looked up, Cort's face had hardened. "I was about to call him on his inappropriateness, but then you arrived and dragged me away."

"How did Emma find these pictures? Did she friend him?"

"I'm not sure what that means, but she said Alan labeled, no, that's not the word she used—"

"Tagged," Cort corrected.

"That's it. She said Alan tagged one photo of me as reading your speech. She has some kind of alert that notifies her when your name appears on the Internet."

"Is there anything unflattering about the pictures he posted?"

"I haven't seen them yet. Emma said there's a picture of me when I was fat paired with one from the fundraiser, like before and after shots."

"So," Cort drawled with hesitation, "this Alan didn't say anything about me or about the two of us?"

"No, he just posted that I was your *speech reader*. Is this something you have to tell Jacqueline?" Brianne rubbed her tongue across her teeth. That woman's name tasted like old pennies in her mouth.

"Probably. What are *you* going to do about it?"

"Nothing. Emma and I think that if I contacted Alan he might wonder if there's more to the photos than just a comparison of me then and now."

"I agree. Let me run it by Jacqueline. I'll call her as soon as we clean up the kitchen."

"I'll clean up. You cooked."

Both of them brought the dishes and food inside. Brianne rinsed while Cort put away the leftovers.

He gave her a quick peck on the cheek. "I'll be in the office."

Brianne loaded the dishwasher and wiped the counter. She sauntered down the hall. The office was through an archway at the back of the living room. She heard the low rumble of Cort's voice. His words weren't comprehensible until he raised his volume.

"Forget it, Jacqueline! It's not an option. I'm not going to discuss it tonight." There was silence as he must have listened to the Ice Queen's response. "I don't care what Bernie thinks is best." More silence followed.

"What would be the point of dropping her now? Everything's going to be over by the end of January."

Brianne whirled back to the kitchen, and the room spun. She placed her hand on the wall and waited. When no longer dizzy, she tiptoed unsteadily to the French doors still open to the patio. The initial shock had faded. Pain threatened to overtake her and turn her knees to jelly. She held onto the back of a wicker chair. The cool night air refreshed her as she breathed it into her lungs.

Inhale. *Never let him see you cry.* Exhale. *Never let him see you cry.*

Brianne continued her mantra until her heart resumed its normal pace. She sat in the cushioned wicker chair, bent forward as though in prayer, her head bowed over clasped hands.

Cort already has a time limit on our relationship? What the hell do I do now?

Maybe, it's for the best. The relationship with Cort exhausted her. Being with him pulled her out of her comfort zone and thrust her into the world of a public persona. With him by her side, she had to be on her toes; armed to deal with intrusions, reactions and comments that would never occur in a relationship with a regular guy.

Her shock and pain now morphed into sad acceptance. Despite Brianne telling Cort that he needed to be worthy of her, she didn't deserve him. He occupied a stratosphere that she aimed for and prayed she wouldn't fall short. Without knowing how or why it occurred, she had earned his love.

At least until the end of January.

His soft step scraped across the threshold. She sat Popsicle-stiff and held her breath.

When he sat in the empty chair beside her, the cushion whooshed out air. "Sorry it took so long."

"That's okay." To her surprise, her voice sounded normal. "What did Jacqueline have to say?"

"She agreed you should just ignore it at this point. She'll monitor what Alan is posting on the Internet, just in case."

She's going to love seeing those fat pictures of me. They'll feed her appetite for revenge.

"Anything you want to do right now?" Cort asked.

"Let's go for a walk." She jumped to her feet. "I've been sitting all day. I need to stretch my legs."

Or hit someone, or kick something, or go batshit crazy.

"Sure. Do you have sneakers with you?"

"In my car. I'll meet you out there."

Brianne hurried through the house, grabbed her keys, and went outside. Cort joined her as she tied her last shoelace. He insisted they stretch first. She set the pace for the walk through his neighborhood with a quick heel-toe stride, arms pumping. In no way did it resemble an evening stroll.

An hour later as they neared his house, Cort placed his hands on his knees, bent forward and huffed. "You can … slow down now … We lost the cops … a mile back."

Chapter 23

THE NEXT DAY at her office computer, Brianne searched online for Cort's publicist. She found a Jacqueline Murphy who worked at PR Media Associates. Bernard Parks and David Ralston owned the firm.

Maybe Cort was talking about someone else, another woman he considered dropping. Other than our relationship, what could be over at the end of January?

Her family and Pam called her out whenever she victimized herself. It was a holdover reaction from years of being bullied coupled with low self-esteem, but sometimes it was legitimate. Brianne grabbed a piece of scrap paper and wrote other explanations. She put down the pen and read aloud what she wrote.

"They were discussing another publicity related topic. *Yeah, right.* He was going to fire a troublesome Hardcort employee after the holidays. *Yeah, right.* A business contract with a female accountant, manager, attorney, or whatever would expire soon so there was no reason to end it now. *Yeah, right.* I'm becoming a pain-in-the-ass and all his relationships have a three month shelf life. Yeah, that's probably right."

#

Pam left work on Friday to spend the weekend in Miami. Since Brianne had the condo to herself, she invited Cort to spend the weekend at her place. He arrived at six PM with his gym bag, a beautiful bouquet of fall flowers, and two shower caps.

Brianne put her hand on her heart. "For me?"

Cort kissed her on the cheek. "One cap is for me. We're going to give your shower a workout this weekend. As for the flowers, I have to keep up with Mark."

They ate crockpot barley vegetable chowder with crusty bread and a spinach salad.

Cort clanked the spoon into his empty soup bowl and patted his abdomen. "That was good. You know, I'm eating a lot healthier because of you."

"I'm glad you liked it."

Cort leaned back in the chair and linked his fingers behind his head. "I'm flying to New York on Thursday morning for a talk show on Friday. They're taping the usual New Year's diet blitz."

"Is it going to be about exercise?"

"Some of it. The show's mainly about how hard it is to keep weight off after you lose it. I'll be there with two contestants from *Weight Loss Wonders* that I trained."

"I thought you were done with the show."

"The contract says I have to do appearances related to the two years I was on until 2015."

"Did the two people you trained gain the weight back?"

"One has regained about fifty pounds, and he was that year's winner. The other one has maintained her weight loss."

Brianne finished her salad and stacked the empty bowl on top of his. "I've always wanted to see New York at Christmas."

"You want to go?"

She jerked her head toward Cort. "What?"

"Could you meet me there on Friday after I finish taping? I'll book the hotel room for the weekend."

Brianne stared at him, wide-eyed. "We can spend the weekend there?"

"Sure."

"Can we see the Christmas tree at Rockefeller Center? Check out the store window displays? Is it too late to get tickets for The Nutcracker ballet? How about shopping for Christmas presents?" Brianne's cheeks prickled with embarrassment when she saw Cort's tiny smile. "I'm sorry. What do you want to do?"

"I hadn't thought of anything beyond you and me in a hotel bed."

Her face fell. "We'd spend the whole weekend in the room?"

"Of course not. We'll go out to dinner." With a smirk, he said, "Just kidding. We'll do whatever you want, sweetheart, including shopping."

She jumped up and hugged him around the neck. He slid back his chair and pulled her down on his lap.

As he rocked her in his arms, Brianne lifted her hand to his face. The stubble of his whiskers scratched across her fingertips. "I love you, sport."

Cort leaned his head into her palm and said, "Back to next weekend. We need to book your ticket as soon as possible. I'll call the hotel to extend the reservation. Keep your fingers crossed they have an available room."

"I'll get my laptop."

Cort got an extension on the hotel reservation, but they would have to move to a different floor on Saturday. Brianne booked a seat on a nonstop flight to New York for Friday afternoon. She whooped with joy when her return trip was on the same plane as Cort's reservation.

"That's great," he said. "Let me pay for it."

"No." She pushed away his American Express card. "I'll handle my own airfare."

He sighed. "I'm in love with an independent woman."

She completed the transaction and closed her laptop. "What's the weather going to be like? I might have to buy some winter clothes. I better start a list."

"You know, sweetheart, if we did what I want, you could pack everything in your purse. I'll make sure the room has a nice view of the city."

"Fuhgeddaboudit," she said in dialect. "I want the whole Noo Yawk experience."

After she put her laptop back in her bedroom, they cleaned up the dishes and put away their leftovers.

Brianne said, "Grab the shower caps. We have more cleaning to do."

They laughed at each other wearing the translucent plastic caps and nothing else.

"It looks like we have on head condoms," Cort said.

They stepped into the shower. His hands were all over her as soon as her body was slick and wet. He imprisoned her against the tiled wall with his muscled body. As he nibbled his way across her shoulder, she spied her hair conditioner on the corner shelf. Stretching her arm past Cort, she grabbed the bottle. The flip top was still open so she squirted a dollop into her other palm.

Cort twisted to see behind him. "What are you doing back there?"

She slid her hands between their bodies. As she sandwiched his hardening cock between her two palms, she massaged him. "Do you like that?"

"What are you using on me?"

"It's just a little conditioner, but it's not working. You're getting harder instead of softer."

She continued to squeeze him as her hands, one after the other, ran up his shaft. His thighs trembled with the effort to maintain control. His arms were braced on the wall behind her.

She stroked until he growled, "Enough."

He pulled her to the middle of the shower and turned her back to him. With one arm wrapped around her waist, he pushed her shoulders forward. She dropped like a rag doll until her palms were flat on the floor. Cort entered her in one quick thrust, eased by the hair product that still coated him. When she raised her upper body, Brianne could control the depth of his penetrations. Cort's hands on her hips held her steady, but she determined the pace. As her climax crested, she locked her knees and moaned in ecstasy.

Cort continued to pump into her with a slow intoxicating rhythm. With her head at her knees, she began to feel dizzy. Brianne stretched out her arms and braced her hands on the wall.

She rode that rhythm until she gasped, "I ... can't. I'm going to fall."

Cort wrapped his arm around her waist and growled, "I've got you."

Sensation shot through her like tiny lightning bolts. She writhed against him and shattered into a million fragments. He followed her with his shout of pleasure. They held onto each other as the water sluiced down their quivering bodies.

#

They never left the condo on Saturday. Cort accompanied Brianne on her Sunday morning walk, which was much slower than the walk after his conversation with the Ice Queen. After he stowed his bag in his car, they strolled to a nearby restaurant for lunch and enjoyed the ocean breeze from an outdoor table. On their way back to the condo, Pam drove past them and honked. Cort kissed her goodbye in the parking lot and then left to visit Lola. When Brianne entered the foyer of the condo, Pam emerged from her bedroom.

In unison, they said, "How was your weekend?"

Brianne gave Pam the go-ahead. "You first."

"I had a good time. Some girlfriends and I went clubbing on South Beach Friday night. I don't know if the people are getting younger or I'm getting older, but it was crazy."

"Did you see Mark?"

"He had to work all day Saturday. I stayed at his place last night. He went to Hardcort this afternoon so I came home. What about you?"

"We stayed in all day yesterday. Guess where Cort and I will be next weekend?"

"Obviously not in Fort Lauderdale."

"New … York … City."

"Shut the front door! Two weeks before Christmas. I am so jealous."

"Cort is taping a talk show on Friday morning so I'm flying in at four PM. You have to help me decide what to pack."

It took an hour to comb through both their wardrobes. Brianne stared at the pitiful amount of cold weather items owned by two full-time Floridians. They prepared a shopping list which included gloves, a long scarf, leggings, and lip balm.

#

Before Christmas, Florida stores contained the same seasonal merchandise as up north. Brianne was able to find all the items on her list and most of it was on sale.

She retrieved her carry-on bag from the back of the closet for the weekend trip. A test pack revealed that cold weather clothes were a lot bulkier than Florida attire. Even sitting on the suitcase and trying to zip it closed between her legs didn't work. She knelt on the top and caught a thick strand of her hair in the fastener.

"Pam, help me!" She waited. "Pam!"

At last, her roommate's legs were visible in the doorway.

"*Chica*, what happened?"

"My hair is stuck."

"Wait, I have to get my phone." Pam's laughter grew fainter as her bare feet slapped on the hallway tile. She returned and in a staged voice, she said, "Tell me again. What did you do?"

"Can't you see? I caught my hair in the zipper." She twisted her neck to look up.

"That's it. Look at me again with that expression."

"Oh, my God! Are you recording me?"

"This is too good not to save for posterity."

"I will kill you if you show that to anyone." When she was finally freed, a dozen strands of hair remained caught in the teeth of the metal fastener. "I'll remember not to do that again when I pack to come home."

At the luggage store in the mall, Brianne bought two vacuum travel bags. Once they were sealed at the top, the air could be squeezed out through a release valve that was then closed to keep them flat. She filled them with her knitted wear. With effort, she was now able to zip her carry-on shut.

#

Cort's flight to New York left early Thursday morning. He told her he had an afternoon meeting with the show's producers and a short rehearsal prior to the Friday morning taping. His promised call to her that evening came in at ten PM.

"I'm sorry it's so late, sweetheart. I went to dinner with Donald and Marie."

"The Osmonds?"

"Donald, not Donnie, and Marie are the contestants I trained. We had a good talk, and I think it'll help when we tape the show tomorrow."

After they discussed their day, Cort proposed down-and-dirty phone sex.

Brianne said, "I don't think I can do it."

"Why not?"

She schooled herself to keep a straight face so her voice would reflect seriousness. "I'm afraid of getting hearing AIDS."

There was several seconds of silence before an explosion of whooping laughs. Between chortles, he said, "Did you just come up with that?"

"It's an old audiology joke from graduate school."

"I was going to suggest setting up our iPhones with FaceTime or using Skype on your laptop so I can watch."

"Let me get used to phone sex first. Besides, cybersex does scare me. You hear stories about hacking and spyware. I would hate for someone to violate our privacy."

"Okay, I understand. We'll just try the no-video kind to start."

Brianne put him on speaker phone so she had both hands free to follow his erotic directions. He offered suggestions on what she could do with BOB. She prayed Pam couldn't hear them through the closed bedroom door.

In a low, sexy voice, Cort said, "Lick that hard cock. How does that feel?"

"Iiittt … ttticklesss … mmmy … lllipsss."

There a moment of silence, then Cort bellowed with laughter. "You can turn BOB off for now."

She used to fantasize sexual scenarios when she listened to Cort's voice as he coached the contestants on TV. Now he commanded her to *do it again, put your hand there, I want to hear how much you want it.*

Before the call ended, he said, "Get here as soon as you can. I don't know if I'll be able to get my hard-on down without you."

#

On Friday, Brianne checked her flight before she left the condo. It was scheduled to depart on time. She drove to the airport and parked in the short term parking garage across from the terminal. Once inside the departure area, she looked at the overhead board to verify the gate number.

Oh no, no, no, no!

Her flight was canceled. Not delayed, canceled.

She dragged her bag toward the ticket counter. She entered the line guide barrier, a flimsy version of the chutes that cattle followed to be butchered at Uncle Homer's slaughterhouse. A grim-faced couple in front of her hefted their bulging backpacks as the line moved forward in miniscule increments.

She asked them, "Are you on Flight 1272?"

The butterscotch blonde whose deeply tanned skin had her well on the way to wizened said, "Everyone in this line is."

"Do you know why the flight was canceled?"

The blonde's male companion scrutinized Brianne with marmoset eyes, magnified behind thick lenses. "We heard it was a mechanical problem. They need a part that will be here tomorrow, so the plane is grounded until then."

You'd think they'd have loaner planes. If the car repair shop can do it, why can't a big airline?

It took over an hour for Brianne to reach the counter. Earlier flights were filled by the time she was able to change her reservation. She had a seat on a plane at nine PM that got into JFK at eleven forty-five. The agent gave her a certificate for a free flight booked within a year and a voucher for ten dollars off a meal at the airport.

Be still my heart. I get an airport dinner instead of one at a premier New York restaurant.

She sighed as she left the ticket counter. Their plans for a romantic dinner and a stroll around Rockefeller Center tonight were gone.

What do I do for the next six hours?

She was sweaty in her heavy sweater and the tights under her jeans. Her attire was based on boarding soon after her arrival and disembarking in a cold climate. In the ladies room, she opened her carry-on, unsealed a vacuum bag, and removed a long-sleeved, cotton top. She changed out of her sweater, peeled off her tights, and put on a pair of socks.

If I get cold travelling from the airport to the hotel, so be it. It's better than being smelly now.

It took her three tries to get the vacuum bag resealed without popping open. She tucked the long rope of her hair inside her top before she climbed onto her suitcase to close the zipper.

She waited in standby for a seat on the two flights before her rescheduled one, but none became available. From the privacy of an empty gate, she called Cort when her original NYC arrival time came and went.

"Are you downstairs?" he asked when he answered the phone.

"I'm still in Fort Lauderdale." Her voice had a teary catch in it.

"What happened, sweetheart?"

"My flight was canceled. I won't get to JFK until midnight."

"I'm sorry you're delayed, but I want you to get here safe."

"I know, but—"

"I'm going to call a car service I've used to bring you to the hotel. Look for the driver in baggage claim. Give me your arrival information."

She recited the flight number and arrival time from her new boarding pass. "I was looking forward to our plans tonight."

"The big Christmas tree will be just as pretty tomorrow night."

"What about our dinner reservation?"

"I'll see what I can do about changing it. Maybe we can do lunch instead."

"No, the restaurant only does dinner." Tears skimmed along the edges of her eyes.

"Brianne, it'll be okay. We'll still have a great time."

She swiped her hand under her nose and sniffed. "I'm just really disappointed. This delay cuts our weekend so short."

"Call me when you land. I'll be waiting in the room. I have a surprise for you that might make up for the delay."

"What is it?"

"You do know what the word surprise means, don't you?"

She laughed for the first time that day. "I love you, sport."

"I love you, too, sweetheart. See you soon."

Chapter 24

BRIANNE ATE A Greek salad and drank two cups of coffee at a restaurant in the airport since she had the time and a ten dollar voucher. She would need the caffeine to stay awake until she got to her destination.

She boarded at eight forty-five. Her seat was in the last row of the plane. At least there was plenty of room in the overhead compartment for her bag. The nonstop flight landed at JFK on time. She called Cort while they taxied to a gate. His phone rang several times before she was sent to voice mail where she left a message about *finally* being in New York.

It was twelve thirty-five by the time she deplaned and got to the baggage claim area. A pretty African American woman in a black coat, her head covered in a multi-colored wool cap, held a sign with Brianne's name on it. Just as she approached, a rich-thin woman swathed in a voluminous fur with lacquered black hair that didn't move, cut her off.

In a supercilious tone, she said, "I'm Brin Gordon. Here's my bag. Be careful with it."

Brianne stood there, stunned. Before she could protest, the driver walked around the haughty woman who appeared to abhor associating with the general public in baggage claim.

She reached for Brianne's roller bag handle and said, "Let me get this for you."

The imposter sputtered, "B-But I'm Brin Gordon."

"No, you're not," called out the young woman as she strode away with the bag.

The phony Brin Gordon shot a frosty glare, or as close to one as her Botoxed face would allow, at the young woman's back. Brianne smiled, shrugged, and followed her bag to the pneumatic exit doors.

Outside the terminal, the driver smiled in greeting as they waited to cross to the parking garage. "Hi, welcome to New York. I'm Serena."

"How do you know *I'm* Brianne Gordon?"

"I don't, but there is no way that witchy woman is Cort Hardison's girlfriend."

They laughed.

The chill night air bit into Brianne's exposed flesh. She hunched her shoulders and turtled her neck into her coat. "She didn't even say my name correctly."

Serena shook her head. "That kind of thing happens all the time."

When they reached the car in the parking garage, Brianne asked if she could sit up front.

She called Cort again and got his voice mail. "I'm in the car on my way to the hotel. I should be there around one forty-five."

Brianne asked the young woman about her job. Serena said she worked part-time at night while her husband babysat their three-year-old daughter.

"Is it safe for you to drive so late?"

"This is my uncle's car service. He vets who I pick up and where. It's even safer than driving a cab during the day."

During the hour long trip into Manhattan, Brianne and the driver discussed Florida tourist attractions, normal speech and language development for toddlers, Christmas activities in the city, and good restaurants, especially for a vegetarian.

At the hotel, the doorman pulled her bag from the trunk. Brianne tipped Serena and thanked her.

She pocketed the money. "Here's my card if you want a ride back to the airport when you leave."

The doorman held the door open for her then escorted her bag to the check-in counter. Brianne handed over another tip. A fresh-faced young man wearing a blazer and tie with the hotel logo awaited her.

Brianne said, "Good morning, I'm here to meet—"

"Are you Miss Gordon?"

She provided her driver's license to verify her identity and was given a key card in an envelope to Cort's hotel room. As she waited for the elevator, she stared at her blank-eyed reflection in the glossy surface of the elevator. A wave of exhaustion washed over her, and she stumbled on the threshold when the doors slid open. Brianne pressed the button for the fourth floor and leaned against the handrail. She exited, located the room, and tapped on the door. Cort didn't answer, so she inserted the key card and swung the door open.

From the dim light emanating from a wet bar, she walked into a large room that was part of a suite. A spectacular view of the New York skyline was visible from a picture window. Twinkling lights in buildings resembled seed pearls on dark velvet. She didn't stop to take off her coat, put down her purse, or release the handle of her suitcase. Like a laser-guided missile, she headed toward a door with light seeping around the edges. She assumed this was the bedroom.

I'm beat. Cort can undress me. He's good at that.

When she pushed the door open, he was lying on his side, eyes closed, the covers pulled up to his bare chest. Brianne had just taken a step into the room when the upper body of a naked woman rose up behind him.

She pushed her blonde hair off her face and said with a tired voice, "Sorry, I fell asleep. Is his girlfriend here yet?"

Brianne stared, transfixed with horror. She couldn't breathe because a bowling ball of pain dropped through her chest and landed on her diaphragm. It caused a part of her to die inside. She kicked her suitcase aside and dragged it to the outer door. On the way, she dropped the key card on a console cabinet. She opened the door and hurried down the hall. As she punched the down button for the elevator, she eyed the nearby stairwell. Someone called her name. It was a woman's voice.

Jacqueline ran around the corner from the hall to the bank of elevators. "Brianne, please stop. Let me explain." The publicist was dressed in an ivory cashmere sweater and black wool skirt. Her French twist hairdo and makeup were immaculate. There was no way she was the blonde woman in Cort's bed. "Brianne, I need to talk to you."

I am getting the fuck out of here.

The doors to the elevator pinged open, and Brianne entered. She punched the lobby button several times.

Jacqueline stepped inside just before the doors shut. "Please stay long enough for me to explain."

Brianne did not look at the publicist or say a word in reply during the descent. The elevator opened into the empty lobby. Her exhausted brain tried to process what to do next. Jacqueline held the door as Brianne stayed rooted in place.

Cort's publicist said, "Where are you going to go?"

She's right. Where can I go at this hour?

Jacqueline maintained a physical distance but talked in a voice used to calm someone with night terrors. "It's the middle of the night. You won't be able to get a flight back until morning. Let me have the night clerk check with the airline. If you decide to leave, he'll change the reservation. We'll contact the car service and see if they can come back and get you. Why don't you sit down over there, and I'll get you some hot coffee?"

Brianne followed her trance-like since she was too numb to think or do for herself. She dropped into a club chair while Jacqueline walked over to a coffee bar. She came back with a steaming cup.

"Do you have your reservation handy?" she asked. Brianne reached into her purse and gave it to her along with Serena's card. Jacqueline put the coffee on a side table and took the paperwork. "I'll be right back."

Brianne reached for the coffee, but her hands still gripped the purse in her lap and the suitcase handle. She dropped her purse with a thump on the coffee table. The suitcase fell over, and the handle banged like a rifle shot on the marble floor. The sharp noise caused Jacqueline and the desk clerk to jerk their heads at her. Brianne gripped the warm china cup in her icy hands.

She chanted as she sipped the black coffee. *Never let them see you cry. Never let them see you cry. Never let them see you cry.*

By the time Jacqueline returned, Brianne was still shattered into unfixable pieces but no longer dumbed with shock. The caffeine helped. A shot of Jack Daniel's would have been even better. As Cort's publicist sat in a chair across from her, Brianne looked at the woman over the rim of the coffee cup. She appeared sympathetic rather than smug, distressed instead of triumphant.

Brianne found her voice. "What the hell is going on here?"

Jacqueline bit her lip then took a breath. "I tried to warn you about Cort."

"You said *nothing* about this."

She sighed. "How much experience have you had with celebrities? I mean, Cort is a rather minor one, but he's still recognized and has a fan base. Have you ever been close to someone who is a professional athlete, an actor, a well-known musician? Anyone like that, other than Cort?"

Brianne shook her head. "No."

"Well, you should know that, regardless of how famous or little known they are, how good or mediocre their talent is, whether they're hunks or dogs, there are groupies and hookers all over the place."

"Who was upstairs in Cort's bed?"

"She's a hooker. Chantel is one of his regulars in the city."

"One of his regulars?" Black dots danced in front of her eyes. The coffee backed up her throat and burned. She didn't want to spit it back in the cup so she swallowed the vile mouthful with a shudder.

Just then the elevator doors opened. A striking blonde who wore a classic red, wool coat with high-heeled boots hurried across the lobby.

"Is that her?" Brianne asked.

Jacqueline nodded. Brianne's face must have displayed a shocked expression. With a hint of scorn, the Ice Queen said, "Come on, you can't be that naïve. Yeah, Tiger Woods' wife was this innocent Swedish au pair that he kept isolated. Maybe she had an excuse for being so clueless. But you've heard all the stories. There are the music groupies that have followed bands around for decades. Scores of women wait in hotel rooms for athletes after the game. Actors have always hooked up with other actors and the film crew on location. Even stand-up comics have groupies. They're called chucklefuckers. The girlfriends and wives of these guys know the score."

Brianne was mute. She neither confirmed nor denied her awareness of the salacious stories. Instead, she worried if this would get in the news. She didn't want to be photographed and asked stupid questions about finding Cort with a hooker.

Jacqueline said, "Even female celebrities do it, although they're usually more discreet and sometimes end up marrying the guy. Their husbands and boyfriends know what's going on when they're away from home. It used to be a well-kept secret. Now even the groupies for the gay and bi celebrities are being photographed and interviewed. You make your deal with the devil when you have a relationship with someone famous. In exchange for the money, the special treatment, and all the perks, you accept that they have another life when they're not with you."

"How did you know Cort was with her?"

Jacqueline raised her arched eyebrows as though to say, *You're such a fool.* "I'm the one he asked to make the arrangements."

You're right. I am a fool.

"I was waiting in my room across the hall for Chantel to leave. When I heard the door shut, I saw you, not her."

"But why? Why did he have you *make the arrangements*? I was on my way." Brianne's voice broke before she fought it back under control.

"He was joking about how horny he was after talking with you last night. I guess he couldn't wait until you got here."

Brianne was gutted. He shared the intimacy of their phone sex with the Ice Queen? Then she recalled his parting words. *I don't know if I'll be able to get my hard-on down without you.*

The desk clerk approached them. "Excuse me. I can get Miss Gordon on a six AM flight that gets into Fort Lauderdale at eight-fifty. There's also a later one at—"

"The one at six will be fine," Brianne said.

Jacqueline held up her finger. "Don't forget to call for the car service."

"The driver is on her way back now. They'll charge the card they used for the trip from the airport." He looked between The Ice Queen and Brianne. "Um, there's also a change fee for the airline."

Jacqueline said, "You have Mr. Hardison's card on file. Use it for the ticket." She checked her watch. "It's almost three. You'll need to be at the airport by four-thirty to allow enough time to get through security. It takes an hour to get from the hotel to the airport. It's best if you leave here in the next thirty minutes."

Brianne put her now-cold coffee on the side table and stood. "Where's the restroom?"

Jacqueline escorted her there. "I'll wait for you out here."

Brianne entered, still in her buttoned-up coat. She held onto her purse and suitcase handle. They were her lifeline back to a familiar place, a parallel universe. She couldn't wait to leave this make-believe world where people looked the same but weren't who you expected them to be. She needed her possessions close to remind her of the old Brianne who was not splintered and crushed.

Jacqueline leaned on the opposite wall and straightened as she walked out. "The car will be here in a few minutes. I know tonight was a big surprise that you weren't expecting."

Had Cort planned a threesome with a hooker?

Is that what he meant by saying he had a surprise when I arrived?

Jacqueline was still speaking. "… told me how much you mean to him. Just remember that. Do you want to leave a message for Cort before you go?"

"Is he awake now?"

"I don't know."

Brianne jumped as her phone rang in her pocket. She fumbled to remove it.

"Is that Cort?" Jacqueline's voice was high-pitched and squeaky.

Brianne looked at the screen in confusion. "No." She lifted the phone to her ear. "Emma, why are you calling?" Her sister was weeping. "Emma, what's wrong?"

"It's Daddy, Bree. He had a heart attack."

"What? When?"

"He was having chest pains at the restaurant last night then collapsed. There were two doctors there, and they administered CPR until the ambulance arrived. They called it a w-w-widow maker."

Brianne shouted into the phone. "Is he dead?"

"No, no." Emma's voice became calmer. "The EMTs got there quickly and stabilized him. They took him into surgery as soon as he got to the hospital."

"Why didn't you call me earlier?"

"There was so much going on here, and you were so far away. What good would it do? Mom and I decided to wait until we had more news."

Brianne's voice rose in panic as a silent scream echoed through her head. "Is he going to die before I get home?"

"The surgeon told mom everything went well. They removed the blockage, but they don't know how much damage was done to his heart. How soon can you get back?"

"I'm on a flight that leaves here at six AM. I should be at the hospital by ten at the latest. Is he at Holy Cross?"

"Yes. He's in recovery now. I can call you with his room number later. Why are you flying back so early?"

Brianne disconnected her phone and slipped it into her pocket. "Is the car here?" She never gave Jacqueline a chance to answer. Instead she raced across the lobby. Her boot heels rapid-fired on the glossy floor.

"What happened?" Jacqueline ran to keep up.

"My father had a massive coronary."

Brianne blew through the front door, just as the doorman unlocked it and swung it open. Jacqueline followed her into the frosty night air. A familiar car glided to halt, and Serena opened the driver's side door. Brianne stomped to the trunk. It popped open, and she threw her bag inside. She walked back to the passenger door.

The Ice Queen shivered with her arms crossed over her chest and her hands tucked into her armpits. "Do you want me to let Cort know about your father?"

Brianne put her face close and looked at Jacqueline with flat, hard eyes. "I don't fucking care what either of you do."

She climbed in the front passenger seat and slammed the door.

Chapter 25

BRIANNE DID NOT speak for several minutes as Serena drove back to the airport. She wanted to cry out, *Do you know what I found when I got to the hotel? My shithead of a boyfriend had a hooker in bed with him!*

Instead she said, "I got a call from my sister that my dad had a heart attack. I have to head back to Florida as soon as possible."

"I'm sorry to hear that. Is he going to be all right?"

"He's out of surgery and now we just have to wait."

Neither woman spoke during the remainder of the trip to the airport.

Brianne went through security in less time than it took in Fort Lauderdale. On the plane, she leaned her head against the closed window and used her balled-up jacket as a pillow. Despite exhaustion which made her eyes burn and her head throb, she was unable to sleep.

In my life I've loved two men with all my heart. How is it possible to lose one and almost lose the other in the same night?

Cort's betrayal consumed her. She wanted to lie in a dark room buried under covers and mourn her broken heart. The anxiety caused by her father's near-death experience made her scream in silence *faster, faster* toward the cockpit. When the plane got to the gate, she became the obnoxious passenger who stood before everyone, grabbed her bag and bullied her way up the aisle.

"I'm sorry."

"Please let me pass."

"Excuse me."

"I've got to get to the hospital."

"Sorry. Thank you."

Passengers stepped out of the aisle and let her go around them. The flight attendant near the cockpit gave her a dirty look as she said the obligatory, "Buh-bye."

Brianne walked as fast as she could without breaking into a run and exited through the doors at the ticketing level. It was closer to the upper deck garage where her car was parked. Inside the vehicle, it took three tries to get the key inserted in the ignition. She needed to calm down before she drove so she closed her eyes.

Inhale. *I'm here now.*

Exhale. *Dad's going to be okay.*

Inhale. *I'm here now.*

Exhale. *Dad's going to be okay.*

She remembered her phone was still turned off and powered it up. It listed two voice mails, one from a blocked number and the other from Cort. She listened to the unknown call first. It was Emma.

"Hi, Brianne. It's nine o'clock on Saturday morning. Daddy is in room four-fifteen. He's doing fine. The doctor just checked on him and said he might be able to go home tomorrow. Can you believe it? We know you'll be here be soon, so drive safely. Oh, Daddy wants to say something."

There was pause, and then her father's weak, but wonderful voice. "I'm okay, baby. Sorry I ruined your weekend. I love you."

"That's enough, Ted," her mother said. "You need to lie still. Here, hang up the phone, Emma."

The call ended, and Brianne's emotional fortification crumbled. Tears rolled down her cheeks and deep, wrenching sobs broke through. With her head cradled on the steering wheel, she cried out her heartbreak and relief. She used all the tissues in her purse to dry her eyes, blow her nose, and wipe up her wet, snotty face that itched from the tears. In the mirror on the visor, her ragged appearance shocked her.

If Dad sees me looking like this, he's going to have another heart attack.

She retrieved her makeup bag from the suitcase. After Brianne cleaned her face with wet wipes, she applied concealer under her eyes, mascara, and lipstick. She sniffed her armpit and sprayed deodorant through her cotton top. A steamy, hot shower would have to wait.

She clicked on Cort's message before she started the car and headed to the hospital.

"Sweetheart, I am *so sorry* to hear about your father. Jacqueline told me she was talking with you in the lobby when Emma called."

So the Ice Queen didn't tell him I made it up to his room.

"I wish you had woken me up."

Not if you knew your hooker was still there.

"I would have flown back with you. I'll contact you as soon as I get home later today. I love you."

She deleted the voice mail and turned on the ignition.

#

When she found the room, she turned off her phone as hospital policy directed. Now she was incommunicado to Cort. No one was there, except her father who was asleep. She laid her fingers lightly on his arm, careful not to wake him. It was enough to feel his warm, living flesh. As his chest rose and fell under the hospital gown, she blinked back tears.

A few minutes later, *psst* hissed from the doorway. Emma and Mom motioned her to come out of the room. Brianne's tears started anew as they enveloped her in their arms.

"He's going to be okay, honey. He was lucky. We're going to have him around for a long time. Don't cry." Her mother swiped the tears off Brianne's cheeks with her thumbs. She pulled a tissue out of her pocket and pinched it against her daughter's nose. "Blow."

"Mom." Brianne pulled her head back, grabbed the tissue, and wiped her own nose.

Emma stood with a foam cup in her outstretched hand.

Brianne asked, "Is that coffee?"

"You want some?"

"Hell, yes."

"Brianne, watch your language," her mother scolded.

Oh, Mom, if you only knew the words that came out of my mouth. I'm not the lady you are.

She took the cup from Emma's hand. "What happened to Dad? Is he going to be all right? What did the doctor say?"

Before Emma or her mother could answer, they had to move aside for an orderly with a patient in a wheelchair.

Candace said, "You girls go drink the coffee and talk. I'll sit with your father."

They went down the hall to a small solarium. No one else was there. They passed the cup back and forth and sipped the awful brew.

Brianne said, "Tell me what happened to Dad. Were you there?"

"No. Mom got in touch with me at home. While Daddy was in surgery, I called some people who worked last night and got the story from them. He complained earlier in the evening that he didn't feel well. Right before he was going to leave, he said his arm and chest hurt."

"Who did he say that to?"

"I don't know for sure, but whoever it was knew something was wrong and told him to sit down. They gave him aspirin, and then he collapsed."

Brianne put her hand over her heart and gasped. "What if he had been driving home when that happened?"

"The cardiologist said that's why this kind of heart attack is called a widow maker. It requires immediate treatment. Someone had already called 911 because the paramedics arrived just a few minutes later. He went right from the ER into surgery to remove the blockage."

"So he's going to be okay now?"

"Dr. Orman seems to think so. He said it doesn't look like Daddy needs bypass surgery right now, but he'll have to be checked regularly."

"And that's it?"

"He can't go to work until he sees the doctor next week. Wait till you hear this." Emma giggled. "After finding out that Daddy owns PrimeTime, the cardiologist told him he has to change his eating habits. He said he needs *a more plant-based diet.* Daddy looked at me and said, *don't tell your sister.*" They laughed as Emma discarded the empty cup in the trash. "Now, why were you flying back here before I called?"

Brianne gave a gusty sigh. "I don't want to talk about it right now. I just want to focus on Dad getting better."

"Did Cort break up with you?"

"No. But I'm going to tell him it's over."

"Why? You love him, and he loves you."

"I know, but it isn't going to work." She leaned her head back on the sofa and covered her eyes with her forearm. "Maybe you were right, Em. I think we are star-crossed."

They returned to their father's hospital room. He was awake. Brianne hugged and kissed him at last.

Ted's face creased with concern as he gazed at his eldest daughter. "Brianne, you look so tired. Why don't you go home and sleep? I'll be fine."

She had been awake for thirty straight hours and was in the light-headed state of exhaustion. "I slept at the hotel and on the plane," she lied.

When his lunch came, Mom shooed her daughters from the room. "You girls should go get something to eat."

Emma said, "I'll go home for a nap and come back this afternoon."

"Good idea." Her mother hugged her goodbye.

"Do you want something from the cafeteria, Mom?" Brianne asked.

"I'm fine."

Brianne rode the elevator down with her sister. In the cafeteria, she got more coffee and a muffin. On her phone, there was a text from Cort. *Be back in FTL at 5PM. How's Ted?*

She debated her reply while she drank the coffee and ate the muffin. Before she powered down her phone, she wrote, *Dad much better. Talk to you later.*

Brianne insisted her mother leave at four o'clock after she caught her catnapping in the chair. She said she would wait for Emma's return. Her sister arrived a short time later.

"I'll stay with Daddy until visiting hours end," she told Brianne.

"You go home and rest," her father said.

Brianne's head ached as though a steel band was tightening around it. Her body was twitchy. On the drive to the condo, she forced her eyes wide open and gripped the steering wheel until her fingers hurt. She sighed with relief when she parked and shut off the engine. After lifting her suitcase out of the trunk, she almost toppled over when it hit the pavement.

A couple approached her as she staggered toward the main entrance. The woman said to her companion, "Did she drive in that condition?"

I'm tired, not drunk.

The hallway leading to the condo seemed longer than usual. She fumbled with her key until the lock clicked, but the door swung open before she turned the knob.

"You're finally home. We've been so worried," Pam said. "How's your dad?"

Brianne lurched inside with her wheeled carry-on. "Good, but he has to be a vegenarian now."

"A vegenarian? What's wrong with you?"

"Nothing, I'm just exhausted. I'm going to bed."

She turned to head down the hall. Someone blocked her way. Hands gripped her arms. She looked up, and everything went dark.

#

When Brianne awoke, she squinted against the bright light that seeped around the edges of the blinds. She used the bathroom and drank a full glass of water. Her mouth tasted like she had eaten burnt toast. As she looked at herself in the mirror above the sink, she was startled by her nakedness.

I don't remember getting undressed for bed.

When she returned to her bedroom, she sat on the edge of the mattress. The alarm clock on her nightstand read ten AM.

Oh, my God! I'm late for work! I have to call the office. Why didn't Pam wake me?

She jumped to her feet and looked for her phone. It was lying on her dresser next to her purse. She pushed the button to bring the screen to life. It read ten-oh-one AM and underneath Sunday, December sixteenth. Then she recalled the horrors of the past two days.

She dropped onto the bed and tucked her knees close to her body. Tears seeped out of the corners of her eyes and dampened the sheet beneath her cheek. The image of the bare-breasted whore with Cort burned behind her eyelids.

I loved him. I had faith in him. I believed that he wouldn't hurt me this much.

At last, hunger forced her to her feet. After she donned panties and a thigh-length T-shirt, she brushed her teeth and washed her face.

Pam sat at the kitchen table with the newspaper.

Brianne opened the refrigerator door and got a carton of yogurt. "Good morning."

"Are you insane?"

Brianne took the seat across from her. "What are you talking about?"

"I'm talking about how dangerous it was for you to drive home yesterday with no sleep."

"I'm here, aren't I?"

"You came stumbling in like a drunken sailor and passed out in the foyer."

Brianne looked up from her yogurt. "I did? How did I get into bed?"

"Cort caught you as you fell and carried you there."

"He was here?"

"He waited with me for you to come home. We figured you hadn't slept in about forty straight hours. I don't how you got here without having an accident."

Brianne hunched her shoulders like a child being scolded. "I admit I was pretty tired. I did okay until I got upstairs."

"Security called me to move your car. You parked it in the middle of two handicapped spaces."

"Oh."

"But you're here now and rested. How's your dad?"

Brianne smiled. "Good, really good. It could have been so much worse. We were lucky it happened where and when it did. He got help so quickly it saved his life." She told Pam about Ted's heart attack at the restaurant and his treatment at the hospital. "I should call to find out when he's being released."

"Emma left me a text this morning. She didn't want to wake you. She said your dad's probably going home after the doctor sees him. They're not sure what time that will be. She'll let you know." Pam picked up another section of the newspaper.

"I guess I'll wait to hear from them. Then I can see Dad at home."

"Cort said he would like to go with you so give him a call." Pam looked up from the newspaper. "*Dios mío*. What's wrong?"

Brianne grabbed a paper napkin to dry the tears that filled her eyes. "I'm breaking up with him for good this time."

Chapter 26

PAM SAID, "WHAT do you mean? What happened? Cort didn't say anything was wrong last night."

Brianne shook her head as she continued to dry her tears. "Remember the double date with Paul when I realized he was just using me to get PrimeTime?"

"What does that have to do with you and Cort?"

"I found out something terrible about him on this trip to New York. Some women are okay with it, but not me."

"What? He wants to pee on you? Wear your underwear?"

"No, but it's bad."

Pam stared at her and cocked her head. "You know you've come to conclusions before that have had other explanations."

"I saw this with my own eyes. There was no misinterpretation this time."

Surprise flashed in Pam's expression. "Saw what?"

"I don't want to talk about it."

"But you need—"

Brianne slapped her palm on the tabletop. "Why can't you accept that I have a good reason to break up with Cort? It's painful and humiliating, and I don't want to discuss it right now."

"Okay, *chi-chi*," Pam said in a calm, civilized voice. "I won't press you. I know it's been a rough couple of days."

I'm yelling at Pam like a crazy woman. What's wrong with me? Oh, that's right. I love a man who keeps regular hookers.

Brianne closed her eyes and took a deep breath to quell the anger that choked her throat. When a trickle of tension ebbed from her body, she opened them and found Pam's usually sunny face frozen in an unrelenting stare.

In a soothing but implacable voice, her friend said, "I *will* want to know what happened."

"You'll be the first person I tell when I'm ready. But today I have to break up with Cort, and he's not going to take it well."

"No, shit. Look what he did after the Healthy Kids fundraiser, and you only had sex once."

"I need your help to do this and to keep him away from me."

"You're sure this is what you want? Maybe you should wait a couple days. Your emotions are running pretty high right now. Take some time. Then talk to Cort before calling it quits."

Brianne was nauseous with dread, but her voice carried conviction. "No, I want to end this now. I would give anything, except my father's life, to keep Cort. But I can't."

Pam sat back in her chair and stared at Brianne, open-mouthed. "It's that bad?"

"Trust me. It's worse than Paul using me to get the restaurant."

"For the record, I don't agree with you rushing to break up with him today. But I'll help with whatever you need me to do." Pam reached across the table and squeezed her hand.

Brianne called downstairs to the security desk. She asked to have Cort's name removed from their guest list again. Pam's phone chimed with a text from Emma. *Dad is at home.*

"Go visit your dad before you see Cort. If he calls, I'll say you're still sleeping."

Brianne showered and dressed. Before leaving for her parents' house, she asked Pam, "How do you think I should tell him?"

"Are you afraid of him or what he might do?"

"No. He would never physically hurt me. I'm afraid of myself. Look how he persuaded me to have you be his therapist, to read his speech, to forgive him after the fundraiser and when he came to Texas."

To have sex at Marisol's party, in the gym, on the phone …

"What about sending him an email or text?"

"That's what a high school kid would do."

"Then call him."

"No, it has to be in person. I don't want to, but it's the best way."

In the end, they decided that Brianne would invite him over, meet him in the lobby, and break up with him there. The security guard on duty ensured that Cort couldn't follow her upstairs.

#

She visited with her parents until two in the afternoon. Mom told Emma and Brianne to go home because their father needed to take a nap. Then she grabbed the remote and switched off the TV.

Dad made a wild grab to get the device back. "Hey! I was watching that, and I don't need a nap."

"The doctor said you need to rest every afternoon until your appointment with him. Goodbye, girls. Let yourselves out."

Candace escorted her husband away from his beloved big screen TV like a recalcitrant child.

From down the hall, their father said, "Sitting in my recliner is resting. I don't know why I have to go to bed if I'm not sleepy."

Emma stopped in front of their cars parked in the driveway. "How are you doing?"

Brianne tried to swallow the lump in her throat to answer her. Tears rose in her eyes, but she clenched her teeth to keep her chin steady. Her bleak expression answered the question.

Emma's eyes raked her sister's face. "You're going to break up with Cort today, aren't you?"

"I have no choice."

"Why?"

"You don't need to know why. Nobody does. I don't want to be with him anymore. Is that okay with you?"

Emma looked as though Brianne had slapped her. "Sorry."

Brianne sighed and pressed the heels of her hands against her eyelids. "No, I am."

After a long moment, Emma asked, "Do you want me to be there with you when you tell him?"

"Thanks for the offer, but I need to handle this on my own."

#

When she returned to the condo, Brianne called Cort and put her phone on speaker so Pam could hear the conversation.

"Sweetheart, how are you?" Cort asked. "You scared the hell out of me last night when you passed out."

"Can you come over here?"

"I told Pam I'd like to see how Ted is doing. Is he still in the hospital?"

"Uh, Dad's fine. He's home now and resting this afternoon. I need you to come to my place."

"You don't sound like you. What's wrong?"

"We need to talk."

Cort was the one who said those words after Emma posted him on PrimeTime's website. She had steeled herself to hear him end their relationship that time.

Will he figure out that I'm the one breaking up with him now?

"Brianne, what's going on?"

"Can you come over?" she repeated.

Cort was quiet for several seconds. "I'll be right there."

The line went dead.

Brianne went downstairs to the guard's station in the lobby. "My boyfriend will be arriving soon, and I'm going to tell him we're through."

The rent-a-cop looked at her in confusion. Then the light bulb went on. "You're gonna break up right here? In the lobby?"

She nodded.

The young man with the too-big uniform looked a little panicked. "Will I need to call the police?"

"No, just make sure he leaves when I go upstairs."

She moved to a sitting area past the elevators and waited. Ten minutes later, Cort came through the door in a rush and headed to the security desk.

Brianne rose and said, "Cort."

He spun around. "What are you doing down here?"

He reached out to pull her into his arms, but she sat and pointed to the chair across from her. "Please, sit."

"First, tell me what this is about."

"I'll tell you as soon as you sit down." She used her professional voice and demeanor. It was her only hope to get through the next few minutes.

He dropped into the chair and didn't take his eyes off her.

Brianne took a deep breath. "I wanted to tell you in person that it's over."

"What's over?"

"Us. I don't want to see you anymore." As much as she wanted to look away, she kept her eyes on him.

Cort looked stunned. "I don't understand."

"I've decided I don't want to continue our relationship."

His eyes narrowed. With razor sharpness in his voice, he spit out, "What did that cunt, Jacqueline, say to you?"

Brianne winced at the offensive word.

What is he going to call me after this?

"It has nothing to do with Jacqueline," she said. "This is between you and me."

"Everything is fine between you and me."

"No, it's not." Brianne's cool composure began to dissipate. "I can't live in your world, Cort. I thought I could, but I can't."

"My world? What are you talking about? You and I live in the same world."

Brianne dropped her head like her neck could no longer support its weight. "No, we don't. In your world, people from all over the country know who you are. They recognize you. Ask for your autograph. They want their picture taken with you."

"That's just kids."

She fought back tears. "No, it's not. You're a television celebrity. You're photographed because of who you are. You have to watch what you say and do. Be careful who you associate with. You have an image and a brand to maintain. You pay people to protect you against bad publicity. In my world, I just need to be a good therapist. It doesn't matter if I'm fat or ugly. No one cares what I do or who I'm involved with. It's not the same for you."

Cort had scooted forward so he sat on the edge of his seat. His elbows were on his knees, and his upper body was bent toward her. He was as close to her as he could get and still respect the physical boundary she had set. "Brianne—"

"I can't do it, Cort. I'm not the kind of woman who can live with you in your world. It's tearing me apart."

His eyes were bleak. "Don't do this. Please don't do this to us. We'll find a way to make it work. I love you with all my heart. I've never felt this way about anyone before."

Oh, God.

"It's because I know you love me that I'm asking you, begging you, to please ..." her voice broke, "please let me go."

His eyes filled with tears.

She stood. Her wobbly knees caused her to sway. What kept her upright was the long icicle of pain in her spine. "Goodbye, Cort."

As she walked to the elevator, the security guard had the phone to his ear. She pushed the up button, and the doors opened. She took one last look at Cort. His face was buried in his hands. The nakedness of his grief caused her to stumble as she stepped inside.

#

The next morning she awoke at four AM. Her body ached like someone had beaten her with a stick. Her eyes were swollen, and her limbs were weak.

Day One Without Him.

She went to the office and worked with her scheduled clients. She did her job with a veneer of normalcy. After work, she went to her parents' house for dinner.

"You're going to be able to eat with us more," her dad said. "Your mother's been scouring the Internet for vegetarian recipes."

She picked at the vegetable lasagna that her mother prepared.

Candace asked, "Is something wrong with it?"

"No, it's fine. I'm just not hungry."

She helped clean up after the meal. Her mother was bent over the dishwasher when Brianne said, "Mom, I broke up with Cort."

Candace straightened and cocked her ear as if she misunderstood what her daughter said. Brianne sat sideways in a kitchen chair. Silent tears spilled from her eyes.

"I'm sorry, honey." Her mother bent and pulled Brianne into a fierce embrace. "It's okay. I know it hurts." Candace straightened and rubbed her daughter's bowed back. Brianne waited for her mother to ask what happened but she didn't. So she laid her head against her mother's body. The heartbeat against her ear was like a soothing clock. Yesterday Emma offered to stay with Brianne when she broke up with Cort. Pam comforted her long into the evening after she told him they were through. Today, her mother offered unconditional love and support. It was doubtful that Lola was comforting him. He had no one else to turn to for consolation.

Unless he calls one of his regular hookers here in Florida.

Her mother said, "You go home and rest. I'll tell your father."

#

On *Day Two Without Him,* Brianne went to the hospital where her dad had recently been discharged. They had a clinic that did free testing for HIV and STDs. Results were available in twenty-four hours. On *Day Three Without Him,* she wept relieved tears behind her closed office door when she called the clinic and was told all her tests were negative.

On *Day Four Without Him,* she came down with the flu. She wasn't sleeping well, eating much, or exercising at all. The viral culprit was likely her shitty weekend on two planes with recycled air.

Her mother called the day after she got sick. "Sorry, honey. I would come take care of you, but I worry about bringing a bug home and your father getting it. I'm sending Emma instead."

She spent the day in bed with a dry cough, sore throat, and a stuffy head. On Saturday afternoon when her temperature spiked at one hundred and one degrees, Pam and Emma took her to an urgent care center. She was put on a steroid inhaler and an antibiotic. The next day she got her period.

#

The family plans for the Christmas holiday changed with Ted's heart attack and Brianne's illness. She and her parents decided to stay home rather than go to Texas. Emma flew with their grandmother to Fort Worth on Monday, the day before the Tuesday holiday.

On Christmas morning, *Day Nine Without Him,* she called her mother. "I think I'll just stay home today, Mom."

"Why? Are you getting sick again?"

"No, I'm fine. I haven't gone shopping, and I'm not very good company right now."

"Brianne Inez Gordon, don't be silly. Christmas is about family being together. When Emma and your grandmother get back from Texas, we'll do a gift exchange then. In fact, don't bother getting us anything. There's nothing we need or want. Just go shopping for your sister and grandmother."

"But, Mom—"

"I'll expect you here by one."

She had not seen her parents since her illness. When Brianne came in the front door, Dad gave her a father-daughter hug. It was one of those clumsy lean-in embraces that started after she got boobs. This one seemed even more awkward, like he was afraid she was now repelled by male contact. She held on to him until he pressed her against him, his arms holding her tight.

When Candace came out of the kitchen, they separated without a word. Her mother studied her face. "You look terrible. Are you still taking your prescription?"

Dad said, "Let me make you some tea with honey and whiskey. That'll put some color back in your cheeks."

"You need vitamin C," Mom said. "I have some in the bathroom."

"Do you want me to start a fire in the fireplace? I can lower the AC if it gets too hot," her father said.

Her mother placed her palms against Brianne's cheeks. "Just this once I wish you would eat some chicken soup. It's called Jewish penicillin because it works, you know."

After they finished their Christmas luncheon and everything was cleaned up, Brianne and her mother went into the family room. Her father was stretched out on the sofa with a basketball game on TV.

Candace smacked his foot and flapped her hands as if to shoo a dog off the furniture. "Ted, get up so Brianne can lie down."

Her father sat up and moved to his nearby recliner. His eyes never left the action on the screen.

"Mom, what are you doing?" Brianne said. "Dad is still recuperating."

"The doctor said his heart is fine. He's going back to work for part of the day tomorrow."

"I'm fine, too."

"No, you're not. Your heart's still broken."

Chapter 27

ON FRIDAY, *DAY Twelve Without Him,* Brianne was at the office and Googled news about Fort Lauderdale. With her illness and the holiday, she had been out of touch. She scanned several headlines.

The breath was sucked from her lungs when she read, *Local Trainer on TV Show.* She clicked the mouse. A photo of Cort appeared. She read the article below the picture.

> Cortland Hardison, owner of area Hardcort Fitness Centers, replaces Ava Kohler next week as a trainer and weight loss coach for the remaining six shows of *Weight Loss Wonders'* fifth season. He is joining long-time trainer, Bill Haney. They worked together during Seasons One and Two.

> A representative for Ms. Kohler cited personal problems which require her immediate attention as the reason for the sudden departure. Other sources close to the show say the remaining contestants, who are finalists for the $500,000 prize, refuse to work with her. "They said all she wanted to do was talk about their emotional problems and not push them physically."

> There is no word yet if Hardison will be rejoining the highly rated show for the upcoming season. "The offer

hasn't been made and I haven't decided yet what my answer would be," he was quoted.

Brianne read the brief article several times. Did he agree to do the show before or after they broke up? Was this the reason for meetings in L.A.?

I guess he'll be in California until the end of January.

A memory synapse triggered. She sat back in her desk chair to recall what she overheard in his phone call with Jacqueline. *What would be the point of dropping her now? Everything will be over by the end of January.*

Was it a reference to Ava Kohler's exit from the show and not about her? A little spark of happiness ran through Brianne but fizzled like a lit match dropped into a puddle. It didn't matter if she misinterpreted the one-sided phone conversation. The hard evidence was what she saw in the hotel room and what Jacqueline said.

Her gaze drifted back to the computer screen. This was why she couldn't live in his world. A newspaper article was written about him when he accepted a temporary new job. She hadn't watched TV in a few days, but there were probably announcements and promotions about his return to the show.

Pam came into her office. "Do you want me to order you some lunch?"

"No, I'm good."

Her friend's eyes flicked to the laptop. "Is that Cort?"

"Do you know about this?" Brianne turned the screen toward Pam.

"Is it about him filling in for the trainer that quit?"

"I guess he changed his mind about doing the show."

Brianne clicked the red X icon to delete the story and opened a client file.

Pam said, "Do you want to talk about what happened? I haven't pushed because you were sick."

"Not yet, Pam. I promise I'll tell you when I'm ready."

#

On *Day Thirteen Without Him,* Brianne was expected at her parents' house at six PM. Emma and Grandma were back from Texas. Despite what her mother said, she bought a present for everyone. When she arrived, her father was outside by the front entrance. He watered pink impatiens plants that grew in big-bellied pots.

"Hi, baby. Everybody's in the kitchen." He leaned his cheek over for a kiss.

Brianne shifted the casserole she carried to give him a smooch. The gift bags that hung on her arms slid and caused her to stagger off-balance.

"Whoa, there." Her father dropped the hose and grabbed her upper arm to steady her. "You okay?"

"Yeah, I think so."

She elbowed open the slightly ajar door and headed toward the back of the house.

In the kitchen, her grandmother said, "Let me tell you, I'd go to Texas more often if I could always travel that way."

"What way?" Brianne asked.

Her mother, grandmother, and sister froze.

In a voice three notches higher than usual, Candace said, "Honey, we didn't hear you come in."

"The front door was open. What were you talking about, Grandma?"

Inez sat at the kitchen table and stared with wide eyes at Brianne like she was a ghost.

"Here, let me help you," Emma said and took the casserole out of her hands.

Her mother lifted an edge of foil on the dish. "What did you make?"

"Butternut squash bread pudding."

"It sounds wonderful." She took it from Emma. "Should I put it in the oven?"

"Sure."

Brianne turned back to her grandmother who fussed with a bold red, white, and blue scarf that was tied in an intricate loop around her neck and shoulders. "Oh, my God, Grandma, is that a real Hermès?"

Inez smoothed her skirt and adjusted the ribbed hem of her cotton sweater. Without looking up, she said, "Do you like it?"

"It looks wonderful on you." Brianne set down the gift bags that creased her arms and kissed her grandmother's cheek. "What was different about the trip to the ranch?"

Emma said, "A limo picked us up at the airport."

"You're kidding. Uncle Junior paid for a limo?"

"He hired a car service. It was way better than riding in his smelly old pickup."

Brianne stood with her hands on her hips. "Wasn't there anybody at the ranch who could drive to the airport?"

Her sister frowned. "No. Equipment broke down. Cattle escaped."

"But a limo?"

"Give it a rest, Brianne," her mother said. "Junior sent a car to pick them up. It happened to be a limo."

What's going on? Why are they acting so weird?

#

After dinner, the Gordons gathered around the Christmas tree. Emma sat on the floor and stacked presents into separate piles. Brianne was sandwiched between her mother and grandmother on the sofa. Ted relaxed in his recliner with the footrest raised and eyed the blank screen of his TV. The tradition was that the youngest family member opened all their gifts first.

Emma unwrapped hers with bubbly enthusiasm. While she oohed and aahed over her presents, a dark cloak of depression drifted over Brianne. A similar feeling enveloped her when she had shopped for her family's gifts.

In the men's department at Macy's, she looked for a shirt to buy her father. Long-sleeved Henley pullovers were neatly folded and stacked on a display table. She picked up one in a deep shade of tangerine.

This color would look fantastic on Cort.

She rubbed the soft cotton against her cheek and imagined his body in it. Her reverie was broken when another shopper bumped into her.

What am I doing? I don't need to buy for him.

She went into Radio Shack to check out a Fitbit activity tracker for Emma. Her attention was diverted by a multiple device charging station.

With this, Cort wouldn't have all those cords on his kitchen counter.

A young salesman asked if she needed help. She shook her head. With rising tears, she left the store.

"Brianne, are you okay?" her mother asked with knitted brows.

She blinked a couple times. "I'm fine."

It was embarrassing that there were more gifts under the tree for her than anyone else. A box from Grandma contained a Hermès scarf like hers but in an orange, black, and blue print. From her parents, she received a beautiful Chanel purse in white tweed, a Narcisco Rodriguez perfume set, and a silk chemise from Victoria's Secret. In a small gift bag was a Cartier box.

Emma said, "I love you, Bree, but until Daddy pays me more, I can't afford real Cartier. I can afford the box though."

When she lifted the whisper-thin silver necklace from where it nestled in the white satin-lined case, there was a folded slip of paper underneath. Brianne opened it and read: *The next piece of jewelry I buy will go on your ring finger.*

She leaned forward and handed the piece of paper to Emma.

"What's this?" Her sister read it. "Shit!"

"Emma, watch your language," Candace scolded. "Ladies don't—"

"What's going on?" Brianne asked. "Why is there a note from Cort with the chain?"

Her family looked at each other like thieves caught red-handed. Finally, her mother said, "He called us after you broke up and was really upset. We couldn't tell him what happened because you hadn't told us. We tried to be supportive and ..."

I felt sorry that Cort didn't have people to comfort him. I didn't have to worry. My family was doing it.

"... invited him to Texas for Christmas. He—"

"What did you say?" Brianne's head jerked toward her grandmother.

"I said I felt sorry for him. So I invited him to go to Texas with Emma and me for Christmas. He had a friend fly us there in his private jet and arranged for a limo to take us to the ranch."

Brianne closed her eyes as her world spun out of control. She put her hand over her mouth as nausea rose up inside.

Maybe if he finds someone to marry, my parents will have the wedding in their backyard.

An arm went around her shoulders. Her mother's voice spoke softly into her ear. "I'm sorry, honey. We shouldn't have tried to pass off Cort's gifts as ours. He just really wanted you to have them."

She opened her eyes when Grandma's thin fingers covered the fist she clenched in her lap. "You know I love you and would never want to hurt you. I'm sorry I asked to him to spend Christmas in Texas."

"It's my fault." Emma cupped her hand on Brianne's knee. "You've been so sad. I wanted you to have some really nice presents."

Ted glared at the contrite women that surrounded his eldest daughter. "I told them it was bad idea, but they wouldn't listen to me."

"I know you all meant well," Brianne forced herself to say as her relatives offered additional confessions, apologies, and explanations. She forgave them but was still hurt by their actions.

Her mother said, "We love you, honey. Don't ever forget that. We're here for you, no matter what. From now on, you tell us what you need us to do, or not do, and we will."

She told them, "Send back all Cort's gifts."

Her grandmother untied the scarf from around her neck.

Brianne stopped her. "No, Grandma. You keep that. It's a gift to you, not me."

Her sister pressed the Chanel bag to her chest and stroked its nubby fabric. "Can I keep the purse?"

"Emma!" her mother said. "Give that to me."

Brianne opened presents that her family did buy her. The mood was now more subdued. Her favorite gift was a one-cup Keurig brewer and a variety of pods. Now she could make her own drinkable coffee.

But all I really want is the man I thought I fell in love with.

#

Monday was New Year's Eve and *Day Fifteen Without Him.* Everyone urged Brianne not to stay home alone. Pam was the most insistent.

"If you want, we can leave the downtown festival and come home right after midnight."

I would rather drag my uncles to a PETA meeting.

Emma invited her to join several friends of theirs at a country western dance club to ring in the New Year.

There's no way I can get drunk enough to pretend I'm having a good time.

Her parents suggested she watch the Times Square show with them and spend the night.

Just what I need. Seeing people have fun in New York City and then sleeping in my old bedroom.

She went to bed early, but was awakened several times during the night. Firecrackers, or maybe gunshots, and the yells of drunken revelers jolted her out of sleep.

Pam came into Brianne's darkened bedroom at noon, opened the blinds, and ripped the sheet off her. "Enough!"

She sat up and shaded her eyes with her forearm. "What are you doing?"

"How long have you been in this bed?"

"What does it matter? It's a holiday."

"When did you last eat?" When Brianne didn't answer, Pam said, "Just as I thought. You can't go on like this, *chi-chi.* I'm so worried about you."

"I want to feel better, but I can't."

Pam sat on the bed and took Brianne in her arms. "You aren't going to feel better lying in bed all the time and not eating. You haven't exercised once since the breakup."

"For the first time in my life, I don't feel like eating. And I've never felt like exercising so there's nothing new there."

"Get up." Pam pulled on her arm and led Brianne into the bathroom. "How much do you weigh?"

"I'm usually around one forty, one forty-five."

"Get on the scale."

When the needle came to rest on one twenty-eight, Brianne looked at her friend in disbelief. "I haven't been under one-thirty since I was twelve years old."

Pam said, "I knew you had lost at least ten pounds. Take a shower, get dressed and meet me in the kitchen. You're eating something if I have to tie you up and force feed you."

#

Starting the first day of January, Pam and Brianne's family made sure she had regular meals. At first, she didn't consume much. Soon she ate enough that her nutrition supervisors were satisfied. Pam monitored breakfast and lunch during the week. Her parents insisted she either have dinner at their house or they brought food to the condo and ate it there with her. She sampled the three new vegetarian entrees on PrimeTime's menu, and Emma took her to lunch on Saturdays. As her diet improved so did her energy levels. But her mind was plagued by a strange restlessness, like the torment of an unrelieved itch.

#

On Wednesday evening, *Day Twenty-Four Without Him,* Emma arrived at the condo in jeans and boots. She pulled her sister off the bed where she was watching TV. "Get dressed. We're going out."

They went to The Roundup which was popular for its country music and dancing. Drinks for ladies that night were free after eight PM. A beginner's line dance class started at seven. Emma pushed Brianne into the midst of the step-counters and feet-watchers.

"I know how to line dance," she protested.

"Act like you don't. Just get moving."

In a short time, Brianne demonstrated the dance steps to the people in the back with her. When the instructor caught her eye, she gave her a nod and said, "Good job."

She managed several dances and one free drink before her tired body gave out. Emma had her home by nine o'clock. She slept through the night for the first time in what seemed like ages. After that, she danced several times a week, with or without Emma. She volunteered to help out the paid dance instructors and worked one-on-one with the less coordinated.

Her weight crept closer to one forty, but her body became leaner and harder. For the first time ever, she tied her shirttails under her breasts and exposed a flat abdomen like the servers and many of the female customers.

#

Three weeks later, Brianne spotted Cort at The Roundup. Or someone who looked like him. She had just finished a country swing dance with Vinnie, one of the resident dance instructors. He asked her to help demonstrate tricks and flips to several couples interested in learning the moves. What caught her eye was the way the dark-haired guy with the baseball cap walked as he headed toward the exit. She elbowed her way between people and hurried to the door. There were several smokers downwind, and a knot of men gathered around a pickup modified with over-sized tires.

"Hey, did anyone see a guy wearing a baseball hat?" she called out.

The cigarette pack shook their heads or shrugged their shoulders. From the monster truck group, a man built like a bull dog with short legs and a deep barrel chest stepped forward with his arms opened wide. On his head was a greasy Texas Rangers cap.

"Here I am. Are you the hot piece of ass that wants me?"

His buddies laughed, and one of them said, "And you wonder why you can't get laid."

Brianne waited to hear a car start or see tail lights pulling out of a parking space. She turned when music blasted from the door that opened behind her.

Emma came out. "What're you doing out here, Bree?"

"I just needed to get a breath of fresh air."

"You ran out like a Kenyan on speed. Looking for someone?"

Her eyes slid away with a quick Pavlovian glance when a car engine roared to life. "No, of course not. Let's go back inside. I'll buy you a beer."

She held the door open for her sister but took one last peek before it shut.

#

Over the next three days, Brianne played the night at The Roundup over and over in her head. She had just come off the dance floor when the guy in the baseball cap turned away. It was that sudden movement that caught her attention. His height and build were similar to Cort's, but the dark hair was much longer. There was something about the way the figure moved that reminded her of him.

She also reviewed the night in New York. The sharp edges of shock from Cort's betrayal had worn off. Her recollection wasn't clouded with pain and humiliation. It was like watching a horror movie over and over again until it lost its impact. She examined the sequence of events like a math problem that didn't add up because of a simple miscalculation.

On Saturday night, Brianne was alone in the condo. She lay in bed and waited to fall asleep. As if her mind was a DVD player, she ran scenes from the night in New York. The drive to the hotel and her check-in at the desk were fast forwarded. In slow motion, the action in the hotel room still caused her sore heart to ache. The conversation with Jacqueline before and after Emma's phone call received her particular attention. She rewound that part several times to view it from different perspectives.

Suddenly she bolted upright in bed and screamed, "That fucking lying bitch!"

Chapter 28

NEAR SUNRISE, BRIANNE drifted off to sleep, her thoughts still ragged with anger. She awoke at noon, showered and made herself a cup of coffee. The condo was too quiet. She was unable to concentrate on anything but explanations for what happened in New York.

One was that she and Cort were both victims of a horrible hoax, and he had been unaware that a naked woman was in bed with him. The other less appealing scenario was that he brought the woman to his room. His intent was either to have her leave before Brianne arrived or he wanted them to engage in a threesome.

There is no fucking way he could have pretty pleased me into that.

He knew she was shy and self-conscious. Although they had only been together a short time, she'd never expressed a willingness to try swinging, and neither had he. They had sex outside the bedroom, but it wasn't for the thrill of getting caught or to fuel a voyeur's prurient interest. Unless her sleazebag radar had gone completely haywire, Cort wasn't into sharing her with someone else.

That left Jacqueline as the engineer of a scene to deceive them both, or she took advantage of the situation to end their relationship. Either way, in Brianne's mind, the Ice Queen was more culpable than Cort. He never would have hurt her like that. She had to let him know what happened.

The Ice Queen could, and probably would, deny her knowledge of the prostitute and their conversation about his out-of-town hookups. Jacqueline told him she talked with Brianne in the lobby. He thought that Emma's phone call came soon after she arrived at the hotel.

Cort doesn't know that I was in his suite.

When Pam came home, she went into her bedroom and unpacked. Brianne stood in the doorway and rubbed one ankle against the other. She was bursting to tell about her revelation.

"What's wrong?" Pam asked. "You look like you have to pee."

Brianne opened her mouth to say she was ready to talk about what happened in New York. Instead, she said, "Nothing's wrong. I haven't been out of the condo all weekend. I guess I'm a little antsy."

"Then let's go out to eat," Pam suggested. "I'm starving. I haven't had anything since brunch this morning."

"Good idea. I'll get changed."

I need more time to think this through more before I start making accusations.

#

Brianne strategized ways to get the information she needed before confiding in Pam and Cort.

I don't want to come across as some crazy woman with a conspiracy theory involving his publicist.

She looked up the address for PR Associates, Jacqueline's employer. They had an office on Commercial Boulevard just east of the turnpike. She drove there the next day on her way back to The Voice Center. The multi-media company was in a building that sat apart from a larger structure that housed various other businesses. A rear door opened into a narrow alleyway with a dumpster. It was barely wide enough for a garbage truck. All the cars were parked out front.

No one entered or left from the main entrance in the fifteen minutes that Brianne was parked there. It was silly to think her nemesis would suddenly appear, and she could …

Do what? Drag her to Cort and demand she confess? Run her over? Stalk her until she called the police?

On Wednesday, Brianne sat in the empty conference room of Sunshine Engineering. Her accent modification class with three new employees had ended. She reviewed and corrected homework assignments designed to improve their grammar and written skills. When finished, she placed the workbooks next to a phone on a side table. Her clients would retrieve them after she left.

Brianne turned to get her briefcase then, without hesitation, she picked up the phone, pressed an unlit button, and dialed a number she memorized. Her heart pounded against her breastbone.

After two rings, a woman said, "PR Associates. How may I direct your call?"

"Hi. Is Jacqueline there?"

"I'm sorry. She's out of the office right now. She'll be back at four. Do you want her voice mail?"

"No, thanks. I'll try her cell." Brianne dropped the receiver like it burned her.

She stood with one hand on her thudding chest and checked her watch. It was one o'clock. In ninety minutes, she had a meeting with a hotel manager in Boca Raton to present a proposal. He was interested in an on-site program to improve his bilingual employees' English skills.

I should be able to get to Jacqueline's office when she arrives.

#

Before she went to her afternoon appointment, she stopped at a Target and purchased a floppy sun hat, a button-down shirt, and a roll of duct tape. Her meeting lasted longer than she expected. Mr. Williamson insisted on showing her around the prestigious hotel and resort. Then the late afternoon traffic out of Boca Raton was horrendous. It was a quarter to five by the time Brianne pulled into the parking lot at PR Associates.

This is probably a waste of time.

She backed her car into a space away from the other vehicles in the lot. Her location had a direct sight line to the front door. While she waited, she took off her tan blazer. Underneath was a thin off-white camisole. She unbuttoned the newly purchased shirt and removed it from the hanger. Brianne dampened the creases in the navy oxford cotton with water from the bottle she kept in the car. She snapped the fabric a few times. The shirt was a size bigger than she usually wore so it fit loosely over her chest. She slipped her arms into it, smoothed it over her camisole and buttoned the front placket.

The cuffs were a little long so she folded them and the sleeves to her forearms. She had to get out of the car and pull down her zipper to tuck the long hem inside her slacks. Crouching behind her open car door, she prayed no one was watching.

I should have researched surveillance techniques before I did this.

At five o'clock, two women exited the building. From her vantage point, she could see that neither of them was Jacqueline. For the next twenty minutes, people trickled out. Brianne tried to look as unobtrusive as possible. She wore her new hat and kept her face lowered.

Just as she was about to give up, Jacqueline came out dressed in slacks and a black silky sweater. She got into a silver Lexus sedan. Brianne started her engine and followed the Ice Queen at a discreet distance. They crossed over the turnpike and headed west. After a few miles, her quarry put on her right turn signal.

Where is she going? Oh, shit!

Jacqueline parked in front of Hardcort Fitness, got out, and entered with a workout bag slung over her shoulder. Brianne eyed the building. This wasn't where she met Cort. It was one of his other locations.

What do I do now?

She could go inside, but because she wasn't a member they weren't going to let her wander through the place. If she expressed interest in a membership, she might get tied up with a salesperson, and Jacqueline would get away.

Besides, do I really want to do this in a place with lethal weights and people around?

The parking space next to the Ice Queen's car was empty. Brianne pulled in and waited. The last of the February daylight faded. Security lights on tall poles clicked on in the parking lot. The front of the building was dark except for backlit Hardcort Fitness letters high on the wall and the lighted rectangle of the main entrance.

The dashboard clock read seven fifteen when Jacqueline emerged. Her blonde hair was skinned into a ponytail. She was makeup free and wore a sweat-darkened tank top and shorts.

Brianne quickly got ready and then said aloud, "Here I go. I hope this meeting with Cort's publicist gets me some answers to my questions."

She opened her door, hustled around the back of her car, and leaned against the rear fender of the Lexus. As Jacqueline headed down the sidewalk, she dabbed at her face with the towel around her neck. She jumped back when she spotted a figure standing next to her car. As if she feared an attack, her eyes darted around then squinted.

Recognition drew her mouth into a sneer. "What do *you* want?"

"I want to talk with you."

Jacqueline gave her a suspicious stare. "How did you know I was here?"

"I went to your office and saw you pulling out of the parking lot. I followed you."

"And you've been waiting until I came out?"

"Yes."

Taking a step off the curb, the publicist said, "Well, you wasted your time. I have nothing to say to you."

Since the Ice Queen had no qualms about lying, neither did Brianne.

Besides, I've got nothing to lose.

"I found out who Chantel is. Remember, the hooker?"

Jacqueline blinked several times. "How do you know my sister?"

Her sister?

Brianne was grateful the parking lot's security lights were behind her. They cast her face and the front of her body in partial shadow. It masked her mouth opening in surprise. "I ... have my ways."

Jacqueline gave her a shrewd and contemptuous look. "So what? There's nothing you can do about it."

"I can tell Cort."

"Are you kidding? He'll thank me for getting his career back on track."

Another missing piece of the jigsaw slipped into place. "Is that what it was all about? His career ... or maybe *yours?*"

"Did you think I did it because I was jealous of you? Don't make me laugh." Now that the Ice Queen could insult Brianne, she regained her arrogance. "I'm too good a publicist for just a two bit gym owner."

One nagging thought that bothered Brianne was why Cort didn't wake up until the next morning. He never drank more than one Scotch or a glass of wine at a time. She concluded that he had to have been knocked out somehow.

"Will Cort also thank you for drugging him?"

Cracks formed in Jacqueline's haughty veneer, but she jutted her chin, lips pinched tight.

Brianne said, "I'm sure your boss, Bernie, wouldn't thank you for doing that to a client."

Jacqueline snorted a mock laugh. "For your information, Bernie will never fire me."

So you're not denying you gave Cort something. Interesting.

"I don't believe that. Anyone can get fired," Brianne said.

"Not me. He and David used to be the hottest publicists in the area, but now they're just the useless, aging figureheads of PR Associates. *I'm* the one who brings in the celebrity clients, not them. And when I start my own agency, all those moneymakers will jump ship with me. So there's nothing you can do to hurt me."

Brianne visibly sagged. "But you can't—"

Jacqueline took a step closer. "I can do whatever I want and you ..." Her face shone with malicious glee when she jeered, "You're just *pathetic.*"

With those words, Brianne turned sideways, her shoulder toward the Ice Queen. Her head drooped like she expected to be slapped, have her hair pulled, or her textbooks knocked out of arms.

In a low menacing voice, Jacqueline said, "Don't fuck with me, Porky. Neither Cort nor Bernie will believe you, and I'll deny everything. Now *get* away from my car."

Brianne stepped to her left and flattened her backside against her Honda. She X-crossed her arms over her breasts like she was ashamed of them. Her posture was the picture of humiliation and defeat.

Jacqueline unlocked the car door, threw her bag inside, and got behind the wheel. As she backed out of the space, she waggled her fingers in a derisive wave of goodbye and beeped her horn to startle her cowed victim.

When the Lexus was out of sight, Brianne walked around her car, opened the door, and sat down. She heaved a mighty sigh and laid her forehead against the steering wheel.

Then she pulled her iPhone from the breast pocket of the dark shirt.

She peeled pieces of black duct tape off the screen, exposed the video button, and tapped it. In the bottom left corner, Brianne touched the image. The recording began with her words, *Here I go. I hope this meeting with Cort's publicist gets me some answers to my questions.* The picture quality was grainy because of the low light. Jacqueline's face flashed on and off the screen, but the audio was loud and clear.

When she had practiced video recording, she discovered that when her iPhone was placed into the breast pocket of a woman's button-down shirt, the lens sat just above the top edge. She used the black tape to hide the backlight. Despite changing the display brightness to its lowest setting, the tape ensured no visible glow could be detected during the recording process.

Now let's see who gets fucked.

#

The TV was on in the living room when Brianne came in the door of the condo. Pam was on the sofa, her feet propped on the coffee table with a bottle of red nail polish. Her toes were splayed with stubby fingers of pink foam.

She aimed the remote and switched off the sound. "Where have you been?"

Brianne sat down and smiled. "I've been making a movie. Wanna see it?" She navigated to the Camera Roll, handed the phone to Pam and pointed. "Click on that. I'm getting myself a glass of wine."

When she returned, the video was ending. She bent down to put her drink on the end table, straightened, and grinned at her friend. When Pam looked up with an open-mouthed and wide-eyed expression, Brianne said, "What do you think?"

Without caution for her just-polished nails, Pam jumped to her feet, grabbed Brianne's hands, and jumped up and down. "You are frigging amazing … brilliant … devious! Let me get that bottle of Merlot, and then you're going to tell me what this is all about."

They settled themselves on each end of the sofa. Brianne turned sideways and stretched her arm across the back cushion to face her friend. She told Pam about the arrival of her late flight to New York City and her inability to make direct contact with Cort upon landing.

"Was he there when you got to the room?" Pam asked.

"He was asleep in bed, but he wasn't alone."

Pam said, "Is this where the sister impersonating a *puta* comes in?"

"Let me finish."

Brianne recounted the rest of the story without interruption. "That's it, Pam. Now you know what happened in New York, and why I broke up with Cort. What do you think?"

"I think we need to call him right now."

With a vehement shake of her head, Brianne said, "No."

"Why not?"

"I still have some unanswered questions. Like is Cort a victim like me or—"

"Did Jacqueline set you up to discover his out-of-town secret?"

Brianne sipped her wine. "Also why was Jacqueline in New York with Cort? He never told me that she would be there."

"Maybe she went because he was going to be on TV?"

"Possibly. But why didn't he tell me?"

Pam looked up from smoothing her fingertip over her toenail. "Shit, I messed this one up. I didn't understand that part in the video about her not being jealous of you."

"Didn't I tell you? She and Cort broke up six months before we got together."

"No, you didn't tell me." Pam threw her hands up in the air. "Men! When will they learn to keep their dicks and their business separate?"

Brianne rubbed her forehead. "Unfortunately, I played my part in her hooker scheme to perfection, and it worked. Cort did *Weight Loss Wonders* again and may sign up for next season."

"Do you think he's going to stay in California? What about his fitness centers and his grandmother?"

"I don't think Lola will ever live alone again. She'll likely go from re-hab to an assisted living center. So that's one tie to Florida that will be ac-counted for soon, if it hasn't been already. As far as Hardcort Athletics is concerned, much of his business can likely be done electronically now. If he has good managers like Mark running the daily operations, then he can oversee them from anywhere in the country."

They speculated on how the hotel scene was set up and whether or not Cort was complicit in it. Two hours later, they called it a night. Although, Brianne was emotionally and physically drained, she had trouble falling asleep. The confrontation with Jacqueline and possibly meeting with Cort again to tell him what happened in New York kept her brain working overtime.

Chapter 29

WHILE THEY ATE supper on Thursday evening, Pam said, "You need to tell Cort what happened whether he has out-of-town hookups or not. He needs to know what the *puta publicista* did."

Brianne sighed. "I know. We hadn't been together very long, but I never had any indication he was a creep that liked hookers. At this point, I trust him more than Jacqueline to tell the truth."

Pam smiled. "I was thinking the same thing."

When Brianne went into her bedroom, she sent Cort a text. *Can you meet me at The Voice Center to talk about what happened in New York?*

After she hit the send button, she held the phone in her palm and stared at the screen. She envisioned seeing messages such as *Eat shit and die* or *I've moved on.*

Three long minutes later she received the message *What time? I'll be there.*

Tomorrow 3PM?

See you then.

Brianne stood on shaky legs and went out to the living room where Pam was watching *Jeopardy.*

She said, "Cort's coming to the office tomorrow afternoon."

Pam scrutinized her friend's face. "Breathe, *chica*. Everything will be fine."

"I'm scared."

"Would it help if I was with you?"

Brianne no longer had a physical reaction, such as tears or a stab of pain, when she saw his one dimensional image on TV or in photos. However, being in the same room with him, breathing the same air, watching him watch her, churned her stomach, and weakened her knees. "No, I'll do this on my own."

"Ah, *chi-chi,* you are a strong, beautiful woman. Getting the *puta publicista* to say what she did proves it. I can't wait for the day when you believe it as much as I do."

#

Brianne finished with her final client on Friday afternoon. During the session, she forced herself to not watch the clock tick down. When they exited the therapy room, she told the choir director to schedule his next appointment with Kitty at the front desk. Pam stood in the hallway.

Brianne whispered, "Is he here?"

Pam nodded, hugged her, and said, "You'll do fine."

As Brianne walked down the hall to her office, she calmed herself with deep breaths. Cort was seated in front of her desk.

He stood. "Hello, Brianne."

Dressed in chinos and a Hardcort Fitness polo shirt, he looked leaner. His hair was longer and brushed his collar. After a nod and weak smile, Brianne walked to her desk and sat down. Her heart hammered in her chest.

"Thank you for coming." Brianne cleared her throat. "Recently, I was able to view what happened in New York less emotionally and more analytically. After several nights of scrutiny, I came to the realization that Jacqueline had engineered a scenario to cause the termination of our relationship."

God, I sound like a boring Power Point presenter.

Cort looked confused. "What are you trying to say?"

She took a deep breath. "Jacqueline put a naked woman in your hotel bed with you."

Cort grabbed the arms of his chair and rose partway up. "What the—"

"Sit down and let me tell you what happened. Then I have a video I want you to see."

Cort listened without interruption. At first, he was in disbelief as evidenced by his wide-eyed, open-mouthed expression. Then his face hardened into a mask, and his body seemed to vibrate with suppressed fury.

Brianne said, "I now believe you were as much a victim as me. I'm sorry I thought otherwise. Once I realized I was duped, I needed confirmation of what happened. Jacqueline could deny everything. So I met her and recorded this conversation." She laid her phone on the desk. Cort scooted forward in his chair. "It was dark out so the picture quality is not good, but ..." she swallowed, "you'll hear what was said."

His eyes never left the screen. With each new revelation, his facial expression and body posture became more ominous. He looked like he wanted to tear her office apart.

When the video ended, she turned her phone around and hit the stop button. Cort nodded and rose to his feet.

"Thank you for telling me." His voice was soft but foreboding. "If you'll email me a copy of that video, I'll handle things from here."

Brianne jumped to her feet. "Cort, what are you going to do?"

After a deep breath, he visibly relaxed. "Don't worry. I won't do anything stupid."

Brianne came around the corner of her desk. "Are you going to talk to Jacqueline about this?"

"First, I'm going to talk with Bernie, her boss. Then I'll meet with the ... with her." He stepped toward the open door.

"Wait." Brianne moved closer to him. "I deserve to be there, too." The words carried her bitter determination to witness retribution but were also frosted with fear.

What if the Ice Queen's right and nothing happens to her but a slap on the wrist?

"Let me get in touch with Bernie first. I'll let you know when we're going to meet." He leaned over and kissed her cheek.

After he left, she placed her fingertips on the spot where his lips had been.

#

Brianne received a text from him on Monday afternoon. *Can you meet at PR Associates tomorrow?*

She checked her schedule. Her last appointment was at eleven-thirty.

Available in the afternoon.

3PM?

I'll be there.

She stared at her phone for a minute then went to Pam's office.

Her friend looked up from her keyboard. "What's up?"

"Cort wants me to meet him tomorrow where Jacqueline works. I need to tell you something." Brianne shifted from foot to foot. "I didn't just break up with Cort because I found him in bed with another woman. I mainly broke up with him because I didn't want to be in a relationship with a celebrity."

"That's not what you told me." Pam's spine straightened as she gave Brianne a hard-eyed look.

"I know. How pathetic am I?"

That's what Jacqueline called me, too.

"Brianne—"

"I broke up with a great guy who loves me because he's a public figure. It's just that I *hate* that kind of life." Her voice cracked. "I don't want to worry about people taking pictures of us, dealing with negative publicity, concerned about how I affect his image. I can't live like that. I just can't."

Pam sighed.

"I know. I'm fucked up." Brianne sniffed and used the sides of her fingers to wipe the dampness along her lower lashes.

Her friend stood and came around the desk. She held onto Brianne's upper arms and looked into her face. "You are *not* fucked up, *chica,* just scared. You've spent most of your life hiding in the shadows because of your weight. Being with Cort forced you into the limelight."

"I was so thrilled that someone like him wanted me for a girlfriend that I never thought about how his public life would affect me. I was *so* not prepared for it."

"I don't think anyone is ever prepared for that, except maybe royalty and even they screw up. You just have to do the best you can."

#

On the day of the meeting at PR Associates, Brianne's nerves got the better of her. She left the building to take a walk and eat her lunch outside. The half hour she spent pacing up and down the pavement while she munched on a peanut butter and jelly sandwich helped.

She had a clearer picture of what she needed to do if Cort wanted to resume their relationship. It would be the second time she made a demand of a boyfriend since she told Paul to get the hell out of her life and the condo. It would be the second time she set a parameter in a relationship since she told Larry at UF that he couldn't film them having sex. It would be the second time she required a boyfriend change his behavior since she insisted Omar not bring yappy, little Paco on dates because he wasn't a real service dog despite the fake vest.

If he agrees, then we'll try it again. If not, then it's over for good.

She returned to the office with a new sense of fortitude and stopped Pam in the hallway. "I'm going home to change and freshen up before the meeting this afternoon."

"Good idea. What are you going wear?"

"I think that black suit I bought on clearance at Sak's."

Brianne fell in love with the pricey outfit. The straight skirt had pretty inverted pleats that flared at the hem. The long-sleeved, fitted jacket sported split cuffs.

Pam smiled. "Wear sheer black stockings, your CFM heels, and put up your hair. You want to dress to kill."

"I'll be sure to put my metaphoric garrote in my purse, too," laughed Brianne.

"Whatever it takes. You want the *puta* to know that you are there to murder any chance that she's getting away with what she did to you and Cort."

#

When Brianne turned into PR Associates' parking lot, she spotted Cort's Mercedes in a space near the front entrance. She checked herself in the visor mirror. Her hair was pulled into a tight bun on the back of her head. She wore darker eye makeup and lipstick than usual. With sunglasses and her black suit, she mimicked a stereotypical female assassin in the movies.

She kept her sunglasses in place until she was led by the receptionist into Mr. Parks' office. Cort was seated in front of the desk. He wore an open-collared white dress shirt and charcoal slacks like the first time he came to The Voice Center for therapy. His eyes moved over her from head to toe.

"Hello, Cort."

He stood and smiled at her as she moved to the chair beside him. Before she sat down, he leaned over and whispered, "You look great."

She nodded to acknowledge his compliment.

Sorry, I can't be more demonstrative. Growing a backbone is new to me. Until this is over, I can't let my guard down.

As she lifted her hand to remove her sunglasses, she caught sight of Jacqueline's boss seated behind the desk. The dark lenses hid her wide-eyed stare. With the name Bernie, she envisioned a short, rotund fellow with a bald head. Instead, he had a full head of silver hair and chiseled features. Bernie was somewhere between his early fifties to mid-sixties. He looked like the actors who play rich men on TV.

Jacqueline's boss stood and reached across his desk with an out-stretched hand. "Miss Gordon, thank you for coming."

"You're welcome. I want to get this situation resolved as soon as possible," she said and took a seat next to Cort.

And I hope the Ice Queen will get what she deserves.

Bernie sat and said, "Cort told me what happened in New York and sent me a copy of the video you recorded. Based on what both of you experienced, I want to tell you how sorry I am for what Jacqueline did. I—"

"But you didn't do anything to apologize for. She did."

"Of course, I understand how you feel." Bernie slid a quick glance at Cort and said, "Jacqueline is wrapping up a photo shoot on Highland Beach. She should be here shortly. Cort and I have been working together the past two days. He has agreed to continue with our agency and has chosen a new publicist, David Cunningham. I know there is no way to compensate you for what you've been through. But I want to offer free marketing and advertising services to your business for the next six months."

Did Cort make him promise that? If he did, it'll make Pam happy.

"I appreciate the offer, but I'll have to consult my business partner first."

Bernie's phone rang. When he hung up, he said, "Jacqueline's here."

A few moments later, there was a tentative knock on the office door, and then it opened. Jacqueline's voice said, "I got here as quickly as I could."

Bernie said, "Come in." He gestured to a chair at the side of his desk.

"You said there's problem?"

Cort turned in his seat. Brianne looked over her shoulder at the Ice Queen.

Jacqueline's eyes bounced between them. "I see. This is a planned ambush."

In a quiet but firm voice, Brianne said, "Karma's a bitch."

Cort looked at her and grinned.

Chapter 30

BERNIE SAID, "SIT down, Jacqueline."

When the woman closed the door behind her and walked to the chair, Brianne faced forward and did her best not to smirk. Once again, the Ice Queen was in a state of dishabille. She wore a pair of wide-legged drawstring linen pants that were limp and wrinkled. On her feet were flip-flops, and on her head was a white cap with her ponytail pulled through the snap back. Her pale pink T-shirt had sweat-darkened armpits.

She sat ramrod straight without her back touching the chair and raised her chin in the air. At the moment, Jacqueline may not be as self-assured and put together as usual, but there was little doubt that in a moment, she could become as vicious as a cornered vixen.

Bernie said, "Cort came to me yesterday and related a very disturbing experience that he and Miss Gordon had in New York."

The Ice Queen shielded her face by tipping her head and smoothing loose hairs behind her ears as though she needed to adjust a mask into place. Her eyes blinked more than usual, which betrayed her nervousness.

"They are convinced," Bernie continued, "that you created a scene to make Miss Gordon believe that Cort used the services of a prostitute."

She shrugged and said, "Maybe he does. I'm not aware of everything in his private life."

Brianne couldn't believe the woman was going to try to weasel her way out of this. She leaned forward and said, "Cut it out, Jacqueline! You told me the woman with Cort was his regular New York hooker, and then I found out it was your sister."

And you were the one who told me.

Bernie said, "At this time, Cort has not yet decided whether he will take legal action against this agency. Instead, he will first sue you and your sister for damages."

Beads of sweat popped up on the Ice Queen's upper lip.

"However," her boss continued, "if you truthfully answer a few questions, he will drop his suit. It's your decision, Jacqueline."

With an impatient sigh, she said, "Fine. What do you want to know?"

Cort said in a voice that dripped icy venom, "Brianne said that you did it to advance my career. Why did you have to break us up for that?"

Jacqueline didn't answer immediately. She seemed to weigh various options as her eyes moved back and forth between the two men. When they finally came to rest on Cort, she said, "We were going places when you were on *Weight Loss Wonders*. I couldn't believe that after two seasons, you quit for no good reason. I've worked hard to get you interested in other West Coast projects. I know you were considering one of them when you met *her*." Jacqueline gestured to Brianne with her chin.

"You broke us up so I would do another reality show?" Cort asked with a hint of disbelief in his voice.

"Why are you so surprised?" she said with disdain. "It worked. She dumped you, and you signed on to finish *Weight Loss Wonders*."

Brianne still questioned Jacqueline's sister posing as a prostitute. "How did you get your sister to go along with your scheme unless she really is a hooker?"

"She's not." Jacqueline snorted and glared at Brianne. "I told her you were hooked on Oxy and other pain killers, but I couldn't persuade Cort to give you up. I was afraid you would destroy his career and credibility."

"Speaking of drugs," he said, "what did you give me to make me sleep?"

"When you joined me at the hotel bar that evening, I slipped two of my Ambien pills in your drink."

Brianne said, "That wasn't a smart thing to do. Don't you know that a side effect of a sedative like that mixed with alcohol is respiratory failure?"

There was an awkward beat of silence in the office, then Cort said, "I remember talking with you in the bar but not much after that. What happened?"

"You were woozy, and I walked you upstairs. After you went into the bedroom, I let myself out, but I took your key card and phone with me. I called Chantel and then waited for Brianne to get there. We went back into your room when she was on her way to the hotel."

An uncomfortable silence echoed in the office until Bernie asked, "Is that all, Cort?"

"Yeah, I've heard enough," he spat.

"Is there anything you want to ask or say, Miss Gordon?" said Bernie.

"Yes, there is. Jacqueline, before trying to break us up, why didn't you just ask me to talk Cort into doing another TV show?"

The woman shrugged, refusing to look at her.

"Come on. Are you that really that fucking stupid?"

Not only did the Ice Queen's head shoot up, but so did Bernie's and Cort's.

Brianne looked at them like she was baffled by their reaction to her F-bomb. Up to now the meeting had been very civil and businesslike. It was time to fight dirty.

"I can't believe that one of the biggest firms in the city would employ such an abysmally bad publicist. When I work with a client who has some-one close, such as a family member or friend, I always enlist their help with therapeutic objectives. It was unprofessional and short-sighted of you to alienate me from the start. Speaking of unprofessional, Bernie," Brianne paused until he dragged his hostile glare away from Jacqueline, "did you know that your employee has such a poor opinion of you? How did you feel when she described you as useless and aging?"

A red flush crept up Bernie's neck and into his cheeks. Not even the Botox in his face prevented his lips from forming into a thin line.

Brianne continued. "Were you surprised to hear *on the video* that she's planning to start her own agency and steal your clients?"

Jacqueline went paper-white and looked like she was about to ralph all over her boss' desk. "W-w-what video?"

Brianne clapped her hand to her cheek in mock dismay. "Oh, I guess we forgot you tell you. I recorded our conversation the other night."

"You didn't—"

"Oh, but I did. You know, you were right. Bernie and Cort might not have believed me, especially if you denied everything. I needed proof, and you exceeded my wildest expectations."

The Ice Queen's spine slumped against the back of the chair as if her bony vertebrae started to crumble.

"Both of them were very interested in what you had to say. Hey, I have an idea." Brianne twisted in her chair to face Cort. "Let's post the video on your website or Facebook page. I wonder if it would go viral?"

He jerked upright and looked like she had just suggested sending Hardcort members to Planet Fitness.

"Now, Miss Gordon," Bernie said, "you don't really mean that."

Brianne cocked her head and gave him a curious look. "Of course I mean it, Bernie. Wouldn't Cort's fans and your other clients want to know what a crackerjack publicist like Jacqueline will do to further her client's career? I wonder if she broke up other relationships or marriages for the good of someone's job prospects."

Jacqueline emitted a loud gasp.

Brianne lifted her open palm in the Ice Queen's direction. "I think we have an answer."

Cort laid his hand on her arm. "Brianne—"

She moved her arm away. "She called me a quack, and you didn't fire her. Instead you insisted she apologize. She did but with the least amount of sincerity possible. Then I overheard her tell a friend that the only reason you were dating me was because I give great blowjobs."

He winced. It was as if her words pierced him like a spear and pinned him to the chair.

"She told you I was responsible for your endorsement on PrimeTime's website when I knew nothing about it. She risked your life with a prescription drug and told me you sleep with prostitutes. This is the world you live in, Cort. The one I didn't want to be in with you."

He looked at her like she had grown another head with the face of a stranger.

This is the new me. Brianne with a backbone. I'm keeping her whether you can love her or not.

There was a stunned silence around the office. No one, other than Brianne, seemed able to move. She sat up tall, as if a string were attached to the top of her head, drawing her up to accommodate her lengthening spine.

Finally Bernie said, "Is there anything you want to say, Jacqueline?"

Brianne doubted that a heartfelt apology would come from that forked tongue. Like any sociopath, the publicist wasn't sorry for what she did. She just regretted it didn't work out the way she intended. The Ice Queen's frozen expression did not change when she shook her head.

Bernie straightened his tie. "As you might have guessed, you are no longer Cort's publicist."

Jacqueline inhaled deeply and nodded. Her now composed expression seemed to say, *Okay. I've taken my licks. Let me get back to work with one less client.*

Bernie interlocked his fingers together on his desk top. His eyes shot furious daggers at her. "And, as of this moment, you are longer an employee of PR Associates."

"But—"

"Security is waiting outside. They are going to escort you to your office to gather your belongings. They will collect your keys, laptop, and cell phone."

"You can't—"

"An email was sent to all your clients during this meeting letting them know that you have been terminated for endangering a client's life and other unethical actions which could result in legal action against this agency."

"That's not—"

"Our tech people have been changing all access codes and discontinued your cell phone service. You will receive a copy of the non-compete agreement you signed when you were hired. You are welcome to have your attorney review it and your termination paperwork."

Bernie rose to his feet, walked to the door, and opened it. A uniformed guard waited just outside. Like an automaton, Jacqueline stood up. Without a word or a glance in Cort and Brianne's direction, she walked out.

Bernie said, "If you two want to talk, you're welcome to use my office as long as needed."

Here we go. The part I dread more than the confrontation with Jacqueline.

The door shut with an audible click. They were alone together.

After a pause, Cort said, "I'm glad all that's behind us now."

Brianne turned in her seat to face him. "Did Bernie offer the use of his office because you're expecting us to get back together again?"

The hopeful look on Cort's face was wiped clean. "It's what I thought would happen after you knew that I didn't sleep with a hooker."

"Except that nothing else in our relationship has changed. If you recall, I told you I couldn't be with you because of your celebrity status."

"But that was—"

"Just my excuse for breaking up?"

"That's what I thought. It's why I was so anxious to find out what really happened in New York."

"The hooker hoax was the catalyst for the breakup, Cort, but not the real reason. I'm still afraid that your celebrity will just ruin another relationship for us."

"That's one of the things my new publicist, David, and I have talked about. He's offered to do media coaching with you. I want you to be comfortable in public with me. You're right. Jacqueline was a lousy publicist for not doing that as well as for insulting you. It was my fault for not firing her right after the fundraiser." He looked down at the floor.

"Did you keep her on because at one time the two of you had a personal relationship?"

Cort's head snapped up. "No. We never dated."

"That's not what she said."

Cort adjusted himself in the chair, as if something prickly had just rubbed his testicle. "I admit we hooked up a few times when we traveled. But that was several years ago. We never dated. It wasn't what she wanted, and it sure as hell wasn't what I wanted either."

Brianne said nothing.

Cort averted his eyes from hers. "I didn't fire her after what she said to you because I was too lazy to go through the hassle of starting with a new publicist. I was hoping everything would work out. I was wrong. Can you forgive me?"

She hesitated.

Cort leaned toward her with a pleading expression. "I know this is the third time I've asked you to forgive me. I can't promise I won't need to ask you again, but I'm learning."

He took responsibility for continuing to employ Jacqueline even after her treatment of Brianne. Had he also learned his lesson when it came to intimacy with someone who was, basically, his employee? Can he be faithful in a monogamous relationship? Will someone as attractive as Cort be able to resist temptation when away from home? She could only hope and, if she wanted him back in her life, she had to trust him.

"I can forgive you again. But it's getting harder to do."

Cort searched her face. "I understand, and I'm grateful." He gave her an expectant smile. "Would you be willing to work with David?"

The coaching and Bernie's offer for marketing and advertising services would help both her and The Voice Center. Pam would encourage her to accept both. "All right. I'll give it a try. But there's something else."

Her concession to working with his new publicist seemed to release the tension he held in check. His eyes shone, and a wide smile split his face. "Shoot."

"I want us to get to know each other."

Cort gave her a puzzled look. "I don't understand, sweetheart."

Ah, the endearment. Don't let that sway you.

"In most relationships, people start out as acquaintances or friends. They become familiar with each other on some basic social level. Then the attraction kicks in. After that, they may become friends with benefits or move to a more committed relationship. We were intimate almost from the beginning, but never achieved intimacy."

"That's just semantics," he said. "Maybe things did move fast for us, but it was because I fell so much in love with you. I've never wanted a woman as much as you. I still do."

"I felt the same way, but it never allowed us to get to know each other. There were so many hidden landmines that blew up in our faces. All we did was cover up the damage with sex. I'm willing to try again, but it has to change. It's crazy if we go back to what we did before and expect a different result."

Cort didn't say anything. Brianne waited. She didn't expect him to agree to her proposal right away.

In a hesitant and guarded tone, he said, "Are you saying you don't want to sleep with me?"

"Are you saying you don't want me if I don't sleep with you?" she echoed.

Cort rubbed his face. At last, he asked, "What are you suggesting?"

"Let's start our relationship again as acquaintances. We'll get together and talk."

"About what?"

"To start, there's your family."

"There's not much to tell. It's just Lola and me."

Brianne said, "I know very little about your parents, about your childhood. Most of what I do know Lola told me. I'm clueless about your feelings and thoughts on things that have happened to you as well as a variety of issues. I know your body, but I don't know you. That might be the reason I believed Jacqueline when she said you used hookers. Without intimacy, there's no trust."

Cort did not look convinced that this was a good idea. His dark brows drew together in a frown.

She added, "You have a right to know more about me, too. Do you know what I think about gun control, abortion, home schooling, plastic surgery, mixed race relationships, having children … all kinds of things?"

"You're right. We have lot to learn about each other," Cort said, sounding a bit hesitant and worried. "But what if one of us reveals something that the other one can't handle?"

"Worse than you having sex with prostitutes?"

Cort's troubled expression was broken by a smile. "Yeah, worse than that."

"If it can't be resolved, then isn't it better to find out now, rather than later?"

Cort sighed. "So what's the first step in this new no-sex relationship of ours?"

"How about breakfast or lunch this weekend?" she suggested.

"I promised to umpire a Little League game on Saturday, starting at nine."

"Perfect. Then let's meet early for breakfast. That way there's a time limit for us. Be prepared to share," she advised.

Chapter 31

THEY MET AT the Harbor Cafe for their first friends-only date. After they placed their breakfast orders, Cort showed her a picture of his tall, heavyset father and tiny Filipino mother on their wedding day. The incongruity of their stature and sizes was almost comic, but the couple looked happy and in love.

"Your father was a big guy," Brianne said.

"Yeah, and he got even bigger. He weighed over four hundred pounds when he died. My mother was killed instantly. The crash made the car careen into a brick wall, and the impact caused the steering wheel to crush Dad's chest. Because of his size, he couldn't move the seat back any farther and still reach the pedals."

"What about his airbag?"

"At that time, not all cars were equipped with them. His wasn't. Even so, he would have survived the crash without one, if not for his weight."

He brought out a picture of himself as a baby. He was a round-cheeked, dark-haired bundle with an open-mouthed, toothless smile. In her mind's eye, a quick image flashed of an infant in her arms with Cort's dark eyes. She looked up from the picture with a wistful smile.

He said, "I know. I was a cute little fella." Then he slid another image across the table to her. "This is one of me a few months before my parents were killed. It was the last Christmas we were together as a family. I was seven years old."

The photograph showed a young boy standing in front of a decorated Christmas tree with a red sled propped on end. He had a wide grin with one front tooth missing. His pajamas weren't just too small, they were way too tight for his chubby frame.

Cort hesitated before he handed over the next photo. "This is when I was in seventh grade."

It was a school picture of a young adolescent. He was even heavier than in the previous picture. His long, dark hair was greasy. Despite the over-sized T-shirt, Brianne could see the start of man-boobs. His face looked longer because of a double chin.

Cort was fat like me?

She laid the pictures side by side and stared at each one.

Was it not his parent's deaths that kept him quiet about his childhood but his own obesity?

She was rendered speechless as warring emotions tumbled around inside her.

"This is the last picture I brought." Cort handed her a senior yearbook photo. The attractive young man was dressed in a tuxedo jacket, white shirt, and bowtie.

Brianne looked closer at the hottie in formal wear. She had a quick memory flash of an older hunk in a tux coming in the front door of her condo. Her expression must have softened.

Cort said, "I've decided to go public about my own childhood obesity. You aren't the only one in this relationship who was an overweight kid. Since I'm the activist in programs for children, I'm stepping forward and personalizing the issue. David and I have been working on it. We're releasing the story and these pictures." He gave her a thin smile. "I have to admit it scares the hell out of me. I'm so sorry for how I made you feel, Brianne. I wasn't bullied like you were, but I should have been more understanding."

The hard, glassy shell that still covered part of Brianne's heart cracked, and a huge chunk dropped away.

#

Their next platonic date was the following Saturday. Cort picked her up, and they drove to an Italian restaurant where he had made a reservation. The din in the main dining room masked their conversation from two nearby tables. Since he showed her photographs from his childhood, she had gone to her parents' house and brought some to show him.

Before she removed them from her purse, she said, "I have a question for you about New York."

"What?"

"When I called you from the airport to tell you my flight was cancelled, you said you had a surprise for me when I got there. Obviously, it wasn't a threesome with a hooker, but what was it?"

He snorted a half-laugh. "I told one of the production assistants for the TV show I couldn't get tickets for The Nutcracker. She made some phone calls, and we were on the Will Call list for Saturday night."

Brianne slumped in her seat. "Really? I would have loved that."

Cort raised his eyebrows. "More than a threesome?"

She gave him a reproving scowl.

"Don't worry, sweetheart. I don't ever want to share you with anyone, including another woman. As far as the ballet goes, we can see it this year."

"Maybe." Right now, she had no desire to visit New York before the Christmas holiday. The bad memories were still too fresh.

After they placed their drink and appetizer order, she opened her purse and handed her childhood pictures to Cort. The progression of photos from infancy to middle school showed an almost bald, wide-eyed baby to a sullen, overweight adolescent.

She said, "By the time I was twelve, I weighed as much as most of the adult women in my family, as my Aunt Eileen often reminded me." Cort studied one photo of her with Emma. Brianne sensed his unspoken question. "Emma and I always had a good sibling relationship. I don't think she ever saw me as fat. I was just her older and bigger sister. But I always considered her my skinny sister."

"What was it like for you in school?" he asked when he viewed a picture from middle school.

"Reading your speech for the Healthy Kids fundraiser brought back memories of being bullied and teased, especially when that photo was taken. I was one of those statistics of obese teenagers who toyed with the idea of suicide." Cort looked at her with a shocked expression. "But I never attempted it because of Grandma and Gary. It would have destroyed my grandmother. I could never do something that selfish to her. And Gary was my rock. We emailed or talked to each other almost every day. I figured if he could endure what the kids in Texas were putting him through, then so could I." Unlike Cort's senior picture where he was a slim, handsome young man, Brianne was at her heaviest. "Despite how big I was, I actually enjoyed high school. Being smart was admired there. The mean kids left me alone when I joined just about every club and organization in the school. I wish I could tell overweight teenagers that hiding from their peers is what makes it worse. The old adage if you can't fight 'em, join 'em worked for me."

#

For the third date, Cort and Brianne went to a major league spring training game. They agreed to hold hands and have one goodbye kiss at the end. It was heaven when the skin of his palm rubbed hers, the tensile strength of his fingers entwined with hers, his hard-muscled forearm brushed against hers.

After Cort parked his car at her condo, he said, "Since I get one kiss, I want it to be good."

"I agree. Let's not do it over the console." She fumbled for the door handle.

Cort laid his hand on her arm. "Let me."

He got out and walked around to her side of the car. With the door open, Cort held out his hand and pulled her up and into his arms. He brushed a strand of hair away from her face. His soft lips pressed hers.

She slid her arms around his neck as she positioned herself against his lean, hard frame. It was like her body had instant recall. Her roundness filled his hollows, her dips moved to where his body protruded. Their mingled breaths quickened. By unspoken mutual agreement tempered with reluctance, the kiss ended. Brianne buried her face in his neck as he hugged her tight. Then Cort walked her to the front entrance and waved goodbye from outside.

#

Over the next weeks, they phoned, texted, or emailed each other every day. The communications were flirty but not erotic. Brianne looked forward to these interactions with Cort. From them, she got a clearer picture of him as a businessman, grandson, friend, future father, and mate. They danced, dined, walked on the beach at sunset, and even got haircuts at the same salon.

One Saturday at the end of March, they drove to New River Villas where Cort's grandmother now lived in her new *apartment*. It was the first weekend in a month that Lola was not involved in a can't-miss activity at the assisted living center. After a morning of shopping and lunch at the flea market in Sunrise, the three of them headed to the parking lot.

Cort gripped the handles of Lola's chair where plastic shopping bags dangled. All morning, he had been anonymous in his Raybans with a baseball cap pulled low. As he pushed his grandmother's wheelchair along the bumpy asphalt path, Brianne trailed a couple steps behind. She had slowed to look at batik-printed sundresses on a nearby clothes rack.

When they passed a row of vendors under pop-up canopies, someone called out, "Brianne. Hey, Brianne."

Cort halted. She slammed into his back and bounced off. With lightning reflexes, he twisted, wrapped his hand around her upper arm, and kept her on her feet. Brianne clutched a handful of his shirt to steady herself. She looked to her right, and Alan Nussbaum rose from a plastic chair. In front of him were tables with boxes of comic books in Mylar sleeves.

Oh shit!

"Remember me? It's Alan. We got dragged to that hokey fundraiser for fat kids."

Brianne still held Cort's shirt in her fist. The muscles in his back hardened into knots. Lola flipped up the brim of her floppy sunhat to view the stranger under the canopy. Brianne wiggled her hand in a weak wave.

She tried to get Cort to move forward with gentle pushes against his back. He remained immobile as her former high school classmate skirted the end of his display table and headed their way.

I have a better chance of re-growing my hymen than getting Cort to leave before Alan gets here.

Alan approached, his eyes focused only on her. He seemed oblivious that she was with a man pushing a woman in a wheelchair. He wore a pair of Madras knee-length shorts, black socks, sneakers, and a Captain Marvel T-shirt.

With a wide unabashed grin, he said, "Hey, did you know I put you on my Facebook page?"

"My sister told me."

"Listen, Comic Con is going to be at the Broward Convention Center next month. I was wondering if you'd like to go. I can get you a free ticket."

Before she could answer, Cort leaned in front of her. "Are you asking my girlfriend out?"

Alan jumped back a half-step. He blinked and shook his head as if awakening from a deep sleep. "Uh ... girlfriend?"

"You heard me."

"No ... no ... I was just offering to get her a ticket." Alan's hand shook as he pointed back at his wares. "I sell comic books." In a rush, he said, "You want a ticket, too?" His eyes shifted to Lola as she wheeled her chair around to present a line of three against one. "Maybe the old lady'd like to go?"

Lola lifted the straw bag on her lap and smacked his leg. "It's not polite to call someone an old lady."

Alan winced when the rough fiber bit the bare skin of his calf.

Cort said, "Let's talk about you posting pictures of *my* girlfriend on *your* Facebook page."

Alan's eyes darted around. He spotted a pimply teenage boy with glasses and a Superman shirt flipping through the boxed books at his tent. "I got a customer. Uh ... let me know if you guys want those tickets." He whirled, quickstepped to his store, and darted behind the folding table again.

Cort grabbed the handles of Lola's chair and turned her toward the parking lot. "Come on. Let's go."

Brianne said, "I'll be right back."

Before he could stop her, she walked to the comic book booth and leaned across the boxes. "Alan, I don't know why you called me a porker at the fundraiser and put pictures from high school on Facebook. You were never mean to me before." The defensive posture he assumed when she approached deflated like a balloon with a slow leak. "In fact, we were both teased and bullied in school, but that's in our past. We're successful business people now." She struggled to say that with conviction as she stood by his folding table at a flea market that doubled as a drive-in theater at night. "So, let's start again and be friends. Okay?" She smiled and held out her hand to him.

He appeared flummoxed. Then Alan reached across the boxes and shook her hand with a damp palm. "I'm sorry, Brianne." He glanced under lowered lids at Cort. "Tell your boyfriend that I'm sorry, too."

"I will. You have a good day." She waved goodbye and joined Cort and Lola.

When they were several feet away, Lola muttered, "I betcha that guy was a weird kid in school. I can still spot 'em."

#

During a dinner date a week later, Brianne said to Cort, "You know, you've become one of my best friends."

"One of them?" He looked at her with arched eyebrows.

"Okay, you're my best friend … with a penis."

"You're my best friend, period."

"Period or with a period?"

He laughed. "Both."

"I was looking at my calendar earlier today. Are you aware that we've been platonically dating for fifty days?"

"I haven't counted. I've just enjoyed the time with you and waited for our next step."

"What I found interesting was that our previous relationship lasted only thirty-eight days."

Cort stared at her open-mouthed. "Are you sure? That can't be right."

"Our first date was on November ninth at your house, and we broke up on December sixteenth."

The check came, and while they waited for the return of Cort's credit card, he asked, "Do you think it's time to talk about where we go from here?"

"I do. I've given it a lot of thought. We have five possible scenarios to choose from."

A frown line creased Cort's brow. "Five?"

"One is that things end right now. We never contact or see each other again."

"Not going to happen," he said with finality.

"Two, we remain friends like on our first two dates, with no touching, just talking."

Cort shook his head.

"Three is what we've been doing the past several weeks as boyfriend and girlfriend." Before he could comment, she said, "Four, we become friends with benefits, but we're not exclusive and can date other people if we want."

Cort said, "I'm assuming that number five means I become your only lover again, and hopefully, something more."

As far as she was concerned, there were only two options for her. One meant a final breakup. The other risked her heart for a future with him. "Yes, that's the last scenario."

Cort looked at her with such an expression of love on his face that she wanted to cry. "Sweetheart, you've never left my heart. I want you back in my life and my bed. In fact, I want you there forever. I'll never stop loving you."

A warm feeling flooded her and filled all the empty, hurt spaces left inside. "I feel the same way. I love you, sport."

The waitress arrived with the credit slip for his signature. Afterward, they walked hand-in-hand to his car. They were parked in a lot that serviced nearby businesses as well as the restaurant.

At the passenger door of his car, she said, "Kiss me like you did the first time on your doorstep. I'm giving you a do-over."

He smiled, put one arm around her waist, and pulled her against him. His mouth covered hers, then his tongue slipped inside. Her shoulder bag slid down her arm. This time she was aware of when it thudded onto the pavement at her feet.

Their kiss became more urgent. Cort leaned back against the still closed car door. She lay against him on a slight slant, her calf muscles stretched until she rose up on her toes. His hand which had been at her waist cupped her buttock. His penis nudged her belly.

"Want to get Chinese?" a voice said.

Cort's head jerked up. "What?"

A man in a rumpled business suit, his tie loosened, stood between their vehicle and the one beside them. "Sorry to interrupt. I need to get into my car."

Brianne moved to stand next to Cort and sidestepped with him away from the driver's door. The stranger's companion, another guy in a business suit, grinned at them over the car roof.

The man opened his door then stopped to look at Cort. "Hey, you're the guy from that TV show, aren't you?"

Cort nodded. "Yeah. Sorry that we got a little carried away here."

The driver took a long look at Brianne and said, "Perfectly understandable." He bent toward the ground. "Miss, you dropped your purse."

She reached past Cort to take it from the man's hand. "Thank you." After the car drove off, Brianne said, "We forgot about our little problem with doors."

Cort laughed. "If this is a do-over, I want to show you my house."

"I've already seen your house."

He opened her car door. "Not this. I'll drive you home after you see my surprise."

Chapter 32

WHEN THEY ENTERED the foyer, he led her to the bottom of the stairs. "Close your eyes and hold my hand."

She shaded her downcast eyes with one hand as her feet climbed the stairs. They stopped halfway down the hallway. A light switch clicked on, and the floor was illuminated.

"Open your eyes."

It was a lovely bathroom tiled in creamy limestone. A glass-walled shower stretched across the far end. To the left of the door was a dark wood vanity with a single sink and a toilet beside it. Although the room had been modernized, the finishes were in keeping with the age and style of the house.

"Wow! It's beautiful, Cort."

She stepped inside then spun in a slow circle looking at all four walls. Something was different. This was not just the ugliest bathroom in the world with new fixtures. She put her hands on the door jamb and leaned out to look up and down the hall. Then it hit her. "You built this into part of the guest bedroom."

"It was a huge room. We just made it a little smaller. It was the architect's idea."

"It's wonderful now." She opened the glass shower door and went inside. "What are all these knobs for?"

Cort pointed to the largest one. "That's the temperature controller. This one is for the shower head, and that one over there is for the two body jets. This bathroom is perfect for me. No more showers at the gym."

Once they were back in the hallway, Brianne touched a part of the solid wall. "It was about here where the door to the old bathroom was, wasn't it?"

"That's right."

"So what did you do with that space?"

"Hang on. There's more." He led her to the master bedroom door. "Close your eyes." Once he positioned her inside the room where he wanted her to stand, he said, "Ta-da."

Brianne opened her eyes and gasped. She faced a smaller version of Marisol's luxury bathroom that they admired the night of her party. Across from the open door was a framed mirror over a marble topped vanity. Hanging crystal pendants lighted the countertop, and a petite chandelier was suspended from the center of the ceiling. A frameless glass shower and hatbox toilet lined one wall. On the opposite side, a slipper tub sat under a large stained glass window. It was a classic room done in soft grays and white marble.

"Do you like it?" Cort asked as he stood beside the doorway.

"Oh my God, I love it!"

"The architect created this from the old bathroom and the unused sitting area here in the master bedroom. Now there are two full baths on the second floor."

"Why aren't you using this one? It's bigger." She ran her fingers across the smooth, cool marble.

"Because it was built for you." Cort entered the room, wrapped his arms around her from behind, and laid his head against hers. She lifted her eyes to his smiling countenance in the mirror. "I didn't want the beautiful woman I love in the ugliest bathroom in the world."

A moment of panic flared in Brianne, and she broke eye contact with him. "Cort, I ... I don't know what to say."

"Say you'll think of this bathroom as a getting-back-together gift, nothing more."

"When did you start this remodeling project?"

"While I was in California doing the TV show. I thought it was a good time since the water was shut off to run new plumbing."

"But that's when we were—"

"I know what you're thinking. Why would I remodel a bathroom for a woman who had just broken up with me?"

"Yes. Why would you do that?"

"I was sick of showering at the gym and figured it was time to remodel anyway."

Because you were planning to sell the house and move to California?

He said, "But during the project I was always asking myself: *Would Brianne like this? Would Brianne pick this?* You were in my head and heart the whole time. Sweetheart, the rest of the house and me with it will come later, if you want."

She turned in his arms and stared at the point on his chest where his heart lay. Then she tilted her head back and smiled. "I accept this wonderful, beautiful, getting-back-together gift. I've never had one better. In fact, I've never had one before."

Cort kissed her with tenderness. She held onto him as she savored the feel, smell, and taste of him.

After a time, he leaned back and said, "I would love a do-over on *this* marble countertop, but it's late, and I know you have to work in the morning."

"Do I get a rain check?"

"Definitely. We have two new showers and a bathtub to break in. It's going to take us awhile."

#

They planned for a quiet dinner at his house the following Friday evening and to spend the weekend in romantic seclusion. Cort had surprised her with a new bathroom, and she wanted to return the favor. However, there was no way to match the scope and cost of his gift. So she bought new Egyptian cotton sheets, fluffy towels, soft microfiber bath mats, and a non-fog shaving mirror for his shower. She also went a little crazy in a bath and body shop.

Brianne arrived in the late afternoon and let herself in with the key Cort gave her. It took several trips to carry everything, including the fixings for supper, from her car. She put the new linens on his bed and placed the items she bought in both bathrooms. When finished, she got supper ready. She cooked two quiches, one with asparagus and leeks, the other with ham and cheese. A pear and walnut salad was ready to have dressing added. In the refrigerator was the tropical fruit cheesecake she made last night.

Cort walked through the French door into the kitchen as she removed biscuits from the oven. When she placed the hot baking sheet on the counter, it rattled and betrayed her jumpiness. He smiled as he ambled toward her.

"Did I startle you, or are you nervous?"

"I guess I'm a little nervous. I don't know why. It's not like it's our first time."

"In a sense, it is. I'm nervous, too."

"You are?"

"I want everything to be perfect."

He nibbled on her bottom lip. Soon his tongue plunged into her mouth again and again. When he lifted his head, his eyes had darkened to black. Cort's body tightened, coiled, hardened. As she reached for his face, he jerked back. She still wore the oven mitts that resembled lobster claws.

With his hand on his heart, he gasped, "I thought I was under attack."

Brianne stalked him around the kitchen island as she hummed the menacing theme from *Jaws*. With the sexual tension cut, he went upstairs and changed his suit pants for well-worn jeans while she put their dinner on the table. During the meal, tenseness knotted her stomach. She ate small bites and moved her food around the plate.

"Sweetheart, relax," Cort said.

She smiled and took a deep breath. It didn't help. After dinner, while Cort loaded the last plate into the dishwasher, Brianne wiped nonexistent spots off the counter.

He pulled the towel from her hand. "Come on."

"Where?" she squeaked.

He led her into the office/TV room and plugged his iPhone into a computer speaker. A song by country artist Josh Turner played. Cort adjusted the volume then held out his hand to her.

"Let's dance."

She glided into his arms. They swayed to the music in the middle of the floor. When the song ended another romantic ballad played.

Brianne said, "Did you create this playlist for us?"

"I spent over twenty dollars buying and downloading songs on iTunes."

"Are they all slow and romantic?"

"I wanted music that keeps you close to me."

During the first song, they had kicked off their shoes. Brianne unbuttoned Cort's shirt while the second one played. His hands slipped under her top and unfastened her bra. To the tempo of the following tune, they undressed each other to a topless state. Her bare breasts brushed against Cort's chest as they moved apart then together again. During the fourth melody, Brianne unzipped his pants, and they dropped to his ankles. He stepped out of them, kicked them across the room, and never missed a beat.

She smiled and lifted Cort's arms to drape over her bare shoulders. They swayed back and forth as she unfastened her slacks. One pant leg slipped off her foot with ease, but the other wrapped her ankle like a boa constrictor. Brianne raised her foot to dislodge it, unaware that Cort stood on the free pant leg. She was anchored to the floor and tipped sideways. He was unable to grab her as she toppled toward the sofa. Her bottom thumped onto the floor.

He dropped to one knee beside her. "Are you okay?"

"I'm fine. Obviously undressing to music doesn't improve my coordination."

"It did get you right where I want." Cort put a pillow behind her head, and she laid flat on the rug. He stretched out on top.

God, I've missed the weight of him on me.

Music played in the background while they kissed and ran their hands over each other's bodies. Cort sat back on his heels, removed her slacks from one ankle, and worked the panties off each foot. He pushed his boxer shorts to his knees and tucked another pillow under her hips.

As he lowered himself, she cupped his face and whispered, "I love you so much."

"Sweetheart, it can't compare with what I feel for you." He nudged himself against the lips of her sex and with a quick thrust of his pelvis pushed inside. His breath hissed out near her ear.

She closed her eyes to concentrate on the sensations she had missed for what seemed like ages. As her hips rose off the pillow to meet him, Brianne quivered. Without warning, she climaxed with a gasp, her back arched.

Cort continued to power into her with fierce lunges. Then he threw back his head and moaned in ecstasy. After long minutes, he looked at her face. "What's wrong, sweetheart?"

She smiled through her tears and ran her fingers over his beloved features. "Nothing's wrong. Everything is perfect."

#

It was early Sunday evening when Cort entered the foyer after he stowed the last bag in her car. "I'm already missing you, and you haven't left yet."

They stood wrapped in each other's arms. Brianne said, "It was wonderful, my love. By far, the best weekend of my life."

"Thank you for my bathroom warming gifts and the new sheets."

"Now you can put clean ones on your bed without having to do laundry."

"It's *our* bed," he said.

They got lost in another goodbye kiss against her car door until teenage boys in a truck drove past and honked. Hoots and whoops reverberated from the cab's open windows.

"You know, maybe we do have a door fetish," Cort concluded.

Brianne recalled when she was on her hands and knees yesterday in the hallway and faced the new bathroom. She was lost in sensation until her head banged into the closed door with a loud thump like someone tried to kick it open. They crab-crawled backwards and resumed without a problem. This morning as they stood against the ensuite bathroom door, her thigh pressed down on the lever handle. It opened, and they stumbled into the room. Cort's quick reflexes and strength saved them from a nasty spill. The second recovery took a little longer as they moved to the safety of the bed.

#

Cort's thirty-first birthday was on the first Sunday in June. It was also the weekend that Brianne's aunts and uncles were in town for the monthly Gordon Enterprises board meeting. Her parents invited him and Lola to join everyone at PrimeTime for a celebration.

Lola and Aunt Eileen together at PrimeTime. Just kill me now.

The night before the party and dinner, Brianne gave Cort her gift to him. When she entered the bedroom, she wore only her cowboy hat and boots. At her side, she carried his new cowhide briefcase.

"Happy birthday, sport." A half hour later, Brianne said, "So, do you want to check out your other present?"

"What other present?"

"Your new briefcase."

"You got me a briefcase? Where is it?"

She sighed.

#

The next evening, Brianne drove herself to PrimeTime. Cort had gone to pick up Lola. She spotted his car in a handicapped space in front and the family's rented limo in the back lot.

Looks like I'm the last to arrive.

When she entered the room, everyone was already seated. Inez was in her usual place with Cort on one side and Lola on the other. The only chair left was next to Aunt Eileen at the opposite end.

Oh shit.

"Hi, everyone," she called out.

Cort pushed back his chair and walked over to her. "Thank God, you're here."

"What happened?"

"Nothing yet. I was afraid you chickened out. I didn't want to do this dinner all on my own."

"Well, considering where I'm sitting, you *will* be on your own."

Brianne kissed her grandmother and waved to the rest of her family. She greeted Lola with a hug then took her seat next to Aunt Eileen.

Uncle Junior's wife appeared alert and clear-eyed. Instead of her usual gin and tonic, a glass of Coke sat in front of her. Her aunt patted her knee. "Finally, I get you to myself."

For the first time in eight years, Brianne ordered an entrée of pumpkin ravioli in brown butter sauce.

After the salads were served, Aunt Eileen said to her, "I need to tell you something important." She took a deep breath. "I haven't had a drink since January, and it's because of you and Cort."

"It is?" Brianne put down her salad fork.

"When Cort spent Christmas with us, he said you broke up with him because you were afraid to be with a celebrity. He was sure it was an excuse for whatever happened in New York. But I knew that you really were scared."

Brianne pushed her half-eaten salad away. "How did you know?"

"Because I was scared, too. Still am, but I'm gettin' help, and I'm gettin' better. Growin' up I was a tomboy and flat as a board. I was bullied somethin' awful. The girls started it, but then the boys did it, too. They called me a dyke and butch all through school. When I met Junior on the rodeo circuit and he asked me to marry him, I was glad to move away from the people I knew as kids. But, unless you deal with your fear, it comes back to bite you. I gave birth to a perfect and beautiful boy who really was gay. Now I had to be strong for him."

Maybe that was why her aunt let Gary dress up as female celebrities and told him she loved him no matter what. During a summer visit when Brianne was ten, Aunt Eileen almost flattened a woman in the IGA when she said, "There's Fairy Gary and his fat friend."

Her aunt said, "And I was strong for my boy. As long as I could drink myself stupid every night after he went to sleep. I know my loose tongue said some cruel things to you. I am *sooo* sorry. Of all people, I know how words can hurt more and longer than punches."

Brianne glanced up. Aunt Jean and her mother observed them from the other side of the table.

They know what she's telling me.

"Trey and Junior were upset with how much I had to drink the day of the wedding. After Christmas, Junior told me if I didn't get help he was goin' to divorce me."

Brianne was shocked. Everyone knew how much her uncle loved his wife.

"I didn't blame him. I thought about you and Cort. He loves you with all his heart. But your fear was makin' you push him away. That's what I'd been doin' to my husband for years. I started goin' to AA meetings in the evenings. Most nights Junior would drive and wait in the car." Her aunt smiled for the first time since she revealed herself to Brianne. "The best news I got was when your mother said you and Cort were back together. One thing I've learned is that fear and happiness cannot live in the same house."

Brianne flung her arms around Aunt Eileen's neck. "You know I love you, don't you?"

"Bless your heart. I love you, too, sweet girl."

When they parted, their server stood behind them. She held two plates with effort. They moved aside so their dinners could be set in front of them. The woman shook the strain out of her arms as she exited the room.

When the meal was finished, Uncle Junior stood up. "I'd like to say a couple things while we're all gathered here." It took a minute until everyone quieted and looked his way. "Last week we got the news that Trey and Kerry will have a little Gordon cowboy or cowgirl in seven months."

Aunt Eileen leaned toward Brianne and said, "My new grandbaby is gonna have a sober meemaw."

When the congratulations, hugs, and handshakes ended, Uncle Junior said, "Next, the Gordon family wants to wish Cort a happy birthday."

Two PrimeTime wait staff came through the double doors into the room with a cake while singing *Happy Birthday.* Everyone at the table joined in the song. Cort blew out the candles to rousing cheers while another waiter wheeled in a cart with presents. Brianne stared open-mouthed. She knew about the cake but didn't know her family bought him gifts.

When the cake was taken away to be sliced, Cort opened the wrapped packages. He received a cowboy hat from Uncle Junior and Aunt Eileen.

"When you come back to the ranch, you won't have to wear one of mine," Junior told him.

Her parents bought him a pair of cowboy boots.

Brianne's mother said, "I checked your size when you took your shoes off at our house. I hope they fit."

Uncle Homer and Aunt Jean gave him a belt buckle embossed with the Double G ranch sign. Her sister gave him a tie tack with the Texas state seal. Next he opened a pair of striped board shorts from Lola.

Two weeks prior, Brianne had taken her laptop to the assisted living center and helped his grandmother place her first online purchase. She was determined to buy her grandson a pair of swimming trunks for his birthday.

"Can you believe it?" she said to Brianne. "Cort told me he swims every day in the nude. I don't care if he is in his own backyard. What would his neighbors say if they found out?"

What would you say if you knew I was often in there naked with him?

After Cort thanked everyone and they shared his birthday cake, Uncle Junior rose to his feet again. "We want to welcome Cort and Lola to the Gordon family monthly dinners. Y'all can join us next month in Fort Worth or back here in August."

"Thanks for inviting me," Lola said. "I had a great time and a killer steak. They don't serve meals like this at New River Villas because most people there don't have their own teeth."

When the laughter died down, Cort rose partway to his feet. "May I say something, Junior?"

Brianne's uncle gave him an open palm gesture and sat down.

Cort pushed back his chair and stood. "I want to thank you for dinner and the presents I received tonight. It's been just Lola and me for years. So we appreciate being welcomed so warmly to share this time with your wonderful family. But, as far as I'm concerned, the best part of your family is sitting right there."

He pointed down the table to Brianne. All heads turned to her. Instead of cringing in the spotlight like she did in the past, she grinned back at them. Then Cort left his end of the table and walked toward her. She turned in her seat to look up at him, her eyebrows arched. He put out his hand, and she rose to her feet.

"What are you doing?" she whispered.

He put her hand on his heart and held it there. "The best day of my life was when I met you. I am the luckiest man alive because you love me, and everyone here knows how much I love you. Lola once told me that I needed to find a good woman because that one quality never changes with time. I not only found a good woman but the most beautiful one in the world."

"Oh, Cort." Brianne's focus narrowed to his eyes that held hers in a romantic thrall. She was flooded with love for him.

He clasped her hand in his, knelt on one knee, and said, "Sweetheart, I hope I'm finally a man worthy of you. Will you marry me?"

Her mouth went slack with surprise at hearing those four words. All her life she'd felt like an outsider because of her weight, her athletic clumsiness, and her bookishness. But this beautiful man who could love any woman in the world was choosing her. Married life with Cort would mean the same joy, heartache, excitement, and disappointment of any marriage but in a more public forum. She'd already experienced life in a world without him, and it was a wasteland. His love was worth the risks and challenges.

There was a collective silence, except for the sounds that drifted in from the main dining room. Lola gasped as if she had been holding her breath and couldn't do it a moment longer.

"Of course, I will, sport." Brianne said, tears springing into her eyes. "I love you."

Cheers and clapping erupted as The Hunk wrapped her in his embrace and kissed her.

Chapter 33

BRIANNE HAD MISGIVINGS about booking her wedding and reception at the Signature Grand. Although the venue was perfect, being there for the Healthy Kids fundraiser colored her recollections of the place with dark, unhappy thoughts. But she couldn't tell her mother that.

Get over it, Brianne. It's time to make a new memory.

That was what happened with Christmas in New York. Cort had insisted on a do-over weekend in December.

He said, "I can't wipe out the heartbreak of that experience, but I can replace it with a better one."

And he did.

He remembered all their cancelled plans. They fought the crowd at night to see the Rockefeller Center Christmas tree lit up. At FAO Schwarz, the famous toy store, they were one of the first ones in line without kids when it opened. Cort dragged her onto the giant keyboard on the floor, but they were unable to toe-tap any recognizable tune. He bought tickets for the American Ballet Theater's performance of The Nutcracker. She was entranced but twice had to nudge him awake. They strolled for blocks past store window displays on Fifth Avenue. The two nights in the hotel suite were magical.

It was three of the best days of my life.

#

With the wedding ten weeks away, Brianne argued on the phone with the wedding planner as she and Pam sat in a crowded downtown café for lunch. "No floral centerpieces. They are a waste of money. How many ways can I say it, Julio? No flowers in vases … Julio … Julio … I don't care. The tables will not look naked. You're going to have to come up with something else." Her finger punched the end button on the phone. "He's a dictator. It's my wedding, not his."

"Is his last name Castro?" Pam asked.

"No. I added the *tator* because we're in a public place."

#

The most difficult decision for Brianne was choosing a wedding gown. She wanted an open back because Cort loved the dress she wore to Trey and Kerry's wedding reception, but the bodice had to provide good support for her bust. She also insisted that it have a skirt in which she could dance. It seemed that everything she liked matched only two of the three criteria. One bridal shop saleswoman suggested she buy two dresses, one for the ceremony and one for the reception.

"That's a good idea," Emma said. "The one for the reception can even be short."

"Forget it. I'm not buying two dresses. I don't want to run and change after pictures are taken. It would be different if the wedding was in the afternoon and the reception was hours later, but it's not."

The saleswoman's lips pursed, and she hauled the rejected gowns out of the dressing room.

One month before the wedding and in a panic, she found the perfect dress. It was a dropped waist ball gown with an illusion bateau neckline and tiny cap sleeves. The back of the dress had a lacy V cut to her waist. The only alteration needed was to have the train of the silk and tulle skirt shortened so she wouldn't trip on it while dancing.

Brianne bucked the trend of identical bridesmaid's gowns. She told each woman to choose a knee-length black dress in a style to fit their body type and preference. Her sister and Pam shopped together and returned to the condo with their purchases to show Brianne. Each dress was similar with one major difference: Pam's was strapless, and Emma's had a halter top. They sent a photo to their cousin, Angie, who was the third bridesmaid.

A few minutes later, Emma's phone dinged with a text message. She checked it and said, "Oh, my God. Bree, you are not going to believe this."

On the screen was a mirror reflection selfie of Angie in Fort Worth. She was wearing her dress, which looked like a duplicate of Pam's and Emma's except it had a V-neckline.

"Just goes to show," Pam said. "This wedding was meant to be."

#

It was a beautiful day in late February, well past the slew of Valentine's Day weddings and before the onslaught of northern spring breakers. The chapel at the Signature Grand was lit by crystal chandeliers and columns topped with floral arrangements in pink and white. Rose petals lined the walkway to the altar where Cort waited with a wide smile on his face. Brianne walked up the aisle toward him on her father's arm.

When they reached the front of the room, Dad kissed her cheek and said to her husband-to-be, "Take good care of my baby."

Cort shook Ted's hand. "I will."

They climbed two steps and stood in front of the minister, who intoned, "Family and friends, we are gathered here to join together Cort and Brianne in a life of mutual commitment."

After his reading of the highlights of marriage, he announced that they had chosen to write their own vows. He turned to Cort and motioned for him to proceed.

With both of Brianne's hands in his, he looked into her eyes. "We met the day you fell at Hardcort Fitness, but little did I know how hard I was going to fall for you. You didn't just become a part of my life, you *are* my life. I'm a better man because of you, and you have the power to make me the best man I can possibly be. I love and respect you more than anyone else on Earth. You mean everything to me."

Brianne sniffed back tears that threatened to fill her eyes. *I knew I should have told the minister to let me go first.*

Cort said, "I promise that I'll be faithful and honest. I'll always honor the trust you've placed in me. I'll laugh with you and be there when you cry. I'll take care of you when you need it and never make you exercise at one of my fitness centers."

Brianne smiled as the wedding guests and the minister chuckled.

"I can't wait to begin our life together as friends as well as husband and wife."

Cort reached into his pocket and handed her a folded handkerchief. She mouthed *thank you,* folded the linen in half and dabbed at the tears along her lash line. After blowing out a breath between pursed lips, she handed the mascara-stained cloth back to him.

She cleared her throat and held his hands again. "You were *my* new beginning. When we met, I began to live my dream. When you wrote that I was worth the work, I began to feel worthy. When you said I love you, I began to love myself. When you asked me to marry you, I began to believe in happily ever after."

Cort's eyes blinked several times. A mighty swallow made his Adam's apple bob.

"I promise to laugh and cry with you. I promise to care for and about you. I promise to buy and cook meat for you."

From his seat, her Uncle Junior said, "That's my girl."

Aunt Eileen scolded, "Hush!"

When the laughter died away, Brianne turned back to Cort. "You are my one true love, and I'll cherish you always. I can't wait for tomorrow, because today is *our* new beginning."

After the exchange of rings, the minister said, "By the power vested in me by the state of Florida, I now pronounce you husband and wife. You may kiss."

Cort placed his palms on her jaw with tenderness and kissed her. She closed her eyes, unaware of anyone else except this man who loved her. Finally, the minister cleared his throat, and they broke apart. Emma handed Brianne her bouquet, and they turned to face their guests. They proceeded down the aisle followed by Emma and her escort, who was a childhood friend of Cort's. Then came Pam and her fiancé, Mark. The last couple was Brianne's cousins, Angie and Gary.

Following the late afternoon wedding, guests headed to the Coconut Palm Atrium for the open bar and appetizers while the bridal party stayed behind for a photo shoot. An hour later, when Cort and Brianne arrived at the reception, they were hungry, thirsty, and ready to party. The room was decorated in beautiful, understated elegance, albeit without floral center-pieces. Instead, low glass vases sat on round mirrors in the center of each round black tablecloth with a thick white candle nestled in undulating waves of pink and white sand.

When dinner was served, Cort gave Brianne his salad. She was the only vegetarian in attendance, so she didn't ask for a special meal. She would just have the side dishes.

After all, it's what I ate at PrimeTime for years.

She slid the chicken breast off her plate next to Cort's New York strip steak. He reached into his jacket pocket and produced a protein bar with a flourish.

"I love you," she said and kissed his cheek.

"I know. It's because I'm such a nice guy."

She cut the Clif Bar into chunks next to the risotto and cooked vege-table medley. "You're my nice guy."

"And you're my beautiful wife."

"Thank you. I've gotten several compliments on my wedding gift from you." She flicked the diamond drop earrings she wore. "I love how they look with my dress."

Cort whispered in her ear, "I'm going to love how they look without the dress."

After dinner, it was time for the wedding toasts. Her father rose to his feet, tapped on the microphone to quiet the room, and cleared his throat.

"I'd like to thank everyone for coming today. I was told I had three *ups* to do. I had to show up, speak up, and pay up. It was only when I was told I would have to give a speech that I wanted to throw up."

The laughter died down, and Ted turned to where the bride and groom sat. "Brianne, you stole my heart the day you were born, and you'll always be my baby, my little girl, my princess. I'm blessed that I could watch you grow up and become the beautiful woman you are today."

Cort handed Brianne his handkerchief again.

"You've just married a wonderful man, the only one I'd could ever let have you. I'm confident that you two are beginning a wonderful journey filled with love and joy. I ask everyone to join me in a toast to wish my daughter and son-in-law a long and happy life together."

More sentiments and well-wishes came from the rest of the bridal party, including Lola.

When her cousin, Gary, stood, Brianne hazarded a nervous glance in his direction. It was hopeless to ask him to give an appropriate wedding toast.

In a camp voice, he said, "Now I promised my cousin, Brianne, that I would not embarrass her with a sexual innuendo during my speech. But I want you to know ... it's hard ... so hard."

When the laughter died down, he said, "All the buzz right now is about gay marriages. Well, shoot, marriage has always been gay. Right, Cort?"

Brianne's new husband looked up as his eyes darted around. He pointed to himself and mouthed, *Me?*

"You're the one who just promised not touch another woman. Gay." Gary pantomimed a checkmark in the air. "You recently bought expensive jewelry. Gay." Another check. "You got all dressed up in absolutely fabulous clothes. Gay." Checkmark again.

Cort laughed with everyone else.

Gary tapped the microphone. "Y'all settle now 'cause I'm about to get serious here. Brianne and I have always been close, 'cause growin' up we were different than anyone else in our family. I wouldn't be here today if it wasn't for her. The love, companionship, and goodness of my cousin gave me strength and a reason for living."

No, Gary. It was the other way around.

"Everyone's love story is beautiful, but Cort and Brianne's is my favorite. Let's toast to their happiness forever."

Cort handed Brianne his handkerchief.

The last person to speak was Emma. She rose to her feet distracted by her cell phone and took the microphone from Gary. She tucked it under her arm as her thumbs bounced across the phone's keypad.

At last, she looked up and put the mike in front of her mouth. "Sorry. It was important. I had to update Cort's Facebook status."

Cort and Ted jerked in Emma's direction.

"Just kidding," she said and pointed a finger at her new brother-in-law. "But I will keep checking it. A year ago November, my sister showed me how much she loved me. She agreed to go with me to her most dreaded place on Earth, a gym. She'll never admit it, but it was to see The Hunk, Cort Hardison."

Brianne covered her mouth with her hand and said, "I'm going to kill her."

"As you heard, that day she fell *on* him, or rather a life-size cutout of him, and he fell *for* her. So you could say I'm the one responsible for where we are today."

A number of people applauded. Someone yelled, "Way to go, Emma."

Her sister curtsied. "One thing our mother, the etiquette optimist, is still trying to teach my sister and me is how to speak like ladies and not use foul language. That's why I'd like to propose a toast to F words."

Brianne glanced at her mother who waggled a warning finger at Emma.

Her sister held her wine glass up high "Here's to family ... friends ... fitness ... forgiveness ... and forever."

Brianne stood and hugged her sister. In her ear, she said, "What the fuck, fitness?"

White-gloved waiters cleared the dishes while Cort and Brianne cut the wedding cake.

Music started for the father-daughter dance. After it ended, Ted handed her to Cort.

The deejay announced, "Ladies and gentlemen, the bride and groom have decided to recreate a wedding dance that went viral on YouTube over a year ago. To Kelly Clarkson's *Don't Rush,* here are Cort and Brianne Hardison. Please give them a round of applause."

They stepped to the middle of the empty floor. Brianne put her hands on Cort's shoulder and in his palm.

He said, "We danced this for the first time at Trey and Kerry's wedding reception and now at ours."

"And Pam wants us to do it at hers in June," said Brianne. "We're going to become famous. Maybe we'll even end up on TV."

Cort laughed as the first few notes of their song began.

www.ingramcontent.com/pod-product-compliance
Lightning Source LLC
Chambersburg PA
CBHW021323250626
47155CB00002B/598